**"You want me to make you hot?" he asked,
his voice low and raspy.**

Sydney's eyes flashed to his.

Morgan swept his thumb across her cheek and she sucked in a deep breath. When his hand caressed her cheek, her eyes closed of their own volition. Time seemed to stand still. She felt his warm breath on her skin.

He slid his thumb down the side of her neck.

She exhaled. "This isn't going anywhere good. You're acting like you want to kiss me and I know that's not true," she joked.

He clenched her hair in his hands and tugged gently. "How do you know that?"

She searched his eyes. "Do you? I mean—do you want to?"

"I do—and so many other things."

His gaze dropped to her mouth as his hand crept up her thighs and rested on her bottom. She jumped in surprise when he squeezed.

Syd placed her hands on his stomach and felt his taut muscles tighten in response. "Caden would kill you."

Morgan traced her lips again with his thumb. "It may be worth it."

THE
FORBIDDEN
MAN

THE FORBIDDEN MAN

An Edge of Scandal Novel

ELLE WRIGHT

FOREVER

NEW YORK   BOSTON

Forever
Hachette Book Group
1290 Avenue of the Americas
New York, NY 10104

www.HachetteBookGroup.com

Printed in the United States of America

First Edition: July 2015
10 9 8 7 6 5 4 3 2 1

OPM

Forever is an imprint of Grand Central Publishing.
The Forever name and logo are trademarks of Hachette Book Group, Inc.

The Hachette Speakers Bureau provides a wide range of authors for speaking events. To find out more, go to www.hachettespeakersbureau.com or call (866) 376-6591.

The publisher is not responsible for websites (or their content) that are not owned by the publisher.

To my beloved mother, though you are no longer with us, your memories regulate my life. You were my EVERYTHING! I am grateful for the love of reading that you instilled in me, the encouragement you gave me to follow my dreams. I appreciate that my first romance book was a gift from you. You were a devoted, dedicated, courageous, soft, kind, and funny spirit. I am thankful for your guidance and the many sacrifices you made for us. You are my inspiration and my Shero. You had a zeal for higher learning that encouraged me and others to succeed. I pray that God gives me the strength to follow your example of showing and teaching Christ's love. I miss you every second, every minute, and every hour of every day. I love you!

ACKNOWLEDGMENTS

Writing *The Forbidden Man* has been a long, uphill, but exciting and satisfying journey. I feel so grateful to be able to do what I love. Without the wealth of support from my family, friends, and colleagues, this wouldn't be possible.

First and foremost, I'd like to thank God for blessing me and keeping me on this long road. Without Him, I'd be nothing.

To my husband, Jason, thank you for everything! From the meltdowns to the nights you had to sleep with the light on so I could write, to the dinners. You've supported me through everything and I love you!

To my children, Asante, Kaia, and Masai; you've inspired me to do better, to be better. I'm so grateful that God blessed me with three beautiful, intelligent, hilarious children. Love you!

To my father, H. Leon Jr., thank you for your support and all the lessons you've taught me over the years, lessons that I infuse into my writing daily. Thank you for always making sure I do something for "me."

To my brother, Lee, I'm so proud that I wrote a book you wanted to read! My life is better with you in it.

To my "Seester," LaDonna, thanks for always listening, for cheering, for praying, for supporting...just for being there.

To my sister, Kim, thank you for reading every version of the book and loving each one. For believing in me since the "first, first" book. You are always hyping me up and I'll never forget it!! Tell Mr. T. he made it all better with just a few words and I'm so grateful.

I want to give a special thanks to my friends, my betas, who listened to me daily about everything from word choice to character names to "too much heat?": Crystal, Danielle, Kimberley, Sheree, Andrea (Buttons), Shannon, Terri, Stacey, Nicole, Danette, Marleta, the Classy Ladies group, and Kenya. Thank you so much for reading and believing in me.

Thanks to my friend Kristina, for helping me in so many ways. You're the ultimate wordsmith.

Also, thanks to my friend and critique partner Christine Hughes. I'm so blessed to know you and be on this writer's journey with you.

To all of my friends and family, I'd be here all day trying to write everyone's name down. But I wanted you all to know that I appreciate your unwavering support. Whether it was just a hug, an encouraging word, a Cutie, a laugh...you all truly mean the world to me.

To my agent, Sara, thank you for taking a chance on me. I would be lost without you.

To Latoya, thank you for loving this book and inspiring me to write more. I truly appreciate everything you've said and done. Thank you for your continued support.

To my editor, Megha, thank you for pushing me further than I expected and encouraging me to tap into more.

Thanks to all the many author friends who have been such

a support to me; authors who have supported me and given good advice; authors who have inspired me to keep writing; and one author in particular, my favorite author, Beverly Jenkins, who has shown me nothing but love. For that I'm ever grateful.

I hope you enjoy the book! Holler at me and let me know what you think!

Thank you!

Love,
Elle

THE
FORBIDDEN
MAN

CHAPTER ONE

Don't move."

Sydney Williams glanced at her watch. "Allina, I have to go. I'm meeting Den in thirty minutes." In a few short months, Syd was finally going to marry her longtime love, Caden Smith, affectionately known as Den.

Sydney flinched when she received a playful whack on the behind.

"I told you to be still. I'm almost finished. There. You can turn around."

Sydney sucked in a deep breath then turned and looked at her reflection. The white silk, floor-length gown fit her perfectly. Smoothing a hand over her hip, she eyed the tiny crystals adorning the plunging neckline. It was simple, understated—exactly how she wanted it.

"What do you think?" Allina said, biting her thumbnail as she stepped back. "I think it looks much better with your hair up."

"It's beautiful. Den's going to love it." Sydney ignored the look her friend gave her and the quick rolling of her eyes. Sighing, she took one last glance at herself, turned around, and raised her arms. Allina unzipped her and she rushed into the fitting room. "I appreciate this, girlfriend. You're truly gifted," she told her from behind the curtain.

Tossing the gown over the door for her friend, she dressed. When she was finished, she slipped into her sandals and pulled the curtain open. Allina was zipping up the garment bag.

"I'm ready to invest when you're ready to go out on your own," Sydney said, rummaging through her purse. "It's time."

"It'll be ready for you Friday after five o'clock," Allina said, changing the subject. She tucked a stray braid that had fallen out into her neat bun.

Before Sydney could go into the countless reasons it was better for Allina to venture out and open her own boutique, her cell phone vibrated. Muttering a curse, she shook her bag and felt around for the cell phone. Sighing heavily, she grabbed a hold of it and pulled it out. After a quick glance at the anonymous number, she was tempted to ignore the call—except she was planning a wedding and it could be someone calling to confirm something.

Grumbling a curse, she answered, "This is Sydney."

"I wasn't sure you'd answer." The nasal-toned voice of her fiancé's ex–booty call, Laney, immediately put Sydney in a bad mood.

"Can't make the right choice all the time. Why the hell are you calling me?" Syd snapped.

"I just thought you'd want to know—"

"And how did you get my number?" She dropped her purse on the chair.

Curiosity prevented her from hanging up on the other woman. It was no secret she couldn't stand Laney, but she couldn't help but wonder why she was calling her. "Look, I'm doing you a favor," Laney said. "The least you can do is treat me with some respect."

Syd's interest turned to dread at Laney's snide tone. The last "favor" from Laney had almost destroyed her relationship with Den. It took months to get over the fact that he'd cheated on her while she was away at graduate school. She gripped her phone. "Laney, what the hell do you want?"

Allina, who'd just returned from the back, stopped in her tracks at the mention of that name.

Placing a hand over the receiver, Syd mouthed to her friend, "I'm fine. Go ahead and finish what you were doing."

Allina didn't look convinced, but walked away anyway, glancing back as she headed toward the counter.

"I'll just cut to the chase," Laney sneered.

"Please do." Something told Syd to have a seat, but she remained on her feet. Although the other woman couldn't see her, she didn't want to give even the slightest impression that she was affected by anything Laney had to say. "I don't have all day."

"If you think you're going to be happy with Den, you're fooling yourself."

"What do you know about it?" Sydney asked with a snicker.

"Everything. I know that Den has been lying to you for months. He told you that you could trust him. That he'd never hurt you again. That he wanted to start fresh, confess everything...the random woman at a bar story...then he realized that he couldn't live without you...couldn't wait to make you his wife."

Syd felt sick to her stomach as Laney droned on. The fact that this woman knew all of her business wasn't the worst part. It was what she feared was coming next that was giving her fits.

"Sydney, did you hear me?" Laney called through the receiver.

She swallowed, then cleared her throat. "Just say what

you need to say and stop wasting my time with this shit, Laney."

"And I'll bet you believed him, too." Laney laughed, and the sound made Syd's skin crawl. "The thing is, he may be ready to make you his wife, but he surely can't keep that promise of never hurting you again, because *I* was the woman at the bar and it definitely wasn't a random hookup. We've been seeing each other for months now—at your house, in your bed."

Closing her eyes, Syd barely flinched when the phone landed on her toes, then the carpeted floor, with a thump.

Allina rushed over to her. "What's going on?"

"Oh God," Syd cried. "This can't be happening."

She vaguely felt Allina nudging her, heard her begging her to say something, anything. It seemed like everything was happening in slow motion. Over the last eight months, she'd spent thousands on the details, the plans, the invitations…Oh God, her family was coming. They'd purchased tickets and paid for hotel rooms. What would they think of her? How would she face them?

"Sydney!" Allina yelled, shaking her out of her thoughts. "What's wrong?"

Syd wouldn't bother calling Den to confirm Laney's story. In her heart, she knew the other woman was telling the truth. She was sure it had happened just the way Laney described. And it wasn't because Laney was such a truth teller. It was only because Den had lied to her more times than she cared to admit, more times than she ever told anyone. He'd promised her he was a changed man, but she knew change didn't come easily to Den. She wanted to drive to his job and embarrass him in front of his employees, demand that he explain himself, order him to do something—anything—to make this seem less real, less devastating. Would there be anything he could say to justify this? Wasn't it her fault for believing the lies, taking him back, and choosing to never hold him accountable every single time he'd hurt her? Yet, even as her heart seemed to split open and the pain crept into her bones, she couldn't muster up any blame for the man she loved. No, there was no one to blame but herself.

Blinking, Sydney zeroed in on her phone lying on the floor and picked it up. She didn't bother checking to see if Laney was still on the line. She turned it off and tossed it into her purse.

What the hell am I going to do now?

"Do me a favor?" she asked Allina, grabbing her keys and heading toward the door. "Call Calisa. Tell her to cancel...everything."

"Wait," Allina called to her before she opened the door. "Don't just leave like this. Something happened. You're upset and crying. You can't drive like this." She walked over and took Sydney's purse from her hand. "Come on. I'm closing up. Keep me company?"

Sydney wiped her eyes angrily then plopped down on an empty chair. "Allina, I know you have an event this evening. You don't have to stay with me."

"I have a few hours." Allina sat down next to her and squeezed her hand. "I'm here for whatever you need, okay?"

"I need a drink." She pulled some tissue from a dispenser and blew her nose.

"I have some wine in the back," Allina offered. "We keep it for bridal parties."

"Bring it out and let me wallow."

"Syd, what happened?" her friend asked again, concern in her brown eyes. She ran her hand over Syd's back.

"He cheated on me," Syd said on a sigh. "Again. With her. Again."

Allina shook her head, disgust playing on her features. "That fucking...piece of shit."

Syd knew that her friend didn't care for Den. It'd been painfully obvious for months. Hell, it'd been years since she'd heard Allina curse, and she'd said "fucking" and "shit" in the same sentence. But Lina wasn't the type to voice her opinion about someone else's relationship. Never had been. She'd always supported Sydney's decisions even if she didn't agree with them.

"You don't have to say it, Lina. I already know you hate him."

Allina sighed heavily, but continued to focus on the end-of-the-night receipts.

The silence from her friend did nothing but heighten her anxiety, and she realized she wanted—no, needed—to hear her thoughts. Exasperated, she told her, "Fine. Say it."

"What's there to say?" Allina shrugged. "He's an ass, but you already knew that."

Ouch. Allina always did have a way of making things very plain. So plain it irked the hell out of her.

"He hurt you again," Allina continued. "I can't say I'm surprised, but I do think it's better that you found out now instead of after you married him."

Syd grabbed hold of Allina's wrist. "Please don't say anything, not even to Kent," Syd begged.

Syd had tried to play matchmaker for Allina and Den's brother Kent for years. But the stubborn duo had refused to see the potential in each other that she had. Instead of dating, they were firmly in the "we're just good friends" camp.

"I never do." Allina smiled slightly and patted her hand.

Releasing her hold, Syd stood up and pulled on her shirt. "Where the hell is that wine?"

Allina disappeared into the back of the store and emerged a few minutes later with a bottle of Red Moscato, Syd's favorite. Pouring it into a cup, she held it out to her.

Instead of taking the cup, Syd grabbed the bottle and put it to her lips.

"Allina?" Syd belched and muttered, "Excuse me."

"Yeah?"

"What am I going to do?" Syd felt like she was going to choke on her tears. It was hard to even think straight. She had no clue where to start. "How am I going to tell everyone? My dad, Red..." Gulping down more of the wine, she covered her mouth when another burp escaped. "Oh God, Red is going to kill him."

Syd knew her twin brother, Jared, or Red as they called him, wasn't Den's biggest fan. He'd always felt that Den didn't appreciate her and took her for granted. Every chance he got, he told her that Den didn't deserve her loyalty.

"Red is going to be fine, Syd. He's an attorney. He knows how to keep his cool."

"It's really my fault," she confessed. "I shouldn't have taken him back again. I knew he wasn't ready. When he proposed, I knew it wasn't right. He did it during my lunch hour, for Christ's sake. Who does that?"

The quick, unromantic proposal had been the talk for weeks within their small circle of friends. Even Den's brothers thought the approach was rather trifling and had told him so countless times. Syd, on the other hand, made excuses for Den: it was romantic to her, they hadn't been able to schedule a dinner, or it was always her dream to get proposed to in an ordinary way. That last excuse was kind of true. She did envision a proposal during a random weeknight dinner or during their favorite television show. Sitting in the drive-thru at Mickey D's? Yeah, somehow that didn't make the cut, but she was happy and couldn't wait to become Den's wife.

Allina scratched her head and peered up at the ceiling.

"Allina, I know you have something to say. You always hold back. It's the reason you never told Kent that you have feelings for him that go beyond just friends, or why you don't have your own shop. You're a kick-ass seamstress, with a good business sense. But you never speak your mind, say how you really feel about stuff."

"Maybe it's not my place," Allina said, her pale cheeks now a dark shade of crimson. "And you promised never to say anything out loud about Kent and my true feelings for him."

Syd smiled. "I'm sorry. I did promise, didn't I? Kent would be lucky to have your tall ass on his arm. You're so beautiful. Just wish you'd realize it." When Allina didn't respond, Syd finished off the bottle and set it on a table nearby. Her friend was modest as this day from hell was long, so it was no use ever paying her a compliment. "You have another one of these?" she asked after a few minutes of silence.

Allina glanced at her before heading to the back. Syd couldn't be sure, but she swore she saw it on Allina's face . . . pity. Her friend thought she was pitiful. Maybe she was.

When Allina returned, Syd reached out to grab the bottle. But Allina held it back. "Syd, maybe you should slow down. You still have to drive."

"I'll slow down when you tell me what you're really thinking."

Sighing heavily, Allina sat down. "Okay. I just think you deserve better. Den is okay—charming, funny, and attentive when he wants to be. I don't think any of us doubts that he loves you. But love and respect are two different things and one or the other isn't enough to sustain a relationship on its own. He's hurt you so much . . . Sometimes it's better to let it go than to keep trying when a relationship isn't working."

"I love him." Her words sounded hollow even to Syd's own ears. Allina hadn't told her anything that she hadn't already thought herself over the past few months.

"I know you do, sweetie. But Den has issues. You said yourself that sometimes you feel like you can't even leave him alone because you're so worried he won't take his meds, or he won't make it without you. In the meantime, it's like you're willing to accept everything he throws at you."

Den's bipolar disorder had wreaked havoc in the lives of those closest to him, especially her and his other brother, Morgan. He had a habit of not taking his meds when he was busy. A part of him always wanted to test the limits, see if he could do without the Lithium.

"You don't understand," Syd told her. "He needs me. And I owe him."

"You don't, Syd." Tears gathered in Allina's eyes and she turned away to wipe them. "I just wish you'd realize that and maybe take this as an opportunity to start fresh."

"Start where?" Syd dropped her gaze to the floor. "I've been with him so long I don't even remember life without him."

"But you've also sacrificed so much for him and the relationship. You've made excuses for his behavior, blamed everything on his disease. What if he's just being himself? Ask yourself why he cheated on you with her in the first place."

Syd had asked herself that question so many times. "I wasn't here. I moved out of the state. How could I expect him to be faithful when I wasn't sure I was coming back?" It was the blanket answer she'd repeated to herself so often she believed it.

"You moved to go to graduate school," Allina said, obviously not accepting the bland excuse. "You went to help your sick father."

"Still, we didn't make any promises when I left," she insisted, even as she realized her defense of Den was more out of habit. The fact was, Den hadn't proven himself worthy of her loyalty in a long time. Just like her brother said.

"Well, you're back now." Allina picked up a safety pin off

the floor and tossed a used tissue into a small waste bin. "It's been years and it seems that you're in this perpetual state of cleaning up behind him."

There it was again. The cold, hard truth. And she couldn't deny it any longer.

"He made a promise when he proposed to you, Syd," Allina continued. "He broke it. You have to decide if you're going to keep accepting that, because you know he's not going to take responsibility for his actions. It's always someone else's fault."

Allina was right. She had given Den more than enough chances and she was tired. The relationship was beyond repair at this point. And even if it wasn't, she wasn't sure she'd want to fix it. As much as she loved him, she had to face the fact that it just wasn't going to work, and he wasn't healthy for her. The wedding was off.

* * *

Morgan tapped on the door to the small storefront, then pressed the bell. He'd rushed over when he'd received Allina's call begging him to come and pick Syd up. She'd spouted something about heartbreak, wine, and weddings, so he dropped everything and raced there. As he waited, he wondered what he'd find when the door opened.

Allina opened the door. "I'm so glad you came."

"What's going on?" he asked, ducking under the low-hanging bell and stepping into the shop. He heard the radio blasting Destiny's Child and what sounded like...singing, loud and off-key.

"I tried to take the bottle away from her, but she's in a mood," Allina told him. "I would stay but I have an event. I tried to call Red, but he's not answering. Calisa didn't pick up either. I even tried Kent. So you're it."

"Where the hell is Den?" Morgan muttered, shaking his head and running a hand over his face. He cringed when Syd hit an awkward high note. "You still haven't told me what's going on, Allina."

She sighed. "That's...not an option. I'm sorry if I interrupted your evening, but I didn't know who else to call. I'd tell you what happened, but I promised I wouldn't."

He muttered a curse under his breath. "Where is she?"

"Back there," she answered, pointing to one of the private bridal rooms in the rear of the store.

Morgan followed her toward the music. Although Allina hadn't technically spilled the beans, he'd already guessed that his brother was the reason Syd was belting out through-with-love songs at the top of her lungs. Obviously, Syd was in no condition to drive. And he wanted to throttle his older brother for undoubtedly breaking her heart. Again.

Rounding the corner, he stopped at the sight of Syd sprawled out on the couch singing Dru Hill's "In My Bed."

"Oh, shit," Morgan grumbled.

"Tell me about it," Allina mumbled under her breath. She stood over Syd and nudged her. "Hey. Morgan's here."

Syd's eyes widened. "Morgan? What is he...?" She pointed at him accusingly. "What are *you* doing here?"

"Syd," he said softly, approaching her. "What are you doing?"

"Singing," she said simply. "And drinking."

He bent down to Syd's level. Pushing a few stray curls out of her face, he took a good look at her, noting that her hazel eyes were bloodshot and her mocha skin had a pink flush to it. Sure signs that she was drunk. "Are you going to tell me what happened?"

"I don't know." Syd shrugged. "Can I trust you?"

He chuckled, amused by the question. "You know you can."

"I don't know." She traced his cheek with her fingers.

"You're his brother. Do you know you have dimples just like him?"

He squeezed her hand and gently removed it from his face. "You can trust me."

"But you don't look like him," she said, her voice low and hoarse. "You have nice facial hair. And you're much taller and thinner. Between me and you," she whispered. "I think Den is going to get fat in a couple of years. He eats too much pizza."

"Tell me what happened," he said, trying to get her back on track.

"He cheated on me with that whore, Laney. Again," she slurred, picking at the mound of curls on the top of her head, pulled into what she often referred to as a bitchy bun. "He fucked me over. I mean, the first time I was away. I gave him that one because I lived in another state at the time. And even though she ended up pregnant…I still forgave his ass." She sobbed and dropped her empty paper cup on the floor.

Morgan remembered the drama surrounding Den's first affair with Laney. The woman had gotten pregnant and couldn't wait to tell the world. Den had refused to 'fess up even though they all told him to tell Syd before she found out from someone else, namely Laney. Eventually, Syd found out the truth when Laney followed her through the mall, taunting her with the sordid details of their ongoing relationship. Shortly after, though, Laney suffered a miscarriage.

Syd squeezed his arm, jarring him from his thoughts. "I forgave him again a week ago when he confessed that he'd slept with some random woman he met in a bar," she cried, her tears falling unchecked down her cheeks. "He said it happened months ago, before he proposed, when we were having that rough patch. But it was really last week. And then I find out it's *her*. He played me. And I let him. Again. She called me, ya know," she babbled on. "She wanted me to know that he fucked her in my bed. He couldn't even take her somewhere else."

"Son of..." Allina groaned. "You didn't tell me that earlier."

"I didn't want to say it out loud," Syd admitted quietly. "Allina already thinks I'm stupid for taking him back in the first place. You probably pity me, too."

"I don't, Syd," Allina said, her voice cracking. She dropped to her knees next to Morgan. "I'm here for you."

"You do," Syd told Allina. "You probably think I'm going to take him back again."

Morgan looked at Allina, who stared down at the floor. He guessed she really did believe Syd would take his cheating brother back. Probably because she always did. Sometimes it would take a few days, a few months, but she always took him back. He'd spent a lot of time trying to figure out why. In the end, he figured her reasons for making excuses for Den's behavior matched his own. He'd spent most of his life doing the same thing, years of ignoring the bad and concentrating on the good. In spite of all Den's flaws, they'd seen the man who protected those he loved with everything he had; the man who could make anyone laugh no matter the circumstance; the smart, talented businessman...a man worth saving.

Glancing back at Syd, anger coursed through him. The Den he wanted to save seemed lost to him. It had been a long time since he felt the need to make excuses for his brother, and that was partly because of Syd. Mostly it was because Morgan resented Den. He'd given up a lot for his brother, but ultimately had made the decision to pull away because he was tired of being pulled into Den's hell. This latest debacle was simply Den being Den—selfish, careless, and impulsive. And he hoped Syd was finished with him for good this time.

"Come on, babe," he said, picking Syd up and cradling her in his arms.

"Are you going to take her home?" Allina asked, her eyes filled with unshed tears. "I mean, are you taking her home with you?"

He nodded as he made his way through the store with Allina right on his heels. "I'll keep trying to reach Red," he told Allina. "In the meantime, I'll make sure she's taken care of. Thanks for calling me."

"Morgan? Her purse," Allina called. She hooked Syd's tote on his arm. "I was going to say tell Den to go screw himself, but just take care of my friend. I parked her car in the garage. It'll be good there overnight."

He nodded. "For what it's worth, I want to kick his ass, too."

CHAPTER TWO

Sydney's eyes popped open and she immediately closed them again. Pressing a hand against her forehead, she groaned and rolled over. Swallowing, she pushed herself upright.

Once the spinning stopped, she opened one eye and tried to focus. Scanning the room, relief washed over her when she realized she was in Morgan's guest room. On the nightstand, she spotted a glass of water and a tiny bottle of Advil.

"Take two and drink the whole glass of water."

She spun toward the door. Morgan stood there, arms crossed. He was dressed in a white tank top and dark sweatpants. His brown skin was damp and she guessed he'd just hopped out of the shower.

"How did I get here?" Syd moaned, rubbing her temples.

"Allina called me last night," he said. He walked over to the window and closed the blinds. "She couldn't lift you up and didn't want you to sleep in the store. I figured you didn't want to go home, so I brought you here."

Grabbing the water, she downed the contents after

swallowing three pills. She rubbed her forehead and leaned back against the headboard. She felt the bed bow under his weight and peered at him out of the corner of her eye. Flashes of the night before replayed in her mind. Wine had seemed like a good idea at the time, but apparently she didn't know when to quit. She remembered Morgan carrying her out of the store and placing her in his truck. They'd shared small talk about weather and...onion rings? "I'm so embarrassed. And I guess I owe you a thank-you for not stopping at White Castle and getting me an order of onion rings. My stomach is in knots. I must have looked like a hot mess."

He chuckled softly, giving her a quick glimpse of his dimples peeking out of his five o'clock shadow.

Covering her face with her hands, she grumbled, "When was the last time you had to take care of my drunk ass?" He opened his mouth to speak, but she forged ahead, "Oh, I know. It was the last time I..." The first time she'd found out about Den and Laney, Morgan had nursed her broken heart and her broken toe when she kicked a wall after leaving a bar. "Den—"

"You don't have to talk about this."

"I know," she told him, meeting his concerned gaze. "And I don't want to."

"Syd, you probably should talk to him." Morgan dropped his gaze and cleared his throat. His normally strong, even voice sounded so foreign to her. Almost like he didn't believe his own words, like he was unsure. "He's been calling around looking for you."

"Are you serious?" she asked, quizzically.

"Laney could be lying. It's not like she's never done that before."

She snorted. "Yeah, right. She was telling the truth. Don't make excuses for him. Don't you get tired of doing that?"

"I could ask you the same question," he retorted.

Ouch. She kicked the heavy comforter off, and frowned at her lack of clothing. Struggling to remember how she'd ended up in one of his shirts, she asked, "Did you...?"

He shook his head. "No. I gave you a T-shirt and you put it on yourself, after you threw up all over my bathroom floor."

She gasped. "I'm so sorry. I'll clean it up."

"Don't worry about it. You're good." He picked up the empty glass and walked out of the room without another word.

She followed him and found him at the kitchen sink.

Although his shirt was swimming on her, she still felt a little exposed. Not that she didn't trust Morgan. Actually, she trusted him with her life. They'd been friends for years, before she'd even met Den. When Morgan breezed into her life, his dark eyes, good looks, cool swagger, and charm had her scribbling his name on stray notebooks. There was a time when she'd thought they could be more than friends, but he was Red's best friend and she was off limits. So, they'd settled into an invaluable friendship. She slid onto one of the stools next to the island, and tugged the shirt over her knees. She absently patted her head and cringed at the way her hair felt.

"Coffee?" he asked, pulling out two mugs. "Or hot chocolate?"

"Coffee, thanks." She watched as he placed her favorite flavor K-cup into the Keurig. "Where's my car?"

"Lina parked it in the garage next to the shop." He turned toward her. "I washed your clothes for you. Figured you didn't want to leave the house smelling like throw-up."

For some reason, that made her feel worse. She plopped her head against the cold, granite countertop. The smell of hazelnut made her stomach do an odd flip. When his strong hand kneaded her tense shoulders, she sat up abruptly and almost toppled over.

"Whoa, watch it." He grabbed her and helped her get her balance. "You okay?"

Turning and looking up at him, she said, "I'd better take a shower. Can you drive me to my car?"

He squeezed her hand. "No problem, but Red is on his way."

She groaned. "Morgan, please don't say anything about this to anyone," she pleaded. She knew he never would, but she couldn't help herself. "I just need to figure out what I'm going to do."

"You know I won't." He set the mug in front of her. "I didn't call him, by the way. I guess he called Allina and she told him I picked you up last night."

The last thing she needed was to deal with her overprotective older-by-five-minutes brother. Her twin never let her live down the fact that he was the oldest. She picked up the steaming cup of coffee and headed back to the bedroom.

The normally sweet coffee tasted bitter, so she dumped it into the bathroom sink. As she stared at her reflection in the mirror, she ran a finger across the faint scar above her breastbone. It took her back to the night Den found her broken and bleeding. The rape didn't define her like it used to, but the scar would always be a reminder.

Bracing her hands against the bathroom sink, she stretched her neck front to back. She turned on the shower, closing her eyes when the steam slowly filled the room. Stepping in, she leaned against the tile, sank to the floor, and cried.

* * *

When Sydney finally emerged from the bathroom, she found her clothes folded on the bed. Smiling, she picked up her shirt, thankful for the always dependable Morgan. As she held it against her nose, taking in the fresh scent of Gain, she thought back to all the times they took care of each other. Whether it be laundry, cooking, or financial support, they made it a point to be supportive of each other. For a while, Morgan had let Sydney drive his car while he was working. And she'd let him and Red crash on her floor more times than she could count during their wild college years.

She dressed quickly, then headed back to the kitchen. The smell of bacon permeated the air and she placed a hand over her queasy stomach. She heard voices as she got closer. Her brother had arrived. *Oh boy.*

"Good morning, sunshine," Red said as she entered the room.

He was sitting at the table, eating bacon and scrambled eggs. Morgan was at the kitchen sink, loading the dishwasher.

Instead of joining him, she went to the stool she'd vacated earlier and sat down.

Morgan glanced at her. "Eat. I made you some dry whole wheat toast and a boiled egg." He brought a full glass of water over and set it down in front of her.

Red pulled out the stool next to her and sat down. "Allina called and told me what happened."

Rolling her eyes, she picked up her fork and cut into the egg. She hadn't been drunk when she'd told her friend to keep what had happened between them.

"You know she didn't want to tell me," Red continued. "I badgered her until she did, so don't be mad at her."

The smell of Red's soap mixed with his signature cologne washed over her. His curly hair was wet. Normally, his presence alone would make everything better, but she didn't want to hear the inevitable lecture. "You didn't have to rush over here to check on me. I'm okay."

"Syd, it's time for you to make some hard decisions," Red

said. "Better yet, you need to just leave him. For good this time."

She glared at her brother, who seemed oblivious to her sour attitude as he devoured the food on his plate. Well, at least she thought he was oblivious, until she noticed that tick in his jaw and the way he stabbed at his eggs.

"I want to beat the shit out of him," he admitted. "But I know you don't want that."

They'd spent a lot of their childhood apart. When their parents divorced, Sydney chose to move with her father to Virginia while Jared stayed with their mother in Michigan. Sydney and her mother didn't get along, and often bumped heads even now because she had chosen to live with her father.

Pushing her plate away, she finished her water and turned her attention to Morgan. He was standing, gazing silently out of the kitchen window. Even in the huge room, he seemed like a giant. At times it was hard to believe he and Den were brothers because they were so different. Morgan was charming, like Den, but the similarities ended there. Although Morgan was confident, he wasn't cocky. He didn't need to be the center of attention. When he walked into a room, though, he commanded it without a word. And when he said he was going to do something, he meant it.

"I told you not to marry him," Red grumbled, interrupting her thoughts.

With her eyes still on Morgan, she snapped at her brother, "Well, I didn't marry him, so just shut up."

"Stop acting like you aren't going to take him back." Red dropped his half-eaten piece of bacon back on his plate.

She cringed at his harsh words. "Leave me alone. You don't understand."

"I do," Red said. "Trust me, I do. You feel like you owe him something. And I understand why you feel that way."

"No, you don't get it." She pushed her glass away from her. "You never did."

"Maybe not," Red conceded. "I know one thing...I hate the way he uses your past with him to continue to act like an ass. He doesn't deserve this blind devotion of yours. He's hurt you time and time again and I'm sick of it."

She stared at Morgan's back and tears pricked her eyes.

Red placed a hand on top of hers and squeezed. "Look, he's not a bad guy, but he has some issues he needs to deal with before he can be in any sort of relationship. I hope he gets it together and finds happiness with someone, but I pray that someone isn't you. I've watched you push yourself to the side too many times and—"

"Red, leave her alone," Morgan demanded. "She had a rough night. She doesn't need this right now."

Syd sighed, grateful for Morgan. He'd always been the peacemaker in their circle of friends.

Morgan finally turned to face her, his dark eyes unreadable. She hated arguing with Red about Den. He'd never been Den's biggest fan, with good reason. Den had betrayed her more than once. And honestly? She would be the same way if the shoe was on the other foot.

"Maybe you can overlook your brother's faults, but I can't," Red mumbled. "You always make excuses for him, always clean up his messes."

"Red, just drop it." Syd pounded her fist on the countertop. "Don't do this right now. My head is spinning." She massaged her temples and prayed her brother would give up. "I just want to go home and get into bed."

"And why is that?" Red asked, apparently unfazed by her outburst. "Because Den hurt you; that's why. You had a wedding planned, dresses bought, invitations sent...and he—"

"Enough!" she yelled, holding up her hand. Of all the

things running through her head, the money spent was the last thing on her mind. It sucked, but not worse than finding out that your fiancé took some other woman to your bedroom. "I'm not on the stand. Stop badgering me. I heard you." Swallowing past the lump in her throat, she croaked, "I need to go to my car. Morgan, can you take me?"

"I'll take you," Red said, taking his plate to the sink. "You have everything?" he asked her.

"Yes," she answered, yanking her purse off the counter. "Thanks for everything, Morgan."

"No problem." Morgan's gaze was fixed on her.

Twisting the strap of her purse around her finger, she nodded at him. They usually said good-bye with a hug, but her feet seemed planted to the ground. It felt as though she should say something else, but what would she tell him? Thanks for cleaning up her puke?

"Let's go, Syd," Red said impatiently as he strode toward the front of the house.

"Bye, Morgan." Sighing, she huffed to the door.

* * *

Sydney gripped the steering wheel, foot on the gas. She was seriously tempted to ram her car into Den's beloved Mustang convertible—the one he'd saved years for and was finally able to purchase a few months ago—with him in it.

Parked in front of their home, Syd slumped forward, leaned her forehead against the steering wheel, turned off the ignition, and tried to ignore the goofy grin on Den's face as he hopped out of his car and approached hers.

Red had dropped her off at her car over an hour earlier and she had decided to go home. But she couldn't bring herself to go in.

The sneer in Laney's tone still taunted her, remained on

a continuous loop in her mind. Dumb asshole slept with *that* bitch. The woman who'd spent many nights harassing them, finding joy in disrupting their lives.

Sydney's chin shook as she fought to control the tears. The disappointment she felt threatened to choke her. Even as she struggled to find a way to excuse this so she could get back to planning the wedding, she knew there was no way she could trust him again. Not that she trusted him anyway. Let's face it, she thought, he hadn't proven himself to be trustworthy. Still, she loved him. Didn't she? And love was supposed to be patient, kind, . . . forgiving, and unconditional.

They had history together, a lifetime it seemed. He was her first love, seeing her through the most traumatic event of her life. After she was raped, he wouldn't leave her side, and for that she would be forever grateful. That night, he wasn't the elusive Den that she'd known only through Red, Kent, and Morgan. He was her own personal Superman. A man who wrapped his heavy jacket around her and carried her to the student health center in the cold. Den stayed with her through the rough ambulance transfer and slept on a chair in the hospital room, even after Red arrived and told him he could go. That man made her love him with everything in her. He was gentle, funny, and smart—her first boyfriend and the only man she'd ever made love with. She took that seriously. Sure, he had his problems. But didn't everybody?

She jumped at the knock on the window. He was still smiling, obviously unaware that his *ex* was a vindictive troll. Sydney wasn't a violent person, never had been. There had been only one other time when she'd raised her hand to strike another person. But the overwhelming urge to slap the shit out of him reared its ugly head. She pushed the door open and jumped out of the car.

"You asshole!" she screamed as her fist connected with

his jaw. His height gave him an advantage because she was aiming for his eye. She wanted to leave a mark.

"What?" Den held a hand to his face, his brown eyes wide. "What's wrong? I thought—"

She shoved him, but he was five-foot-eleven, two hundred twenty pounds of solid muscle and didn't budge. "Fuck off!" she shrieked. "How could you do this to me again?"

He hunched his shoulders. "Syd...What? Where have you been? I've been worried sick—" He reached out to grab her hand and she yanked it back.

"I talked to Laney," she roared. "She called me to gloat about it."

He froze, eyes wide and mouth hanging open.

"Her?" she howled, smacking him again. "You cheated on me with that...Ugh, I'm so done with you."

"Syd, I'm sorry," he said frantically. He reached for her again and she smacked his hand away. He clasped his hands over his head, then let them fall to his sides. "I'm sorry. Let me just—"

She pushed him. "What is your problem? How many times am I supposed to forgive you? Why?"

He didn't answer.

"Why?" she sobbed, not caring that their next-door neighbor, Mrs. Eldridge, had stepped outside of her house and was eyeing the scene.

"I-it's not...It just happened. I don't want to hurt you, Syd." His eyes filled with tears, but she refused to let him get to her this time. He needed to feel her wrath, feel how much he hurt her.

"Then why do you keep doing it?" she demanded.

His shoulders slumped forward and he shoved his hands into his pockets. She folded her arms across her breasts and waited.

"I can't do this anymore!" she cried. "Every single time...

I forgive you. And you hurt me again. You don't even care enough about me not to bring that shit into my own home. I've stood by you through everything, Den."

Although Den owned a successful construction company, he had many demons. Watching his father mistreat his mother for years hadn't been a cakewalk. Neither was being removed from his childhood home by Children's Protective Services at the age of thirteen. He'd been through hell and she wanted to be a person he could count on. But...

"You're not blameless in this," he said softly, wiping a tear from his face. "You've completely pushed me to the side, working so much I barely see you."

Sydney knew the past few months had been hectic with her job and her new business venture. But she'd assured him that things would die down once the bar opened and she could quit her full-time engineering job.

"I call you and you don't even answer your phone," he added. "I cook dinner and you can't even come home to eat it."

"So you cheat on me?" she blared, stepping back. Brushing a few tears off her cheeks angrily, she pointed at him. "I can't believe you're even trying to turn this around on me. That is not okay, Den."

He sighed. "I'm sorry, Syd. I was wrong. You have to forgive me. I love you—"

"Get out." She needed to get away from him before her resolve cracked. He'd always had this ability to suck her back in. While she'd love to say she didn't know why, she knew exactly why he'd pulled her back time and time again. It was because he was always sincere. He never *wanted* to hurt her and she believed that. But she couldn't take the torture anymore.

His eyes widened. "Syd, we can fix this. I want to be with you. We can go to counseling or something, but don't give up on us."

He reached out to touch her, but she turned her shoulder, dodging his advances. "Don't touch me. Get your shit. You can't stay here anymore."

"Don't do this," he begged.

She whirled around and glared at him. "The wedding is off."

Sydney wondered if she should feel some sort of satisfaction at the pain etched in his face at her declaration, but disappointment clouded her emotions. She turned her back on him again, intent on running into the house, but his hand on her shoulder stopped her.

"Syd, we can work through this," he pleaded. "We can work through anything as long as I know you're with me. I'll be better. I promise."

She hopped back in her car, slammed the door, and locked it. *Shit*. She slammed her hands against the steering wheel and screamed, "Don't be here when I get back!"

CHAPTER THREE

$\mathcal{I}$t was dark, and the volume on her stereo was turned low. The driver's side window was open. The cool March breeze whipped across her face as she contemplated her next move, causing the tears to fall faster. She'd driven around for hours and ended up at her mother's house. She could always go in the house and explain why she had been sitting in her driveway for over an hour. Then she'd have to hear about how she always wasted precious time being dramatic. Then her mother would tell her she was being ridiculous for kicking Den out. She was one to talk since her mother valued little about any man, including her own father. Her mother couldn't be bothered to support her father even when he was seriously ill, but she'd encouraged Syd to stick with Den. Probably because her mother had cheated on her father for years behind his back and had the nerve to act insulted when her father had said "no more." Resting her head against the steering wheel, Syd sighed.

Headlights shined as her brother's black Lexus pulled in beside her.

"Hey," Red said, approaching her car and bracing his

arms on the top. "Mom called. She said you've been sitting out here for a while. She's worried sick. You okay?"

"I haven't been sitting out here that long." She looked pleadingly at him. "Can you just tell her I'm fine? I don't feel like dealing with her." She leaned her head back against the headrest, finding it hard to believe her mother was that concerned, especially since she never called or even came outside to check on her.

"You can tell her yourself when you go inside."

Syd muttered a string of curse words and crossed her arms, burrowing her back into the seat. Going inside wasn't an option.

Red drummed his fingers against the car. "I'm sorry about earlier," he said, meeting her gaze. It was almost like looking in a mirror. They had the twin thing down—from their light skin and matching hazel eyes, deep dimples and wavy hair, to simple mannerisms like biting the insides of their cheeks when they were irritated. "I can't stand to see you like this. Fine," he said, with a heavy sigh. "If you don't want to go inside, come with me. We can go shoot some pool or something, anything to get you out of this car so Mom can stop blowing up my phone."

"I just want to be left alone, Red," she whined. "I can't go in the house because Mom will drive me crazy with all the questions and the accusations. And I don't want to shoot pool in a crowded bar." She let out a humorless chuckle when her stomach growled.

He opened the door. "Scoot over. I'll drive."

She climbed over to the passenger side and waited for him to get in the car.

He adjusted the driver's seat. "It's about time you let me behind the wheel."

Maybe he was right, and she needed the distraction of stale smoke, meaningless chatter, and loud music. Anything was better than fighting with her mom, Den, or anyone else, for that matter.

Sucking in a breath, she took in the new car smell. She'd finally purchased her dream car, a cream Cadillac CTS Coupe.

"What do you have a taste for?" he asked, backing out of the driveway.

She ignored his question and stared out into the dark. "I know what everyone thinks of me," she admitted, her voice low and flat. "Everybody thinks I'm a fool for dealing with Den. But you remember how it was for me when I moved back to Michigan for college?" She turned to face him.

He nodded and traced the steering wheel with one hand.

"I went through a lot my freshman year, and Den was there for me. He was one of the first friends I had outside of you and Morgan." It was true. When she arrived for her freshman year at the University of Michigan, she met Den through Morgan. Morgan and Red had played high school basketball together. Morgan had visited Virginia with Red a few times and he spoke often of his older brother. She'd only seen Den a handful of times before she was raped, but after that, he was a constant fixture in her life.

"He wasn't your only friend," Red said.

Sydney stared at the overhead dome light and thought about that time of her life. She'd been a shy, slightly over-weight nerd. It was hard for her to leave her father and move to Michigan with a mother who had never shown her much love. But she'd wanted to be near her brother. They'd spent far too much time apart. And she'd missed him.

She wasn't in town long when, after studying late at the library, one of her teaching assistants followed her. He approached her and offered to walk her home. She'd been surprised that the good-looking man even knew her name and agreed without hesitation. As they were walking, he told her that he found her very attractive. She still remembered the soft kiss he planted on her cheek, the first kiss she'd ever received, and the flutter in her stomach when he grabbed her hand. It wasn't until she realized that instead of walking toward the well-lit area, he was pulling her into the dark. Before she could fight back, he punched her in the face, stuck a knife in her side, and pinned her down in the bushes. He'd raped her for what seemed like hours. When he finally stopped, he dug the knife into her skin. She begged for her life, promising she'd never tell if he let her live. But her pleas didn't stop him from plunging the knife into her chest. He left her there shivering, bleeding, and crying in the cold.

When she'd heard voices, she'd recognized Den's immediately. He was with a woman. It was a strange coincidence and one she'd considered fate. After a few tries, she managed to scream his name loudly enough that he heard her. He saved her that night. She always felt that she would have died if he hadn't been there.

"Syd?" Red squeezed her shoulder, bringing her back to the present. "Come back, now. I know it's hard, but don't go back there. You've come a long way since then."

"I know, Red. But it did have an impact on my life and the choices I've made so far. Den saved me that night and I made a vow to always return the favor. He slept on a fold-out chair in my dorm room for weeks, until I felt like I could sleep alone. He's wrong, Red, but...look at his childhood. His parents sucked. He's fought so hard to live a normal life."

Not only did Den suffer from bipolar disorder, but he'd struggled with alcoholism as a teenager after he was removed from his parents' home by CPS. Every now and then, he fell off the wagon, which always seemed to coincide with being off his medication or arguing with her. It was during one of those dark times that he'd met Laney and slept with her the first time. It was also the reason she rationalized the cheating and took him back.

"He's not the only person in the world to have a bad childhood," Red said with a furrowed brow. "We didn't have a walk in the park. You can't save him, Syd. For starters, he has to want to be saved. He has a family now that would give him the clothes off their backs, if he needed them. I know for a fact that Morgan has sacrificed his own happiness for Den countless times."

Sydney knew that. Morgan had turned down a basketball scholarship to the University of California–Los Angeles to stay in Michigan, close to Den. "You don't know him like I do, Red. It doesn't matter anyway." She shrugged and stared out the window. "I don't want to talk about this anymore."

"I agree," Red grumbled. "I'm tired of talking about him. Let's just go to the bar, shoot some pool."

Knowing she shouldn't drink another ounce of liquor and actually not drinking were two different things. She picked up her phone and punched in a number.

"Sydney? Thank God," her friend Calisa answered. "I've been calling you all day."

"Hey, Cali. I know. Red and I are headed to get something to eat and shoot some pool. Want to meet us at the Sidetrack?"

"I'm on my way," she said.

Sighing, Syd turned her phone off and tossed it in the glove compartment. Calisa wasn't the only person who'd been calling her all day. Den had been calling nonstop for hours. She glanced at Red, told him they were all set.

As he sped down the I-94 toward their destination, she watched the lights of the city streak by. Ypsilanti was a small suburb next to Ann Arbor; her mother had lived there for years. It was a typical college town and the Sidetrack bar was one of the more popular local hangouts.

* * *

"Syd, did you want some of these wings?" Allina asked, before dipping a flat piece of chicken into the ranch dressing.

"No, thanks." Syd wondered why she had let Red talk her into a group night out. She wasn't in the mood for conversation. "How did your event go last night?"

"It was awesome." Allina munched on the wing. "I made some great connections. I wanted to talk to Calisa about possibly working together on a few projects."

"Makes sense," Syd said. Hearing that made her smile. Allina was wasting her potential working in that bridal shop. "You should totally look into it."

Allina glanced at her with sad eyes. "I'm sorry about telling Red. He wouldn't leave me alone until I caved. Have you talked to Den yet?"

"Don't bring him into this bar tonight," Red ordered. "We're supposed to be keeping her mind off the jerk."

Allina smacked his arm when he swiped a wing off her plate. "Get your own."

"Why?" He swiped a piece of celery from her. "You're not going to finish it."

Her friend Calisa joined them at the table and took one of Allina's fries. "Hey, got here as soon as I could. Hi, Lina." She hugged Syd. "Love you, honey."

"Did you see me sitting here?" Red asked Calisa, a gleam in his eyes.

Calisa waved him off while she pulled out a cloth to clean her glasses. "I did, but I'm not sure you're worth my time today. You irritated me last night with your attitude."

Syd laughed softly at her friends. Calisa was like a short ball of fire. She was everything Red claimed he didn't want in a woman—career-driven and fiercely independent. She didn't need anyone and made no secret of it. And Red was smitten.

"Can I talk to you for a minute?" Red stood and wrapped an arm around Calisa's shoulder. "Alone."

"I'll be right back," Calisa grumbled as Red led her toward a remote corner of the bar.

Sydney stared at her full shot of Patrón. Twirling the small glass between her hands, she contemplated taking it. Her initial intent was to drink away her sorrows again, but she couldn't bring herself to do it. Allina was mumbling some nonsense about Kent and a "date" and Calisa and Red were having a heated discussion on the other side of the bar. She was quickly losing interest in the scene. Kent entered the bar and gave her his signature, dimpled smile.

Syd glanced at Allina, who was pretending not to watch Kent. She didn't understand why her friend didn't just admit that she was into him. Kent was dark-skinned, and built like a linebacker. But it was his infectious charm and dry sense of humor that distinguished him from other men. More than a few women at the bar broke their necks to get a look at him as he approached their table.

Kent slid into the booth. "Hey, baby." He glanced at Allina and snatched the pickle off her plate. "Hey, Lina."

"Hi," Allina murmured.

"Hi, Kent," Syd said, grinning at one of her favorite people.

When CPS had removed Morgan and Den from their parents' home, Kent convinced his parents to let Morgan come and live with them. It was quite the scandal for their town when one of the more prominent families was exposed for running a prostitution and drug ring in their quiet suburb. Morgan had refused to split up from Den and the Smith family ended up taking in both brothers. Eventually, they made it official and adopted them.

Syd and Kent had known each other for so long, but it

wasn't until they went to work for the same company after graduation that they grew close. Now, she couldn't imagine life without him—without any of them.

Kent wrapped an arm around Syd and squeezed. "You okay?"

"As okay as I can be. I have so many calls to make, vendors to cancel, deposits lost. Since I missed work today, and probably tomorrow, I'll have to catch up Monday morning. Not to mention my heart feels like a brick in my stomach. But I guess it could be worse."

Without another word, Kent tossed her shot of tequila back, filled the glass again, and slid it over to her. "Drink up. It's Thursday."

She laughed. A sincere laugh that turned into a sincerely gut-wrenching cry. Her life was anything but funny. Not only did she have to cancel her wedding, but she had to figure out where she was going to live. Was she going to fight Den for their house? Would she be better off starting fresh? It was a lot to think about. Kent held her tightly. Rubbing her nose on his cashmere sweater, she took comfort in his smell. Tears streamed down her face into the soft material, but he didn't let go until the tears subsided.

Pulling away, she wiped her face. "I'm sorry," she said, pushing the full shot glass away from her. "Didn't mean to cry all over your nice sweater."

"What the hell did you do to her?" Morgan asked, sliding into the booth across from them.

Opening her eyes, she peered up at his concerned face. Her eyes welled up in tears again and she averted her gaze. "He didn't do anything." She swiped at her eyes with a tattered napkin. "I'm just being emotional." She scanned the area around the booth. "Where's Lina?"

"She tapped me on the shoulder while you were crying and said she had to take a call," Kent told her.

Morgan frowned at her. "You okay, Syd?" he asked, taking her hand.

She willed herself to stop the waterworks, but the tears kept falling. It made her angry. The last thing she wanted to do was cry like a baby. Snatching a few pieces of Kleenex from the small box she'd brought with her, she rubbed at her eyes furiously, choking back a sob. She balled up the tissue when the tears wouldn't stop and peered up at the ceiling.

When she finally met Morgan's gaze again, he reached out and, with his thumb, swiped a tear that managed to escape. She leaned into his hand as it lingered over her cheek and closed her eyes, comforted by the gesture. "I know it hurts now. But it's going to be okay."

Red and Calisa walked over to the booth, drawing her attention away from Morgan to them. Syd smiled at the way her best friend seemed to have her brother tied up in knots. He couldn't stand the attention she drew from the men in the bar—and even some of the women—with her beautiful brown skin, pretty smile, and expressive brown eyes. Syd wasn't ashamed to admit that she'd often wished for Cali's figure. They used to joke that Syd had the hips and the butt, but Cali had the boobs, and she never failed to flaunt them.

"Syd, let's go," Red said, looking at his watch. "I have an early deposition tomorrow."

"I'm not ready to go yet," she said, pouting. "I want to stay and pretend I'm drowning my sorrows."

"I'll take her home," Morgan offered. "I'm off tomorrow."

"Cool. I'll take your car back to Mom's." Red glanced at Calisa, who was applying fresh lip gloss. "Are you coming with me or are you still acting like you hate me?"

Syd rolled her eyes at her friend and her brother. They'd been sleeping together forever, but refused to acknowledge it in public, even though everybody knew. Red made it clear that he wouldn't allow any woman to lock him down and

Calisa was fine with her life the way it was without the complication of a boyfriend.

"I have my own car and I'm going home when I leave here," Calisa stated, crossing her arms. Sydney knew it was a lie designed to throw everyone off, but judging by the "yeah right" looks on Morgan's and Kent's faces, they really weren't fooling anyone.

"Calisa, you don't have to stay," Syd assured her.

"Syd, you need me." Cali clasped Syd's hand between her own. "If I hadn't been held up with a client, I would've been able to share an appetizer and take a shot with you."

"Trust me, I'm fine," Syd said. "I don't want to talk about Den, our relationship, or the wedding that is not to be. You have an early meeting. Go on home."

"I'll call you tomorrow, Syd," Calisa said, hugging her tight. "We're doing lunch."

Syd gave her a half-smile. A crowded bar wasn't exactly the best place to have a "girlfriend" moment, so it worked out.

Allina returned, yapping on her cell phone. When she hung up, she explained that she had to run to the shop and finish up an alteration.

"Do you want me to walk you out?" Kent asked Allina.

"We're heading out. You can walk out with us," Calisa offered.

They said their good-byes. As Syd watched them leave, she pushed her plate away. Any appetite she had walked out the door with them, leaving a bit of indigestion behind. *Oh, God.* "I need to go to sleep. Greasy fries after going months without fried food to get into my wedding dress . . . not agreeing with me right now." Dropping her head on the table, she groaned. "I guess I really can't hang like I used to."

Kent stood up and helped her to her feet. "You don't look too hot. We should get you out of here."

She grabbed Kent's shirt and let him lead her out of the bar. The temperature had dropped and the air hit her like a ton of bricks. "Oh my God, it's chilly out. I thought we'd seen the worst of this cold weather," she said, wrapping her arms around herself.

"Take this," Morgan said, wrapping his coat around her shoulders. The thick blazer immediately knocked the chill off and she pushed her arms through the sleeves and pulled it closed.

Kent led her to Morgan's truck. "You sure you don't want me to take her, Roc?"

Sydney giggled. For some reason, she was always tickled pink when someone called Morgan by his nickname "Roc." His biological mother had given him the nickname because he used to always bump his head as a child. She'd tell him his head was hard as a rock. The name stuck. But what she found hilarious was that he really was hardheaded. Stubborn as the day is long and pretty set in his ways. The name seemed to fit him in more ways than one.

"It's on my way," Morgan said simply.

She climbed into the truck and blew a kiss at Kent. "Bye."

Kent grinned. "See you." He placed a soft kiss on her forehead. "Let's do lunch, okay?"

"Sure. Maybe one day next week?"

"Sounds good. I'll put it on your calendar. All right, Roc." He gave Morgan dap before he disappeared into the night.

The car ride was quiet, but her thoughts were screaming in her head. When they turned down her street, dread seeped into her soul. Would Den be there? What if he hadn't packed up and left like she'd asked? What if he had?

Her questions were answered soon enough when they passed by her brightly lit home. "He's still there," she croaked. "I told him to leave."

Morgan stopped the car in front of the house. "What do

you want to do? Do you want me to go talk to him? You let me know. I can kick his ass out for you if he won't leave."

She chuckled. "I don't want you in the middle of this. You've done enough just listening to me and taking care of me. I appreciate it. Can you just take me to my mom's house?"

"You're sure?" he asked, with a knowing look.

"Oh, God," she groaned when she saw the front door open.

Den stood, arms crossed in the doorway. After a few seconds, he walked out of the house and approached the truck. She cracked the window open a bit.

He nodded a quick greeting at Morgan, then looked at her. "What are doing, Syd? I've been waiting on you to come home. We need to talk."

"No we don't," she said through clenched teeth. "I told you to leave. You can't even respect me enough to get out of my house."

"*Our* house," he retorted. "And you can't just kick me out. We can work this out, Syd."

"No, we can't!" she shouted. "You cheated on me in my own fuckin' bed. I deserve better."

Den tried to open the car door but it was locked. "Let's not do this out here. Come inside so we can talk alone."

"I said no." Crossing her arms, she shifted to face front.

"Den, just go back inside," Morgan said, his voice low and controlled. "This isn't helping."

"Stay out of this, Roc," Den snapped. "This is between me and Syd."

"You're the one standing out here acting like you're not wrong," Morgan growled.

Out of the corner of her eye, she noticed Morgan's fists were clenched, and thought maybe she should just go talk to Den to keep the peace between the brothers.

"Just leave her the hell alone," Morgan said, the warning

in his tone clear. "You fucked up. Accept it and take some goddamn responsibility for your own actions, for once."

Den reeled back on his heels. "What did you just say to me?"

"You heard me," Morgan grumbled. "This is on you, Den. She asked you to leave and you didn't. Now you're trying to get her inside when she obviously doesn't want to be bothered with you."

"She's my fiancée. And this is *our* house. Syd?" Den continued to call her name until she finally looked at him. "Please. Don't do this."

Syd closed her eyes. Every *please*, every *sorry*, every *tear*...they always seemed to be her undoing. And she didn't want to forgive and forget this time. Not like the forgetting part ever worked anyway. The pain she felt seemed to fill every space in her body and mind.

"If you won't leave, I'll go." She hugged herself and forced herself to focus on the road in front of her. Getting him to leave would be a battle she was not up to having. "It's probably better this way. I'll have Red draw up a quit-claim deed and...you can have the house. I don't want to fight, Den. I'm tired of fighting. I just want my things. You can have the furniture, everything except for the Christmas stuff. Don't make this harder than it has to be."

Den punched the side of the truck, startling her. When Morgan reached for his seat belt, Syd placed her hand on his. The last thing she needed was for Morgan to jump out of the car.

"Den, just go back in the house!" Syd shouted.

Morgan jumped out of the car before she could stop him and walked up to Den. He had more than a few inches on Den in height, but Den outweighed him. She'd seen them in physical fights before, but she hated the thought of them fighting each other—especially over her.

"What the hell is wrong with you?" Morgan sneered. "Are you trying to scare her?"

Den shoved him. "I told you to stay out of this, Morgan."

"You brought me into it the minute you chose to come out here." Morgan pushed him back. "Syd already told you to leave her alone. She shouldn't have to keep telling you. Look at her; she's tired." He pointed at her. "She doesn't feel good and you come out here acting like she owes you something. You always do this. Nobody owes you shit. If anything, you owe her for putting up with your ass all these years."

"I don't want to do this," Den snarled. "I just want my fiancée to get out of your car and come inside so we can work this out."

"She's not coming," Morgan growled. "And if you don't take your ass inside, I will beat the shit out of you."

"Really?" Den stepped back and tilted his head at Morgan. "You're serious, right now? You're going to kick my ass for trying to fix my relationship. I know Syd is your friend, but I'm your brother."

"Yeah, you *are* my brother." Morgan glanced back at Syd before turning back to Den. "But you're wrong. And I'm not going to stand here and watch you try to make her feel guilty for your mistakes."

They stood, facing each other, Morgan's fists clenched to his sides, Den's arms folded across his chest.

Sydney rolled the window down all the way. "Morgan, please . . . Get back in the car," she begged.

Morgan backed away slowly, then hopped in the truck, started it, and pulled off, leaving Den standing outside in front of the house.

After they'd been driving for a few miles, Morgan pulled over and pounded his hands against the steering wheel.

Placing a hand on his back, she whispered, "I'm sorry."

He turned to her, fury in his eyes. "Don't. Stop apologizing for him. He's a grown man. We both have to stop doing that."

Morgan had done his fair share of making excuses for his older brother, just like she did. And he'd suffered for it over the years. A gifted basketball player, Morgan had been recruited by numerous teams including his first choice, UCLA. But he decided against going to California to stay closer to his brother, because Den was in a bad place. Syd didn't understand the dynamics of their relationship at the time, but she knew Morgan was driven and had a plan mapped out for his life. Denying himself that dream was big for him, but he'd decided to just play for Michigan.

During the last semester of his senior year, their biological mother died and Den spiraled even further out of control. In a drunken tirade, Den climbed behind the wheel of a car, intent on doing some damage to himself. Morgan jumped in with him and Den drove them into a tree. Luckily, neither of them was seriously hurt. But Morgan's leg was injured, effectively ending his basketball career.

"I guess you're right," she said. "It seems like I've spent too long making excuses for him."

The car descended into silence. As it stretched out even longer, she thought about their confrontation. Morgan had been so angry with Den. She'd noticed that Morgan had backed away from Den in recent months, but she figured it had something to do with his job. He worked long hours trying to make partner at the architecture firm. In that moment, though, she realized it was something more personal. As the heater blared, she warred with herself on broaching the subject with him.

"I hate when he acts like this," Morgan admitted quietly. "Reminds me of my father. And we all know how I felt about him."

Morgan wasn't the type of person who talked about his

past. He rarely brought it up. Den told everything, though. And she remembered him telling her that Morgan hated their father so much that he'd refused to be called by his true name, Nathan, because that was his father's name. That's why everyone called him by their last name, Morgan. Once the Smiths adopted them, he'd changed it legally to Morgan Smith.

"Thank you for having my back," she said. "I know it was hard for you. I hate that this is happening and I wish—"

"How about I take you to my house?" he suggested. "It's quiet there. You can sleep in peace."

"Okay, that sounds good." She'd table her questions for later. It was obvious he was done talking about Den and she couldn't say she blamed him.

CHAPTER FOUR

Morgan held the door open for Sydney, allowing her to step into the house. He watched as she twisted a finger around her purse strap. He tried to make eye contact but she avoided his gaze.

As she stood against the door—shoulders slouched—he twisted the lock. After he'd made the decision to bring her back there, no words were spoken. Instead she'd turned the music up and stared out the window. But he'd heard her—crying softly.

"You want a seat or are you going to stand there all night?" he asked.

With red eyes, she peered up at him through wet lashes. He towered over her by at least six inches, even though she was wearing heels. She gave him a smile, but it didn't reach her eyes.

When he opened his arms, she walked into his embrace. He held her for a few minutes, stroking her back and listening to her soft cries until she pulled away from him.

"Come on," he said, holding out his hand.

Taking his hand, she let him lead her farther into the

house. When they entered the kitchen, he flicked on the recessed lights under the cabinets, pulled out a chair, and motioned for her to take a seat.

Morgan watched as she tapped her tiny fingers against the granite countertop and wondered how he always ended up in this position. The question was one he asked himself often, yet he already knew the answer. If she needed him, he had no choice but to be there for her. In a sense, he felt guilty for the way Den had treated her, but there was more to it.

Over the years, she'd become more than his best friend's sister. It was during a summer vacation in Virginia that he realized his life wouldn't be complete if he never got the chance to kiss her. Unfortunately, Red had made it very clear that his sister was not an option. Being the type of friend Morgan was, he respected Red's declaration and never made his feelings known. Once college started, he played the role of the overprotective brother's best friend. He became her confidante, a person she could be herself with, and she was the same for him.

After she was raped, she was so fragile, so scared. Neither he nor Red could reach her. Den was the only one who could back then. It was a relief that she had someone to confide in. Not only did it help her get through the hard recovery, but being her hero helped Den. Morgan noticed subtle changes in Den's behavior at first. His brother started to care about his life again, made plans for the future. That was a good thing and Morgan was grateful. A little over a year after the rape, Den asked Syd out on their first date. They'd pretty much been together ever since.

Morgan's friendship with Syd didn't suffer for long after her rape, and they continued to grow closer even as she fell in love with Den. Things were good for a while, but Den's mood swings continued to plague all of his relationships, and had especially taken a toll on Syd. Morgan had watched

her give up so much of herself for his brother and it angered
him, mostly because he'd been there himself and he knew
what it was like to live in Den's bottomless pit. He wanted
more for Syd, but she wouldn't give up on Den.

He eyed her as she fidgeted in her seat.

"Coffee?" he asked.

"Tequila," she responded.

He hesitated, wondered if he should insist that she drink
some tea and go to sleep since she'd said her stomach was
hurting earlier. Or should he indulge her request and let her
drink until she passed out? Deciding to let her have her way,
he pulled a fifth of Patrón out of the freezer, grabbed a shot
glass from the cabinet, and set it on the countertop. Tequila
was her drink of choice when she was depressed, hurt, or
angry. He smirked when she grabbed the bottle of liquor,
popped the lid off, and poured a shot into the glass.

"Thanks." She sucked the shot down.

"You're welcome. But—"

The plan was to warn her about drinking too much again,
let her know that she should only take a few shots. But then
she let out the cutest hiccup. He covered his mouth to hide
his smile.

"Are you laughing at me?" she asked.

"No," he lied.

Then she grabbed the whole bottle by the neck and shuffled to the den.

* * *

Sydney sat on the large sectional, staring at the roaring fireplace. Morgan's house was always a wonder to her, probably because he'd designed it himself. His signature was all
over it, from the imported sofas and glass tables in the living room to the sunken den with the big screen TV, leather

sectional, and attached game room with a huge nine-foot pool table. The kitchen was fully equipped with smart appliances, glass-front cherrywood cabinets, and granite countertops. The finished basement housed his home office and theater room. Having been there more than a few times, she knew the layout well and felt comfortable there.

She noticed an open book, his glasses, and a half-empty beer bottle on the coffee table. He must have been reading before Red called him to the bar. One of the things she loved about Morgan was that he loved to read. Picking up the book, she skimmed the first few pages before putting it back in its place.

Morgan entered the room and headed straight to the recliner—on the other side of the room. She slammed a shot glass on the table and poured another. "Take one," she ordered, sliding the glass over the wood toward him. "There's no way I'm drinking alone tonight."

When he downed the contents, she filled it up again. He picked it up and she tipped the bottle in his direction. "Here's to my fucked up life. Cheers!" Only she didn't follow up her toast with another drink.

Resting her head against the couch, she gripped the bottle in her hand. "How pathetic is this?" She glanced at him out of the corner of her eye.

"You're not pathetic." His voice was barely above a whisper.

"Yes I am. Don't lie." She pointed the bottle at him. "Everyone warned me, even you. You told me not to accept the proposal, not to get sucked back in by his promises and lies, but I didn't listen. I knew it wasn't right and I did it anyway. Now look at me."

"You couldn't have known he would do this. Things happen."

Sydney watched Morgan quietly for a few minutes, stared

into his concerned eyes. "I should have listened to you. You want to know the worst part?" She took another swig and frowned as the liquid burned her throat on its way down.

He nodded.

"When Laney called and told me he cheated on me with her, I was relieved at first," she admitted softly. "It's not like this is the first time he's disappointed me, broken my heart. But you already know that." Everybody else knew about the cheating and drinking, but Morgan knew everything else. All the other things, like the times she'd had to call the police because Den was in a rage or had disappeared for days. "At first I thought, 'This is my chance.' Then it hit me...what this really means."

"What does it mean?" he asked.

She wiped some excess liquor from her chin with the back of her hand. "Never mind."

"I hate when you do that." He leaned forward, resting his elbows on his knees. "Say it."

Using the sleeve of her sweater, she rubbed her mouth. "There's really nothing left to say—nothing to do except move on."

"Are you sure you don't want to work this out with him?"

Sydney glared at him. *Was he serious*? "What? Work it out?" she asked incredulously. "How am I supposed to do that?"

He shrugged. "I'm not saying you should. But you have before, so you need to be sure that you don't want to work it out."

The liquor was doing its job—numbing her brain. She embraced the deadening of emotions. "That's the last thing I want right now. And don't look at me like you think I'm full of shit."

"I'm just trying to help." He guzzled down the rest of his beer.

They sat in silence for a few minutes. "You're mad?" she asked.

His eyes flashed to hers. "No."

"You're mad, Morgan. I'm sorry I snapped at you. I'm so upset." She slid to the other end of the sectional—the side closest to him. Her eyes welled up with fresh tears.

"I'm not mad." He tapped the empty bottle against the table. "But you've been in this situation before. I just want you to be sure."

"Oh, believe me, I am."

"Good." Sighing, he leaned closer. "He's my brother, but he doesn't deserve you."

He rubbed her cheek and she leaned into his hand as he stroked her. She captured his hand, held it against her face. He'd always made her feel safe, and she needed that. Reluctantly, she let go and smoothed her hair back.

A couple of minutes passed and the silence was getting to her. Needing to put some space between them, she jumped up and paced the room. As she moved from one end to the other—back and forth—her mind was filled with all sorts of questions.

On the fireplace mantel, Sydney smiled at a picture of all of them—Den, Kent, Red, Morgan, and her at the bar. She picked up the frame and ran a thumb over the edges. They were inseparable, all of them preferring to hang out with each other rather than anyone else. The massive crush she'd had on Morgan back in high school never went anywhere. In the end, it was for the best, because he was one of her best friends. They understood each other.

Clearing her throat, she set the picture back on the mantel and turned to Morgan. "Can we listen to some music?" She tugged at her collar and released the top button on her blouse. "It's hot in here."

Morgan walked over to the built-in shelves against the

wall that contained his DVDs and CDs. "You know I don't have a lot of that old, old-school music you like." He picked through the discs.

"I have one." She rummaged around in her Coach tote and pulled out a CD. "I think this one might work."

He smirked then and her stomach shifted. "You carry around CDs in your purse?"

She shrugged. "You know I'm always prepared." She pulled the CD out of its case and held it out to him.

"For what?" He loaded it into the player.

Sydney didn't answer him. She was busy taking in his smell. It seemed as if Morgan made it his mission to smell delicious enough to eat—spicy, fresh, and male. Issey Miyake, his favorite cologne. When her stomach fluttered, she closed her eyes.

Maybe I should have taken it easy with the tequila?

The music of the Isley Brothers floated to her ears and she couldn't help but sway back and forth as her favorite song permeated her soul. *Can I go on my way without you? Whoa... how can I know?* She hummed the tune as the verse played on. She'd never thought about the meaning before, but as she listened she figured it was about two lovers connected through space and time; two lovers who've always come back to each other. Her eyes fluttered open, but she resisted the urge to look at him. She wobbled on her feet and slyly rested her hand on the mantel to keep herself upright.

Glancing back at him over her shoulder, she sang the chorus. "I'll always come back to you." She smiled up at him. "Dance with me?"

He raised a brow.

"Please?" she asked again.

He took her hand and pulled her close.

As they swayed to the music, his massive hands rested on the small of her back and his chin on top of her head. She relaxed her head on his chest and snuggled against him. His arms were like a warm cocoon. She felt the heat emanating from his body. It seemed to light a match inside of her and shoot through her body.

The guitar strings plucked away at her senses and she thought of Den. After she was raped, Den proved to be what she needed—a savior. She was scared of everything those first few months, even her shadow.

Over the years, she'd gone through so many changes. No matter what was going on with her and Den, though, one thing remained solid—her relationship with her "boys." Red, Morgan, and Kent rallied around her and made sure she was protected, scaring off anyone who came within a few feet of her. They were a close-knit group and met at their favorite bar every Friday night for happy hour. Once or twice a year, they planned elaborate vacations to warmer climates and ski trips to lavish northern resorts. More often than not, she was charged with planning the excursions, but Morgan always volunteered to assist.

She appreciated that he always made himself available to her and loved being around him. They discussed any- and everything, from politics to old television shows to sports. They checked in with each other daily, updating one another on significant events in their lives. He shared his relationship woes with her and she vented about hers. When she was arguing with Den, Morgan almost always took her side, often giving her a shoulder to cry on. He never let her down—unlike his brother. She'd never admitted it to anyone, but she found herself thinking about him even when he wasn't around—yearning for the comfort that only he provided, the understanding that he gave her. It had always been that way between them.

Stepping back, she let out a heavy sigh. "I need to go to sleep and put this day behind me."

"Good idea." He shoved his hands into his pockets.

"I'll be out of your hair tomorrow," she promised. "I can just go stay with Red until I find a place."

"You don't have to, ya know?" Morgan scratched the back of his neck. "You can stay here. I have plenty of room and Den won't bother you here."

"You've already gone above and beyond the call of duty."

He tucked a strand of hair behind her ear. "We're friends. And Den is fucked up. We both know it."

Syd stepped back, putting space between them. "I don't want you to feel like you have to clean up his mess by taking me in."

A smile spread across his face. "You do know me, right?"

She laughed. "What's that supposed to mean?"

"Take care of Den, yes. Cover for him, sometimes. Enable him, pretty much. Let his girlfriend stay with me because I feel responsible for his trifling ways…never. Look, we have our own relationship. You're not just Den's fiancée. So when I offer you a place to stay, I'm offering *you* a place to stay."

"Okay, but I'm not moving in with you," she said emphatically. "I do appreciate the offer, though. It's really time for me to make some decisions about where I want to be. I've spent so many years pushing myself aside to please others. It's time to stop and please Syd. And I can start by taking some time." She picked up his empty beer bottle, the shot glass, and the bottle of Patrón. "Actually, I think I'm going to get a room tonight."

He took all three from her hand and set them down on the coffee table. "You don't have to leave, Syd."

"No, I do." Turning, she fluffed the throw pillows and folded up a blanket that was lying on the couch. "I want to be alone. I need to think and sleep and make some plans. Do you mind taking me?"

As she bent to grab the empty glasses again, his hand on her back gave her pause. Swallowing, she turned to face him.

"Sydney, stop," he said, his voice low, husky. He rarely called her by her full name. Her cheeks grew warm and she ducked her head. "You don't have to clean my house."

The hint of tequila mixed with beer on his breath made her pause. Her heart seemed to be beating louder than ever and the urge to bolt took over. Turning her back to him quickly, she let out a slow breath. "I'm going to call the new hotel by the mall and see if they have any rooms."

Patting him on his shoulder, she hurried to his home office. As much as she wanted to stay with him, everything in her was screaming that it wasn't a good idea. Besides, she needed to deal with her life and not hide from it.

CHAPTER FIVE

$\mathscr{M}$ichigan weather sucks," Sydney murmured to herself. The temperature had dropped even further. That's what she deserved for putting her winter coat away too early. She heard Morgan cursing his tire to hell and back from outside the truck.

She felt guilty that she'd begged him to take her to a hotel for the night. It had started snowing and he'd hit an ice patch and skidded off the road.

A blast of cold, snowy air whooshed in when Morgan opened the door and climbed back in.

"Morgan?" Sydney said.

He glanced at her out of the corner of his eye. "What?"

"I'm sorry." She dropped her chin to her chest and rubbed her hands together.

Shaking his head, he tapped a button to increase the heat. "It's cold. Put this on." He tossed her a University of Michigan hoodie he must have gotten out of the trunk. "I don't have my tools with me. Triple A has an hour wait for roadside assistance. I called Kent, but he's in Detroit. It'll take a while for him to get here."

"What's wrong with your tire?" She put the oversized sweatshirt on.

He shrugged. "I blew that shit out. Rim is bent. I'll need to replace it."

She pulled the hood on over her head and rubbed her hands against her thighs. "How long do you really think it will take for the tow truck to get here?"

He shrugged. "I can't say. It's snowing pretty badly. Hopefully it won't take too long."

"What possessed me to leave the comfort of your warm house in this weather?" Shivering, she burrowed into his side and he rubbed her shoulder.

"You *needed* time alone," he murmured. *Sarcasm evident.*

She closed her eyes. "I'm glad you're here."

"I'm going to bill Den's ass for this," he said, mumbling another curse under his breath. "That was a brand-new tire."

She cringed when he mentioned Den's name. In a way, Den was responsible for this mess—in a roundabout way. Mostly, she felt responsible.

"It's not your fault," he said.

She wasn't surprised that he knew what she'd been thinking. That seemed to happen a lot. Sydney thought back on a similar conversation she'd shared with Morgan years earlier—when she'd found out Den had gotten Laney pregnant.

"What a night, huh?" she said. "I mean, technically, it *is* my fault. And you know why?"

Morgan tilted his head to the side, looking her in the eyes. "Why?" he asked.

"Because I'm the one who kept taking him back." The telltale signs had been there for a while. In hindsight, she could see that the quick, unromantic marriage proposal was a desperate attempt on his part to hold on to her. He knew he'd messed up. And he also knew that if they were married when the truth finally came out, it would be harder for her to leave him. "I put myself in this situation again. I just… I thought if I loved him enough, showed him enough support, he'd get his act together. He'd stop playing the blame game and become the man that we all know he can be. He was doing so well. He was taking his meds consistently. He runs a successful construction business. Why couldn't that be enough? Why wasn't I enough?"

"He's an idiot. You *are* enough." Morgan squeezed her. "And you're not wrong for feeling the way you do. You deserve better."

"He sure knows how to make me feel like I'm overreacting." She stared down at the engagement ring on her finger, twisted it around. "Forget it. Let's just not talk about it anymore. I'll figure this out in the morning."

Pulling a flask from his wool pea coat, he took a sip and handed it to her. "Want a sip? Maybe it will help with the cold."

"No thanks." She grimaced at the thought of more liquor. "Do you have something to eat in here? I'm hungry."

He opened the glove compartment and pulled out a Snickers bar.

She ripped it open and took a bite, scowling at the stale taste. "Yuck. How long has this been in there?" He was staring at her when she looked up at him. She felt heat rush to her cheeks when he smirked at her. "Don't look at me like that." She grabbed the flask, took a few sips, then shoved it into his chest. Scowling, she told him, "That stuff tastes like gasoline."

"Yeah." He chuckled. "Yet you keep taking sips."

She was having a hard time focusing on anything, considering her eyes were filled with tears and the bourbon was working its way through her body. "You don't happen to have a bottle of water in here, do you? I've never tasted a bitter chocolate bar before."

He flashed a smile. "Guess I should've thrown that out last year, huh?"

Laughing, she punched his arm and he nudged her back playfully. Before she could stop herself, she ran a finger over his chin. Her eyes widened and she jerked her hand back. *What the hell am I doing?* "I'm sorry. You had some..." She scratched the back of her head.

"Are you still feeling cold?" he asked, adjusting the heater and finishing off the contents of his flask.

"Actually, I'm feeling pretty hot." She jumped when he started coughing. "Are you okay?"

He wiped his mouth. "I'm straight."

"You sure?" Syd studied his face as she smoothed her hand over his back.

"Yeah." He closed the flask and tucked it back into his pocket. "It's the liquor."

"Huh?"

"The bourbon." He patted his pocket. "It's making you hot."

"Somehow I doubt that," she mumbled.

"What?" he asked, leaning in closer.

I doubt it's the liquor. "Forget it. I'm cold again." She burrowed into him.

"You want me to make you hot?" he asked.

Her eyes flashed to his and her lips parted.

"I meant..." He cleared his throat and shifted in his seat. "Uh, I can turn the heat up."

"No." She forced a smile and lowered her gaze. "It's fine."

When his hand caressed her cheek, her eyes closed of their own volition. Time seemed to stand still. She felt his warm breath on her skin above her lips. "I think—" She dug her nails into his knee. "Maybe you should call Kent again. See where he is."

He slid his thumb down the side of her neck.

She exhaled. *So this is what Terry McMillan meant when she waited to exhale?* "Because this isn't going anywhere good. You're acting like you want to kiss me and I know that's not true," she joked.

He clenched her hair in his hands and tugged gently. "How do you know that?"

She searched his eyes. "Do you? I mean—do you want to?"

"I do—and so many other things."

She let out a nervous giggle. "I think you're feeling the effects of that gasoline you're drinking, Morgan."

His gaze dropped to her mouth as his hand crept up her thigh and rested on her hip. She jumped in surprise when he squeezed. "Actually, I don't believe I'm drunk enough," he said. "At this point, I know exactly what I'm doing, which means I'd be held responsible for my actions."

Syd placed her hands on his stomach and felt his taut muscles tighten in response. "Den would kill you. So would Red."

Morgan traced her lips with his thumb. "It may be worth it. Let me..." Then, his mouth was on hers, drawing a low moan from her mouth. The simple touch of his lips to hers set off a fire in Syd that seemed to burn brighter and hotter with every second.

She wrapped her arms tightly around his neck as he continued to assault her senses with his kisses. He slid his tongue across her bottom lip, demanding entrance, which she happily granted. She gripped a fistful of his hair as he pulled her onto his lap. He rocked into her, introducing her to his rock hard erection. She braced her other hand against the window as she grinded into him. He trailed hot, wet kisses down her throat and cupped her breasts in his hands. As his thumbs traced her nipples, she cried out and he captured her cry with his hot mouth.

Reluctantly, she tried to pull away, but he latched onto her bottom lip with his teeth and sucked. He obviously wasn't ready for this to end…neither was she.

Syd ran her fingers through his short hair, scraping her nails across his scalp. He groaned as she rocked into him in a slow rhythm. *Damn.* As wrong as it was—kissing a man that should be forbidden to her for so many reasons—she couldn't stop. It felt too good, too right to stop. She wanted him so badly. She felt him—hard—against her. She needed to ease the constant ache between her legs.

Slowly, he snaked his hands under her shirt inch by inch. He finally broke the kiss and tugged both the sweatshirt and her shirt over her head at once. He flicked off the overhead light and dipped his head to take one covered breast into his mouth. She cried louder as he dragged his tongue over her nipple. She felt light-headed, like she was floating on air. His smell seemed to infuse into her skin and the hair on her nape stood on end. A warmth spread through her body. Her brain screamed at her to push him away even as her body demanded more.

"Damn. I want you, Syd," he breathed out after grazing her swollen bud with his teeth.

Unable to form any words at that point, she rocked harder. He unbuttoned her jeans and she gasped when he slid his hand into her soaking panties. "Oh God," she murmured. "Please…"

"Shit, you're so wet—for me." He parted her slick folds with his finger and began strumming her clit like a guitar. She arched her back as pleasure washed over her and her hips moved in time with his ministrations.

Pulling her head up, he devoured her mouth in a desperate kiss. He unclasped the front hooks of her bra with his free hand and it fell open. Her stomach quivered as his hand snaked its way up her stomach. Then he stopped.

Sydney's eyes popped open, disappointment clouding her mind.

Morgan removed his hand from her panties and groaned. "We can't do this." He rested his forehead against hers and pulled her bra closed, refastening it.

"Yeah, I know," she agreed, even though she really wanted to grab his hand and put it back where it had been.

"I want to. Damn, I want to." He grabbed her hips and rocked them into him again.

"I can tell." The feel of his hard-on sent a shiver straight through her body down to her core. She brushed her lips against his, unable to help herself.

He cocked a brow. "You have no idea."

"I think I do." She smirked. "But you're right. We probably shouldn't do this. We'd regret it in the morning."

He sighed heavily. "I can't do that to him—he wouldn't take it too well. Not to mention, we may never be able to come back from it."

"I know." That was all she could say at that point. "This would be catastrophic. I can't even believe I—I'm sorry." Clarity started to rear its ugly head and guilt slammed into her. She fumbled for her shirt and pulled it on quickly. Neither of them spoke as she slipped the sweatshirt back on.

When she shifted to get off his lap, he squeezed her thighs. Groaning, he pulled her into another intense kiss.

Placing her hands against his chest, she reluctantly pulled back. As she slid off his lap, she buttoned her pants. When she peered up at him, she was struck by the heat blazing from his eyes, the intensity of his gaze. "What is it, Morgan?"

He rubbed his face. "I need to apologize to you." She opened her mouth to speak, but he continued before she could. "Hold on. Let me finish." She clamped her mouth shut. "I shouldn't have taken advantage of the situation. I don't want you to feel like anything that happened tonight is your fault. It was a mistake—on my part."

"I think we're both adults," she said, unable to take her eyes off of his full lips.

"Yes, but you just broke up—with my brother, of all people. I shouldn't have kissed you." He moistened his lips. "Sydney, this can't happen again and no one needs to know about it."

A light shined into the car. He grumbled a curse and adjusted his pants.

"You're right." She swallowed hard and adjusted her clothes. "Let's just not bring it up. Ever."

Casting another glance at him, she caught him staring back at her, his chest heaving. Kent knocked on the window, snapping her back to reality. She watched him hop out of the car to greet Kent and vowed to never put herself in that position again or there would be hell to pay.

CHAPTER SIX

$\mathscr{W}$hen they got back to the house, Morgan watched Sydney pour herself a shot of tequila and then pace the room. He'd cursed himself the whole ride home because he'd kissed her. Well, he'd done a hell of a lot more than kiss her. Although he suggested they never speak of it again, he thought maybe he should address it at some point. *Or maybe not.*

Taking a seat, he studied her movements. Initially, he'd had a hard time trying to figure out why she was attracted to Den. He understood that they'd bonded in the aftermath of the rape and subsequent trial, but they were complete opposites. Den was compulsive, with far too many vices. Sydney was cautious, deliberate. Still, he saw that they gave each other something they both needed at the time. Red had almost blown a gasket when she announced that she was in love with him, though. Of course, he'd had to defend his brother to Red, but he definitely couldn't blame his friend for being skeptical of the relationship.

He loved his brother, but Den was incapable of truly loving anyone. He hadn't grasped the concept that it wasn't all about him and what he wanted. It had everything to do with how they were raised, and was the reason Morgan preferred nonrelationships: dinner and a movie...breakfast in the morning before he made up some excuse to get whoever he'd brought home out of there.

But Syd...she wasn't like any other woman he'd met. She never judged him or made him feel bad for his choices. He wasn't an emotional person by any means, but he'd been able to share a side of himself with her that he'd never shown anyone else. After everything she'd gone through, she doted on the people she loved. She believed in him, telling him once that she'd always be on the sidelines of his life rooting for his success. That unwavering support and love inspired him to live up to it, to be a better man.

In recent years, she'd blossomed as she came into her own. Ultimately, he had a feeling that the person she was becoming would outgrow his brother. She became a social butterfly who could talk to anyone—from the hood all the way up to the boardroom. She had ambition and wasn't content to stay stagnant. No, she had dreams she wanted to attain and she worked hard every day in an effort to get where she wanted.

She tugged at the collar of his sweatshirt and finally pulled it off, fumbling with it when the fabric caught on her earring. She swore, and sent the shirt sailing across the room. *Beautiful, sexy—and drunk as hell.*

Turning to face him, she stumbled to the couch. Along the way, she tripped over her own shoe and landed firmly in Morgan's lap. He placed both hands on her hips to hold her steady.

He squeezed her waist and swore she felt it, too—the spark that passed between them. It took every ounce of restraint he had not to move his hands over her ass, which was one of his favorite things about her. She wasn't a stick figures she had curves in all the right places.

He brushed a stray piece of hair away from her eyes. "Maybe it's time to put the tequila away," he told her.

She pouted. "You're no fun. Things just got a bit serious for a minute. One more drink?" she asked, holding up her index finger.

"Okay, one more. Then coffee, then sleep." He stared at her mouth, engrossed in her pink tongue as she moistened her lips.

She slid onto the seat next to him. They tossed back one more shot together and made small talk. After a while, she plopped her head back against the chair and closed her eyes. "I'm so drunk, Morgan."

"Pretty much. For two days now," he snickered.

She giggled. "Right. I guess I better rein that in, huh?"

"Yep. But you've had a lot going on." They both laughed.

When she rested her hand on his knee, he swore silently. Who knew one person's touch could make him want to risk everything to feel it, to do anything to erase her worries? He touched her hair, ran his thumb over a curly lock. She gasped softly, her hazel eyes turning noticeably darker.

She squeezed his knee. "Let's not talk about me anymore. I want to hear about you. What do you want?"

Is she flirting with me? Just to be sure ... "Excuse me?"

"You spend so much time taking care of everyone. If you could do anything in the world, what would you do?"

You. He cleared his throat in an effort to keep himself from blurting it out loud. "I don't know."

"Yes you do. You're very driven. You get what you want most of the time, and you don't let anything stand in your way."

Not all the time. "Sometimes you can't have everything you want." He'd learned that at an early age. When his father had beat the shit out of him for saying the wrong thing, or even thinking the wrong thing, he would pray to God to save him from his bleak existence. His life had changed when he met Kent. The Smiths offered him a safe haven, but they also provided his father with a means to punish him. If Morgan fought back, he'd keep him from visiting the Smiths.

"What do you want?" she whispered, interrupting his thoughts.

Swallowing, his gaze dropped from her eyes to her pouty mouth. "Somehow I think you already know."

She blinked as if she was shaking her mind free of something. "What makes you think that?"

He hunched his shoulders and smoothed two fingers over the small crease in her forehead. "Maybe because you want the same thing." Even if she wasn't flirting with him, he was definitely flirting with her.

He reached out and pushed that wayward strand of hair back behind her ear, letting his fingers linger there until he trailed them down her neck slowly.

She closed her eyes and leaned into his hand. He leaned closer, as if he had no will of his own. They were a mere breath apart, so close the tips of their noses bumped. Then her eyes popped open and she jerked her head back. She gasped, touching her parted lips with her fingers. Bolting to her feet, she stretched. "Maybe we should get that coffee."

"Sydney..." He struggled to keep his voice even.

"Yes," she breathed, shooting him a quick glance before looking away again. "What is it?"

He wanted to taste her, to feel her lips against his again. He chickened out. "Coffee it is."

When they entered the kitchen, Morgan willed himself to keep his mind out of the gutter. There was no sense in traveling down this road. Syd was unavailable to him. Period.

He busied himself, pulling mugs out of the cabinet and setting them on the island.

Turning to Syd, he noticed her eyes were puffy and red. He'd been so preoccupied with his own thoughts he hadn't realized she'd been crying. "I'm sorry, Syd. I'm sorry that you're hurting."

"Don't." She rubbed her nose with a paper towel. "You know I'm a crybaby. Guess I just can't believe everything that's happened."

"Let me get you some Kleenex." Staring into her glassy eyes, he had an overwhelming urge to drive over to Den's house and kick the shit out of him for breaking her heart again. He couldn't understand how his brother cheated on her.

"I don't need it," she insisted, waving a hand at him. "What I need is this." She moved close to him and entwined her hands with his. "I need to feel safe—here with you."

Without saying another word, he wrapped his arms around her tightly. His stereo was still on from earlier and smooth jazz blared from the speakers in the other room. They began to sway to the music again.

He closed his eyes when she slid her hands down his arms and back up his chest. When he opened them, she was watching him through hooded eyes.

"I want to thank you for this, Morgan." Her fingernail scraped the skin under his collar. "You've been a good friend to me over the years—more than a friend."

"It's gonna be okay." He kissed her forehead, letting his lips linger. He pulled back and noticed a tear fall and kissed her under her eye where the tear drizzled down her cheek. She stood on the tips of her toes and wrapped her arms around his neck again and hugged him to her. He wrapped a hand around her neck and squeezed lightly. Visions of kissing her until she didn't remember anything, most of all Den, filtered through his mind. "Morgan," she said, her voice thick with emotion. "Don't let go."

He let her words convince his hands to explore further. He ran his fingers through her curly mane and down her neck. He traced the base of her neck with his thumbs, enjoying the way her eyes fluttered. He leaned closer to her, rubbing his nose against hers. "I won't, Syd. I won't let go."

Just like that, they had crossed a line. And he knew that this time they would never be able to go back.

CHAPTER SEVEN

It had been a week since Sydney had scandalously made out with her ex-fiancé's brother in his car. And if it hadn't been for her bladder screaming at her, they could've taken it even further than that at his house afterward. Instead, she'd gone to the bathroom and locked herself in the guest room for the rest of the night.

She'd avoided him since then and threw herself into work, putting in twelve-hour days. Graduating with her degree in chemical engineering had been a huge accomplishment, but she'd always wanted more. At a young age, she'd announced to her father that she wanted to own a bar, a place where adults could go to eat, listen to good music, and drink.

One night in college, she and Morgan had stayed behind while the crew went to a fraternity party on campus. He'd been shocked, but encouraging, when she shared her dream with him. He told her that if she was serious, he'd help her. And that's exactly what he did. She was closer than ever to realizing her dream and she couldn't wait until she could quit her job and devote her time to her business.

Now, after a particularly stressful day at work, her concentration was shot and she left early to take a drive. She drove around for half an hour, running through her list of things to do in her head.

Pulling up at a construction site, she parked her car and walked around the lot. Six months ago, she'd entered into a partnership with Red, Kent, and Morgan to build her dream—the Ice Box, a hometown bar and grill. It was her baby and she'd come up with the concept, the decor, and the business plan. She'd asked Den to jump in with them, but he'd decided against it saying he "wasn't into that shit." It had hurt her at the time—and she'd made home life a living hell for a bit—but Den had made up for his lack of interest in the partnership by offering to complete the construction for a minimal price.

Morgan had put up most of the capital upfront for the purchase of the building, with the caveat that the company consider it a loan, payable in equal installments over ten years. The brothers had come into a lot of money when their grandmother died. Den had blown all of his inheritance fairly quickly, but Morgan was smart with his. He built his house and put the rest in the bank. She suspected he had enough saved to live on for the rest of his life.

Even before he'd found out about the trust fund he'd already saved a small fortune, being the financial wizard he was. He had a keen mind for investments and made sound judgments, which paid off handsomely.

Kent was a promotional wizard with a knack for coming up with innovative ideas. He was a smooth talker and possessed a wealth of business contacts that were more than willing to throw their hats in the ring with the group. Although he'd graduated from MIT with a degree in computer engineering, he was extremely talented in art and graphic design.

Red had finished law school, passing the bar exam on his first try and landing a coveted position at a top law firm in town. After winning his first ten cases, he was promoted to junior partner, which made him the first African American to hold the title in the firm. He was a gifted litigator and was glad to contribute to the venture, offering healthy investment and legal services for a piece of the pie.

Using her key to open the door, Sydney entered the building. It was mostly finished and it would soon be time to move the new furniture in. As she walked around the bar, she thought of Den. On paper, he was quite the catch. He owned Smith Construction, and he'd recently received a contract to build a new casino and mall complex in a nearby city.

Although he had a reputation around town for being a hothead—an asshole—there was a side to him that others rarely saw. Being with Den had been easy at first. He had been patient with her through the trial and the subsequent fallout on campus. She wiped a tear from her cheek. *How did everything fall apart so badly?*

She slid into one of the booths. In her heart, she knew Den was sorry for what he'd done and would take things back if he could. He wasn't perfect by far, but she loved him anyway. Or at least she thought she did.

Sydney scanned the massive space, noting the dirty tarps covering the pool tables and scattered paint supplies. Soon the last remnants of the Mic Mac would be gone, replaced by new fixtures, furniture, and brand-new pool tables. Their old hangout would become their new adventure. The Mic Mac had been a refuge for her when she arrived in the area and she'd spent hours here shooting pool, laughing, eating, and drinking.

The sound of the door opening jarred her from her thoughts. She stood up, praying it was one of the workers and not a killer. When Calisa appeared in the doorway, she sighed.

Sydney smiled at her best girlfriend as she stepped into the bar. "You came?"

"Of course I did," Calisa said, tossing her bag into an empty chair. She pulled her hat off and ran a hand through her long, black hair. "And I brought food."

She set a brown paper bag on the table in front of Syd.

"You're the bomb." Syd smiled at Calisa. "Smells good. I've had a taste for Chinese."

Calisa took a seat and they dug in. After a few minutes, Calisa asked, "Are you ready to talk?"

"Not really." Syd pushed her food around on her plate, then peered at her friend. "Tell me about you."

"Red's an ass. But you already know that."

"Are you finally admitting that you and Red are friends with benefits?" Syd asked with a wide grin.

"Never. Besides, I wouldn't really call us 'friends.'" Humming, Cali tilted her head from side to side as if in thought. "More like thorns in each other's sides."

They burst out into a fit of laughter.

"Where's Allina?" Calisa asked. "You didn't call her?"

Syd shook her head. "I can't talk to her right now. She won't understand. She'll just tell me to pray and everything will be all right."

"I hear ya," Cali said, nodding her head. She dipped her fork into a container and pulled out some more lo mein. "She sees things in black and white. I always try to show her the gray areas in between, but she's pigheaded. She thinks I don't know she has a crush on Red."

"Well, as far as she's concerned, he's single," Syd teased, knowing that Allina's heart was firmly in Kent's camp, not Red's.

"Whatever. So what won't Allina understand?" Cali paused and set her chopsticks down. She lifted her gaze. "You're taking Den back?"

"I wish it was that simple," Syd told her.

Calisa and Syd had understood each other from their very first meeting. They were college roommates and hit it off instantly. They'd agreed to never judge each other and always be there—no matter what.

Syd met Calisa's concerned gaze. "I did something. And now I don't know how to fix it."

"What is it? Whatever you did, it couldn't be worse than taking Den back," she muttered. "Please tell me you didn't take him back, Syd. It's time to let him go."

Syd figured Calisa must feel strongly about this if she said it aloud. She was never one to tell her what she should or shouldn't do.

"I'm not taking Den back," Syd assured her. "This isn't about him—well, not exactly." She pondered her next move. Did she really want to tell Cali about Morgan?

"You're scaring me," Cali said, waving a hand in front of her face to get her attention. "What did you do?"

"I kissed someone."

Calisa's eyes widened and her fork slipped through her fingers and hit the table with a clang. "Seriously?"

Syd nodded.

"Who?" Calisa asked, with a smirk. "Is that all you did?"

"Shut up," Syd hissed. "You can't say a word about this to anyone, especially not Red."

"Please. I wouldn't even tell Red about my day at work, let alone something about your potential sex life, which by the way is awesome to say out loud." She clapped her hands with glee. "You may have a sex life that doesn't consist of boring ass sex with Den."

"Oh my God, Cali." Syd covered her face with her hands and slid down in her seat. "You were never supposed to say that out loud. And it was only the one time."

Calisa waved her off. "One boring time is one too many."
She winked.

Giggling, Sydney picked at her food. "You're too much."

"Well, I'm waiting. Spill."

"It was—" Syd hesitated.

The front door to the bar slammed and the confession
died on Syd's lips when Morgan walked in.

* * *

Morgan approached them. He'd spotted her car outside and
decided to check on her. They hadn't spoken since the night
they almost broke every rule in the book.

Syd offered him a sad smile. "Hey."

"Are you okay?" he asked. Glancing at Calisa, he asked,
"What's up, Cali?"

Calisa waved at him and popped a piece of sweet and
sour chicken into her mouth.

"I'm okay," Syd sat up straight and pushed her plate away.
"Cali brought me food. What are you doing here?"

"I was driving by, saw your car." He scanned the room to
avoid eye contact. "Everything seems to be falling into place
here."

"Yeah, it is." A slow smile spread across her face as she
looked around the huge room. It had been the first genuine
one he'd seen in a while. "It's exciting. I was thinking about
old times before Cali got here. We had a lot of good memories here."

"That we did," he agreed.

"Remember when that girl stabbed Red with a fork
because he was ignoring her calls?" she asked, giggling
softly. "And she got you instead, Morgan?"

Calisa groaned. "I remember that one," she chimed in. "I
told him to leave those crazy 'hos alone."

"Yeah, but it wasn't a laughing matter at the time." Morgan chuckled. He hadn't even flinched until he'd looked down and saw all the blood. Then the pain came and lasted for hours.

"And Kent threw his beer in her face because he didn't want to hit her," Syd added, hugging a knee to her chest. "He was pissed."

"Right." Morgan traced the edge of the table with his thumb. "That shit hurt like hell. Thank God Kerry was there." Kent's ex-girlfriend Kerry had been a resident at University Hospital at the time and she had tended to Morgan's wound. "But the highlight was when you hauled off and clocked that bitch," he said, mimicking a right hook. "Shocked the hell out of all of us."

Calisa burst out into a fit of laughter. "That's right. She fell like a ton of bricks, too."

"I'd never punched anybody before," Syd said, palms up. Her eyes were bright with an inner glow that was contagious. "I was shocked, too."

"I knew you had it in you," he said.

"Well, I didn't want Kent to go to jail for hitting that girl. Throwing his drink in her face didn't do anything for his temper." Syd rested her chin on her knee, a slight smile still on her face. "Life was very different then."

"Not that different." He kicked an empty can of paint to the side.

She frowned, cocked her head to the side. "But you have to admit it wasn't so complicated then."

Calisa was watching him with a curious look on her face, so he told Syd, "Well, I just wanted to check on you." He turned to leave.

"Morgan," Syd called after him. He stopped and glanced back at her over his shoulder. "How's Den?"

He shrugged. "Still upset. He's been calling me every hour asking if I've talked to you."

Calisa gathered up the empty containers. "I'm going to toss these in the trash and give you two a few minutes."

He watched her disappear into the back and inched closer to Syd.

"This is hard," Syd whispered. "I'm not sure what to do—about him, about the—"

"No need to bring it up because we said we wouldn't." Of course they said they wouldn't. She was his brother's ex-fiancée, one of his closest friends. So why couldn't he look her in the eye?

Only he knew why he couldn't meet her gaze. It was the same reason he'd picked up the phone a million times to call her over the last week. He couldn't forget. He'd kissed her like he didn't have a care in the world. He'd stuck his hand in her—

"Morgan?" She asked with raised eyebrows.

"Huh?"

She leaned forward. "Did you hear me?" she whispered.

Had she been talking? "What did you say?"

"I was just saying I should've said something to you sooner." She tucked her hair behind her ear. "I felt a little . . . awkward. Then, at your house, afterward . . ."

"Me too. I don't know what came over me." Of course, he did. *She's cute, vulnerable.* He wanted to be her hero, make her feel better. *That's it. Yep.*

They stared at each other. There were unspoken words he wished he could say and he figured she felt the same way.

"I better go," he told her, unable to take the silence between them any longer. "I'll talk to you soon."

She opened her mouth to speak, but nothing came out and she clamped it shut again.

He had a feeling she wanted to say something important, but instead of waiting it out or asking her what was on her mind, he decided to leave well enough alone and left.

* * *

Syd stared at Morgan as he walked out. Who knew a heated kiss in his truck would leave her tongue-tied around him? It was unacceptable.

"It was him, wasn't it?" Cali asked.

Syd jumped, startled by Calisa's entrance. "You scared me," she said, sliding back into the booth.

"It was him." Calisa slid in across from her. "Spill. Right now."

"It was a mistake," Syd admitted. "We were stranded on the side of the road—and alone. I was sad—and had been drinking. And it just happened."

"What's his excuse?" Cali asked skeptically. "Was he drinking?"

Syd shrugged. "A little." Honestly, she didn't know what Morgan was thinking. The only thing she knew was there had been a shift in their relationship. He'd kissed her like she was his and she'd enjoyed every minute of it—until reality hit.

"Oh my God, you kissed Morgan." Cali shook her head and pressed a hand against her chest. "You're so dead."

Frowning, she smacked Calisa's other hand. "Stop. I'm not dead, Cali. It was an accident."

"What?" Cali asked, lifting a single eyebrow. "You fell on his lips?"

"No. Not an accident, it was unexpected," Syd explained. "And wrong on every level. We promised we wouldn't say anything about it again and pretend like it didn't happen."

"Only you can't do that," Cali mused. Syd wanted to wipe that smirk off her friend's face. "You're thinking about it. And judging by the way your face turned bright red when he walked in, you liked it."

Covering her face, Syd felt her neck and cheeks grow

warm with a blush. It was the worst part of being fair-skinned. She could never hide a blush, turning a shade of crimson whenever she was embarrassed or flustered. And boy, did Morgan bring it out in her that night.

"You have to stop, Cali," Syd ordered softly. "It wasn't like that."

"Well, then tell me what it was like." Cali leaned forward, her gaze fixed on Syd like she was a lab specimen.

Syd took a deep breath. "It was just a kiss," she lied.

"You're lying to me."

"Okay, we made out a little bit." She squeezed her eyes shut and waited for Cali's response. When it didn't come, she slowly opened her eyes.

Her friend was grinning now. "How little is 'a little bit'?"

"None of your business." Syd blinked rapidly and sat back, creating some distance between them. Cali wouldn't give up. She was as relentless as Red. *They're made for each other*, Syd thought.

"Did any clothes come off?" Cali prodded.

She gaped at her nosy friend. "No," she lied.

"Bra undone?"

Silence.

"Ha!" Cali smacked her palms down on the table and cackled loudly.

"You're getting too much pleasure from this," Syd said, her voice flat.

"Get out!" Cali shook her head as if she still couldn't believe what she was hearing. "What are you going to do?"

Needing some space, Syd jumped up from the table and paced the room. "Nothing." She brought a shaky hand up to her forehead, then smoothed it over her hair. "I'm not going to do anything. It's over and it'll never happen again." She bit her thumbnail. "I would appreciate if you didn't bring this up again. We're already uncomfortable around each other now. The last thing I need is you smiling at him when we're all together this weekend at Red's dinner."

Crossing her arms, Calisa watched her with narrowed eyes.

"What?" Syd asked, fidgeting.

"For anyone else, a kiss wouldn't mean anything. But you..." Cali pointed at Syd. "You don't make mistakes like that."

"I did. I made a mistake and I want—no, I *need*—to forget it. So let's drop the subject, okay?"

"Okay," Cali muttered, rolling her eyes. "Sit your ass down and stop pacing around here like a mad woman."

Sliding back into the booth, Syd stabbed at her sweet and sour chicken. Maybe if she kept saying it out loud, that the kiss didn't mean anything, it would be true.

CHAPTER EIGHT

After countless calls from Red to convince him to talk to his brother, Morgan knocked on Den's door and waited. When Den answered, he held the door open for him.

"Long time, bruh," Den said, kicking a pair of shoes out of the way. "You're right on time. Mama's in the kitchen cooking up some dinner."

Morgan hadn't talked to Den much since the altercation on the lawn that night. When they did talk, it was basically filler. It had been a tradition in recent years to eat with Mama one Sunday a month. Kent had thought of the idea after Papa died in an attempt to make sure Mama wasn't feeling too alone in the world. It was the least he could do for a woman who'd given him so much love without ever wanting anything in return.

He walked into the kitchen and smiled at the sight of Mama at the stove stirring something in a big pot. He wrapped his arms around her and gave her a kiss on the cheek. "Smells good, Mama."

She grinned at him. "Hey, stranger. I'm so glad you're here." She held the spoon up to his mouth and gave him a taste of the simmering beef stew. "I figured I'd come over and help your brother out."

Morgan nodded. "That's good." He opened the refrigerator to get something to drink and noticed a six pack of beer. Shaking his head, he hoped it was for show, because Den had no business drinking. Grabbing a bottle of water, he twisted the cap off and gulped it down at once.

"You know I want to take some of that home," Morgan told Mama, sneaking another spoonful when she opened the cabinet to pull something out. There was something about her cooking that made everything better. He didn't know how or what he was going to say to Den, but he couldn't deny the smell of seasoned beef and potatoes made him feel a little more at ease.

He walked over to the table and sat down across from Den. "We need to talk."

Den assessed him quietly. "Let me guess. This is about Syd."

Morgan nodded, giving Mama a quick glance before turning his attention back to Den. "You need to leave her alone. Red is talking PPO." And Morgan had just been subjected to a half hour of Red cussing and fussing about Den's inability to leave Syd alone, before threatening to get a Personal Protection Order against Den. "I know you feel like you're doing the right thing, but—"

"How would you know that?" Den asked, a frown on his face. "You haven't been by to talk to me, to help me with anything."

"Have you been drinking again?" Morgan asked, changing the subject.

His brother snorted loudly. "Would you care if I was?"

Morgan lowered his gaze and focused on a groove in the wood table. It was a gift, made by him for Syd and Den's housewarming. Woodwork was a hobby of his and something he did to decompress. He'd worked on the table for months, spending countless hours making sure it was perfect. Syd had been elated when he'd presented it to them and suggested he start selling pieces. But he'd never had the desire. It was something he wanted to keep for himself.

"I thought it was best if I stayed away," Morgan lied. The truth was he couldn't bring himself to face Den. He'd acted like a jealous, brooding jerk that night in front of Syd, then turned around and kissed her like she wasn't his brother's girl—ex or not. He couldn't explain why he'd done it. The fact that he couldn't scared him, because he had never lost control like he did that night in the car with anyone. He prided himself on the fact that he maintained control in any circumstance. He'd had to when his parents had trotted hookers and drug users in and out of their house, when the authorities had barged into their home and took his mother and father out in handcuffs, when he'd lost the ability to play ball. Control was his thing. But he'd thrown caution to the wind with Syd in that car. He'd done something he never would have done before.

"After you almost fought me in my yard," Den added, squinting his eyes at him.

"Wasn't my finest moment," Morgan said. "But you have to admit it wasn't yours, either. Continuing to hound Syd isn't going to make this right."

Den leaned back in his chair, crossed his arms. "You don't know her like I do. She wants to work things out and we will. I have to pursue her. That's what she wants."

"You cheated on her in your house!" Morgan roared. "Then you proposed to her to cover it up, to ease your conscience. If you think she doesn't know that, then you're a fucking idiot."

"Boys, stop," Mama said, approaching the table. "I won't have any yelling. Whatever is going on can be worked out using inside voices."

"I'm sorry, Mama," Morgan mumbled. "I'm just...I was simply trying to tell Den he needs to back off of Syd, give her some space."

"Have you talked to Syd?" she asked him.

Den snorted. "Of course he has. Why do you think he's here? It's definitely not to see me."

"Den." Morgan glared at his brother.

"What's going on?" Mama asked, squeezing both of their hands. "I hate seeing you at each other's throats."

"Red called and asked me to talk to Den," Morgan confessed to Mama. "I don't want things to get worse than they already are. Apparently, Den has been calling her, showing up at Red's house, Syd's job...He needs to stop."

Den rolled his eyes and pushed himself away from the table, jerking his hand out of Mama's grasp. "I don't understand why everyone has an opinion about my relationship with Syd!" he hollered.

"Den, sit down," Mama ordered.

Den plopped back down into the chair without another word, crossing one leg over the other.

"Caden," Mama continued, "I love you. But I think it's time for you to let it go. You've hurt Syd—"

"Mama, stop," Den groaned, shaking his head slowly.

Mama grabbed Den's chin and pulled his attention back to her. "Listen to me. You can't expect her to keep forgiving you time and time again."

"I love her," Den said. "We can work this out."

"I know you're hurting, but you did this to yourself." After a few seconds, Mama let go of Den and dropped her hand to her lap. She glanced over at Morgan, a grave expression on her face. They'd both seen Den like this. And they knew it wasn't good.

"All I'm saying is just give her some space," Morgan added, knowing that space wouldn't be enough. He didn't doubt that Syd would always love and be there for Den, but *being* with Den in a relationship was a different story. "She needs time."

"Have you talked to her?" Mama asked Morgan again.

"I have," Morgan said.

"How is she?" Mama asked. "I've been meaning to contact her, but things have been hectic."

"She's doing all right, working and trying to move on." He looked at Den. "I didn't come over here because she asked me to, Den, despite what you may think."

Den shrugged. "Whatever. Bottom line is you're *my* brother and—"

"You know what?" Morgan asked. "That's your problem. You think everyone owes you something. It's Den's world. Everybody else better recognize, huh? What kind of brother would I be if I didn't tell you the truth? You fucked up." *Boy, he had a lot of nerve.*

"You're supposed to have my back." Den pounded his fists against the table.

Morgan gritted his teeth. The fact that his brother failed to see how much he'd sacrificed for him burned him up. "I need to go." He stood up. Mama's hand around his wrist gave him pause. He peered down at her. "Mama, please. If I stay, it won't go well and I won't disrespect you like that."

"Morgan, sit down." Mama squeezed him slightly. "I don't want you to leave like this."

"Let him go, Mama," Den said, flapping his hand. "Can't count on him anyway."

Tilting her head, she met Morgan's gaze. "Please, sit."

Morgan bent down and kissed Mama on her forehead. "I love you, Mama. But I have to go."

Pouring the rest of his water out in the sink, he set the bottle on the table and walked out.

* * *

Sydney walked around the empty space. It was bittersweet, but she'd finally purchased her own condo. Den fought her all the way, but Red was a wizard with the gift of gab and had some key friends in the judicial system.

"It's nice," Red said from behind her. "Now all you need is furniture. I wish you'd let me take Den to court for that."

Shaking her head, she ran her hands along the granite countertop. "It's not necessary. He can have everything. I'm just happy to get out of your house."

Syd had wanted to strangle Red every day for the past five weeks since she'd been staying with him. It wasn't enough that he lectured her day in and day out about going back to Den, but he ate all of her food and drank every ounce of her Minute Maid fruit punch. It was way past time for her to leave.

"No overnight guests, Syd," Red ordered.

"You're not my father, Red."

He placed his hands on her shoulders and squeezed. "I just want you to be okay. We've been here before. Den hasn't given up and he has this way of getting under your skin. Don't let him."

Den had been calling her daily, imploring her to change her mind, to take him back. She'd actually considered it more than once, but she couldn't bring herself to do it.

"I told you, I'm done," she said.

"Well, let's celebrate," he suggested, pulling out his cell phone. "I'm going to call Kent and Roc over...Calisa and Allina, and we're going to eat pizza and break in your new furniture."

"Look around you," Syd said, her arms open. "I don't have any furniture. And I don't really want company."

"Please, you're having company." He punched several

keys on his phone while she waited in silence. Finally, setting his phone down, he said, "Text sent. And we're going to Art Van and buying you a dinette set and a La-Z-Boy chair. You can order frou-frou couches and throw pillows and other girly shit later. Then we're going to Walmart and buying paper plates, cups, and plastic utensils."

"My God, you're pushy." She glanced around the condo. An uneasy feeling had settled in her gut and she wondered if she could really go through with this. It was so easy to say she was fine with the change in her life and ready to move on, but a lot harder to do. "I can't leave."

"Why the hell not?" Red asked.

"Because the furniture is coming in half an hour." When he gaped at her, she smirked. "You should've known your sister is always prepared. I ordered my furniture last week."

* * *

"Hi, Syd!" Calisa said, breezing past her into her new condo. Syd still liked the sound of that—her *new* condo. If only her life felt *new*.

"Hey, girlfriend." Syd gave her friend an affectionate hug. Red strolled in with five pizzas from the local joint. "I got your favorite, Syd, even though I can't stand feta cheese on pizza."

"I brought the wine." Calisa held up a huge bottle of Moscato and waved it at her. "And I'm taking my own tour, too."

Red watched Calisa disappear into the back.

"You've got it bad, brother," Syd said, helping him with the pizza boxes. "I'm not sure why you don't just tell her you love her and be together."

"This conversation isn't happening right now," Red said with a grimace. "This is all about your new place. I called everybody that matters. They should be here shortly."

"I'm here now," Kent announced from the doorway. He entered with Allina right behind him.

Syd hugged Allina, then Kent. "Glad you guys could come." She grabbed the lemon meringue pie Allina had in her hand. Gesturing toward the back hallway, she said, "Cali's already showing herself around if you want to join her."

Allina laughed. "I think I'd like *you* to give me a tour."

Syd noticed the frown on her friend's face and figured it had something to do with Kent. "Sure, come on back. It's not that big of a space, but it's perfect for me."

Syd made quick work of showing Allina the master bedroom and headed toward the staircase to the loft-slash-office and additional bedrooms.

"Thanks for saving me," Allina whispered as they walked up the stairs, arm in arm. "He irritates the hell out of me right now."

"Maybe it's because you secretly want to jump his bones?" Syd nudged her friend with her shoulder.

Allina shushed her. "Don't say that out loud. The walls have ears, remember?"

Shaking her head at her stubborn friend, Syd finished up the tour. When they walked back into the living room, Morgan was there.

Memories of the last time she'd seen him flooded her mind and she gave him a brief wave before heading into the kitchen to grab a big glass of wine.

Tossing a throw pillow onto the floor, she sat down and scanned the faces of her closest friends. Syd had truly hit the friend lottery, because she couldn't imagine her life without anyone in the room.

"Thanks for coming over," she said, her voice thick with tears. She tapped a loose fist against her heart. "You just don't know how much I appreciate you all."

"Man, stop being all mushy," Red ordered. "Pizza and mush don't mix."

She laughed at him, grateful that he interjected before she turned into a bumbling mess. "Hey, I can be however I want in *my* house, jerk."

"Did you bid down?" Kent asked. "I hope so, because my co-worker just bought in this subdivision and paid much less than asking."

"Of course she did," Red said before she could answer herself. "Who do you think brokered the deal?"

"Yes, Red brought his 'A' game to the table." She smiled at her relentless but lovable brother. "I came in at $10,000 less than asking so I'm happy."

And she really was—for the most part. She'd directed the movers and the delivery men all afternoon and when they were gone she couldn't help but feel proud of herself. But she'd be lying if she said it wasn't bittersweet. She'd always envisioned buying a bigger house with Den after they married.

"I love this room," Calisa said, with a slight wiggle of her eyebrows. "Vaulted ceilings, fireplace...You should have Morgan make you some shelves." Cali winked at her and smiled.

Mortified, Sydney narrowed her eyes, bit the inside of her cheek, and looked at her friends to see if anyone else caught Cali's attempt at humor.

"Well, he does know how to do all that shit," Red said, obviously missing the mischievous glimmer in Cali's eyes. "And since Den...Well, we won't bring him up. Anyway, Roc can probably even install recessed lighting in here as well."

Syd's gaze met Morgan's across the room. He hadn't said much since he'd arrived and she wondered if he felt as awkward as she did. "Sure," she croaked, squeezing her throat.

"If Morgan has the time, I'd love him to come...over. Would you mind, Morgan?"

Taking a swig from his beer, he nodded. "It shouldn't be too hard to build you something. But the recessed lighting, as good as I am, should be contracted out."

"Thanks." She swallowed as their gazes lingered. "I'm assuming you know someone. Can you send me their information so I can give them a call?"

"You got it," he said.

Exhaling, Syd focused on the pizza in front of her. The conversation didn't stop there, though—neither did the laughs, courtesy of Red. She sat there trying to join in. Unfortunately, it was pointless because her mind kept wandering back to her problems. While Cali had handled canceling the resort and getting refunds from the booked vendors, Syd still had to take care of a few things pertaining to the wedding. What drained her, though, was dealing with Den and the constant phone calls begging her to give him a chance. He'd come to her job armed with Gerbera daisies and chocolate. He'd shown up at Red's house at odd times. She'd spent many nights calming Red down. Den had turned on the charm in every situation, but she could see the desperation in his eyes. It scared her and she worried about his emotional health.

Cali and Allina were trying their best not to mention it, but it would've been her bridal shower the next day. Instead of opening scanty pieces of lingerie, she was preparing to send Thanks-but-we're-not-getting-married letters to her invited guests.

"Damn, Allina, will you just take the damn piece of pizza," Kent blared, drawing her attention toward the far side of the room, where he and Allina were sitting.

"No," Allina said, crossing her arms. "I told you I didn't want it. Eat it yourself."

"I have no idea what the hell you're going through today, but I wish you'd get over it," Kent grumbled, biting down into his slice.

She shoved him and the pizza fell onto his plate. "Maybe you shouldn't be such an ass. Did you ever think of that? I bet it never even occurred to you that *you* did something wrong. It's always me."

"Okay, this is pretty weird," Red said, surveying the scene. "I don't think I've ever heard Allina yell at anyone. And she said 'ass.'"

"Shut up, Red," Calisa said. "Obviously she's upset. It's just like a man to downplay it or say it's weird."

Syd looked at Morgan. He smirked and she knew he was thinking the same thing. *How in hell did we end up surrounded by not one, but two crazy-ass not-so-couples?*

"Syd, we're leaving," Red announced, glaring at Calisa, who ignored him.

Jumping to her feet, Syd turned to her brother. "You're leaving? Why?"

"You look tired," Red said, rubbing his brow, "and judging by the way Allina is shooting death glares at Kent and Calisa is getting on my nerves, it's probably better if we leave you to the solitude of your place. It's a powder keg in here right now."

"Okay, I guess," she said. "I am tired. I'm just going to get into bed and watch some TV."

Allina yanked her purse off the table and rushed up to her, pulling her into a tight hug. "I'm sorry, girlfriend. I have to get out of here. Talk to you soon."

"Wait," Syd said. It was too late, though, because Allina all but ran out and Kent muttered a few choice curses before he gave her a quick kiss and scrambled out after her friend.

Calisa tossed her plate into the trash and set her wine glass in the sink. "He's right, babe. It's probably time to get out of here. I'll see you tomorrow. Maybe we can go to the spa or something." She planted a kiss on Syd's cheek and pushed past Red on her way out the door.

"I swear, that woman…" Red grumbled. "I'll see you later, sis." He gave her a strong hug.

"Well, I guess that's my cue," Morgan said, standing up. He took his empty plate and glass into the kitchen.

When he returned, he gave her an awkward side hug and hurried toward the door.

"Wait, Morgan," Syd called before he walked out. "I was wondering if you could do something for me."

They hadn't mentioned the make-out session. Well, they hadn't really talked about anything. Their interactions seemed to have been reduced to "bar" business. He'd taken on some of her "bar" responsibilities and she was grateful. But the ease with each other had been replaced with long pauses and brief hugs.

"What's up?" he asked.

She rummaged through her briefcase and pulled out a manila folder. "I was wondering if you could handle this— the inspection is scheduled for Tuesday and the plumbing needs to be checked before they come." Holding the folder out to him, she waited until he grabbed it to continue. "I've already hired JP's Plumbing and they're coming Monday. Can you be there? Oh, and we've been getting tons of employment applications and I was wondering if you could review them and let me know your impressions."

He skimmed through the paperwork in the folder, closed it, and set it on the table. "No."

Frowning, she asked, "Excuse me? No?"

"You heard me," he responded in a sharp tone. "No. I'm not doing it."

She crossed her arms and glared at him. "Why? What's wrong with you?"

"I could be asking you the same question." The hard line of his jaw let her know that he wasn't happy with her. Narrowed eyes assessed her, unnerving her. "What the hell is wrong with *you*?" He asked, throwing his hands up. "You've been passing all of your responsibilities to me for weeks. This is a partnership. We all have things to do. But you're not doing anything. You're sitting here, letting your life pass you by. You've stopped calling your friends, you don't go anywhere, you're barely here."

"I just need some time," she shouted. "Is that too much to ask? Time!"

"You've had plenty." He stalked away from her, then came back. "And, with all due respect, you don't need time. You need to get off your ass and do something. Stop feeling sorry for yourself. Instead of thinking of what you lost, think about what you gained."

"What is that, exactly?" Her heart thundered in her chest. It seemed as though she felt her pulse through her throat. Swallowing hard, she asked, "My self-respect? That was gone a long time ago. What?" she yelled. Her cheeks burned and her chin trembled. "I'm starting over from scratch. I poured equity and sweat into that home and I lost it. I put hours, days, and years into my relationship and I lost it. What did I gain? Huh? You tell me."

"You gain a little bit of your self-respect every time you wake up in the morning sane," he said, gripping her face in his massive hands. "You didn't lose everything. You still have family, friends, a job, and a new business in the works. You're better off than a lot of people."

"I don't feel better off." She choked back a sob and backed away. "I feel empty. I feel tired."

"Get over it, Syd," he demanded. "You're not dead. You're still alive; breathing, healthy. Your life is not over. You're not this girl. You're not the girl who pulls the cover over her head when she gets news she doesn't want to hear. You're a fighter. You're strong. You're beautiful."

"What do you want from me, Morgan?" she screamed. "I'm doing the best I can."

Gripping her arms, he pulled her toward him. "I want you to fight your way out of this funk you've been in. Be the woman I know you are."

"Let me go, Morgan," she ground out between her teeth.

"Not until you promise me you're going to beat this." He shook her slightly. "Not until you grab that folder and put it back in your briefcase."

Yanking her arms free from his hold, she backed away slowly. "Get out." She pointed at the door and opened it. "Now."

He picked up his jacket and walked to the door. "You can be angry all you want. But you know I'm right."

"Don't tell me what I know," she hissed. "You have no idea how I feel. None of you do. You don't think I know what you all really think about me?"

"That's an excuse, Syd. Everyone here tonight loves you. We all want you to be okay. But you're on this pity train, feeling sorry for yourself. And I don't like it. Nobody does. Get your shit together."

She shoved him, using all of her strength, and he stumbled backward but remained standing. "Stop telling me to get my shit together." She pushed him again. "I have my shit together. I will take care of *my* business. I don't need you or Red or anybody else telling me what I have to do. If I have to take a month off to clear my head, then I will do that. You know why? Because I'm a grown-ass woman. My father lives in Virginia. And the last time he told me what to do, I moved out of his house. I'm so tired of everyone acting like they know what's best for Syd." Jamming a finger into her chest, she continued, "I know what's best for Syd and I am doing what's best for me! And if you don't like it, get the hell out of my house and don't bother coming back."

Syd couldn't be sure, but something had changed. Her breathing was heavy, but her eyes remained on his. They didn't move, didn't speak. But he was looking at her differently and she couldn't place it. Was it anger? Disgust? Pity? Suddenly, she couldn't take the silence anymore, the scrutiny.

"I've had enough," she said, turning her back on him. Sucking in a deep breath, she said, "You need to go. Now."

"Shut up," he said.

Rage, blinding and hot, rushed through her body and coated her insides like Pepto-Bismol. She whirled around. "Don't tell me to shut—"

Before she could get "the hell up" out, he pulled her to him and kissed her.

CHAPTER NINE

*M*organ would've never believed such a turn of events could happen. But it did. And he'd kissed Syd—again.

He felt the sting of her hand connecting with his cheek seconds later. "Stop!" she cried, running a shaky hand down her face.

A half-ass apology was all he could get out because he couldn't wrap his brain around the fact that he'd done it.

"What the hell are you doing?" she demanded, her eyes wild.

"I don't know what I'm doing," he admitted, hanging his head low.

And he didn't. He'd thought of her a lot over the past month. His attraction was growing by leaps and bounds. It wasn't like he'd been immune to her all these years. His friendship with Red and her subsequent relationship with Den had prevented him from ever exploring the burgeoning feelings he'd had all those years ago. Syd was attractive, but it was better left unsaid and mostly innocent—until he kissed her.

Sydney paced the room, barely sparing him a glance. He

couldn't help but smile at the way she muttered to herself. It seemed as if she was talking herself out of something.

He often found himself impressed with her. He guessed it was because she was complex and hard to figure out. She'd managed to pick up the pieces of her life when others would've thrown in the towel. She loved with her whole heart and was loyal to a fault. Other qualities that normally would've annoyed him in a woman seemed to draw him to her even more—like the fact that she dreamed big. He was practical, but he could believe in her dreams. She saw the best in people when he tended to see the worst. She was a survivor. That was why he'd pushed her earlier, urged her to fight out of a depression that could otherwise overtake her.

When Morgan looked up, Syd was standing in front of him. *How long has she been staring at me and when did she get so close?* Her fingers flitted across his cheek. "I'm sorry I hit you. You just took me by surprise."

Her eyes made him want to fix everything in her life. And as he peered into them, he realized he wasn't that sorry. Wrong, yes. Sorry—not quite. The reality of that thought slammed into him and he backed away.

She grabbed hold of his wrist. "Morgan?"

"What?"

Her chin quivered as tears sprang to her eyes. He brushed one away as it fell down her cheek. Had he done that?

"Don't cry, Syd," he begged. He pulled her into his arms and hugged her close. "We're good. We're okay. I didn't mean it. I'm sorry." He murmured those words so many times he lost count. Turning his nose into her hair, he begged her to accept his apology.

Pulling back, he was prepared to say it again, but then... His lips were a whisper away from hers. He could feel her sweet breath on his lips, smell the wine on it. Her cheeks were red and her eyes were wide and her lips were—

Kissing him?

Unable to help himself, he cradled her face in his hands and pulled her deeper into the kiss. She wrapped her arms around his neck. In that moment, his need for her overpowered every shred of sense he had. It overwhelmed him with its intensity. He pulled her toward the loveseat, unbuttoning her shirt along the way with shaky fingers. Once the back of his knees hit the edge, they tumbled down onto the cushions. She pulled his shirt over his head and tossed it on the floor.

He pulled her blouse apart, baring her caramel skin to his hungry eyes. Kneeling down, he kissed her belly button, then trailed lazy kisses back up her body to her mouth. Urged on by her soft moans, he nipped her bottom lip and traced it with his tongue. He deepened the kiss and plunged his tongue into her mouth, playing with hers. He snapped her jeans open and slowly unzipped them.

"No," she bucked up and dashed to the other side of the room.

Groaning in frustration, he stood. He grabbed his shirt and tugged it on quickly, muttering a string of curses. Should he say something? Morgan was many things, but unsure wasn't one of them. The thought of facing what had just happened, or even a discussion of what had happened in his car, made his head hurt. Clearing his throat, he said, "I'm going to go now."

"Please don't," she murmured.

He couldn't be sure he'd heard her right.

"I don't want you to go," she repeated. As she moved closer to him, he wondered what she was thinking. Her eyes were unreadable.

He swiped his thumb over her bare earlobe. She shivered under his touch; her hazel eyes turned darker.

She rested her forehead against his chest and he pulled her to him. Obviously, she just needed someone to comfort her. She needed a friend. And he was going to be that person for her—a good friend. All he had to do was stop thinking about her body, her face…her mouth. He definitely had to stop touching her like *that*. If only it were that easy. *Damn.*

* * *

Sydney held in a breath as Morgan's hands slid over her body, stopping at the small of her back. Their eyes met and he smiled at her. She ran her finger over the deep dimple on his right cheek. There was no denying that she wanted him. She wanted him to continue touching her. She wanted him to touch her in other places. *How selfish.*

"What are we doing?" he murmured against her ear.

She tensed up as her mind continued to battle her heart and her body and she started to pull back.

"Don't," he commanded softly.

The word stroked her senses like she wished he would stroke her. She quickly snapped out of that thought. "Coffee?"

"No." He grazed her cheek with his fingers. "We need to deal with this."

"I can't…" She pulled away but he held her still.

"There is something going on here. Talk to me."

As she looked into his eyes, she felt heat creep into her face. He'd always seemed to make her feel like she was the only woman in the world. She often wondered if he looked at everyone like that. If he did, it was no wonder women fell all over themselves to get with him.

Why wouldn't they? His skin was the color of dark, rich caramel. He was built like a rock with broad shoulders and a sculpted physique. Every time they went out, he was dressed to the nines, which drew plenty of stares from every type of woman imaginable. Even when he was in jeans and a T-shirt he looked like he belonged in *GQ* magazine. All of that was coupled with the fact that he was a genuinely nice guy—and she was very attracted to him in that moment.

That's why Sydney knew this wasn't a good idea. But he wasn't running and screaming the other way. She felt the heat emanating from his body—the electricity in the room. Judging by the way he'd kissed her, she guessed he felt something for her. She definitely felt something for him. *Will one of them stop this before it goes too far?*

"Morgan?" Sydney said, gazing into his dark eyes.

"Yes." His voice was low.

"This can't end well," she whispered. She closed her eyes when she felt his hands squeeze her waist.

"I know," he murmured.

For a minute, time stood still. Neither of them moved.

"Look at me," he commanded softly. "We have a decision to make. We either stop this now or not. If we don't do this, then we're good—still friends. But if we do this...once I start, I don't think I can stop."

* * *

Morgan watched Sydney mull over his words. He knew it was wrong wanting her the way he did, although she was technically single. He couldn't help himself, though. His desire for her was clouding everything.

He dropped his head, his gaze landing on her breasts. Her blouse was unbuttoned, giving him a glimpse of her red satin bra. *That has to go.* Vaguely, he heard her say something, but his mind was already planning his seduction, thinking ahead. There were so many things he wanted to do to her.

Sydney skimmed her fingertips along his jawline, bringing his gaze back to hers. "Morgan, did you hear me?"

No. Her soft palm against his face felt like a bolt of fire, and as she stroked the stubble on his chin he became more distracted.

He was admittedly torn between fulfilling his desire for her and his loyalty to his brother. Den would never forgive him, but damn it he wanted her—more than he wanted to breathe in that moment. Shit, Den would flip if he knew about that night in his truck—the way he'd touched her, kissed her. His brother would probably try to kill him. Fortunately for him, Den never pulled his head out of his ass long enough to pay attention. Then again, they hadn't exactly been talking much.

He'd crossed a line with her, physically and emotionally. He felt things for Syd that screamed betrayal of the worst kind. Of course, he convinced himself that those fleeting moments, those times he'd let himself think "what if," or the times his gaze lingered on her for too long, were nothing because they never went anywhere.

But he wanted to make love to her. And judging by the way she responded to him, he was pretty sure she wanted it just as much as he did. The family dynamic would change forever and Den would never be able to get past it. *Maybe it would be different if he'd broken up with her—a little different anyway. Okay, not that different.* The fact that Den had fought her purchase of the condo with everything he could think of cemented that he wasn't going to let her go.

"Morgan?" Syd called.

His eyes flashed to hers and he loosened his hold on her. Thinking of Den provided a "cold shower" of sorts. Frustration had him turning around and stalking to the refrigerator, leaving her standing there.

Pouring a tall glass of cold water, he took several breaths to collect himself. He thought about the confused look on Syd's face. It should have never gone that far, but Morgan definitely wanted everything she had to offer. That made him feel guilty. He slammed the empty glass on the counter.

"I'm sorry," he said.

"Me too," she murmured, pressing her hands against her cheeks. "I should've...it's just...you always make me feel secure. You never judge me or treat me like some precious china doll, or put me on a pedestal that's impossible to reach."

In Morgan's eyes, that was the biggest problem in Den and Syd's relationship. Den had placed Syd on a pedestal, like she was something to attain. For all her talk about Den saving her, it was really the other way around. Den needed her to feel like a human being, to feel redeemed. That's why his brother always fought so hard to keep her. It was also why he would always fall short and disappoint her.

"You know me," she continued. Her eyes shone bright, like a beacon of light in dark, stormy waters. He found himself wanting to go to her, but his feet refused to cooperate. "I mean, you really know me and accept who I am. That feels so good and I just let myself get carried away with you." She glanced away for a second. "I'm sorry. It's not fair to either of us."

"It's not your fault." He focused on her lips and the way she pulled her bottom lip into her mouth and nibbled on it. "I don't want you to be sorry."

"It's okay if you...Never mind."

He filled up another glass with water and slid it over to her. "Drink this. It helps."

She picked it up and did as she was told. "Thanks." She wiped a tear from her chin. "You probably think I'm an emotional wreck, huh?"

He shook his head. "I know who you are, remember? Emotional, yes. Wreck, no."

Her hands shook as she peered at him over the rim of her

glass. She followed his movements as he crept closer to her, stepping behind her. As he inched closer, she set her glass down on the countertop. He massaged her shoulders, drawing a soft moan from her.

"I don't want you to think I don't want you," he whispered against her ear. "I do. It's hard to resist you."

She leaned her head back against his shoulder, allowing him a glimpse at the valley between her breasts.

He closed his eyes, stifling the urge to cup them in his hands. Turning his face into her deep curls, he inhaled the soft scent of her shampoo. "Syd," he groaned.

Morgan slid his hands down her arms and over her stomach. She arched her back as he drummed his fingers over her trembling skin. Peering up at the ceiling, he wondered why he'd put himself right back in the same situation. *Who knew drinking water was sexy?*

Resting his chin on her shoulder, he brushed his mouth against her neck, groaning when her body trembled under his mouth. She whispered his name as he nibbled at her skin. He kissed her earlobe and took it in his mouth. She jumped when he grazed it with his teeth. He placed short, wet kisses down her jawline toward his destination. He wanted to feel her tongue against his, hear her call his name over and over again as he made love to her.

When her mouth parted slightly, he gently bit her neck. He smirked against her skin, hit by an urge to leave a mark on her skin so that everyone knew he'd been there. *Rational?* Not at all.

"I need you to be sure this is what you want," he murmured. He'd already made his decision. If she was willing, he would make love to her. They'd deal with the consequences later. "We're almost past the point of no return."

She turned around. "I do want you, Morgan."

As he peered into her eyes, there was no doubt she

wanted him. Her hazel orbs were black with desire. Still, he needed more. If he was going all the way, he wanted to hear her say the words. "I know you want me, Syd. But are you sure?"

Instead of answering him, she pulled him into a kiss, throwing her arms around his neck tightly. She ran her tongue across his bottom lip, coaxing his mouth open, and deepened the kiss.

He poured everything he had into that kiss, delving his hand into her hair and letting the strands wrap around his fingers like vines. They only broke apart to breathe before diving back in for more. He moved his other arm around her back and pulled her tight against him, lifting her off the ground and backing her against the wall. He sucked her bottom lip until she moaned his name in his mouth.

"Morgan," she whispered. "Make love to me."

Her soft command drove him into a frenzy. He pressed his mouth against hers with an urgency, breathing her in like this was the first *and* last time they would be together. For all he knew, it was. He thought of taking her right there in the kitchen, but she deserved better. He planned on worshipping her—slowly.

"Morgan," she breathed.

His thumb slid from her chin, down her neck, with his tongue following close behind. He kissed his way over to her shoulder, peeling her shirt off as he moved. Her smell—a burst of citrus—heightened his senses as he tasted her bare skin. He pressed into her, making sure she remembered how much he wanted her.

* * *

Sydney felt like she was going to burst into flames. She'd never been so turned on in all her life—never wanted anyone like this. She moaned loudly when he ran his thumb over her covered nipples.

"Be patient," he whispered, squeezing her wrists gently when she tried to unhook her bra. "We'll get to that part when I'm ready."

As he continued his ministrations, the dull ache between her thighs grew in intensity. Her stomach fluttered as his fingers circled her belly button. Then he stopped.

She opened her eyes and found him looking at her. Frowning, she asked, "What's wrong?" *Please tell me he doesn't want to stop now?*

He rested his forehead against hers. "Syd, we can't come back from this." He pressed both hands against the wall. "People will be hurt. Are we really going to do this?"

He was right. If they slept together, there would be no turning back. Lives would change.

"I need you to be sure." He moved a piece of hair from her face.

She bit the inside of her cheek, running down a mental list of everything that could go wrong if they slept together. "What if I'm not sure?"

"Then we won't go any further."

"What if I want to go further?" she asked.

"Sometimes you can't have everything you want, Syd," Morgan replied. "This isn't a no-name one-night stand. You won't be able to erase it and pretend it didn't happen."

"I know we can't pretend," Syd admitted. "I'm not sure of much, but I know one thing." She lifted herself on the tips of her toes and brushed her lips against his jaw. "After I found out about Den, I didn't think I could feel anything until you kissed me." When she thought about a word she could use to describe the growing need she felt for him, she came up short. There were no words to explain what she felt for him. "I want that again. I need it. I need you, Morgan."

She smoothed her hands down his chest as she placed light kisses down his neck. She traced the sculpted muscles of his stomach with her fingers.

He kissed her forehead. "That's always good to hear, but—"

"I want you to hold me." She grasped his hands and squeezed.

"I want to do more than hold you, Syd," he told her.

"I want your best," she whispered in his ear. "Can you give it to me?"

He arched a brow. "Can you handle everything I want to give you?"

"If I couldn't handle it, I wouldn't be asking for it," she teased, tracing his lips with her tongue. She enjoyed this little game they were playing, baiting him. It made her feel powerful, like she'd taken control of the situation. She palmed his erection and squeezed softly. "Do you need another invitation?"

When he pinned her hands above her head, she figured he didn't. He further confirmed that when he smirked and shook his head. Their fingers were intertwined when their mouths met in another fervent kiss. She groaned into his mouth as his hands moved down her extended arms slowly.

He popped the remaining buttons of her shirt and yanked it off as she squirmed in pleasure.

"So beautiful," he whispered against her mouth.

She tugged at his shirt and pulled it off, tossing it on the floor. Now they were touching—skin to skin. He lifted her up and she instinctively wrapped her legs around him as he carried her through the house, to her bedroom.

CHAPTER TEN

Sydney's head hit the pillow as she tried to even out her breathing. Sex had never been something she enjoyed and she figured that was because of the rape. She'd once compared it to watching golf—just not that interesting. Closing her eyes, she thought back to the way Morgan had held her, the movement of their bodies, how in sync they were. This definitely wasn't your average golf match and Morgan was definitely "in the zone." Her skin still tingled from the pleasure that rolled through her. Smiling to herself, she turned to Morgan, whose eyes were closed. She eyed the messed up bed, looking for the bedsheet. When she spotted the rumpled cover, she pulled it over her naked body.

He tugged it off her. "Don't cover yourself up. Don't hide from me now." His voice was gentle yet firm.

She let her hands fall to her sides, tapping her fingers against the mattress. Normally, she'd hop up and go take a shower, so she was unsure of what to do next. The only sounds in the room were their breathing and the low hum of the ceiling fan. She glanced at him out of the corner of her eye. He was lying on his side watching her—his eyes piercing.

He swept her curls off her face as she struggled to keep her eyes open. "You all right?"

She rolled over and rested her head against his chest. Nodding, she said, "More than all right. I never knew it could be like this. I can't stop thinking about it." A blush crept into her cheeks. She laughed, covering her face.

She felt his body tremble beneath her as he laughed. "It was pretty intense." He traced slow circles on her back. "You tired?"

"Nope." She touched her lips to his in a lingering kiss. "Why? Are you?"

"Not even a little bit."

Giggling, she dropped her head on his chest. "Don't look at me like that."

"Like what?"

Sydney shrugged and rolled onto her back. "I don't know, like you know something."

"I do." He trailed his index finger around a nipple and down to her belly button. Although she wasn't completely comfortable with her nakedness, he was slowly stoking a flame in her. She closed her eyes as his hand traveled down to the juncture between her thighs. He took her nipple into his mouth, suckling it gently.

"You know what I know?" he murmured against her skin.

"What?" she breathed, trying to focus on his words and not on his hands.

He placed short, wet kisses down her stomach, causing it to flutter with excitement. When he stopped, she opened her eyes. He smirked. "I know how to make you call my name."

She smacked him, unable to hide her grin. "You're silly."

"Well, it's true. Isn't it?"

"Um..." She bit her lip. "I think the true test is whether you can do it twice."

* * *

Sydney woke to the sun streaming in through the blinds. She turned to Morgan, who was softly snoring. She reached out and ran her hand over his chest, tracing his six-pack. *Perfect*. She frowned and sat up, running her fingers through her tangled mane. What had she done? She was in bed—after making love countless times—with her best friend, her ex-fiancé's brother. She buried her face in her hands, trying not to think about the way he'd touched her or how he'd made her feel. *Euphoria*. If she could describe the feeling in one word, that would be it. She plopped back into the soft down pillow and rolled over on her side. *What now?*

Morgan's strong arms snaked around her and pulled her close to him. "It's early," he murmured, placing a kiss on her collarbone. One of his hands squeezed a breast and the other gripped her thigh. "What are you thinking about?"

A smile tugged at the corners of her mouth as she remembered him waking her up a couple of hours ago to take her again from behind.

"You okay?" he asked after a few minutes.

Sure. I'm great. I just hooked up with my ex-fiancé's brother. But damn it was good. Her thoughts were racing. Did she want to share them with him? There were plenty of reasons to not sleep together, but they both had jumped in like they didn't have a care in the world. Once she'd made the decision to make love to him, she hadn't looked back—until now. Lying there in her bed with him, after they'd given in to a passion she hadn't realized was there, seemed to tilt her world on its axis. It wasn't like she and Morgan could hold each other's hands and walk into the sunset together.

A few months ago, he'd been her best friend and soon-to-be brother-in-law. Any feelings she may or may not have had back when she was teenager were long gone. *Weren't they*? She didn't know what was what anymore. She cleared her throat. "I'm good."

He chuckled and nipped her ear. "What are you thinking about?" he asked again.

She finally turned to face him and looked into his eyes. She slid a finger down his chin. "I..."

"What is it?" he asked, concern in his eyes.

"Calisa is supposed to come by this morning. We're going over color palettes."

He frowned. "Well, I guess I better get out of here, huh?"

Holding the sheet to her body, she sat up on the edge of the bed. She felt the tips of his fingers on her back and turned back to him. "Yeah, I guess."

"Okay. I understand."

She wondered if he did. They'd spent the night together. And she was kicking him out first thing in the morning? Before she'd even cooked him breakfast? She wouldn't have understood if the shoe was on the other foot. But what else was she supposed to do? Declare her love for him? The situation was already complicated enough. As much as she wanted to, she couldn't bury her head in the sand and pretend it was okay to be with him. In fact, it was pretty much *not*.

"I wish you didn't have to just get up and leave," she told him, avoiding eye contact with him and focusing instead on a loose thread on her pillowcase.

"I understand," he repeated evenly.

There it was again. He understood. "Are you sure?" She tried to ignore the tightness that settled in her chest. "I've never done this before, so I don't—"

"It's okay," he assured her, brushing his hand down her back gently. "I get it. Really."

Morgan probably did understand. He wasn't accustomed to staying nights with women. Knowing him, he couldn't wait to get out of there. She leaned closer and kissed him. When she pulled back, she ran her fingers across his jaw. She wanted to say something, but the words escaped her. Deciding to leave it at that, she hurried into the bathroom to take a quick shower.

Her body ached, but the hot water helped. After her shower, she wrapped a towel around her and walked back into the bedroom. Morgan was still lying in bed, his arms behind his head, staring at the ceiling. She swallowed and glanced around the room. Frowning, she realized that she had no idea where her—

"What's wrong?" His voice interrupted her thoughts.

"I'm trying to remember where my underwear is," she admitted with a soft laugh. She remembered him tossing them away, but she had no idea where. Spotting them on her dresser, draped on one of her bottles of perfume, she picked them up. "Here they are. Calisa likes to make herself at home. Knowing her, she'd spot these in a minute and ask for an explanation." She tossed the panties into a hamper.

He snickered. "Your bra is in the den."

She hurried to the den, picking up stray clothes along the way. When she walked back into her room, Morgan was sitting on the edge of the bed. He smiled when she handed him his shirt. "Thanks."

"I'll walk you out," she offered.

He stood up, giving her a glimpse of his nakedness once more before he disappeared into the bathroom. *Damn, he's fine.*

Emerging fully clothed, he squeezed her hand and pulled her to him. "I'm not sure what to say. You don't have to walk me out, though." He kissed her temple then her forehead. "We'll talk?"

Gripping her towel closed, she nodded. "Sure."

Not that she knew what they would talk about. It would be kind of hard to talk about the weather or the price of milk or a basketball game.

"'Bye, Syd."

"'Bye," she whispered, after he disappeared through her bedroom doorway.

CHAPTER ELEVEN

A couple of weeks passed. Morgan hadn't spoken to Sydney since he'd walked out of her house the morning after they had spent the night together. It was strange that they hadn't talked and Morgan wanted to reach out to her. He hadn't been able to stop thinking about her, but he figured it was best that he didn't. He needed time to process everything and come up with a plan on how to address it.

After receiving numerous phone calls from Mama urging him to be there for his brother, Morgan decided to go over and see him. It was high time he faced him. As he neared Den's house he noticed Syd's car, so he slouched in the car seat. He was tempted to drive right past, unsure about being in a room with Syd and Den at the same time, especially before he'd had a chance to talk to Syd. Then there was the chance that he'd see her and want a repeat of that night.

Might as well get this over with. He parked in front of the house and walked to the door. Before he could knock, the door swung open and he was face-to-face with Syd.

Her mouth fell open and a hand flew to her chest as she

shuffled backward. "Oh my God," she breathed. "You scared the shit out of me."

"I'm sorry." He reached out to touch her but then pulled back. "Is Den here?" he asked.

"Yes, I am," Den said, appearing behind her.

She flinched, taking a deep breath and closing her eyes. "Den, you know I hate when you sneak up on me."

Den rubbed her shoulder. "I'm sorry." He glanced at Morgan. "What's up, Roc? Come on in."

"I have to run out to my car and grab my bag," Syd announced.

Morgan watched as she jogged toward her car. His thoughts went back to how she'd looked lying underneath him, the glow on her face and the insatiable look in her eyes. Shaking his head, he turned back to Den and stepped into the house.

"What brings you my way?" Den asked.

Morgan followed Den through the house to the family room, where Den plopped down on the couch. Following suit, Morgan had a seat. "I just stopped by to see how you were. We haven't talked in a while."

Den cocked his head. "Really?" He scratched his jaw. "Well, the last few times we spoke, things were kind of tense."

Nodding, Morgan shifted in his seat. "Exactly. That's why I figured it was time we talked."

"Are you sure it's not because Mama sent you?" Den asked with a smirk.

"Well, that's part of it," Morgan admitted. "How are you?"

"I'm okay." Den took a sip from a glass of water that was sitting on the end table. "I have a few projects that are keeping me busy. I actually just left the bar. My team is working hard to get everything completed by the end of the month."

Morgan clasped his hands together and leaned forward. "That's good. Glad you're busy."

"And you would be happy to know that I've taken your advice about Syd and backed off."

Morgan had fooled himself. Talking to Den was harder than he thought it would be. He wanted to repair the damage done to his relationship with his brother, but it seemed to him that too much had happened. Things had built up over years. And he'd made it worse by sleeping with Syd.

A loud crash, followed by a string of high-pitched curses, drew their attention toward the hallway. Syd was on her knees scooping a bunch of Christmas ornaments into her arms.

Morgan wanted to go to her, but held back when Den rushed over, knelt down next to her, and picked up the scattered Christmas decorations. "Aw man, Syd," Den said, picking up a broken bulb and holding it out for her to see the crack in it. "It's one of your favorites."

Syd continued to place the decorations back into the bin. "It's okay. I wasn't paying attention," she muttered, shooting Morgan a brief glance. He wondered if she'd heard their conversation.

Once everything was tucked away and the lid secure, Den picked up the bin. "I'll take this out for you," he offered. "Is that it?"

She shook her head quickly. "I have another box in the basement." They followed Den toward the door.

Morgan stared as Syd directed Den to the backseat with the box. When Den cracked a joke and Syd laughed softly, Morgan's hands tightened into fists. Turning away, he stalked over to the refrigerator and pulled out a bottle of water. Shaking his head rapidly, he took a deep breath. When they came back in the house, Den was talking animatedly, telling a joke. Syd listened intently, her eyes smiling.

Morgan didn't hear the punchline, but Syd laughed out loud, slapping her knees with glee. The longer they laughed, the more irritated he became.

He wondered if he'd missed something. Syd hadn't even been able to look at Den without crying a few weeks ago. Had something changed between them that he didn't know about? As he felt his body temperature rising, he rubbed sweaty palms against his jeans. If something had changed between his brother and Syd, what would it matter? No promises had been exchanged between them, just sex. They couldn't be together, even if he wanted to. Since when had he ever thought about *being* with someone anyway? Frustrated, he yanked his keys from his pocket. He needed to get the hell out of there.

"I'm going to go," he announced, interrupting their prolonged giggles.

Syd's eyes flashed to his and her face went slack. All the humor in her eyes seemed to evaporate. Unable to look at her, he turned to Den and told him he'd holler at him later. "Bye, Syd," he grumbled on his way out.

The drive home didn't do anything for his mood. Morgan stomped into his house, slamming the door behind him. Heading straight for the kitchen, he pulled a beer out of the fridge and gulped it down. *What the hell just happened*?

Syd was, for all intents and purposes, his best friend. Sometimes friends slept together and maintained their friendship. Hell, he'd done it before with no problem. Why was this different?

He smacked his forehead with his hand and pulled out his phone. Staring at the black screen he pondered his desire to call her. They definitely needed to talk, but he needed a plan before then. Several contingency plans too, because there were so many ways a talk with Syd could go. This was a woman who meant a great deal to him. She was worth an uncomfortable conversation and a sincere attempt to save their friendship. The attraction he felt for her would just have to take a backseat.

He missed her.

According to Red, she'd been considering taking a leave of absence from her job to get herself together and to focus on the bar. He guessed the talk he'd had with her worked. Still, he wanted to hear all of this from her. He was sure he would've been the first person she told about it—if they hadn't slept together.

The doorbell chimed. He frowned, wondering who it could be. He wasn't expecting company and didn't really feel like being bothered. When he opened the door, Sydney brushed past him into the house before he could say "Come in."

She paced the floor, grumbling under her breath and wringing her hands together. Honestly, he didn't even bother trying to make out her words. He focused on the sway of her hips, thought about tugging off her yoga pants and taking her against the door—which totally went against everything he had just decided. Peering up at the ceiling, he let out a heavy sigh. *Lord, please don't lead me to temptation again.*

"Morgan?!" Sydney shouted.

He snapped out of his thoughts. "Hmm?" When he looked at her, she rolled her eyes at him.

She crossed her arms over her breasts and tapped her foot against the ceramic tile. "You didn't hear a word I said," she hissed.

"What were you saying?" He walked over to her and squeezed her arms gently.

"Maybe you should've been listening to me," she roared. "I spent the last couple of weeks trying to figure out what I was going to say to you and you didn't even hear me."

He reached out to caress her face, unable to resist the urge to touch her. "I'm sorry. What did you say?"

"I was just saying..." Her voice trailed off as his hand slipped down to her neck.

His gazed dropped to her mouth. It was so ready to be kissed. He arched a brow and smirked.

A wisp of a smile crept over her face, then she seemed to snap out of it. Frowning, she slapped his hand away. "No. This wasn't a good idea. I didn't come here for this. I came here to set the record straight, especially after that awkward encounter at Den's house."

He sighed. "What's wrong?"

"I need you to listen to me—not caress me and certainly not seduce me." She smacked him again.

"Ouch." He rubbed his shoulder. "Seduce you? I haven't seduced you. Did you want me to?"

"No!" she screeched, flailing her arms wildly.

"Just checking, Syd. Let's talk." Tears gathered in her eyes and he wanted to kick himself for everything he'd done to make this more complicated.

"Morgan?" she muttered, wiping her cheeks. "We can't do this."

He swiped a thumb under her eyes, catching an errant tear. "Okay, Syd, I'm listening."

"It was a mistake to sleep together and we can't do it again. It was wrong. I'm—I'm sorry."

He could feel irrational anger bubbling up in his gut so he chose to remain silent and let her finish.

"This won't work out," she continued. "You understand why this can't work, don't you?" She gazed up at him and looked away quickly. "That's what I needed to say. I have to go." She turned and opened the door. Before he could think about it, he pushed the door closed. Neither of them moved. She didn't turn around to face him and his hand was glued to the door.

The worst part of this was that he knew she was right.

He *should've* known better than to sleep with her. Not only because of Den, but because she was his best friend's sister and one of his best friends. But they'd crossed a line and, God help him, he wanted her again.

"Syd," he whispered. "Turn around."

* * *

Taking a deep breath, she turned to face him. He was standing so close to her—too close. She eyed the strong arm extended above her, holding the door. She leaned back against the door and waited.

"Before you bust up," he said, tilting his head to meet her gaze. "Don't you think we should talk about this?"

"What is there to talk about?" she asked. "Sleeping with you was wrong, regardless of how good it was. There's really nothing to talk about."

"I can think of plenty. First of all, we *slept* together, Syd. That deserves a conversation."

She peered up at the ceiling in a futile attempt to keep more tears from falling. "Everything...it's too hard now."

"What is too hard?" he asked, his eyes blazing.

"Us!" she yelled, throwing her hands up in the air out of frustration. "This!" She motioned between them. "I can't sleep with someone and pretend like it doesn't mean anything."

"Who said it didn't mean anything?"

They'd argued before, but this felt different. It was almost surreal. She'd never dreamed that she would be fighting with Morgan about *not* sleeping with him. But here they were—arguing. "All I'm saying is...it meant something to me. But I don't want to hurt anyone. And I don't want to get hurt."

"I wouldn't hurt you," he murmured, pinching the bridge of his nose.

"You wouldn't try, but you could." Her voice cracked, her mouth went dry. "I know you. You don't do love and relationships. And even if you did, this would be impossible, considering my relationship with Den. I still love him. Part of me probably always will." She'd managed to keep her eyes on other things, like the edge of his wife beater tank, a black dot on his wall, and the earring in his ear. If she met his eyes, she would fall apart.

"I can't let you just walk out like this. There's a lot at stake here."

She finally met his gaze. "What we shared was... You were there when I needed someone, like you always are. But let's not pretend that it can be more than what it was."

He narrowed his eyes. "What do you think it was?"

"Sex? Comfort? We're friends, but... it's too close. I'd rather be your friend than lose you altogether." She ran a hand through her hair. "What if I fell in love with you?" His eyes widened, but she forged ahead. "I mean it's not that big of a leap. I've loved you for years; I'm on the rebound. We're connected. But what we did... could ruin your relationship with your family and destroy the bond you have with your brother. And I wouldn't be able to deal with that. Let's just chalk it up to despair and bad choices and—"

Her speech ended when his mouth met hers. *Damn tears.* They flowed freely as he feasted on her lips, and then she was done. Lost in his kisses. She moaned into his mouth and wrapped her arms around his neck.

There was no point in fighting it. Over the past few weeks, she hadn't been able to stop thinking about being with him. She wanted him. And judging by the bulge in his pants, he wanted her, too. He pulled at her shirt, finally pushing it up and undoing her bra while she unbuttoned his jeans and pushed them off. He untied her pants, shoved them down to the floor, and lifted her up out of them. She wrapped her legs around his waist as he pushed her against the door, grinding into her. She groaned when he pushed her panties to the side and delved into her in one fluid motion.

Pleasure washed over her as he thrust in and out of her. She purred when he yanked her shirt open and nipped at one of her aching buds. Gripping his shoulder, she pushed back at him, grinding into him with a force she'd never felt before.

Moaning, she grabbed his head with her hands, pulling him into an intense kiss and biting down on his bottom lip. He cursed, breaking the kiss, but didn't break the rhythm. She cried out his name as his teeth dug into her neck and groaned when his tongue swept across the sore spot.

Her orgasm threatened to choke her with its intensity. She dug her nails into his back, enjoying the sharp intake of his breath against her skin. Her head fell back against the door as she trembled. He grabbed her hair and pulled her into a deep, passionate kiss. Screaming out his name against his mouth, she shook as she fell over the cliff. He followed her over the edge, groaning her name.

She collapsed onto his shoulder and let her breathing even out. She felt a sensation, as if she were floating, and realized he was moving. Squeezing her legs around his waist, she buried her face in his neck as he walked over to the couch and plopped down on it.

They sat in silence for a few minutes. He stroked her back slowly. "I can't believe this," she mumbled against his skin.

"Me neither."

She sat up, her eyes filling with tears. "I told you we have to stop. Oh my God." Jumping off his lap, she raced to the door and picked up her pants, tugging them on clumsily. She braced herself on the wall when she almost toppled over. "I have to go."

"Wait," he said, slipping his pants on. "Don't go, Syd."

She held a hand out. "Don't do this. Don't come any

closer." Her clothes were a twisted mess. Her bra was hanging off and her shirt was draped off her shoulder, her curls wild around her face.

Yet, despite the way her nerves still tingled and her heart shifted, she felt terrible. Was it possible to feel so good and so bad at the same time? She'd gone there to tell him they couldn't sleep together anymore and she'd let him take her against the freakin' door.

"Syd?" he called softly.

"Stop." She pushed a bra strap up. "It's cool. I have to get out of here."

"I want you," he said.

"Do you even realize what you're saying?" she asked, holding her hair back then releasing it.

"I said it, didn't I? Why do you think I slept with you?"

She shrugged. "I don't know. I'm still trying to figure that out." She wrapped a hand around the base of her neck. "We argued and our guards were down? I was hurting over Den's betrayal."

"I knew exactly what I was doing—*both* times," he said. "I made a conscious decision—*both* times. I probably should regret it, but I don't."

Lord help her, she wanted him too. She sagged against the door, her energy sapped. "What are we going to do?"

"We don't have to make a grand decision right now," he said. "You needed me and I was there for you. We're not in love." He scratched the side of his neck with a finger. "We... had fun. Why can't we let it be that?"

"You know why," she argued. "We're risking a lot, including our own friendship, so that we can... what? Have fun?"

"Don't be like that."

"How am I supposed to be, Morgan? Seriously, what's in this for you?" Her heart pounded as he appeared to mull over her question. It wasn't like him to be so cavalier with her feelings. There had to be something more, something he wasn't saying out loud.

"I don't know," he said finally. "I don't want to lose you. At the same time, I'm not ready to make a quick decision just for the hell of it. Obviously there's something between us that doesn't want to go away. We need to discuss what that means."

In a normal world, a discussion could go one of two ways. Either they'd stop or not. But she wasn't naïve enough to not see all the gray areas in the situation. It wasn't that simple. "What do you think it means?"

"I don't know," he repeated. "You mentioned how we're risking so much by being together. But when I'm with you all I feel is this connection. In the moment, I'm not thinking about consequences or hurt feelings—just you."

"I don't know what to say," she whispered.

"What *can* you say? It's fucked up. And I can't even reason with myself about it," he admitted, approaching her. He skimmed the back of a finger down her chin. "Right or wrong, I'm where I want to be."

Sydney wanted to forget all the reasons they shouldn't be together, wrap her arms around him, and hug him tight. But she couldn't . . . not again. Someone had to stop the train. His lips grazed her neck, sending shivers up her spine again. "I have to go," she said. "'Bye, Morgan."

Ignoring his pleas, she yanked open the door and ran to her car.

*C*HAPTER TWELVE

*S*ydney burst into Red's bedroom. "Get out, Red. I need to talk to Cali."

Red jumped and fell over the edge of the bed while Calisa grabbed a pillow to cover her naked chest.

"Syd, what the hell are you doing?" Red roared.

"I told you I need to talk to Cali," she shouted. She grabbed Calisa's discarded shirt off the ground and tossed it to her. "Please, Red...just leave."

"You can't bust in my house, looking all crazy, and kick me out," Red complained.

Syd touched the top of her hair, wondering how she looked to them. She could only imagine based on the fact that she'd cried the whole way here.

"Red, just go." Cali pulled on her blouse and climbed off the bed.

"How long am I supposed to be gone?" he asked.

"A long time," Syd said.

"Are you okay?" He squeezed Syd's shoulder. "I'm worried about you."

When she didn't answer him, he turned to Calisa and sighed. "I'll be back...later."

After he left, Syd closed the door and plopped down on the bed. "I'm so dead," she grumbled.

With her hands on her hips, Calisa tapped her bare foot on the floor. "Syd, what is going on? Red is right. You're looking crazy—unhinged, to be exact. Your hair is a mess; you have these little tissue pieces on your face." She picked at Syd's cheeks. "What is the problem? And can you pretend that you didn't walk in on me and Red in a compromising position?"

"I could care less that I caught you with your bra off with my brother," Syd assured her bestie. "This is important. I did something."

"Please, for the love of God, don't tell me you took Den back," Calisa said, checking her makeup in the mirror and popping a piece of gum in her mouth.

"I wish you'd stop saying that. I didn't take Den back. And I'm not going to."

"What did you do?" Cali asked sarcastically. "Kiss another guy? Or did you actually move to second base?"

"I slept with Morgan," Syd blurted out.

Calisa's mouth fell open and the gum fell out onto the carpet. "What?"

"Morgan and I did it—twice."

Sitting next to her, Cali said, "Wait...what?" She picked up the gum and tossed it into a nearby trash can.

"Do I have to repeat myself again?" Syd clutched the comforter, dreading the conversation but knowing it had to happen. "We got busy, more than once."

"Get out." Cali grabbed Syd's arm. "You had sex with Morgan? More than once? I can't even believe this," she said. "Was it good?"

Syd shoved her lightly. "Don't play around with me. It was a mistake, Cali. And now I don't know how to fix it."

"A mistake? Girl, 'bye," Cali said, waving a hand as if she was dismissing Syd. "Haven't I taught you anything, Syd? A mistake is one time. You get one mistake, not two. Unless you did it more than one time in one night. Then maybe we could make a case for a mistake because after the one time, you always go for seconds—or maybe even thirds." She tapped her chin. "But if this is two times on two different days, that is not a mistake. It's a choice."

Syd thought back on Morgan's assertion that he'd made a conscious choice to be with her. Even so, what they'd done could still be classified as a mistake. "No, it really was a mistake. It shouldn't have happened. I didn't go over there to have sex. In fact, I went over to tell him to forget about the first time."

"Then you just fell on him and your clothes miraculously disappeared?"

"Bitch," Syd grumbled under her breath. Cali had a way of making her feel stupid sometimes. It was just her way. "Please, you have to help me," she begged. "You know I don't do stuff like this. I don't know how to handle sex without strings. I'm overly emotional right now. I can't think straight because I'm always thinking of having sex—with Morgan."

"Wow," Cali said, grinning widely. "He must have put it down."

Syd glared at her amused friend. "Can you focus? Do you know what this means?"

Her eyes darted around the room then she frowned. "It means you had sex with Morgan?"

"No." Syd stood up and paced the room. "It means I'm a 'ho. And not just any 'ho. This is like some *Jerry Springer– Maury Povich–not your baby daddy–backwoods trailer trash–ghetto fabulous* drama. I slept with my ex-fiancé's brother. I'm a tramp."

"Don't get carried away, Syd," Calisa said. "And sit down. You're making me nervous with all this pacing back and forth shit."

Syd leaned against the dresser. "What am I gonna do?"

"What does Morgan want to do?"

Shrugging, Syd could feel the panic rising in her again. "I don't know. Should I even care?"

"Calm down, okay? You're not the first person to sleep with someone and regret it. I do it all the time with Red."

"Oh please." Now it was her turn to dismiss Cali. "You like sleeping with Red. You've been doing it for five years now." When Calisa gaped at her, she continued. "We all know it. We were just letting you think we didn't. And that's okay. You know why? You're single, Red's single . . . and he's not your ex's brother."

Calisa smirked. "He's my best friend's brother."

"And your best friend doesn't care," Syd told her, shrugging half-heartedly. "So let's stop talking about you and start figuring out how I'm going to get myself out of this."

"Maybe there's nothing to figure out," Cali suggested. "It could be an isolated incident, or two. Morgan is sensible. He doesn't just have sex . . . Well, he wouldn't do that with you."

Everyone knew Morgan was a player, preferring meaningless flings with women he cared nothing about to long-term relationships with flowers and candy and visions of engagement rings.

"Then why did he do it, Cali?" Syd pushed her hair out of her face. "He's discriminating. He doesn't take just anyone to bed."

"I have no idea." Calisa shrugged. "Your guess is as good as mine. But don't you think you need to ask him that question?"

"He wanted to talk, but I bolted. I can't even look at him without . . ." *Wanting him to finish where he left off?*

"You liked it a lot, huh?" Calisa grinned at Syd with a gleam in her brown eyes. "I need some details."

"No," Syd said, fiddling with her sleeves. "It doesn't matter anyway, because it'll never happen again. Besides, it's better forgotten."

"Damn. Defensive, much? Listen, you're going to have to talk to him. He's your friend and your business partner. If it's really never going to happen again, then talk to him. But something tells me you're worried about a third *mistake*."

"You're such a... I should've talked to Allina."

"Yeah, right." Calisa folded her arms. "Good luck with that one. She's too wrapped up in whatever she has going on with Kent to focus on anything right now."

The night of the impromptu pizza party at Syd's house was the last time she'd seen Allina. They'd talked on the phone a few times, but when Syd asked her to meet her for lunch or dinner, her friend always made an excuse. Kent hadn't mentioned anything, but they all assumed it had to do with him.

Syd sighed heavily and ran a jerky hand through her hair. "This sucks."

"Pretty much," Cali agreed with a nod. "But not as bad as you think."

"Seriously? This was the worst possible thing I could've done. What if Den finds out?"

"So what?" Cali leaned back, her lips curling in disgust. "Den has no room to judge anyone, Syd. You didn't do anything wrong. You're single. You didn't cheat on him. Give yourself a break. There are so many other things to worry about. This isn't one of them. You and Morgan are friends and this won't come between that. Just talk to him. Tell him how you feel and leave it at that."

Syd smiled gratefully at her BFF. "Thanks. You're right. We'll get past this. Eventually. Then things will go back to normal." Yet even as she said it, she knew things would never go back to the way they had been. Never.

* * *

Morgan rushed to the front door when the bell rang. He hoped it was Syd. He'd been trying to call her since she'd bolted out of his house earlier, but his calls kept going straight to voicemail. Thinking about the conversation they'd had before and after he'd taken her against the damn door, he regretted downplaying what had happened between them. While he thought it would ease her fears, it only served one purpose—to make him feel better. It was so much more than a "fun" time. *She* was more than that.

He yanked the door open and was surprised to find his best friend on the other side. Letting out a heavy sigh, he stepped aside to let him in.

"Expecting someone?" Red asked, walking in. Morgan observed his best friend as he sat down on the couch—hard. It was obvious by the tick in his jaw and the way he stared at the clock on the wall that something was on his mind.

Unable to help himself, Morgan checked his cell phone. When he looked up, Red was eyeing him, a slight frown on his face.

"What's going on, Roc?" Red asked.

Morgan glanced at his cell phone again. "Nothing," he lied. "I'm good. What's up? You never stop by without calling."

Leaning forward, Red rested his elbows on his knees. "Syd came over today," he said, scrubbing his eyes. "She barged into my bedroom—without knocking—looking a hot-ass mess."

Morgan froze. The thought of Syd hurting... *What the hell have I done?* He should have gone after her earlier.

"Her eyes were puffy," Red continued. "She was agitated, disheveled. I'm worried about her."

Me too. Tugging on his collar, Morgan peered down at his phone. Instead of excusing himself so he could try to call her again, he forced his attention back to Red, who was silently studying him again.

"Roc, I can leave if you're expecting someone," Red said.

Clearing his throat, Morgan gave his phone a quick glance again, and then tossed it on the couch. He sat down on the chair across from Red. "What makes you think I'm expecting someone?" he asked.

"Probably because you keep checking your phone every two seconds," Red retorted.

"I'm good," Morgan repeated, rubbing his palms over his jeans. "So what happened with Syd? Did you talk to her?"

"She kicked me out so she could talk to Cali," he grumbled.

"Shit," Morgan muttered. He was hit with an urge to tell his friend everything. Red had been like a brother to him. They'd been through more than a few tight situations together. But this wasn't about a random woman; it was about Syd. And Red was an extremely overprotective brother. He'd never asked Morgan for much in their many years of friendship, except one thing—not to fuck with his sister.

"Have you talked to her?" Red asked.

Morgan's eyes snapped to Red. "Me?" He blinked. "No. I…Why do you ask?" Cursing himself for stammering like a fool, Morgan jumped up. "Beer?" he asked, heading toward the kitchen.

Once they were in the kitchen, Morgan pulled two beers out and offered one of them to Red. His friend opened it and took a long pull. "She's a wreck," he continued, leaning against the counter. "You know something, don't you?"

Red was like a vulture. He was an attorney, trained in the art of tripping people up on the witness stand. It was a gift that often came in handy in his personal life as well. Normally, Morgan wouldn't be fazed. But this wasn't a *normal* situation.

Morgan shrugged. "I saw her earlier." He turned the water on, rinsed off a breakfast plate, and loaded it into the dishwasher. "I don't know, Red. Maybe you should just ask her."

"Tell me what she was like when you saw her," Red insisted.

Avoiding eye contact, Morgan wiped off the countertop. "We didn't really talk," he said. *That much was true.* They were too busy getting it in to do that. "She came over and we...didn't talk."

Judging by the tight expression on Red's face when he shot him a sideways glance, Morgan figured he'd fucked up somewhere. His friend didn't look convinced. Red only confirmed it when he asked, "What happened between you and Syd?"

Turning slowly, Morgan asked, making sure to keep his tone even, "Why would I know what's wrong with Syd? And if I did, why would I tell you?"

"Because I want to know," Red demanded, crossing his arms.

And he deserved that much. They had become fast friends in high school and had similar philosophies on life. They played hard and studied harder. One night, Morgan had had an altercation with one of the star varsity basketball players. Well, it wasn't really an altercation—the asshole had sucker-punched him then turned around and slapped his girlfriend for daring to talk to him. After Red jumped in and beat the crap out of the guy, Morgan had known he had a friend for life. The principal had threatened to kick them both off the team as well as suspend them. Red took the case, defending them in the disciplinary meeting. In the end, the varsity player had been suspended for starting the fight and had to apologize in front of the team. It was Red's first successful case.

"We're friends," Morgan said, wiping his hand on a towel and dropping it on the counter.

"What *kind* of friends?" Red asked.

Morgan stepped back, lowering his brows into a frown. "If you have something to say then say it. Stop beating around the bush."

"Okay, you've been a good friend to Syd and I appreciate it. But something's off. You're both acting out of character. You're loyal, guarded…moody. But never distracted and rarely defensive. It's not hard to put two and two together. Whatever is going on with her, you're involved."

"Maybe you should talk to your sister," Morgan said.

"I'm talking to my best friend. Roc, we've been through a lot together. We're opening a business in a couple of months. Don't you think you can trust me? Now, I know my sister and she's hiding something."

Morgan cast another sideways glance at Red and dropped his head, sighing heavily. His friend wasn't going to let this go, and he owed him the truth.

Apparently Red didn't need it explained, though, because he asked, "When?"

"A couple of weeks ago," Morgan admitted. "After that little impromptu housewarming."

"My next question would be why?" Red asked, cracking his knuckles.

"Why do you think?" Morgan asked. "Do you really need an explanation?"

"You slept with my sister, Roc," he said through clenched teeth. "I think I deserve one. Is this the first time?"

"What the hell is that supposed to mean?"

Red shrugged. "Hey, I had to ask. What now?"

"I don't know," Morgan murmured. "I can't stop thinking about her."

"That's not new," Red grumbled. When Morgan glared at him, he hunched his shoulders. "What? You act like I don't know you've wanted my sister for years. I'm not stupid. I peeped that a long time ago."

"You're an ass." Morgan slumped forward. "And you're wrong."

Red dismissed him with a wave of his hand. "Whatever."

"This wasn't an intentional thing. It just kind of happened." *More than once.*

"Sex doesn't just *happen*, unless you were drinking." Red frowned, and Morgan knew where he was going. "Were you drunk?"

"Nope."

"Was she drunk?" Red asked, eyebrows raised.

"Hell no. I'm not a pervert. I wouldn't take advantage of a drunk hooker, let alone an inebriated Syd."

Peering up at the ceiling, Red shook his head. "Well, this is awkward."

"Try being me for a day," Morgan said, finally taking a sip of his beer.

"What are you going to do?"

"Syd's important to me," Morgan said, tapping his finger against the countertop. "I guess that's not new either, huh? I mean, it is what it is." He picked at the label on the beer bottle. "We can't change it. We just have to figure out where to go from here. There are other factors to consider, like the fact that she was engaged to Den."

"True," Red agreed. "That's messed up."

"Thanks. Not only that, but I wish I could say for certain that it wouldn't happen again. I'm pretty sure it will."

"Really, Roc?" Red asked, covering his ears. "That's too much information."

"Well, it's the truth. I can't seem to control myself around her."

"How does she feel about this?"

Morgan wished he knew. But knowing Syd, he may never know. "I'm not stupid enough to think this is some type of *love* thing," he said. "She still loves Den. And I'm cool with that. She's confused."

"They were together a long-ass time and headed to the altar before he couldn't keep his dick in his pants," Red grumbled.

Morgan knew Red was still furious with Den for cheating on Syd. He'd often shared with Morgan his concerns about the relationship. And Morgan couldn't blame his friend for feeling the way he did. It hadn't been the first time, or even the second, that Den had cheated on Syd. Still, Syd took him back, and Red couldn't stand it. Then there were Den's mood swings—the times that his illness had pulled Syd into that dark space. Red couldn't deal with the fact that she was touched by it.

As far as Red was concerned, Syd never should have accepted Den's proposal in the first place and he let it be known.

"I'd be lying if I didn't say I'm relieved that the damn wedding is off," Red admitted. "It wasn't right. He is not good for her. I do wish she'd broken off the engagement for the right reason, though."

Morgan finished off his beer. "What would've been the right reason?"

"Love?"

"She does love him," Morgan said matter-of-factly. It was a truth he'd rather not admit, but he was a realist.

"She just thinks she loves him," Red countered. "I'm not that convinced. And if his way of loving her is cheating on her in her own bed, then he can keep that shit."

"I don't want to talk about this. Just…" Morgan tossed the empty bottle into the recycle bin. "Do me a favor? Don't say anything to her about this. Let her tell you if she wants to."

"Look, Roc, I'm not mad at you or even surprised that you two were together. I just don't want her hurt any more than she already is. And I don't like seeing her like she was today. You need to fix this, since you broke it."

CHAPTER THIRTEEN

*M*organ closed the door and locked it. After two beers and more badgering, Red finally left. He'd probably said too much, but he knew it wasn't going anywhere. Red was one of the few people he could trust.

Picking up his phone, he tapped it on. *Two missed calls.* He dialed Syd.

"Morgan," she whispered.

Frowning, he asked, "Syd, what's going on?" He could make out the sounds of people talking and a crying kid in the background, and wondered where she was.

"We need to talk," she said breathlessly.

"Why are you whispering?"

"There are too many people around. I'm in Target, the one close to your house. But I don't think I should come over there."

"Why don't we just meet for dinner or something?" he suggested. "A neutral setting?"

"Where?" she asked, a hitch in her voice. "What if people see us together?" He waited while she exchanged a greeting with someone in the store, presumably a store clerk, because she asked where they'd moved the wine. He heard a response, but couldn't make out exact words. After a few seconds she said, "Okay, I'm back."

"It wouldn't be the first time people have seen us together, Syd," he said, picking up the conversation where they'd left off. "We go out all the time."

"Yes, but that was before."

He smiled when she cursed Target and damned the store to hell for not carrying her favorite wine. "Before what?" he asked after she was done with her tantrum.

"Before you'd seen me naked," she hissed.

"O . . . kay. Fine. Would you rather just talk on the phone?"

"Hold on," she ordered.

He waited, listening to the click of her heels as she moved.

"Okay." He heard the jingle of her keys, and seconds later the slamming of her car door. "I'm back in my car," she said in a normal voice.

He drummed his fingers on the end table next to his chair. "Are you going to talk?"

Right then, he should've been annoyed. But he was amused. He could picture her sitting in her car, biting her nails, trying to figure out what she was going to say.

"Syd?" he asked when the silence stretched on. "I'm happy to sit here on the phone forever if that's what you need. But my phone will probably die and we have that big meeting tomorrow at the bar."

"I know, I know. I don't know where to start."

Chuckling, he asked, "How about you start by telling me how you feel?"

"About you?" she asked in a high voice.

"About anything, but preferably about us."

"It's not that simple," she admitted softly, so softly he strained to hear her. "I feel like we're setting ourselves up for a huge disappointment."

"How so?" he asked.

"Well, for one, you're Den's brother. I may not want to get back together with him, but I do still love him."

"I know that." He tried to ignore the pulling in his gut at her admission. "I expect that. Sure, a part of me hates that you do, but that's not because of what happened between us. It's because you deserve better. But you two have a connection. Hell, I have a connection to him."

"And that's why—"

"We can't be together," he finished for her, his tone dry and more agitated than he expected. "You don't have to tell me all the reasons we can't do this again. I know we can't be together. But there's a problem here: we're always around each other. With the opening of the Ice Box, we're going to be around each other even more. It's inevitable that we're going to find ourselves in the same position as before— tearing each other apart against the door, or making love in a supply closet."

"You've thought about this—a lot."

She was smiling. He could tell by the inflection in her tone and the way her voice hitched. He relaxed in his chair and imagined her eyes. It was probably a good thing they were talking on the phone because if she'd been in front of him right then, he wouldn't be able to keep his hands to himself.

"Hell, yeah." He laughed. "I know myself and it'll be hard to stay away from you."

"What if Den catches us?" she asked. "What if Kent walks into the supply closet while we're ... sneaking?"

Realizing that she'd considered the possibilities, too, he smirked. "I guess you've thought about it, too?"

"Truthfully?"

"Of course."

She sucked in a deep breath. "I've never done anything

like this before," she told him. "I don't know if it's the rush or the need to just feel free, or you. We've been friends forever. Nothing like this has ever happened between us. Not even close. It scares me. I'm not that girl. I don't have sex for fun, I've never wanted to have a 'friend with benefits,' but I can't stop thinking about you. It's wreaking havoc on my life. I don't know how to fix it."

"Come over. Let me fix it for you." *Damn*. He'd just put it out there. Was she going to bite?

She didn't speak for what felt like an eternity and he wondered briefly if he'd played his cards too hard and fast for her. Syd wasn't like the women he normally messed around with.

"We're playing with serious fire, Morgan," she said softly.

"Are you coming?" he asked.

More silence.

"I'm on my way," she said, disconnecting the call.

A while later, Sydney burst into the house.

"Hi," she said absently. She tossed her purse onto the couch before plopping down on it herself.

"What's wrong?" he asked, taking a seat next to her. "What took you so long? I thought you were close."

She tucked her legs under her and sighed heavily. He couldn't help but notice her attire. She must have gone home and taken a shower because she smelled like a mixture of Dove soap, Gain detergent and Snuggle fabric softener. Red said she'd looked crazy, but she was far from it.

Her eyes flashed to his, fury laced in them. "I stopped at another store and bumped into Laney. She had the nerve to follow me around the store, making snide comments about how I couldn't keep Den happy in the bedroom and that's why he turned to her. The more she talked, the angrier I got. It took everything in me, but I managed to get out of there without responding."

He squeezed her leg. "You did the right thing."

"I refuse to let her take me there, no matter how angry I am." She stared down at his hands and traced the veins gently. "I have no room to talk, but how could he do that to me?"

"What are you talking about, you have no room to talk?" he asked.

"Well, I'm not exactly at home knitting." Her gaze met his. "I'm here with you."

"But you're not with Den, and you haven't been for over a month. Bringing Laney into your home has nothing to do with us," he argued. "You know better than to listen to her. She's full of shit—always has been."

Laney was a thorn in his family's side. Hooking up with her had to be the worst thing Den had ever done. She'd never given him anything but trouble. Yet, Morgan figured that was the attraction. They'd hooked up when Den had been off his meds for some time, blaming it on the fact that Syd left him. He'd claimed he wanted to feel something instead of numbness. According to Den, the Lithium made him feel like a shell of himself. And Laney fed the part of him that wanted to embrace the darkness inside. She was bitter, cold, and calculating, and he'd fallen right into her trap. Next thing the family knew, she'd gotten pregnant and demanded he support her. Morgan had supported Den when his brother had decided to step up and be a father to his child, and even through the subsequent miscarriage. And Morgan had never shared with anyone that he suspected she'd faked the pregnancy anyway.

"I can't believe he slept with her again," Syd said after a while. "He cheated on me with that skank. What the hell was his problem? And I feel bad because all I could think about after I got in my car was getting over here to see you. What does that make me? A hypocrite? Because that is exactly the way I feel."

Morgan picked up her hand and brushed his lips over her palm. "You have to stop being so hard on yourself. We're friends before we're anything else. It's not a bad thing to want to come see me."

"It is when all I want to do is feel your arms around me," she said. "We still haven't figured this—"

Before she could finish her sentence, he pulled her into a kiss. As the kiss deepened, he pulled her on top of him. She breathed out his name when he squeezed her ass and rocked into her. She braced her arms on the back of the couch as she undulated against him. He was okay with admitting that he seemed to have a one-track mind around her lately, but she was right. They hadn't solved anything. But it was hard to concentrate on anything else when his desire for her seemed to eclipse everything.

Breaking the kiss, he rested his forehead against hers. "You're right. We probably should come to some sort of conclusion. At the same time, I kind of feel like there's nothing to solve. We know there'll be consequences." He lifted her up and set her down next to him. Standing up, he paced the floor. "The question is—as harsh as it sounds—are we going to continue to do this anyway?"

Her eyes widened. "I-I don't know what to say to that."

He eyed her, letting his gaze travel up from her thighs to her mouth. She bit her bottom lip. "Say yes . . . or no," he said. "That's it. Look, so much has changed between us. But I'd like to think the most important thing hasn't—our friendship. Whatever you decide, I'm okay." He paused, wondering how those words even escaped him. There was no way he would be okay if she said no. But he wanted her happy more than he wanted to be with her. *Whipped.*

Every sound seemed to echo in his ears and his nerves felt raw, exposed. Waiting for her answer brought out a paranoia in him he'd never experienced with any woman.

"Morgan, I..." She rolled her eyes and rested her head on the back of the couch. "This is a hot mess. But I want you. I'm going to say..."

He knelt down in front of her and placed a hand on each of her thighs. "Whatever it is, you can say it. We've always been able to talk about anything. There's no reason that should change now."

"Yes."

That was all he needed to hear. He gripped her thighs and tugged her to him. He hooked his fingers under the waistband of her shorts, peeled them off slowly, and tossed them behind him.

Positioning himself between her thighs, he brushed his lips over hers before he lifted her shirt up and off, throwing it behind the couch. He ran his fingers over the bare skin of her stomach and under the elastic band of her lace panties. Taking her bottom lip into his mouth, he kissed her again—harder.

He trailed kisses down her neck to the tops of her breasts. She felt so warm, smelled so good. Wanting to taste her fully, he unhooked her bra. He traced a nipple with his tongue before taking it into his mouth, suckling it. Her soft cries stoked his senses and he kissed his way to her other nipple, giving it the same attention. When he was satisfied, he brushed his lips down her stomach and dipped his tongue in her belly button, enjoying her quick intake of breath. He couldn't let her go. A warmth spread through his body at the sight of her beneath him, a feeling he wouldn't trade for anything. She was his drug, a high he'd never before experienced. He wanted more. He wanted to explore every bit of her, lay her down on every surface of his home and make love to her.

She shivered under his palms as he ran his tongue along the thin line of her underwear.

"Oh Morgan," she moaned. "What are you doing to me?"

He peered up at her and smiled. "Not half of what I really want to do to you."

Then he threw her legs over his shoulders and touched his tongue to her.

She purred and raked her fingers through his hair. He tasted her, savoring her essence. It wasn't long before her first release tore through her, but he didn't stop. He continued to ply her, loving the feel of her beneath his tongue. Every time she whispered his name, his chest seemed to expand. He hissed against her when he felt the bite of her nails digging into his shoulders. But he continued his ministrations, slipping two fingers inside her.

She screamed his name out as her body rocked under the force of another climax. Her legs tightened around his head in a death grip and he waited. Once her grip loosened and her legs fell open, he went in for more, circling her clit with his tongue and sucking it into his mouth. It was only a few minutes before she came again, moaning his name.

Morgan stared at her when she slowly opened her eyes. She lifted herself up and looked down at him. He didn't move, though, and she fell back on the couch as his tongue darted out again and stabbed at her core until she begged for mercy.

"Morgan," she breathed, pushing at his shoulders.

He hummed against her as he continued to strum her clit with his tongue.

"Please," she begged.

"So good," he murmured, savoring the taste of her sweetness.

"Oh...Oh God...Morgan," she cried as another release coursed through her.

When her body went limp, he lifted her up, cradling her. He carried her through the house to his bedroom, kissing her along the way. Kicking the door open, he hurried to the bed and set her down gently. Stumbling as he tried to kick off his pants, he grumbled in frustration. Finally, he bent down, yanked them off, and flung them across the room. He made quick work of the rest of his clothes and joined her on the bed. Resting his weight on her, he slid home. At least, that's what it felt like to him. A calm settled over him, a peace that couldn't be explained. He felt complete for the first time in his life.

As they made love, Morgan realized that it was fast becoming his favorite thing to do. He wondered if he'd ever be able to get enough of her. He watched her face as he thrust in and out, picking up the pace. Her eyes were closed tight and her skin was a soft shade of red.

"Open your eyes," he commanded softly.

Her eyes opened and locked on his. Taking her bottom lip in his mouth, he grazed it with his teeth before kissing her deeply.

As he quickened the pace, his felt his control slipping. His stomach quivered with the need to complete the act, but he wouldn't come without her. He felt her inner walls tremble and knew she was close. Hooking his arms under her legs, he pushed into her—harder. She fell over the cliff first, with him following shortly after.

They lay still for a few minutes, then he rolled over onto his back, pulling her with him. She rested her head against his chest as he stroked her back.

He placed a kiss on the top of her head. "I think we've passed the point of no return, baby."

He felt the rumble of her laughter before he heard the sound. She peered up into his eyes, a smile gracing her lips. She kissed him soundly. "I would say you're right."

*C*HAPTER FOURTEEN

*S*ydney scanned the documents in her hands, struggling to keep her attention on the matter at hand. Seated around the conference room table were her business partners—Kent, Red, and Morgan. Joining them were representatives from Den's construction company. They had scheduled the meeting to finalize some last-minute additions to the building. Earlier, they'd met with the interior design company to go over ideas. Red had finally received a copy of the liquor license, which had everyone on edge because the approval process was so daunting—not to mention the expensive price tag. Everything seemed to be falling in line. The Ice Box would be opening in a matter of weeks.

She glanced across the table at Morgan, who had his nose buried in paperwork. Red nudged him in the arm and passed over the amended contract for the construction. Once he signed on the dotted line, he handed the document to Kent, working nearby on his laptop. Kent scribbled his signature and set it in front of her.

Still unable to concentrate on business, she snuck another glance at Morgan, noticing the slight furrow in his brow.

She wondered what he was thinking—if he'd thought of her while he was away. They hadn't seen each other in two weeks because he'd had to fly out of town on business.

When he was away, she'd told herself countless times to end things before one of them got hurt. She even wrote him a letter because she realized that telling him in person would prove futile. Her desire for him was stronger than ever. Forcing her attention back to the contract in front of her, she skimmed it and then signed on the dotted line.

Looking up, she caught Kent smacking Morgan on the back. "Roc," Kent said, shoving a folder in his face. "Stop daydreaming and sign this paper. It's the last one."

Morgan jerked the folder from Kent's hand and scribbled what she assumed was his signature on it.

She had tried not to stare, but her eyes were glued to him. She felt like she was back in high school, staring across the classroom at an unrequited crush. But she was far from the fourteen-year-old girl who'd been enamored with the star athlete on the football team. Now she was a grown-ass woman—who was crushing on her best friend.

She bit down on her pen as Morgan and Kent carried on a conversation with each other in muffled tones. She couldn't help but smile when they both laughed and gave each other some dap. Morgan had such a beautiful smile. He had dimples, but the little creases that framed his mouth when he was happy made her stomach do somersaults. *Damn, he's sexy.*

It'd been two whole weeks since he'd made her climax so hard she could barely move or breathe. She watched him moisten his lips with his tongue. His perfect tongue—on her skin, in her mouth, on her... *Oh shit!* Wasn't she supposed to be concentrating on the business at hand?

She shifted her attention back to the papers in front of her and tried to focus on color palettes. Still, she couldn't help but peek up at him again. Closing her eyes as she remembered that wicked tongue of his, she mused to herself that he definitely lived up to his hype. She smiled and opened her eyes to find him staring at her with a smirk that let her know he knew exactly what she was thinking about. She cleared her throat and raked a hand through her hair before she turned back to view the material swatches in front of her.

Once every "i" was dotted and every "t" crossed, the group let out a collective sigh. Caden's account representative excused herself and the interior designer left behind the designs for the group. Red tucked the paperwork and liquor license in his briefcase.

"Well, this is it," she said. "Thank you all for helping to make this project a success. I have a feeling we're going to be in business together for years to come."

"As long as we are each committed, there shouldn't be a problem," Red added.

Sydney opened her planner. "Right now, we're actually ahead of schedule. We've booked the caterer and Morgan's already hired a deejay. All the decorations for opening night were purchased at a discount, thanks to Cali. The main thing to focus on right now is promotion. One of Den's clients has offered to sell us a billboard and Kent is almost finished with the design."

Kent scribbled on a piece of paper. "I'm done, actually. I already sent it off. I also put in a call to a friend at the Mix radio station who agreed to plug opening night at the top of the hour for the whole week leading up to the opening. Flyers are at the printers."

"Morgan and I have already hired most of the staff and training has already started for management," she added. "It would be nice if we can schedule a meeting as soon as possible so employees can meet all of you. I understand schedules are different, but let's make it happen."

They all nodded in agreement.

Red stood up. "I'll get back to you with my schedule for next week. But right now I need to get back to the office. Talk to you later."

"Yeah, I need to make a move." Kent said, glancing at his watch. "I have a project meeting. Check you later."

Realizing she was now alone with Morgan, she jumped up and started packing her briefcase. "I guess I better get going, too. I need to get with Cali and finish the event details."

As she stuffed her laptop in its case, she felt Morgan walk up behind her. *Shit.* She froze.

"Should I expect you tonight?" he whispered in her ear.

She covered her face with her hands. "Why are you doing this to me? Can you stop being so damn irresistible?"

He turned her around and gently pulled her hands away from her face. "Can you stop being so damn dramatic? I want to see you."

She eyed him warily. "It's not a good idea. I'm supposed to be staying away from you."

He smiled. Her stomach flip-flopped. "Says who?"

When he grabbed her earlobe between his teeth and tugged gently, she shivered. Her mind was quickly becoming a pile of mush. She placed her hands on his chest to hold him at bay. "Says me! I told myself that I wouldn't sleep with you again."

He brushed his lips below her ear and down her neck. "You didn't tell me that."

A small moan escaped her lips, and her head fell back. *I'm so easy.* "I know...I...I was...going to send you an e-mail."

"An e-mail?" he asked, chuckling. "Is that what we're reduced to?"

She groaned when he nipped at her neck. "Morgan, you know we can't talk in person."

He continued his assault on her neck, then worked his way

back up to her chin. "Maybe we should stop talking. Did you ever think of that?"

She gasped when he bit her chin gently. "We never settle anything."

He leaned closer to her, touching his lips to hers. "I thought it was pretty much settled. I missed you."

Her heart tightened. She'd missed him, too. "It has been forever since I've seen you," she admitted. Unable to help herself, she kissed him. "You were gone for two weeks."

"It couldn't be helped. My boss needed me to secure an account. So, should I expect you?" he murmured while nibbling on her bottom lip.

"No. Yes." Her eyes fluttered as he ran his thumb down her neck. *Damn it*. She couldn't think straight.

"Which one is it?"

She gave up. Her body was already screaming at her to stop playing coy and just do him on the conference table. "What time should I be there?"

"Why don't you come around seven? I have a project to finish up at the office," he said, kissing his way down her throat. His hands slid up her thighs, pushing her dress up.

She trembled as he continued to work on her neck with his magnificent tongue. "Seven it is."

"Good." He kissed her deeply and possessively.

Sydney knew they were taking a chance; any of their friends could come strolling in. She was helpless to stop him, though. Reaching out, she grabbed the waistline of his pants, unbuttoned them, and pushed them to the floor. She gasped when he yanked her underwear off.

She wanted to shout *yes!* when he perched her up on the conference table, shoving everything away. Then he grabbed her thighs and entered her in one smooth motion. She purred as he filled her completely and began to move in and out of her. It wasn't long before she felt that heaviness in her stomach that signaled she was close. She closed her legs around his waist and pushed against him, biting down on his neck when her orgasm ripped through her. He thrust into her two more times before he came, exploding inside her.

Seconds later, she was finally able to move again. He pulled away from her, tugged her dress down, and she hopped off the conference table. As they quickly scrambled to get dressed, she wondered if she'd ever be able to be in the same room with him without turning into a wanton woman. Shit, she lost her underwear again. She frowned as she scanned the area around the conference table.

"Looking for these?" he asked, the thin fabric dangling from his finger.

She smiled and snatched her panties away from him. "Thanks," she said, sliding them on.

Deciding it was best to escape before she wanted a second go-round, she collected her things. Unfortunately, they were strewn across the table, so she had to practically climb on it to gather everything. As she reached for her laptop bag, she felt him behind her and stilled as he pressed into her.

He swept her hair off her neck and kissed it. "I can't get enough of you, Syd," he murmured against her skin. "When I was gone, I couldn't stop thinking about you."

"I hate to admit it, but I'm glad." She relaxed against him.

"You're glad, huh?"

"I'm glad I wasn't the only one." Leaning forward, she picked up her pen and dropped it into her purse. "I don't know what you've done to me, but it was definitely something you shouldn't have been doing."

He gently smacked her butt. "Hey, I don't do anything you don't want me to do."

"That's the problem," she admitted, fanning through a stack of papers. "My mind turns to liquid Jell-O whenever we're in the same room. I can't think straight. I had it all planned out...how I was going to tell you I wasn't sleeping with you again." She purposely didn't turn around to look at him. "I even drafted the e-mail. But...well...you know how that turned out. Here I am, sitting in the middle of a business meeting and can't stop thinking about that last time we were together and the things you did to me. And instead of telling you I can't sleep with you anymore, I end up letting you do me on the conference table."

He laughed as he wrapped his arms around her and placed a sweet kiss on her cheek. "You're so cute when you're all riled up."

"Cute, huh?" she asked sarcastically. "Will I be cute to you when we get disowned by your entire family?"

"Stop thinking all doom and gloom. Seven o'clock, baby. Be on time." He nipped at her chin then let her go.

She picked up her bag and slung her purse over her shoulder. "Since I'm incapable of making a decision and sticking to it when it comes to you, I'll see you at seven." She hurried out of the room.

*C*HAPTER FIFTEEN

*M*organ dashed through the house when he heard the blare of a car horn. He'd spent the rest of the afternoon at work trying to pretend he wasn't anxious to see Syd.

Even though he'd run into an old girlfriend who'd offered to blow his mind (among other things) while he was out of town, Syd had been the only one in his thoughts. He couldn't get the image of her out of his head—the way her eyes glistened when she laughed and the way her back arched when he touched her. He wanted to feel her in his arms again.

Their little dalliance at the Ice Box after their meeting wasn't enough for him. The more he made love to her, the more he wanted her.

Opening the side door he pushed the garage door button and watched as the heavy door opened. Syd pulled into the empty space next to his truck and hopped out of her car. Once she walked into the house, he closed the garage door, hiding her car from view.

"You're late," he said. "I was wondering if you were going to stand me up."

She smirked. "Yeah, right. You knew I was coming. But

I'm sorry I'm late. I ended up staying a little later at the office."

He helped her out of her jacket and tossed it on a chair. "Are you hungry? I bought dinner."

"Hmm...What did you get?"

"I had a taste for pasta," he said, wrapping his arms around her waist. "Italian sound good?"

"Sounds wonderful." Pulling away from him, she headed to the kitchen table. She picked up the bottle of Italian red wine and set it back down. "I'm starved."

He grabbed a couple of plates from the cabinet and set them down on the table while she opened the bag from the restaurant and removed the cartons. Once everything was set up, he poured her a glass of wine and joined her.

"This is good," She said, taking a bite of her pasta. "You know I love Carraba's."

"And it's always good to eat a full meal so that you'll have plenty of energy." When her gaze met his, he knew she had caught his meaning. No use denying his intentions for the evening.

She pointed her fork at him. "One of these days I'm not going to be such a sure thing."

He snickered. "You think I think you're a sure thing?"

"Yes," she said, nodding. "See how easily you were able to distract me this afternoon?"

"And that makes you a sure thing?"

"I'm here, aren't I?" She giggled and sipped her wine. "You never had any doubt, did you? And I know you don't want me to eat for energy if we're going to...talk."

"We can talk, but it won't change anything." He took her hand and brushed his thumb over her knuckles. "I have definite plans for tonight."

Her hazel eyes darkened and her skin flushed. He loved making her blush. It did something to him to know that he'd caused it, to see it start from the base of her neck and creep into her cheeks. That meant he was doing something right.

She arched a brow. "What kind of plans?"

"I think we have a lot of time to make up for—two weeks, to be exact." He cleared his throat. "How about this? To prove to you that I don't think you're a sure thing, I'm going to let you set the pace. Whatever you want to do, I'll do— even if you want to watch a movie and cuddle. Or not. You decide."

"Really?" She looked at him skeptically. "Whatever I want to do?"

He nodded. "You pick the agenda."

She swirled her fork over her plate of food. "What if I told you your agenda was fine with me?" Putting down the fork, she stood up and sauntered over to him. "What if I told you that I wanted you for dessert?" She unbuckled his belt and slid it off slowly. His breath caught in his throat. "What if I told you it was time for me to take control of the situation?" She tugged him to his feet and unbuttoned his pants, letting them fall to the floor.

"What about your promise to yourself?"

"Shut up." Her hands were on his face, pulling him into a kiss. "It's my turn."

Before he could respond, she dropped to her knees, jerked his boxers down and peered up at him, a slow smile spreading across her face.

* * *

Sydney watched Morgan as he slept. He looked so peaceful that she hated to wake him. They'd spent hours "talking," but now it was morning. She'd spent another night with Morgan. She ran a finger down his chest, over the ridges of his six-pack. Leaning down, she kissed his jawline.

"What time is it?" he murmured, bringing a hand up and running it through her hair.

"It's six o'clock. I have to get ready for work." She rested her chin on his chest. She'd requested a leave but her boss had asked her to take on a new project instead, so she'd settled for a reduction in her hours for the time being. "Although I could sleep for a couple more hours. I'm dead tired."

"You should be. You worked your ass off last night." He smacked her ass lightly.

"Stop." She pinched him and sat up, drawing her knees to her chest and resting her chin on them. "What time do you have to be at work?"

"I don't. I'm off today." He ran a finger down her spine, sending a shiver through her.

"Lucky you."

"You know it's Kent's birthday." He brushed his mouth over her shoulder. "I'm supposed to get with him and Den this morning for the traditional stack of pancakes and a game of horse at the park."

"Sounds fun," she said, unable to hide the sarcasm in her voice.

"What's wrong?"

Waking up in Morgan's room, naked in his bed, while he brings up Den like it's normal conversation? "Are you serious?" she asked, glaring at him over her shoulder.

"Um, I asked, didn't I?"

She pulled the sheet around her. "Morgan, can't you see how crazy this is? We woke up in your bed talking about how my ex—your brother—is hanging out with you today for friendly breakfast and basketball. And you want to know what's wrong?"

It was definitely time to go home. She stood up, taking the sheet with her. When she looked back at him, lying stark naked on the bed, she froze. Turning away from him she asked, "Can you please put something over you?"

He peered up at the ceiling, his hands behind his head. He made no move to pull the big comforter up off the floor to cover himself.

"Don't start acting shy now," he said, a slight edge to his voice. "You pulled the covers off of me in your hurry to once again point out all the wrong that we've been doing."

She whirled around to face him. "That's because we're wrong."

He rolled his eyes. "Yes, Syd, we're definitely wrong. Is that what you want to hear?"

She wanted to hit him in the head with her shoe, but she couldn't find it. "What is your problem, Morgan?"

"I don't have a problem."

"Obviously."

"So why did you ask me what my problem is if I *obviously* don't have a problem?" Shaking his head, he got out of bed and stomped to the master bathroom. She was right on his heels. He turned on the shower and reached behind her for a towel.

"Morgan?" She called.

He ignored her.

"Morgan, I—"

"Don't," he ordered, slicing a hand through the air. He stepped in the shower and proceeded to completely ignore her presence in the bathroom.

As much as she wanted to walk out and leave, she couldn't. She knew she'd started that little argument because *she* felt guilty. She couldn't blame him for being irritated with her. Hell, she was irritated with herself.

"Morgan?" she called again, ready to apologize for going off.

When he didn't answer her, she sighed, yanked the shower door open, and stepped in—sheet and all.

* * *

Did she step into this shower in a sheet? Morgan moved back slightly, staring at Syd in disbelief. Her arms were crossed over her breasts, her chin held high. She was definitely sexy when she was riled up, but damn if he wasn't tired of trying to justify what was going on between them.

His gaze dropped from her face to his drenched sheet. "I envisioned taking a hot shower with you, but I never imagined it would be like this. What the hell were you thinking jumping into the shower in a sheet?"

"You wouldn't talk to me," she said, her eyes flashing.

"So, you throw a fit and soak up my bedding in the process?" He threw his hands up in frustration. "And I'm still not talking to you with that on."

"Asshole," she hissed. Opening the shower door, she tossed the wet sheet on his ceramic floor.

Morgan wanted to continue ignoring her because, frankly, he was irritated. But of course, he was a man. Gazing at her firm, wet body, he tried—unsuccessfully—to fight his body's natural response. Sighing, he said, "Syd, can we make an agreement to stop talking about Den and how wrong we are because I know the ramifications of our actions? I don't need a daily reminder."

Okay, so he'd managed to get his point across without pinning her against the shower wall and fucking her senseless.

"Morgan, I know. I probably shouldn't have gone there this morning. I still feel guilty."

"That's fine, but don't take that shit out on me." He nudged her. "Can I take my shower now?"

"Fine." She rolled her eyes. "I'm going home."

He grabbed her arm and tugged her to him. "I don't want to fight with you, Syd," he whispered against her ear.

"I don't want to fight with you either," she agreed, pressing a palm to her eyes. "I'm sorry. I shouldn't have started it."

In all the years they'd been friends, they'd rarely argued. They almost always came up on the same side of most issues.

Her eyes welled up with tears. "My feelings are all jumbled up. So much has happened. I broke up with Den, called off the wedding. If all that hadn't happened, I would be going over seating charts and finalizing menus right now. Then I see you and I can't seem to—I know that we're always going to be friends but things are different. No matter what we've said, things will never be the same. It's scary. You've always been my voice of reason. And I don't want to lose that. I guess I'm not handling this too well."

He traced her cheek with the palm of his hand. "That makes two of us. It's kind of hard to concentrate, though, when all I want to do is make love to you."

"I feel the same way," she whispered. "I'm not sure what to do."

Her skin glistened under the spray of the shower as steam filled the bathroom. He watched the rise and fall of her breasts and felt himself hardening. God, would she always have this effect on him? He reached out and ran a finger over one of her nipples. She moaned when he pulled her closer, their bodies touching.

"This is only going to hurt us in the long run," she said.

"You don't know that." He dipped his head down, rubbed his nose against her cheek. Then he kissed her—hard, tilting her head to get a better angle. She gasped when he backed her against the cool, wet tile. Pulling away, he grinned when her eyes remained closed and her mouth open. "God, I want you so bad. Do you even realize how much?"

She shook her head. "I-I—"

His mouth covered hers again. He pulled her against him so she could feel how much he wanted her.

"Morgan," she breathed, digging her nails into his shoulders.

"Feel that?" he murmured against her ear. He nipped her earlobe. "That's for you."

She arched her back and rocked into him, murmuring her approval. "Oh God," she groaned.

She whimpered when his hand slipped between her thighs and two fingers slid into her. Resting his head on her shoulder, he worked her, moving his fingers in and out of her. He kissed his way down from her shoulder to her perky breast and suckled the tip into his mouth.

After paying the same attention to her other breast, he worked his way back up to her lips, snaking his tongue into her mouth. He raked his hand through her wet curls and gripped her hair in his hands, holding her to him. He wrapped his free arm around her waist and lifted her off the ground. Once she wrapped her legs around him, he didn't waste any more time—he slid into her easily. Bracing himself, he paused to give her time to adjust to their position.

Her head fell to his shoulder and he tugged on her hair. "Look at me," he commanded in a low voice.

Their gazes locked as he moved inside her, pumping in and out as if he'd never get another chance. Her soft mewls egged him on and he increased the pace. He wanted to steal every bit of fear from her.

Although he felt the water lose its heat, he couldn't stop. He wanted to see her come. She obviously didn't notice the change in temperature because she whispered, "Don't stop."

Was that the doorbell? If it was, he didn't care. He wanted to finish. Gripping her ass he pounded into her, and she met his thrusts with a fire of her own. She screamed his name as tremors rolled through her body. The sheer force of her orgasm seemed to milk his from him and he followed soon after, roaring out her name.

The sound of the doorbell ringing jarred him from the

moment. He froze. Then the chill of the cold water finally registered and he jumped out of the shower with her still in his arms. Setting her down, he quickly turned off the spray and pulled a towel around his body.

"Stay here," he said. "If it's Kent or Den, they have a key."

She nodded and he rushed out of the bathroom. As he dashed through the bedroom into the hallway, he remembered they'd left a trail of clothes from the kitchen to the bedroom in their haste to get down to it the night before. After he noticed the first sign that he had female company—her sandals—he snatched them up and threw them into the spare room.

In the kitchen, he grabbed her jacket and scanned the room. *Where the hell is her dress?* He searched the floor around the island. *Shit.* Frowning, he tried to remember where he'd tossed it.

"What's up, Roc?"

Morgan whirled around, fists up. "Shit, Kent." He opened his hands and let them fall to his sides. "What the hell are you doing here?"

"I could be asking you the same question, but I'm not sure I want to know." Kent scowled at him, holding up the missing dress. "Looking for this? Or maybe Syd misplaced it?"

Morgan snatched the dress away from him. "What's up?" he asked, deliberately side-stepping the question.

"Did you forget that we were supposed to go out this morning?"

"Aren't you here early?"

Kent pulled down his sunglasses, looking at Morgan over the rims with a cold glare. "Den is on his way," he said. "Maybe you should get dressed before this gets worse than it already is?"

"Maybe you should mind your own business," Morgan retorted. "You don't know what's going on."

"I know that either you went out searching for someone with the same taste in dresses as Syd, or you have the real thing in your bedroom. And since the likelihood of you finding some chick that happened to be wearing the same outfit on the same day is pretty low, I have to ask, what the hell are you thinking?"

Morgan gripped his towel, pulling it tightly around his waist. "Kent—"

"What the hell are you thinking?" Kent repeated. "Shit, Morgan, do you realize what this means—what's going to happen?"

"Calm down, Kent. It's not what you think," Morgan lied. He racked his brain trying to come up with a suitable excuse, but he knew it wouldn't work with Kent. He knew him better than anyone.

"What is it, Roc? What do *you* think I think?" Kent paced the room, grumbling curses under his breath. "Where is she?"

"I'm not talking about this right now. I have to get dressed, as you so aptly pointed out." He turned around and left Kent in the kitchen. *Shit. All hell is about the break loose.*

CHAPTER SIXTEEN

Syd waited for Morgan anxiously, chewing on her thumbnail. It had been a few minutes since he'd left her, and she knew something was wrong. Her clothes were strewn all over the house so getting dressed wasn't an option, but she couldn't sit there in a towel either. She pulled a robe out of Morgan's closet and slipped it on.

Morgan rushed in the room, slammed the door, and let out a string of curses.

"Who's here?" she asked, biting down on her lip.

"Kent." He dropped her clothes on the bed and yanked his towel off. He pulled some boxers out of a drawer and slid them on.

She plopped down on his bed. "He knows I'm here?" It wasn't really a question—more a statement. Judging by the way Morgan was jerking on his clothes, she pretty much had her answer.

"He saw your dress in the kitchen." He bowed his head and gripped the edge of the dresser, letting out a slow breath. "I'm sorry."

Can you say "busted"? She approached him, placing a hand on his back. "It's not your fault. I should've left when I woke up."

He turned to face her, caressing her face in his hands. "I wanted you to stay. I should've kept my hands to myself, but I couldn't see past what I wanted." He kissed her, then slipped on a T-shirt. "I'm going to go. Can you stay here? At least until I leave. I can pretty much guarantee that Kent won't say anything."

She nodded, silently thanking God that Kent was the one who'd found them, because he wasn't the type to share secrets with anyone. "I hate that he knows I'm here."

"He's cool," he assured her, bending down to put on his socks. "He's not happy, but he won't say anything." He walked to the door but then turned back. "I'll be out of here in a few, okay? I'll call you later."

She crawled into his bed after he left and waited.

* * *

Den was waiting with Kent when Morgan walked into the kitchen. He opened the refrigerator and grabbed a bottle of water. "What's up, Den?"

"Not much. What do you feel like for breakfast?"

"Since it's my birthday, I say we go to the gym first," Kent said. "We can eat when we get done."

"Roc, you seen Syd?" Den asked.

Way to change the subject. "Why?" Morgan asked, glaring at Kent. "You looking for her?"

"I tried calling her, but I couldn't get an answer." Den shrugged and guzzled from his bottle of water. "Last time I saw her, we actually were able to talk to each other without fighting. I started seeing someone, a counselor. I've been taking my meds. I told Laney there's nothing between us. If

I can prove to her that I'm willing to work on myself, maybe she'll give me another chance. This can't be it between us. I can't lose her for good."

Den's confession hit Morgan like a ton of bricks. He'd officially become a dirty bastard. He was actually listening to his brother talk about winning Syd back and, at the same time, vowing it would never happen—not if he had anything to say about it.

A few hours later, the brothers returned to Morgan's house. Den and Kent made themselves at home in the game room while Morgan grabbed a few more bottles of water. *Too early for beer.* He tossed a bottle at each of his brothers and plopped down on the recliner.

It had been a long time since he'd hung out with both of his brothers and it felt good. No matter what was going on in their lives, they always spent the mornings of their birthdays together. Despite what had been going on in recent months, they were able to push all of that aside and just enjoy each other's company.

"I think I want to go out tonight," Kent announced after taking a long swig of water.

"We can do something," Morgan agreed. "It's Friday."

"Maybe we can invite some people here?" Kent suggested. "Roc has plenty of space."

"Good idea," Den said.

Morgan frowned at Kent, wondering where he was going with this. After spending the morning shooting baskets and avoiding eye contact with Kent, he was surprised his brother wanted to have a gathering at his house. Morgan began to question if this Syd thing would be the one secret Kent would blab—to everyone. Every time Den had brought her up, Kent had shot Morgan a pointed glance.

"Who's going to come here on such short notice?" Morgan had a sinking feeling that something was going to go down soon—and it wasn't going to be pretty. The last thing he wanted was a whole bunch of people at his house.

"It doesn't have to be big," Kent said. "Just the usual suspects. I'm sure we can get Syd and Red to come over." Kent glanced at Morgan. "Besides, it's my birthday. And you both owe me a good time. And you never know when we'll all be able to get together like this again."

"I can throw some stuff on the grill," Den offered before Morgan could respond to Kent's sly remark. "I'm sure Syd can make her famous potato salad."

"Whatever," Morgan said, standing up. "Let yourself out. I'm going to get in the shower."

Okay, so he was an asshole *and* a dirty bastard. Part of him felt bad for copping an attitude, but he didn't care. Needing a break from his brothers, he stalked into the bedroom and slammed the door. Only, he wasn't prepared for what awaited him. Lying on his bed, still in her robe, was a sleeping Syd. *Shit.*

He sat on the edge of the bed and turned to face her. Unable to help himself, he reached out and smoothed his thumb over the furrow in her brow. He let his gaze roam over her sleeping form. The robe had fallen open, giving him a view of her smooth shoulders and long legs.

Morgan gently nudged her. "Syd?" he whispered. She didn't stir. He bent down to her ear. "Wake up."

She moaned, stretched, and rolled over on her back. "Morgan," she said, her eyes still closed. Then she sat up straight, seemingly realizing she was still in his room. "Shit!"

He placed a finger over her mouth. "You have to be quiet. Den and Kent may still be in the house."

Her eyes widened. "Oh God."

He squeezed her thigh. "It's okay. You're fine. I told them to leave. Let me check and see if they're actually gone yet."

"What if they walk in here?" Syd said, panic in her voice. "What time is it?"

"They won't. And it's eleven o'clock."

She dropped her face into her hands. "What was I thinking? I missed work, too."

Morgan rubbed her back in an effort to calm her down. "I told you everything's fine."

"And I'm still in your robe," she hissed, throwing her hands in the air.

Deciding to try another approach, he slid his hand under the robe and stroked her inner thigh. "Calm down. I told you everything was going to be okay."

She punched him in the stomach, causing him to grunt. "Morgan, this is not the time. Den could be right out there. Kent...oh my God...what—"

"Don't panic. They may be gone already. I'll be right back."

She smacked her forehead and fell back against the pillow, tears welling in her eyes. "I—"

"Morgan?" Den called from the hallway.

He jumped up and rushed to the door, motioning and pointing Sydney to the bathroom. She hopped off the bed and hurried toward it.

"Den?" Kent called loudly from the other side of the door. "What's going on?"

Morgan leaned his ear against the door to listen

"I wanted to ask Roc if he could get in touch with Syd about tonight," he heard Den say.

"He's probably in the bathroom," Kent replied. "Why don't *you* call Syd later and ask her to come?"

Morgan felt Syd come up behind him and turned around. "What are you doing?" he mouthed to her. He pointed back to the bathroom. She shook her head and put her ear to the door.

"You were together for a long time," Kent continued. "You should be able to talk to her. Oh, make sure you get me a nice rib-eye when you pick up the meat."

As the voices traveled farther away from the door, Morgan cracked it open and poked his head out, just to make sure. Not wanting to take any more chances, he waited a few minutes before he headed toward the kitchen, kicking himself the whole time for not getting the alarm fixed. If he had, he would've heard the "front door open" announcement in his bedroom. But he was glad it worked in the kitchen, so when the monotone voice stated the door was closed, he hurried back to Sydney. Kent had saved his ass—again.

"I'm sorry," she said as soon as he entered the bedroom.

He hoped this wasn't going to turn into another one of those *we're-so-wrong* discussions. "What are you sorry for? You didn't do anything wrong."

"I did." She pressed a hand to her chest, her eyes wide. "I fell asleep when I should've put my clothes on and left. It's bad enough that Kent knows I was here, but what if Den had come in here?"

"Baby, it's fine," he assured her.

She tightened the belt on the robe and grumbled a curse. "This can't happen again." She stalked toward the bathroom.

He dashed to the door to block her entrance. "Don't start this again, Syd. I thought we had an understanding." Well, at least, he thought she understood that he wanted her and *no, we can't be together* wasn't in his vocabulary at that point. Maybe tomorrow, or even tonight. But not while she was standing in front of him in nothing but his robe.

"I do understand." *See!* She did get it. "I understand that this was too big of a chance to take." His stomach tightened. *Not again.* "Spending the night here was just not a good idea."

He was relieved she wasn't going to go into all the reasons they couldn't be together again. He gripped the belt of the robe and pulled her closer. "You can stay here," he said. "The only reason Kent knows is because he found your dress in the kitchen. It's not like he saw your car."

"I know." She pulled away from him. "But it could've been Den who found my dress. Oh my God," she gasped. "What if it had been Mama?"

"She doesn't have a key."

Syd shoved him out of the way and went into the bathroom. "I have to get out of here," she said, slipping on her panties. She hooked her bra and pulled her hair back into a sloppy ponytail. "I was supposed to be at work hours ago."

He stared at her, so entranced by her movements that he couldn't offer her any words. Not that he needed to, because she continued mumbling as she washed her face and brushed her teeth with his spare toothbrush.

Then she was standing in front of him. "I guess I'm going to have to call my boss and tell her I won't be in," she said, chewing on her finger. "I might as well use this time to take care of some Ice Box business. I could try to meet up with Calisa about the opening. What's this about a get-together here?"

"Kent wants to have something here for his birthday," he grumbled.

"Okay. I probably won't be here. I don't even think I can look Kent in the eye again—especially after he found my dress."

"I told you Kent won't say anything."

She stood on the tips of her toes and brushed her lips against his. "Can I have my dress back?"

Frowning, he looked down at his hands. He hadn't realized he was holding it. He didn't even remember picking it up off the bed, where he'd dropped it earlier. But deciding to roll with it, he grinned. "I will—on one condition."

Squinting at him, she asked, "What condition?"

He wrapped his arms around her waist and tugged her to him. "You can have it back if you take another shower with me."

She laughed loudly. "I am *not* getting into the shower with you again, Roc."

He loved when she called him "Roc." It happened rarely, and he couldn't help but find his nickname sexy coming from her mouth. He moved his hand up to tangle in her silky hair and leaned in, inhaling her shampoo. "You should probably jump in the shower again," he murmured. "You're all sweaty."

"Only because your sweaty ass is all over me, Roc."

He *loved* it.

She placed her hands flat on his chest and nudged him back. "Come on, Roc. Give me my dress back."

Loved it.

Dipping his head down, he crushed his lips over hers. She looped her arms around his neck as his tongue slipped into her warm mouth. Fueled by her soft moans, he pulled her toward the shower.

When he broke the kiss, she let out a frustrated groan—replaced by a purr as he trailed moist kisses down her throat. His thumbs found her strained nipples underneath her bra and he nipped at her skin as he pushed her against the shower door. If she let him, he would make love to her all day.

Just when he thought she might give in, she shoved him—hard. He stumbled back a step. "Morgan. We can't do this. I have to get out of here." When he tried to grab her again, she dodged him and snatched up her dress, which had fallen on the floor. *Damn.*

Taking a deep breath, he followed her and ended up running right into her. "What—"

Kent was standing in the doorway.

*C*HAPTER SEVENTEEN

*S*yd was rendered speechless at the sight of Kent standing in the bedroom. She opened her mouth to speak, then clamped it shut. What exactly would she say? *I'm sorry I slept with both of your brothers?*

Morgan quickly stepped in front of her. "What the hell are you doing, Kent?" he roared. "What part of 'knock before you enter' don't you understand?"

"So tell me again how it's not what I think," Kent snarled.

She couldn't form a sentence if she tried. Actually, she felt faint. She looked down at herself, still in her bra and panties. Why hadn't she slipped her dress on? *Dummy.*

"I'm not getting into this with you right now," Morgan said. "Get the fuck out of my room, Kent!"

Kent pointed at her. "Syd, get dressed." Then he stalked out of the room.

Morgan bolted out of the room after Kent while Sydney struggled to slip her dress on. She put her jacket on and then followed them. *Oh Lord.* She didn't want them to fight. She'd been around the brothers a long time, had been there when they'd gotten into some physical scrapes.

When she entered the kitchen, they were standing—face-to-face.

"I can't understand what goes on in your fucking mind!" Kent yelled. "Den could have just as easily walked into your bedroom. You're damn lucky I caught him before he did."

"How did you know I was still here?" she asked, finally straightening the twisted mess of her belt.

"Your keys?" Kent growled, holding them up in the air. "Damn, if you're going to have an affair, do a better job of hiding that shit, Syd." He threw the keys on the counter.

She lowered her head, shame rolling through her like waves.

"Don't talk to her like that," Morgan demanded. "And we're not having an affair. We're both single. Actually, get the hell out of here right now."

"Hell no. Your stupid ass can't even see past what you want and think about the consequences of your actions. I mean, damn." Kent threw his hands up in frustration. "How long has this been going on?"

Her eyes flashed to his. "Not long." She swallowed past the lump in her throat. "It hasn't been going on that long, Kent. We weren't sleeping together while I was with Den, if that's what you think."

"Does it really matter, Syd?" Kent said through his teeth. "As far as Den's concerned, you're just on one of your little 'breaks.' He thinks this is all going to blow over with some therapy. He's not going to care when it started."

Shuddering, she stepped back. She felt like she was going to throw up.

"This is wrong as hell, Syd," Kent said, his voice softer. "You have to know that."

She peered at him, tears welling up in her eyes. "I—"

"Even if she knew that, how is any of this your business?" Morgan said. "This is between us."

Kent frowned at Morgan. "Roc, you're fuckin' around with the woman your brother is in love with. He was here telling us how he hoped they could get back together. He still thinks he has a chance with her. And you were hiding her in your room the whole time."

"You know it's not like that." Morgan slammed his fist on the counter.

"Then you tell me what it's like," Kent ordered.

She slipped between the brothers, who were both standing with their fists closed, chests heaving. "Kent, it just happened. It wasn't planned. I've never done anything like this before."

Kent snorted. "Syd, don't you think I know that about you? Shit happens. I know that. You weren't in the frame of mind to make a good decision. I know who seduced whom here," he said, glaring at Morgan.

"What the hell is that supposed to mean?" Morgan shouted. "I didn't plan on sleeping with Syd. It just happened."

"Come on, Roc." Kent crossed his arms. "I know you."

"Obviously not well enough if you think I would take advantage of her like that."

"You wanted her, right?" Kent said. Sarcasm laced his words.

"What the hell is your problem?" Morgan asked angrily. "You should know that I would never willingly get myself into this mess."

Syd whirled around, surprised at Morgan's words. "What?"

Morgan sighed. "I didn't mean it like that. All I'm saying is, I wouldn't go out and start screwing Den's ex-girlfriend."

She shot him another wary look, but turned to Kent to address him.

"Syd," Kent said. "I'm not sure what's really going on between you two, but you have to realize this can only end badly."

She glanced back at Morgan. He wouldn't look at her, but he didn't have to. She knew what he was thinking. Turning back to Kent, she said, "I know what we did and are doing is wrong. I'm sorry if you're upset with me. I...I...there's no justification for it. But this is not Morgan's fault. I'm a willing participant. I could've stopped it, but I didn't, even though I knew the consequences."

"Okay, so it happened," Kent said. "You could stop now—before it gets worse."

As much as she hated the disappointed look in Kent's eyes, she couldn't tell him that she wouldn't see Morgan again. It would be a lie. "I can't, Kent. I guess I could tell you that I'll stop. But I know it would be a lie. I'm sorry that I put you in this position in the first place."

"What is this?" Kent asked.

She shrugged and looked over at Morgan, who was watching her. "I don't know, Kent. I just need you to promise me that you won't say anything right now. Den isn't ready for this yet. I know it would hurt him and I don't want to do that."

"Syd, can you leave us alone?" Morgan asked.

She didn't bother to hide her surprise at Morgan's question. Instead of arguing that she should stay—she wanted to stay and make sure things were settled—she said, "I guess I'll go then."

"I put your shoes in the spare room," Morgan said.

Nodding, she grabbed her keys and went to grab her sandals. She left without saying good-bye to Morgan.

* * *

Morgan opened the fridge and pulled out two beers. After he handed one to Kent, he twisted the cap off and took a long pull. "It's not her fault," he said.

"Whose fault is it?" Kent asked, setting his bottle on the counter.

"Why does it have to be anybody's fault? Shit happens. You said it yourself," Morgan explained. "There wasn't a sinister plan to fuck Den over. It wasn't this grand seduction. She was falling apart. She needed something."

"And you gave it to her?" Kent asked sarcastically.

Morgan nodded. "You were there. She wasn't working. She barely ate, her eyes were dead. She wasn't talking. She asked me to take care of something for her. I confronted her and begged to fight her way out of this. But she was so lost— so sad and angry and...beautiful."

"Morgan, I'm going to ask you the same thing I asked Syd. What is this?"

He took another long pull of his beer. "I don't know."

Kent's shoulders dropped. "Like I told Syd, this isn't going to end well. At this point, Den isn't the only one I'm concerned about."

Morgan knew Kent was concerned for him, too. If he was being honest with himself, Kent had a reason to be concerned. The consequences of his actions were liable to put a serious strain on the whole family. Morgan could lose the only biological family he had.

"I want her," Morgan admitted. "I tried not to. I mean, it's Syd. She's been a fixture in our lives for years. There, but forbidden. Nothing I ever expected. After it happened, we agreed it could never happen again. Then it did. And now that I've had her, I'm not sure if I'll be able to let her go." He felt relief at finally telling that to someone other than Syd. But he didn't want to put Kent in the middle.

The silence seemed to drag on for minutes. The only sound in the room was the hum of the refrigerator, signaling the icemaker filling with water.

Finally Kent asked, "What are you going to do? Den

is going to blow up when he finds out. You're going to do irreparable damage to your relationship with him. Is this worth it?"

"Why does it have to be either or?" Morgan finished the rest of his beer and slammed it on the countertop. "Den cheated on her, Kent. And it's not the first time. He didn't treat her right. Why shouldn't I get the chance to treat her better?"

"Because, Roc, Den is your brother and he's still in love with Syd."

"Maybe he should've thought about that before he fucked Laney in their house. As far as I'm concerned, he's always been this way. He does these idiotic things and then expects everything to be forgotten once he apologizes. Den is selfish—always has been. He never deserved her."

"And what?" Kent asked. "You do?"

Morgan drummed his fingers against the countertop. "Probably not, but Den doesn't deserve her either."

"This is not a competition. Syd's a part of our family. Do you really think you're going to be able to live happily ever after with Den's ex-girlfriend? It's not realistic."

Morgan stalked out of the kitchen. Feeling the need for fresh air, he opened the patio door and stepped out onto the deck. He gripped the rail.

"Syd doesn't deserve to be in a relationship with someone in secret," Kent said, stepping beside him and leaning against the rail. "Why would you put yourself through this when you know it's not going to work? It can't last. What happens when she takes him back?"

"Kent, you don't know what you are talking about," Morgan replied. The thought had occurred to him that Syd could take his brother back, especially in the beginning. But things had progressed too far. He couldn't see that happening. "They aren't getting back together. It's not going to happen."

"Because of you?" Kent asked.

"No," Morgan growled, shaking his head. "Because of Den's cheating ass. He cheated on her with the worst possible person. Laney? Come on now. He obviously didn't give a damn about Syd's feelings, so why the hell should I give a damn about his?"

"Well, for one thing, who made you Syd's number one protector? And why does what he did justify *you* sneaking around behind his back with her?"

Touché. "I didn't say it justified anything. I'm just saying...he fucked up."

"Roc, you're in love with her," Kent said, eyeing him.

Morgan glared at him. "What?"

"You're in love with Syd. Admit it."

"Kent, drop it." Morgan warned, rolling his neck in an effort to relieve the tension that had set in. "Are you going to say anything to Den about this?"

"You know I'm not going to say anything," Kent said.

"So this conversation is done, right? I have a barbecue to prepare for." Morgan jerked the tarp covering the grill off. It irked the hell out of him that his brother knew him so well.

Kent dragged a patio chair over near the grill and plopped down in it. "I won't say anything to Den, but you need to take a long hard look at what's really going on here. Look at you. You're so mad at Den because he cheated on Syd that you're conveniently overlooking what you've done. There has got to be a reason you would risk your relationship with him for this. And it's definitely not sex. You can get that from anywhere. Why Syd? Just admit that you're in love with her."

Morgan poked at the grill. Kent was right. The situation was messy and complicated. He knew Kent was coming from a good place. He loved Syd like a sister and wanted all of them to be happy.

"What difference does it make, Kent?" Morgan asked finally. "Is it going to change anything if I tell you I love her? Is it going to make this any less wrong?"

"No," Kent said. "Maybe more understandable."

Morgan dropped his head. He thought about a conversation he'd had with Syd recently. He had told her that it wasn't a love thing. Even then, he'd known he was lying. "You already know the answer to your question. Why do you keep asking?"

"Maybe I want to hear you say it." Kent shrugged when Morgan glared at him. "You're not disloyal. You've never gone after someone else's girl."

"She's not his girl anymore." Morgan slipped on an old pair of work gloves he kept by the grill.

"Keep telling yourself that and you might really believe it one day." Kent swatted at a fly. "I love Syd; you know that. And I was happy when Syd moved out and broke things off. She does deserve better. But better can't be you."

"What the hell do you want me to say?" Morgan dumped a handful of charcoal out into a trash bag. "That I'm in love with Syd? That I can't go ten minutes without thinking about her? Is that what you want me to say? You want me to tell you that I'm glad that Den cheated on her—gave me a shot at her?"

Once he'd emptied the grill, he shook off the gloves. Lowering his voice, he told Kent, "Den fucked her over—after she twisted herself in knots to be with him, gave him chance after chance to get his shit together. Den doesn't deserve her and he lost her. Is that what you want me to say? Don't you think I know I'm an asshole? I know I'm wrong as hell. But I don't care because I love her that much. You keep asking me 'What is this?'" He shrugged. "How the hell would I know? I've never been in this situation before. What I do know is I *know* her. Everything about her is ingrained in my memory."

He tapped his temple with his finger. "From the way she smells—sometimes like grapefruit and vanilla, other times like daisies—to the tiny flecks of color in her eyes. Is that what you're waiting for me to say?"

Kent stared at his brother, obviously surprised at the outburst. Morgan had never been emotional. He rarely ever lost his cool.

"I do love her," Morgan admitted. "And it's driving me a little insane—but it's better than anything I've ever felt before."

"I don't know what to say," Kent said, approaching him. "The thing is...it won't be easy. Syd is wonderful, beautiful, and you could do a lot worse. Under different circumstances, I may even be willing to admit she's perfect for you. But Den loves her, man. And now you do, too. It's a disaster waiting to happen." He patted Morgan on the back. "I'm sorry."

Morgan shrugged. "It is what it is." Focusing his attention back on the grill, Morgan continued cleaning. Kent was closer to him than Den had ever been. They'd been "brothers" since the sandbox at their elementary school. By the time his parents were arrested, he'd already been a fixture at Kent's home and the Smiths loved him like a son. He'd forever be grateful that Kent had begged his parents to take Morgan in when CPS was set to ship him off to Tuscaloosa, Alabama, to live with his grammy.

After a long pause, Kent said, "I wish things didn't have to be this way with you and Syd. I can see how much you love her. Unfortunately, your relationship with Den will never recover if he finds out. But you should know, I'm still your brother and I'm still going to be here. I got your back."

Morgan nodded. "Thanks."

"Just leave me out of it when this shit hits the fan," Kent added with a chuckle.

"You wouldn't stay out of it if I paid you to."

"Whatever. I'm not getting involved in this mess." Kent glanced at his watch. "By the way, I think you hurt her feelings."

"I'll talk to her," Morgan said.

"What's up?" Den asked, stepping out onto the deck. "Why are y'all looking so serious?"

Maybe I should rethink letting them have keys. "We're not," Morgan said, trying to keep his tone even.

"Did you get everything we need?" Kent asked Den.

Den nodded. "Yeah, I also called Syd—like you suggested—and she finally answered. She wasn't going to come, but I managed to convince her to come for you, Kent. She agreed to bring coleslaw. And she's going to let Red know."

Morgan swiped his hands together. "Good." Without speaking further, he left them, went into his bedroom, and closed the door.

CHAPTER EIGHTEEN

The barbecue was already under way when Morgan heard the doorbell. The usual suspects were already at his house that night: Kent, Red, Den, Allina, and some random girl Red brought as a date. When Morgan answered the door, his heart tightened. His gaze swept over her body—her hips, the curve of her ass, and the little peek of her stomach. He wanted her. She was wearing low-rider jeans and a halter top that accentuated her breasts and bare smooth shoulders. She was holding a bowl, more than likely full of coleslaw.

Sydney must have sensed his perusal because a pretty blush worked its way up her neck. "Sorry I'm late," she murmured, pulling her shirt down. She handed him the bowl. "Is the food ready?"

He shook his head. "The food is not even close to being ready." He leaned in closer, catching a whiff of her soft perfume. "Listen, about earlier…"

She held a hand up. "Morgan, you don't have to explain anything to me."

Kent staggered into the living room. "Hey, Sydney!" He pulled her into an embrace, giving her a kiss on the corner of her mouth. That was a "Kent and Syd" thing. Morgan hated it.

"Kent, you all right?" Syd asked, pulling away. "A little tipsy, huh?" She grinned when Kent shot her a humorous look.

"You know I'm feeling good, baby." Kent wrapped his arm around her shoulder. "Come on in here and get something to drink with me." Kent dragged her out of the room, leaving Morgan holding the bowl.

Morgan took the coleslaw to the kitchen. When he stepped into the family room, Syd was sitting next to Allina. He could hear Red's boisterous laughter from outside on the patio.

"I'm so happy you're here, Syd," he heard Allina say. "I thought I was going to be stuck with these fools."

Syd laughed out loud. "You could've talked to Red's date."

Allina scrunched her nose. "I tried, but she's not the most intelligent person. Wish he'd have just brought Calisa."

"Cali has an event tonight," Syd explained. "And he wouldn't have brought her anyway. They're still pretending they're not together."

Kent shoved a drink toward Syd. "Here, take this."

Grabbing the glass, she took a sip and scowled. "Damn, Kent, are you trying to kill me?" Syd asked, holding her chest.

Kent smirked. "Too strong? Let me take that one." He took the glass and downed the contents in one gulp. He pointed at her. "By the way, we do need to talk." Morgan didn't have to guess what he wanted to talk to Syd about.

"Hey, Syd," Den said, stepping in from the patio. "I thought I heard you. How are you?"

She gave Den a polite smile. "Hi. I'm good. How are you?"

"Okay, I guess." He turned to Morgan. "Roc, I need your help with the grill."

Morgan followed Den out to the patio.

* * *

Sydney had enjoyed her night with her friends—good food, laughter, plenty of drinks—just what she needed. And best of all? No drama. Morgan pretty much stayed away from her, but every so often, she could feel him watching her. Den was busy trying to get on her good side again, while Red pretended to be interested in his date. By ten o'clock, Allina was holding Kent up because he'd drunk too much. *Yep, everything is normal.*

Deciding it was time to clean, she scooped up a few dirty dishes and headed to the kitchen. As she loaded the dishwasher, she hoped for more carefree nights like this with her homies. Unfortunately, she had a feeling this would probably be the last time a gathering with all of them would be this peaceful.

She heard footsteps behind her and, without a doubt, knew it was Morgan. "You're almost out of Cascade."

"We need to talk," he said in a husky voice.

"No we don't." She placed the last fork in the tray and closed the dishwasher door. Grabbing a dish towel, she wet it and wiped the countertop. "You don't have to explain yourself. I understand why you told me to leave and why you said what you said. It's okay."

"I still feel bad. I felt like it would've been better for me to talk to Kent in private."

He smelled like a mixture of spice and leather. She took a shaky breath, tossed the dish cloth in the sink, and turned to him. "I told you . . . It's okay."

He stepped closer to her and she retreated until the edge of the countertop dug into her back. "I still want to talk later. Can you stay?"

"I'm not sure it's a good idea," she said, sinking her teeth into her bottom lip.

Morgan reached out and brushed a finger down her bare shoulder. A shiver shot through her at his touch. "Baby," he whispered, leaning closer to her.

Closing her eyes, she willed herself to not fall into anything with him. But her body had reacted to his warm breath against her face, the smell of his cologne. *Too close.* It was dangerous to be so close to him.

He leaned against her, both hands on the counter on either side of her. Dipping his head down, he nuzzled against her neck, then rubbed his nose under her chin. *Is he going to take it further with a house full of people?*

"Stay. Baby, stay with me tonight." He brushed his lips against hers.

She framed his face with her hands. "I want to." Their lips were barely touching and she wanted to kiss him—fully.

"Syd?" Red's voice called out, startling her. She jerked away from Morgan and turned to face the sink.

"In the kitchen!" she shouted, gripping the countertop. Her heart was racing.

When she turned around, Red was standing in the doorway, a frown on his face. "I didn't know you were in here, Roc," he said, his gaze darting from Syd to Morgan.

She gave Morgan a sidelong glance. "He was helping me clean the kitchen," she lied.

"Good." Red's frown disappeared and was replaced by . . . a smirk? No. A smile. "I'm actually glad you're in here, Roc. We're out of beer."

Without a word, Morgan opened the fridge and pulled out another six-pack and handed it to Red. "Here ya go. Last one."

"Thanks, Roc." Red glanced at Syd, then back at Morgan. "You know this isn't enough beer. The night is still young. You mind running to the store and picking up some more, Roc? We're running low on tequila, too."

Morgan nodded. "Okay."

Red smiled slightly. *That's definitely a smirk.* "Take Syd with you."

He knows. Her eyes flashed to Morgan, who didn't seem as surprised as she was.

"Okay?" Red asked, bringing her attention back to him.

Syd nodded, keeping her gaze on Morgan, who was suspiciously avoiding eye contact. "Okay."

Red excused himself from the kitchen, announcing that Morgan and Syd were making a store run.

Morgan motioned with his head toward the garage and she swept her purse off the countertop and headed out. As she stepped into the dark garage, he walked behind her and kissed her shoulder.

She jerked away from him. "Red knows," she said, whirling around to face him. "And you know he knows."

"I know," he murmured against her jawline.

Oh shit. He's so not playing fair. She gripped the back of his head and arched back as he placed a line of kisses down her throat. "When did he find out?"

Stopping abruptly, he opened the passenger door. "Remember the day you busted in his house and kicked him out? He came over to my house." She climbed into the truck while he rushed around and slid into the driver's seat. He kissed her chin and then her full lips.

Will he always make me feel this dizzy? She found it hard to concentrate on the conversation, but got a reprieve when he started the truck, tapped the garage door opener, and zoomed out. "Is that when you told him?"

"I didn't tell him. He figured it out." He squeezed her thigh as he sped down the road.

"God, I can't believe you didn't tell me." Anger would have been the appropriate emotion, but she couldn't manage it when his fingers were blazing a hot trail up her thigh.

"It slipped my mind. If you recall, we were doing other

things that night." Morgan grabbed her hand, brought it up to his mouth, and placed a kiss on her palm.

Devil. She shifted in her seat, crossing her legs, then uncrossing them. She really needed to get ahold of herself. The desire for him seemed to flow through her like a tidal wave whenever they were near each other. "I guess I should talk to him. Maybe he's been waiting for me to say something this whole time." Unable to resist touching him, she swept a finger across his jaw and massaged his neck gently.

"Maybe you should," he said. "You know Kent wants to talk to you, too?"

Sydney nodded. "I know, but I kind of want to avoid that conversation for a while."

The rest of the ride to the store was quiet for the most part. No talking, but plenty of...petting. Of course, once they were in the store, they pretended to be the "good" friends that everyone in town thought they were. When they finally made it back to his house—after a few detours—Syd's shirt was hanging off and her pants were unzipped.

As he pulled into the garage, she struggled to fix her clothes. Her hands were shaking uncontrollably, which made it all the more difficult to untwist her bra and blouse. He was already opening her door when she finally straightened everything. Hopping out of the truck, she tugged on her shirt once more and turned to him. "How do I look?"

He smirked. "Thoroughly satisfied."

"Morgan, stop." She hit him lightly. "Seriously, do I look okay?"

"Of course you do." He leaned down and gave her a sweet kiss on her forehead, then her lips, before opening the door to the house.

"What took you so long?" Den asked, a frown on his face.

CHAPTER NINETEEN

Speechless, Sydney watched Morgan walk past Den to the refrigerator to unload the bags.

Guilty much? She swallowed, pulling at the bottom of her shirt. "We weren't gone that long, Den."

"Can we talk for a minute?" Den asked. "I was waiting for you."

Still unable to look him in the eye, she lowered her head. "What about?"

"Alone?" She peered up at Den then. His attention was on Morgan.

"Okay," she said, sensing a shift in the atmosphere. "We can talk. But I don't want to get into anything serious here. It's supposed to be a party. Morgan, can you...?"

"I'll be in the other room," Morgan grumbled.

Once they were alone, Den approached her. "Syd, I miss you. I'm so sorry about everything that's happened between us. I need you to forgive me."

Syd closed her eyes. "This is not the time to talk about us. But just so you know, I've already forgiven you."

His eyes widened. "If you've forgiven me, why can't we

give this another shot? We can make this work, Sydney. I love you."

She held up her hand when he inched closer to her. "No you don't. You don't love me. If you did, then you wouldn't have cheated on me. The fact that you did tells me a lot about our relationship, though. As much as what happened hurt me, I know it was for the best. " He opened his mouth to speak, but she had to get this out. "Let me finish," she rushed out. "Den, I know you're sorry. I'm sorry, too—for so many things." Needing space, she walked around to the other side of the island. "I wanted things to work out between us so badly that I refused to see what was right in front of me. I should have never accepted your proposal."

"I do love you," he insisted.

"And I love you. But I can't be with you."

He frowned, confusion etched in his face. "Are you serious?"

She gripped the countertop, digging her nails into the granite. "Yes, I am."

"So, you love me, but you can't be with me. When did you come to this conclusion?"

"You fucked another woman in our bed," she said. She'd tried to be rational, calm. But it still stung. "You don't think before you act and I'm tired of being the casualty of your mistakes. I deserve better. You promised me you wouldn't hurt me again."

Being with Den, loving him, was like a battle she couldn't win. The more she fought, the more she hurt. Just when she thought they were moving forward, he'd pull them back. When she tried to walk away, he begged her to stay. And she always let him back in. It was time for one of them to let go.

"I didn't want to hurt you, Syd," he said, his voice thick. "Please don't give up on us."

"Give up?" she asked. *Unbelievable.* After everything

he'd done, he had the nerve to tell her not to give up on them. Anger built up in her like steam in a pressure cooker. "I gave you everything I had!" she shouted, stomping toward him. "Against my better judgment, I forgave you time and time again. I trusted you to keep your promise and you disappointed me every time."

Den turned his back on her and she shoved him. "Don't turn your back on me," she snapped. "Look at me. *You* couldn't keep your dick in your pants. So you're going to listen to me. I can't keep doing this. You've destroyed everything. I love you, yes, but I'm not *in* love with you. And I don't want you anymore." She immediately regretted her words when Den rocked back on his heels. For all her bravado, she still felt responsible for him. "Den, don't make this worse."

Den threw his hands up, then pounded his fist onto the counter. "Worse? I know I fucked up, but I wanted to marry you. I gave you a ring. We planned to spend our lives together. We can fix this."

"You gave me a ring after you cheated on me! It was like you were trying to trap me or something. It was calculated, deceitful. How do you expect me to feel about that?" She bit the inside of her cheek and counted to ten. "This can't be fixed. You didn't just fuck up; you broke my heart."

"I told you I can be better, Syd." He reached out to touch her but she backed away quickly. "With your help I can be the man you love again. I told Laney we're done. I'm even seeing a shrink, like you suggested. I'm making an effort. Don't close the door forever, Syd. I need you."

She heard the creak of a door and glanced up. They had company: Morgan, Red, and Kent were standing in the doorway to the kitchen. *Great, things just got worse.*

Den whirled around to face them. "What the hell are you all doing here? I'm having a conversation with Syd."

"You call this a conversation?" Red asked calmly. "Everyone can hear you."

"It's okay, Red," Syd assured him.

"You heard her," Den snarled, glaring at Red. "She doesn't need you to protect her from me, Red."

Red rolled his eyes. "Whatever, Den. I know Syd doesn't *need* me to protect her from you, but I'm *going* to step in anyway because you've hurt her enough."

Red was baiting Den. Her eyes caught Morgan's and she silently begged him to step in. She could tell Den was about to hit the roof the way his eyes were narrowed on Red. And Red? Backing down wasn't his style.

When Morgan didn't move, she guessed their ESP wasn't as strong as she thought. "Please," she said, squeezing Den's arm. "Let's not do this."

Den yanked his arm out of her hold and pointed at Red. "What are you going to do, Red? Huh? You want to kick my ass?"

Red glowered at Den, his jaw ticking. "You fucked that bitch Laney in the house you shared with my sister," he sneered. "Hell yeah, I want to beat the shit out of you. But since I know she doesn't want that, I'm just going to be happy that Syd is away from you. She moved out; she's happy."

Den snorted. "And you know what's best for her?" His hands clenched, then unclenched. "You've always tried to interfere in our relationship, from the beginning."

Red arched a brow. "Not really. Believe me, I wanted her to leave your ass a long time ago. That's on her. But you're not going to stand here and throw some sort of temper tantrum and browbeat her into taking you back. Leave her alone."

"Red, this isn't helping." Kent stepped between the two men.

Sydney exhaled, glad that someone realized the situation

was a train wreck. Red hadn't been a fan of Den's for quite some time. Things had gotten much worse after Sydney accepted Den's proposal. Red had been adamantly against their marrying. It was almost as if Red blamed Den because she'd agreed to marry him, which was completely irrational. Accepting Den's proposal had been her decision to make. And since Red knew about Morgan, she wanted to make sure that tempers didn't flare so much that something slipped out. That would be a disaster.

"I'm just letting him know," Red replied, his voice flat.

"Stay out of this, Red," she hissed. "Why don't you go back into the game room with your girl?"

Den leaned against the counter and crossed his arms over his chest. "Yes, Red, let us finish our conversation."

Before Red could say another word, Sydney covered his mouth with her hand. "Can you please?" Red pushed her hand from his face and stormed out of the room.

She ran a hand through her hair, trying to calm her frayed nerves. Turning to Den, she said, "Den, I'm sorry if you don't want to hear it. But I'm done. I really wish you well in therapy. You need something that I can't give you. It's probably the reason you slept with Laney again," she repeated, hoping to drive the point home.

Den stepped closer to her. "I didn't like having to schedule an appointment to talk to my girlfriend or have dinner with her. Laney was there. I made a mistake," he said, crowding her space. She backed away. "There's no other reason!" he bellowed, swiping the plates off the island.

Then Morgan was there, between her and Den. "You need to step back."

Den backed away slowly. "I'm sorry, Syd. Please. We've been through so much together. This doesn't have to be the end. We're made for each other. You know me. You understand me."

"I do know you," Syd agreed, keeping her tone even. Maybe if she remained calm, everybody else would, too. Clearing her throat, she said, "But you're not the man for me."

"Don't say that, Syd," he growled, smashing his fist into the wall. *Zero to sixty in less than two seconds.* As if the damage to the wall wasn't enough, he toppled over a plate that was sitting on the edge of the sink. It fell to the ground, shattering into pieces.

Morgan lunged at Den, but Kent pulled him back. "Den, chill out," Kent ordered.

Syd hadn't realized she was crying until she felt a tear streak down her face. Den was wildly angry, but he would never put his hands on her. Unfortunately, throwing glass, breaking furniture, and pounding walls was his way of releasing tension.

When her gaze met Morgan's again, she was hit with an overwhelming urge to go to him and let him hold her, but that was impossible. Fury was bleeding through his body—his fists clenched, his chest heaving.

"I know you're upset, Den," Kent said into the quiet, tense air. "But this is not the place, nor time, to talk about it."

Den tilted his head up toward the ceiling. "Kent, why are you here?" he asked, annoyance dripping from his voice. "Why can't I talk to my fiancée without an audience? And for once, can you please have *my* back? You're always there defending and stepping in—for everyone else."

"What does this have to do with having your back?" Kent hollered. "Here you are—in the middle of *my* birthday party discussing your breakup with Syd—loudly. You already broke Morgan's dishes; you've punched a hole in his wall. Having common courtesy has nothing to do with getting your back."

"Whatever," Den sneered. "You don't understand."

"Shut the hell up!" Morgan yelled, slicing a hand through

the air. "This isn't about you, Den. It's not about having your
back. If you want to talk to Syd, talk to her another time—
somewhere else."

Den walked up on Morgan, not backing down. "Don't
worry, brother. As far as *you* having my back, I didn't hold
my breath waiting for that." A flash of something in Den's
eyes gave her pause. He was angry but it felt like something
else. "I know whose side you're on," Den growled. "You
made that perfectly clear."

"Get out of my fucking face, Den!" Morgan thundered.
"Or I will kick your ass out of *my* house."

"Roc, you think I don't know that you have Sydney's
back—no matter what?" Den continued, his voice a low
rumble. Sydney braced herself. The air had changed again.
Morgan was quiet, calm…So was Den. It was the perfect
storm, before all hell broke loose. "I wonder why." Panic
shot through Sydney's bones at Den's change in demeanor
and she wondered if he suspected something. "You want me
to talk to Syd another day? Why? Did I interrupt *your* time
with the 'perfect' Syd?"

Deciding not to take any more chances, she tugged Morgan away from Den. "Stop, Den!"

"No, you stop!" His voice trembled with fury.

"Go home!" she snapped. Things were liable to escalate
even further if one of them didn't leave.

Den blinked hard, then she saw the tears. *Oh, shit.*
"Fuck you."

She gasped. "What?" Den had a potty mouth, but he'd
never said anything like that to her before. Sure, he was a hot
head, but he was never crass toward her.

"You heard me," Den murmured. "I wanted to spend the
rest of my life with you."

Hearing Den curse at her like that threw her off, made her
want to lash out at him.

"How many times did you call me Laney when we were in bed?" Morgan and Kent whirled around to face her, surprise evident judging by the way their mouths hung open. "How many times, Den?" she asked again, her temper flaring. "So don't stand here and act like you love me and I was the reason you went to Laney." She drew in a slow, steady breath, angry at herself for revealing something she'd told herself they'd gotten past a while ago.

Den sighed. "I love you, Syd. You're my angel. I know you're hurt. And it was my fault; but I love you. And I'm not going to give you up without a fight. I need to get out of here." He stomped out of the room. A few minutes later, the front door slammed. He was gone.

CHAPTER TWENTY

Sydney couldn't sleep. It had been hours since her argument with Den. She was unhinged. The party was ruined and everyone had left Morgan's house saddened by the events of the evening. She'd called both Kent and Morgan to see if they'd heard from Den, but neither had since he stormed out. She couldn't shake the feeling that something was wrong.

The sound of the house phone ringing startled her, and she snatched the phone off its base. "Hello?"

"Sydney?"

"Yes. Hi, Mama."

"It's Den," The older woman's voice was shaky.

Syd's heart sank and she braced herself for the news. "What is it?"

"There's been an accident."

Jumping out of bed, Syd ran into the bathroom. "What kind of accident? What happened?"

"I don't know." The woman Syd considered a second mother sounded tired. "The police think he fell asleep at the wheel or something. He ran into a pole."

"Is he—?" she gasped.

"No. We're at University Hospital."

Slowly, the breath she'd been holding seeped out. "Okay, Mama."

"Can you please come? He's unconscious. I think if you were here..."

"I'll be there right away."

When Sydney ended the call, she held the phone against her chest. She tried not to think the worst, but... *What if he never wakes up?*

* * *

Sydney's heels clicked against the white floors of the hospital. She couldn't let her mind wander to what she would find when she got to Den's room. The only thing she could think about was why—and how. How had it come to this?

Other hospital personnel scurried past her as she raced through the maze of hallways at the University of Michigan Medical Center. She walked past a nurse's station and absently touched the paper tag stuck to her jacket. The hospital insisted every visitor wear a blue visitor I.D., using driver's license photos to identify each guest.

It didn't take long for her to reach Room 614. The door was closed. She hesitated, then pushed it open.

The room was dim and quiet. The only sounds were of the many machines beeping and buzzing. Den was lying on a small bed, his eyes closed. She knew he was unconscious, but he looked like he was just taking a rest. He worked hard and would often come home and lie on the bed with his eyes closed—relaxing. She wished that was the case this time.

She inched closer to the bed and placed her hand on his arm. She listened to the blood pressure cuff inflate on his other arm and closed her eyes. "Den, I'm so sorry." She smoothed the hair on his arms. "I'm sorry you're here. I wish we could go back and do things over, Den. How did we get here?"

She watched the rise and fall of his chest as he struggled to breathe. "Den, wake up." She dashed a tear away from her cheek. "Your family needs you." She paused. "I need you to survive. Please... wake up."

Sucking in a deep breath, she noticed a chair in the corner. She walked over to it, set her purse down on a small table, and plopped down into the seat. There was nothing she could do now. She would wait.

"You're here?" Mama said, stepping into the room a few minutes later.

Sydney dashed a tear from her cheek. "Yes. I just got here." Mama had been out of town for a couple of months, visiting family. "When did you get back?" She embraced the older woman, who was the mother she wished she'd had growing up—loving, accepting, and giving. Nothing like her own mother.

"Tonight."

Mama Smith was a tall, thin woman. Although she was in her early sixties, she had aged very well. She kept herself dolled up at all times—makeup flawless, clothes fitted. You'd never catch her without her lipstick. But today she looked pale. Her hair was pulled back into a haggard bun, and she wore loose-fitting sweats.

Syd remembered meeting her for the first time, the night of the rape. Den had called her and she'd dropped everything to come to the hospital. When the nurses prodded and poked her, Mama Smith took it upon herself to supervise. She held her hand and prayed with her, told her she'd get through it. Then she'd insisted Syd call her "Mama." From that moment on, Syd was part of the family.

Mama had always wanted a little girl, but it wasn't in the cards for her. After Kent was born, she'd gotten very sick and the doctors ended up having to take her uterus, preventing her from having more children. Even before Syd had started dating Den, Mama used to tell her that God blessed her with a daughter that cold night.

Mama dashed the tears from her face. "The doctors are optimistic, but he was hurt pretty badly."

"Was he drinking?" Sydney whispered, praying that their altercation hadn't driven Den to the bar.

She shrugged. "They don't know what happened. But according to the preliminary tests, he didn't have any alcohol in his system. Like I told you on the phone, they think he fell asleep behind the wheel." She walked over to the bed and gently pulled Den's blanket over his chest. "Kent and Morgan left to get me something to eat."

Sydney nodded, relieved that Den hadn't been drinking.

"Sydney, I've been meaning to come and check on you," Mama Smith said.

"I know you've been busy. Besides, Den and I…" She let her voice trail off. Den was lying in a hospital bed, clinging to life. No sense in bringing up their relationship.

Mama squeezed her hand reassuringly. "I love you regardless of whether you're with him or not."

Syd's chin trembled as relief washed over her. She didn't know why she'd thought Mama would act any differently. "I love you," she said, sniffling. "And I appreciate you. I'll always care for Den, but… being with him is not healthy for me."

Mama wrapped her arms around Syd in a tight hug. "I know. It's okay."

Seconds later, Mama let go of Syd and turned to Den, brushing her hand over his. "The doctors are saying that if…" Her voice cracked. "If he wakes up, they'll be able to better assess the damage done, what type of help he'll need."

Sydney felt like time stopped with Mama's admission. Her throat seemed to close up and everything seemed to lose focus. The thought of Den not waking up... "If I can help, I will. No matter what has happened between us, I do love him. I want him to be okay."

As Sydney looked into Mama's worried eyes, she wanted nothing more than to soothe her worries. She could tell Mama was desperate for anything that could possibly help her son. After the sudden death of Papa Smith, Mama had been inconsolable, like her life was over. Eventually, Mama was able to get through it, but it had been a long hard road.

Mama slumped over the bed, sobbing quietly as she prayed over Den. Swallowing, Syd rubbed her back and joined her, praying that God spared his life.

* * *

Hours passed and Den still didn't regain consciousness. Sydney paced the small hospital room like a caged animal. There was no doubt about it—she felt guilty. Den had left the house after an angry confrontation with her, and ended up in the hospital clinging to life. If he died...

She heard the door creak and stopped pacing.

Morgan poked his head into the room and stepped in. "Mama told me you were in here." He closed the door behind him. "How is he?"

Syd looked down at Den. "No change. I just don't understand. What was he doing?"

Morgan hunched his shoulders. "I'm still trying to figure that out myself."

Syd couldn't help but feel responsible. "He could die."

His eyes flashed to hers, hurt reflected in them. Her heart dropped to her chest. Den was Morgan's brother after all, his only blood relative left. This had to be hard on him, too.

He let out a haggard breath. "I feel bad, too. But you can't blame yourself. And he's not dead."

She squeezed her eyes shut and scrubbed her face with her hands. "Well, he's barely alive."

"Stop." He placed his hands on her shoulders. "I know you're scared, and feeling a little guilty but—"

"A little guilty?" she asked. "I'm probably the reason Den ran his car off the road."

"Syd, he was upset, but he wasn't suicidal. He probably just lost control of the car."

"I told Mama I would help any way I can."

He dropped his arms to his sides. "Okay. That's nice of you. What does that mean, exactly?"

She averted her eyes. "Basically, it means that I'm willing to do whatever it takes to help Den recover. Despite everything, Den helped me. I want to help him. I owe him that much."

"Okay, but you still haven't told me what that means. Or why you felt the need to say that to me?"

Honestly, she didn't know why she'd said it. All she knew was, Den was lying in front of her, unconscious. And one of the last things she'd said to him was "get out." Although they'd been through so much, she still couldn't imagine her life without him in it. No one had ever hurt her more than he had, but she still needed him to survive. She needed it like she needed her own breath.

She pointed toward the bed. "Morgan, we can't do this here."

"Do what?" he asked, confusion in his eyes. "I'm just asking you a question."

A loud beep sounded in the room and Syd looked over at the bed. Her gaze darted to Morgan, then back to Den. She approached the bed with Morgan by her side. "Do you think we should call the nurse?" she asked.

He squinted up at the monitor. "Maybe I should just go get someone. It looks like his blood pressure is going up."

Nodding, she ran a hand over Den's. Smiling to herself, she remembered the first night they spent together. Afterward, she had watched him sleep. He always looked so peaceful in his sleep—innocent, almost childlike.

"Wake up, Den," she said.

The machine beeped again. It looked like his pulse was going up. She looked back at the door, wondering what was taking Morgan so long. When she looked down, there was a frown on Den's face. Seconds later, his eyelids jumped, then his eyes fluttered open.

Her eyes widened when their gazes met. "You're awake?"

He swallowed visibly, wincing.

She squeezed his hand, felt her tears threatening to fall. "We were worried. You gave us all a scare."

"What happened?" He croaked, clearing his throat.

She picked up a cup from the bedside table. "Drink this." She adjusted the bed, raising his head up slightly. She held the cup to his mouth. "It's water."

He sucked the straw, sipping the water. Once he had his fill, he turned his head. She took a step back. "How did I get in the hospital?" he asked.

"You were in a car accident." She set the cup down. "Do you remember anything?"

"I was driving," he explained. "I was angry—at you, Morgan, and Kent. I went to the bar to shoot some pool, but it was too crowded. I remember heading toward the house, but that's it."

A nurse entered the room with Morgan on her heels. "Is everything okay?" the short woman asked. "Oh Mr. Smith, you're awake." She began checking his vital signs.

"Den?" Morgan approached the bed. "I'm glad you're awake, bruh. You scared everybody."

Den nodded. "That's what Syd said. Is Mama here?"

Morgan pulled his phone out of his pocket. "She went

home to change, but she'll come right back once I tell her you're awake." He looked at Syd. "I'm going to step outside the room while the nurse is looking him over to call Mama and Kent."

While the nurse poked and prodded, Syd turned away. Her eyes darted around the room. Every time she turned Den's way, he was looking at her, studying her, his expression blank.

She felt a pain in her stomach. Although she was relieved, the guilt hadn't abated. She'd been carrying on with Morgan behind Den's back for weeks. A sudden urge to bare her soul had her stepping forward, her mouth open and ready to confess everything.

"Mr. Smith, I'm going to page the doctor and let him know that you're awake," the nurse announced. Syd closed her mouth, covering it with her hand. "Are you in any pain?" the nurse asked.

He nodded. "I have a headache."

"Well, I'll see what we can do for that, okay?" the small woman smiled kindly and left the room.

Syd straightened the thin hospital blanket. It wasn't the right time to try to ease her guilt. "I'm going to call Red." She patted his chest. "I'll be right back."

He held her hand against his chest. "Syd?"

"Yes."

"I'm glad you're here," he said. "I hope this means that we can move forward."

Leaning down, she kissed him on the cheek. "Get some rest. I'm so glad you're up."

CHAPTER TWENTY-ONE

Sydney dashed down the hall toward Den's room. Mama had sent her a text telling her to come when she got home from work. It had been a week since Den was admitted, but he'd made a remarkable recovery.

She was sure he'd be released any day, but she wasn't so sure he was ready. She'd gone to his house to get some things for Mama a few days earlier, and what met her when she walked in nearly made her sick to her stomach. The house was a mess: shards of glass and empty beer bottles everywhere, dirty clothes strewn around. Briefly she questioned whether he was actually taking his medication like he'd claimed. When Den was in a depressed state, his urge to destroy everything reared its ugly head, and drinking exacerbated that urge. Luckily, the doctors hadn't found any substance other than traces of Lithium in his bloodwork the night of the accident. So she guessed he had been telling the truth when he said he was taking his medication. It still didn't explain why he was living in such filth.

Pushing the hospital room door open, she peeked in. Den's doctor was there along with Mama and Kent.

"Syd." Mama waved, a smile on her face. "Come in."

Clutching her purse, Syd entered the room. Her eyes darted to Kent before she asked Mama, "Is everything okay?"

The doctor slid over, giving her a glimpse of Den. He certainly looked healthy. He was sitting up, sipping on a small drink box of apple juice.

"Hey, Syd." Den gave her a half-smile. "Good news. The doctor told me I could go home tomorrow."

"That's good, Den."

"He certainly has made a quick turnaround," Mama added. "The thing is, we're a little concerned about him being by himself. That's where you come in."

Syd's gaze locked on Mama Smith. "What do you mean?"

"Well, as you know, he broke a few ribs upon impact," the doctor said. "And with the injury to his leg, he's going to need some help."

"I told him he didn't have to worry," Mama said. "That we'd all be there for him."

Sydney eyed Kent, who was standing in the corner, arms crossed in front of his chest. "What are you asking me, Mama?"

"Syd," Den said, his voice hoarse. "I know it's a lot to ask. We're not together and you've made it clear that you're done...Never mind. It's too much to ask. And—"

"No, no," Syd jumped in. "What is it, Den?"

"It's just that the cost for a stay in a rehab facility and subsequent physical therapy—even with my insurance—is a lot. It would really help if you would stay at the house for a week or two."

"He can't be alone and the boys have some things coming up, as do I," Mama said. "I got a call this morning from my sister. She has to have surgery and she needs me to come and help her out." Mama scratched the back of her neck. "It would only be a little while. Kent has already agreed to assist. I haven't spoken with Morgan yet but I'm sure he'd help."

Mama went on to explain the plan in further detail. They'd all take turns staying with Den overnight. A nurse aid would come to the house for a few hours a day as well.

After a while, Mama's words started to run together. All Sydney could think was, *Morgan is going to have a fit.* Even so, she found herself nodding. "Sure. It won't be a problem. I'm happy to help."

* * *

Morgan opened his front door after hearing the doorbell ring. He smiled at Syd. "I was wondering when you would get here." He pulled her into the house and into an intense kiss. He took her purse and dropped it on a chair. When she pulled back, he groaned.

"Morgan, can I get in the house first?"

He placed a line of kisses from her ear to her chin. "I put a couple of steaks on the grill. You hungry?"

She shook her head. "Not really. I was hoping we could talk."

Uh-oh. That's never a good thing. "You know how we are when it comes to talk," he joked. When she frowned, he groaned. "What's going on, Syd?" He followed her into the kitchen.

She grabbed a bottle of water from the fridge. "Den's getting released from the hospital tomorrow morning."

He leaned against the counter. "I heard. Just got off the phone with Kent. That's good."

"Yeah, it is." She took a swig. "Did Kent tell you about Mama's idea?"

Kent had mentioned to him that Mama was supposed to give him a call, but he hadn't heard from her. He wondered why Kent hadn't told him about an "idea" when he talked to him.

"She wants me to help out, too," Syd added.

"Okay," he said slowly, an uncomfortable feeling settling in his gut. "What's the plan?"

"That we take shifts spending the night with Den while she's in Phoenix."

In an effort to control his temper, Morgan stepped out onto the patio and headed for the grill. Lifting the top, he stabbed the thick pieces of beef with the fork.

"Morgan." She touched his shoulder. "Are you going to talk to me?"

"I think it's better if I keep my thoughts to myself."

"Why?" She walked around to stand in front of him, tilting her head as she peered up at him.

"What did you tell her?" he asked.

He was met by her silence.

"I guess that answers my question."

"It's temporary," she argued. "I told you before, I feel like I owe him. You have to understand that."

Closing the grill, he asked, "Temporary or not, do you really think it's a good idea?"

"I think it's necessary," she replied.

"I can understand helping out, but I just don't think it's a good idea to spend nights over there."

"You're worried I'm going to want to get back together with him, aren't you?" she asked. "You don't trust me."

"Wrong." Morgan had no problem with Syd helping Den out, but he felt there needed to be boundaries set, some distance. Syd staying with Den would only enflame the situation and possibly give his brother false hope. "Of course I trust you. I just don't think it's a good idea. Can't you just go over during the day, take him meals, or clean the house?"

"I think you're making this bigger than it is."

"Well, tell me what you're thinking, then, because I don't get it. Syd, we're sleeping together. At some point, we're going to have to make a decision about what the hell we're doing. Do you plan on sleeping with me while you're 'staying' with Den? That's not going to happen. It's unrealistic. A bad idea on every level."

"The entire situation is unrealistic," she argued. "I still don't see what the difference is if I go over during the day as opposed to sleeping there and leaving in the morning."

"How about perception? What happens when Den thinks you're going to get back together?"

One of the cutest things about Syd was her naïveté about men and sex. It made him want to teach her a lesson, show her how things worked, using a hands-on technique. But it was also one of the most frustrating things about her, because she tended to gloss over important things. For instance, men didn't have women at their house after eleven o'clock, by themselves, if they didn't plan on making a move. Period. Den repeatedly made it very clear that he loved Syd and wouldn't give up on her. Putting them in close proximity at night was asking for trouble.

"I don't like it," he said.

He heard a tap on the glass and turned toward the patio door.

Kent stepped outside. "What's up, Roc? Syd?"

"Hi, Kent." Syd looked down, her curls falling over her face like a curtain. "I was telling Morgan about the living situation with Den."

"Yeah, it's something, huh?" The sarcastic tone in Kent's voice was unmistakable.

Morgan snickered. "Some bullshit," he murmured.

"Thanks, Morgan." Syd crossed her arms over her breasts.

"Well, you have to admit it's awkward considering... everything," Kent added. "Hate to burst your bubble, Syd, but this is definitely not a good idea."

"It's temporary, Kent!" Syd exclaimed, plopping down on a patio chair.

Morgan closed the top of the grill and turned around. "Seriously? Syd, you're not that naïve."

Syd glanced at Kent. "Kent, you understand that I feel like I have to do whatever I can to help Den, especially after everything we've been through?"

Kent bowed his head. "I do understand and I hate that this has happened. But I'm with Roc. There has to be another way to ease your guilt."

"But—"

Kent held up his hand. "Wait, let me finish. I know you care about him, but this isn't right."

Sydney sighed deeply. "Fine. You don't agree. I get it. But I already promised your mother. So...I'm going to do it." She peered up at Morgan. "Morgan, I hope you can give me some time to make this right."

"Do whatever, Syd." Morgan said. "You're going to anyway. I don't like it, but I'm not going to force you. And you don't owe me anything. We didn't make any promises. You're free to do what you want to do."

Syd flinched as if he'd lifted his hand to slap her. Her mouth opened, but no words came out. She stared at him a long time, pain in her eyes. Then she broke eye contact. He'd hurt her.

"I'm sorry," he said softly. "I didn't mean to hurt you. I understand that you feel like you're doing what's best. Trust me, I appreciate that you want to help out. I want my brother to make a full recovery. At the same time, you're not just anybody. The situation is destined to blow up."

"Okay," she said, her voice thick with emotion. "But you'll see. It's going to be okay, Morgan."

"Whatever you say," he said.

Stepping on the tips of her toes, she pressed her lips to his. He froze, surprised that she kissed him in front of Kent. She nipped at his lip, eliciting a low groan from him before he kissed her back. She wrapped her arms around his neck. "I have to go. I told Den I'd bring him a frosty." She eyed Kent, then Morgan. "I'll call you later?" She gave him another quick kiss.

He licked his lips. Nodding, he said, "Later." She slipped into the house, leaving him with a grinning Kent. "Don't say anything," he grumbled before turning back to the grill.

CHAPTER TWENTY-TWO

*S*yd stared out at the city from her balcony. It was a cool June night; perfect weather, in her mind. Too bad her life was a crazy, hot-ass mess. As the soft breeze whipped across her face, she closed her eyes. *What the hell am I supposed to do now?*

It had been a week since Den was released from the hospital, and Syd had been staying with him. Morgan and Kent had been right. While the idea had seemed good at the time, it simply wasn't helping the situation. It was uncomfortable, awkward. But she tried to keep everything in perspective. She was there for a reason and that was to help Den.

She hadn't seen Morgan in a couple of days because he was out of town on business. He hadn't called either. She wanted to call him, but didn't. *Maybe he needed the time to himself?*

Sydney sat on her balcony with a bottle of Moscato, immersed in her thoughts. She'd only been with Den one night before he'd started talking about getting back together again. It could never happen, but how would she tell him again? The last time she had, he drove off the road and almost killed himself.

She thought about the night of the accident. She had been so angry—at Den, but mostly at herself—for letting the argument get that far in the first place.

"Syd?" Calisa called out from inside the house.

"Out here," Syd yelled. She'd called Cali over for a "wine" down girlfriends evening.

Calisa stepped out onto the balcony. "I see you started without me, honey." She plopped down into the seat next to her.

Syd glanced at her friend. "It's that kind of day, babe. You sounded crazy on the phone, too. What's going on?" She watched Calisa fill her empty wineglass.

Calisa smiled at her. "One guess. Your brother gets on my last nerve. Every single time I tell him that I'm tired of this thing we have going on, he throws it in my face that I started it. Well, maybe I want to finish it. I'm just tired of the booty calls."

"What are you talking about? Are you saying you want a relationship with Red?"

She shrugged. "No, I'm not saying that. I'm not even sure I want to be with him at all. It's getting old. Then, he's been on this mission to find his daughter, which is great. I hope he does find her, but that's a lot to deal with."

Syd nodded. Red had recently found out he was a father—to a six-year-old little girl. But instead of letting him get to know his child, the mother had left town and seemingly vanished off the face of the Earth. The search had begun to consume her brother's days and she knew he wouldn't give up until he found her.

"So tell me," Calisa said. "What's going on with you and Morgan? Last I knew you were happily getting your groove on. And now you're staying with Den again? Red is pissed."

"Yeah, well, he can join the club. Trust me, I heard it from everyone. It's only a few weeks—gosh. They're acting like I sold my condo and moved back in with him."

Calisa smacked Syd on the leg. "That's for having such an eventful life while I'm wallowing in uncertainty. I told Red we had to take a break. No sex for a while, so no action for me right now."

Syd laughed. "I'm sorry. But in my defense, you don't want this eventful life."

Calisa stood up with her arms open. "Hot sex with a fine-ass man who adores you? That's a good life. Come here, heffa. We both need hugs."

Syd jumped to her feet and hugged her friend. Before she could stop them, the tears came and Calisa let her cry in her arms. That's why they'd hit it off in college. Calisa never judged her and vice versa. She wouldn't trade their friendship for anything.

Once Syd calmed down, they both took their seats again and sipped on their wine silently. A few moments later their calm, peaceful moment was interrupted by the buzzing of her cell phone.

Calisa refilled her glass. "Are you going to answer it?"

Shaking her head, she said, "I don't really feel like being bothered right now."

"Who is it?" Cali asked.

Sydney paused. "Den. He's been calling me all day." Den had pitched a fit when she told him she had arranged for Kent to stay with him, so that she could go home to her place for the night.

"You're going to have to deal with this, Syd. You can't keep doing this to yourself. You've done everything you can for Den."

"I can't deal with it. Not right now. He's not stable enough. He's still jumpy and his moods are everywhere. I'm just concerned that he will let himself go." Sydney looked down at her phone when it began ringing again. Frowning at Den's name flashing on the caller ID, she pushed the ignore button.

Calisa watched her. "Have you heard from Morgan?"

"I haven't heard from him. He's out of town for work." Morgan's outburst, his assertion that she didn't owe him anything, had hurt her. They hadn't defined who they were to each other, but she felt like she owed him everything. That's why she'd kissed him in front of Kent. Yet, even though he'd kissed her back, apologized for hurting her feelings, she felt like things were different between them. "His firm is trying to establish a satellite office in Maryland. Kent has been helping me with the remaining staff interviews and training in his absence."

"Why haven't you called him?"

Syd shrugged. "I don't know. What am I supposed to say? I fucked up? Besides, I need to focus on the opening. It's in three weeks."

"How about you call him and tell him the truth?" Cali suggested. "Tell him that you fucked up. Don't push him away, honey. You have a real chance at happiness here."

"How can I be happy breaking up a family?" Syd asked, rubbing her eyes. "And what about Den? What would he do if he found out about Morgan?"

"I could give less than a damn about what Den would do," Calisa said. "I'm sorry, Syd, but what are you going to do? Be miserable for the rest of your life because of someone else? Den is a grown-ass man. You can't protect him forever."

Sydney gulped down the rest of her wine and set the glass on the table. "Cali, I'm sleeping with his brother. That makes me a straight-up 'ho."

Her friend gasped, before she busted out laughing. "Syd, you're not a 'ho. Stop saying that. Okay, so maybe you made a little 'ho-*ish* move. That doesn't mean you intentionally set out to hurt him."

"I love you for having my back," Sydney said, grinning at her friend. "But you know there's no excuse. I can't justify getting between two brothers. I feel sick to my stomach just thinking about the fallout from this."

"Morgan doesn't seem to care, though. Kent doesn't care, and he knows about you two. Red... You know he's all about your happiness. Everyone that you really care about is aware of the situation and has not banished you to the dark side. So why not be with the man you're obviously in love with?"

Syd pointed a wobbly finger at her friend, feeling the effects of the wine already. "See, there you go. Who said I was in love with Morgan?" Calisa shot her a *bitch, please* look. Syd laughed. "Okay, so I'm in love with him. However, it doesn't change anything."

"I don't agree," Cali said, shaking her head. "It changes everything."

"How so? We're not in a relationship. We're basically sex buddies." She gasped. "Wait, we're you and Red."

"Ha Ha," Cali said, tossing a throw pillow her way.

Ducking, Syd chuckled. "Sorry. That was a low blow, huh?"

"Real low," Cali grumbled, rolling her eyes. "Anyway, that man loves you. You have to know that. Listen, you've always done what everyone else thought you should do. Do what you want to do for a change."

Syd pondered Calisa's words. All her life, she'd made decisions based on what everyone else thought was best. Could she change that now after so many years? She knew she was in love with Morgan. Just the thought of him was doing things to her body that she definitely couldn't say out loud. Was she willing to take the risk and be with him? That was a question she was not prepared to answer.

Her phone vibrated on the tabletop. She stood up from her seat and walked inside, leaving it on the surface.

Calisa was on her tail as she headed to the refrigerator. "Where are you going?"

Pulling the fridge open, she pulled out another bottle of

Moscato and handed it to her bestie. "I'm doing what I want to do—like you said."

"I hope this means you're going to call Morgan?" Calisa asked, tapping her fingers on the countertop.

Syd opened the freezer. "No, I'm getting some ice cream." She set the huge tub of Oreo Cookies 'n Cream on the counter. "This is what I want."

Calisa rolled her eyes. "Whatever, Syd. Pass me a spoon."

* * *

Morgan walked into the Ice Box and flicked on the lights. He smiled at the progress made while he was gone. His plane had landed an hour earlier and, as tired as he was, he had wanted to see how everything looked. He scanned the newly decorated space. The tables were set up, and the furniture in place. The only things left to do were finishing touches and they'd be good to go.

Work had been kicking his ass, and he wanted to relax with a beer and a game of pool. Kent should arrive any minute. He'd called him as soon as he'd exited Detroit Metro Airport. He pulled the tarp off one of the pool tables. They were going to break it in tonight.

Sydney was constantly on his mind while he was gone, but he'd chosen not to call her. He was getting a little wary of the whole situation. He really needed to unwind. Hooking two fingers in the knot of his tie, he shifted it back and forth and loosened it. He heard the latch on the door click open. He rolled his neck to relieve some of the tension that had set in and racked the balls.

Kent strolled in and dropped his briefcase on a chair. "What's up, Roc?"

Morgan picked up a stick and chalked the tip. "Shit. Tired from the flight, but ready to get this game in."

"You okay?" Kent asked him.

"I'm good." Anxious to focus on anything but his feelings for Syd and the entire situation with Den, Morgan said, "Go ahead and break."

Kent aimed his stick and took a shot, scattering balls around the table and landing the three in a pocket. "Solid. What's up?"

Morgan watched as Kent sunk another ball in the corner pocket. "Nothing much. I was offered a new opportunity with the firm. Partner."

Kent paused before he took his shot. He straightened to his full height, leaning on the stick with a grin. "That's good news."

Morgan went over to the bar and found a bottle of Rémy Martin and some glasses, came back, and set the bottle on a high-top table next to them, and poured for them both. "There's one problem." He downed the contents of his glass with one gulp.

"What's that?" Kent asked, eyeing the table. He tapped the corner pocket with his stick.

"I'd have to move to Baltimore."

Kent peered at him as he lined up his shot. "Wow. That's...far."

"Not that far," Morgan said. "A lot of money, though."

"Shit," Kent groaned when he missed his shot. "Well, is the money worth the move—especially since we're opening up in a few weeks?"

"It may be worth it to get away from here." Over the past week, Morgan had thought a lot about his choices, starting with sleeping with Syd in the first place, and falling in love with her. Being away from her had helped him get some perspective. When his bosses had offered him the promotion, it seemed like a solution. Maybe not a perfect one, but a good one.

"Have you talked to Syd?" Kent asked.

Morgan rolled his eyes, and leaned down to take his shot. "No."

"I have."

That got Morgan's attention. He looked at his brother expectantly. When Kent didn't say anything, Morgan set his stick on the table. "Well?"

"We went to dinner the other day," Kent explained. "She mentioned that you hadn't called her. I told her that she should talk to you and deal with this—sooner rather than later."

"That's it?" Morgan had hoped that Kent would be able to enlighten him, tell him something he didn't already know.

Kent shrugged. "That's all I'm willing to say to you."

Immediately irritated with Kent for starting a conversation he knew he wouldn't finish, Morgan jerked the stick up and played his turn. "How is she?" *I'm such a sap*.

"She's good. We've hired all the staff and scheduled a meeting for tomorrow night at five o'clock. Is that going to work for you?"

Morgan nodded. "I'll be there. Don't tell her I'm back yet, though."

"That's real mature, Roc."

"Whatever. I'm irritated." Morgan leaned against a bar stool.

"Are you going to tell her about the promotion?"

"Hell, no. Why should I? I'm not even sure if I'm going to take the job. And I'm definitely not sure what Syd and I are doing. She's too busy trying to protect Den's feelings. I mean, I am, too, but at some point we have to make a decision." He paced back and forth, massaging his temples. "She pissed me off agreeing to stay with Den, even for a short time. I mean, what the fuck?"

"Is that why you haven't called her?" Kent asked.

"Part of it," Morgan admitted. It certainly hadn't helped

that she was first on the stay-with-Den schedule. "It's not like things are like they were even a month ago. There are so many unanswered questions. The big one is what *are* we doing? It's not like she can sneak me into Den's house for a quickie. So I figured it would be best if I just kept my distance while she's there." Sighing, he pinched the bridge of his nose. "I keep trying to tell myself not to push her, but shit. I'm risking a hell of a lot by being with her in the first place. And I'm not just talking about Den and the family." He took another swig of his drink. "I'm starting to feel like I'm the sorry, whipped, mushy guy for expecting more from her."

Kent grimaced. "I'd never consider you mushy."

"I know how I feel about her," he said. "You know how I feel about her. Hell, everybody knows how I feel about her except her and Den. Then, there's this pull she has to him. I'd be lying if I said it didn't bother me that she feels like she owes him so much. She says that she won't go back to Den, but I don't know if I can trust that. They have a history. He's comfortable to her, and I'm not."

Kent sat down on the edge of the pool table. "Have you considered telling Sydney what you told me? From what I gather, she still thinks you two are just kicking it."

Morgan looked at Kent. "When did you give up your 'you and Syd are so wrong' spiel?"

"Whatever," Kent said with a smirk. "You know that was a one-time deal. Besides, I don't actually think you're *that* wrong."

Frowning, Morgan finished his drink and slammed it down on the wood table. "Really? That's not what you said before."

Kent shrugged. "Well, I also told you that I would support you—no matter what. After listening to Syd yell at Den and go over all the reasons they're done, what's left to say?

I guess I understand a whole lot better. Sometimes people make errors in judgment—mistakes. Syd and Den don't work anymore. I think she'll always love him—in that pure and innocent, first love kind of way. But they're not the same people they were when they got together. That relationship couldn't survive with all the hurt between them. And why should the both of you suffer forever because of it?"

Morgan snorted. "Well, it looks like I'm the only one suffering. I'm in the worst position. Now I'm in love with the girl and have no idea what she's thinking."

"Trust me; you're not the only one suffering." Kent poured himself another drink. "She blames herself, you know. Don't you think she loves you?"

"I don't know. If she does, I might be waiting forever before she finally told me." Morgan thought he knew how she felt. He swore he could see it in her eyes, but he needed to hear it from her. "I need to know that I'm putting myself on the line for something. I can't be the only one showing my ass all the time. There's a good chance Den will never trust me again even without knowing about me and Syd. You heard him; he knows that I don't have his back when it comes to her. How fucked up is that?"

Kent scratched his jaw. "Well, the whole situation is fucked up. Speaking as your other brother—as much as it will hurt Den in the end—don't let Syd get away. Tell her how you feel. And then see what happens."

Morgan stood there in thought for a minute while Kent lined up his next shot. The sound of the door opening drew him out of his thoughts. Kent looked up as Morgan turned around. Syd was standing there with Calisa by her side.

CHAPTER TWENTY-THREE

*S*ydney hadn't expected Morgan to be there. Her plan had been to show Calisa the progress they'd made and go over some last-minute details for the opening.

Gripping her purse tightly, she approached them. She wondered what Morgan was thinking staring at her so intently. He set his pool stick on the table and crossed his arms over his chest. *Oh, God, I've missed him.*

"Hey," she croaked. She cleared her throat. "I saw your car out front. I didn't think anyone would be here. When did you get back in town?"

She shifted when he stared at her silently.

"When did you get back?" she repeated.

"Tonight," he said finally. "My plane landed an hour ago."

"Oh," she said, trying not to show her disappointment in not hearing from him. "How was your trip?"

"Enlightening," he said simply, pouring more cognac into his glass.

"Uh…" Kent said. He pointed toward the far side of the room. "Calisa, let me show you what we've done with the… kitchen."

"Oh," Calisa said, nodding quickly. "Yes. I've been wanting to see some good kitchens."

Sydney watched the other two scurry off to the kitchen. She turned to Morgan. "Enlightening? How so?"

"I had plenty of time to think about things...mostly about us."

She ran her thumb over the edge of the pool table. "Really? What about us?"

"That's the question—what about *us*?"

Suddenly, she felt nervous. "What do you mean?" She could tell he wasn't too happy with her. But she still couldn't keep her eyes off him.

He inched closer to her and she dug her nails into the wood of the table. "I mean, *what about us*? What is this?" He motioned back and forth between them. "We've yet to define it, and from where I'm standing, we don't seem to be an 'us.'"

"Oh." She couldn't blame him. They had been talking around the issue ever since they'd slept together the first time. The only thing they agreed on was that they wanted each other.

"While I was away, I thought about the conversation we had about you helping Den out and staying with him. It's not right." He held up his hand when she opened her mouth to speak. "Before you say anything, let me explain. Up until now, I guess it probably seems that I could care less about Den's feelings, considering...well, since we've been sleeping together. But this seems a little over the top for you to do after everything we've gone through in the last few months."

"I told you why I did it, Morgan."

"I know you did. I know that you believe in the reasons you did it. But what am I supposed to do with that? You're so busy trying to protect Den—trying to be there for him. And you want me to understand."

She swallowed as his gaze traveled over her body like a sweet caress. Even when he was obviously irritated with her, he still knew how to make her weak in the knees. She averted her gaze and focused on a small ridge in the pool table, scraping her thumb across it. "I asked you to understand because—"

"I know, Syd. It's temporary," he said, lifting a single eyebrow.

She closed her hands together, squeezing her fingers. "Well, yes. I know it is."

He tilted his head, searching her eyes. "We have so many issues, Syd. A major issue—aside from Den—is that we've never defined what we're doing or what we are to each other. I know you want me." He swept his thumb under her chin. Her eyes closed. It was the first time he'd touched her in a week and she wanted to savor the feeling. "I feel it when we're together, when I'm making love to you. It's all good then. But when the lights come on, I'm left wondering... What am I to you? Maybe we should categorize what *this* is. If we're going to stay friends, fine. If we're going to become more, then we need to talk about how to make it happen, starting with when we're going to tell Den. Either way, I need to know because that would determine my reaction."

"Morgan, you know you're not *just my friend*."

"What am I, then?" he asked.

Her eyes fluttered closed as he rubbed the sensitive skin beneath her ear lobe. "I don't even have a word to describe what you are to me."

She looked at him then. Her breath caught in her throat at the intensity in his eyes. From the moment he'd kissed her, she'd looked at him differently. Even though she'd tried, she couldn't deny the connection between them. She wanted to tell him that she loved him, that being with him made her feel whole. The idea of doing so scared her and made her want to run and hide. Yet, the thought of not being in his presence made her feel sick.

Then there was Den. She loved him, too. Being with Morgan would devastate him. "Um." Her voice cracked, and she coughed. Every word seemed to die on her tongue. The silence grew.

His shoulders slumped and he dropped his hand to his side. She immediately missed the contact. He turned and headed back to a seat on the other side of the pool table, creating an even further distance between them. "I think maybe we should cool it," he said, hunching his shoulders. "It's obvious you're not ready."

"Morgan, I don't want to lose you."

"I don't want to lose you, either. This started as a thing, two friends being there for each other. It's bigger than that now. You have to know that."

"I don't know what you want from me," she said, bowing her head. "I told you, I don't want to lose you."

"Tell me that *this* is worth it," he said.

"Stop," Sydney said, frowning.

"Why? We have to be realistic. I'm risking a hell of a lot by being with you. Den is my brother."

She couldn't forget that if she tried. "What do you want from me?" she asked. "You just said everything that I've been thinking since we've started this. Den *is* your brother. The only family you have left. Nothing about this is simple."

"Then why continue this? Why are were still doing this?" He lowered his chin to his chest. "Every time we're together, I'm risking that relationship and every other relationship in my family. I'm creating a situation that would put my family in the middle. You asked me what I want from *you*? I already told you: I want you to tell me how you feel and what you want from me." He stood up and leaned against the pool table, his hand flat on the felt surface. "I love you."

She peered at him, her lips parted. Her heart hammered in her chest.

"Syd, I love you. And because I love you, I accept you—even the parts that infuriate me. If you can't do this, you need to say it. I'll be hurt, but I'll move on. I know you're scared. But I can't keep doing this with you, Syd. We're going around in circles. We either stop or we don't. If we don't, then you have to be with me." He pointed at his chest. "Be willing to fight for *us*."

"Morgan, I—" She held a hand to her chest.

"What is it, Syd? What is *this*?" he pleaded. "What do you expect from me?"

She couldn't take the distance between them anymore, so she walked around the table, stood next to him. "Morgan, I hear you. I don't know what I expect from you or even if I have a right to expect anything at all."

He gazed at her. "What do you want to do?"

She squeezed his arm and leaned her head against his shoulder. "When you were gone, I did a lot of thinking, too. The biggest problem is we never talk much anymore." She thought of all the forgotten talks they were supposed to have—and what they'd been doing instead. "We probably should've been doing that all along."

"I guess you're right."

"Your feelings do matter to me," she said. "We've been through a lot over the years. The truth is, after Kent's birthday at your house—and the confrontation with Den—I almost choked on my guilt."

She finally let go of his arm and perched herself on the edge of the pool table. Still needing the contact, she took his hand in hers.

"I spent years with him," she said, taking a deep breath. "Our relationship was intense. He protected me so fiercely when I needed it the most. I loved him with everything I had.

You know that. I didn't think there would ever be anyone else for me."

Morgan clutched her hand in his.

"When I had to call off the wedding, I tried so hard to get to the point where I wasn't thinking about him all the time—and everything we went through. But then something changed. I'm not sure when it did, but I started thinking that this wasn't the worst thing that could happen to me. Breaking up with Den, after all those years, was the best decision for me. I've always felt like I owed him. He did literally pick me up and put me back together after I was raped."

"He didn't do that, Syd," he told her. "You did. He may have saved you that night, protected you when you needed it, but you're the one who refused to give up. Some women would have dropped out of school after what happened to you. But you got out of the hospital and went to class with cuts and sores on your legs and arms. That was all you."

"Yes, but Den helped. He did. I was damaged goods, with damage so severe that the doctors doubted I could ever get pregnant and have kids of my own."

Syd hadn't wanted much growing up, but she had always wanted to be a mother. She'd been devastated. Den had never left her side, though. The others tried to get through to her, but she'd pushed everyone away at the time. But Den refused to let her push him away. He made her laugh when she wanted to cry. She trusted him. That trust grew into love.

"Knowing I couldn't have kids was one of the reasons I forgave him when he cheated on me with Laney the first time and got her pregnant," she continued. "But that's a whole different story. The point I'm trying to make is, I never thought we wouldn't grow old together. Then I realized that I'm not dead. If anything, I feel more alive now than I have in a long time. And I know that part of that reason is you."

He eyed her. "What are you saying?"

"Morgan, I never want to hurt you. Allowing myself to be with you on this level is big for me. You're so not safe," she confessed. "I knew it from the moment you kissed me. I couldn't stop myself from wanting to explore it. I didn't know much then, but I knew that I wanted you—I needed you. At the same time, I was horrified at what I'd done. Den was the only man I've ever been with. I don't have forbidden affairs. But I couldn't stop thinking about it. It still scares me. I have a tendency to get lost in you."

"Sydney—"

"Wait," she rushed on, needing to get the words out. "If I don't say this now, I'm not sure when I'll get the nerve again. You always make me feel so many things at once, Morgan. And that's what is so overwhelming about you. I've made so many mistakes, and I've never been so wrong in my life. But my feelings are clear." She held his face in her hands. "I love you," she whispered. "You're my best friend. You accept me as I am, even though I get on your nerves."

He laughed softly. "You really do."

She loved to hear him laugh. She giggled. "You know me better than anyone else and you've never tried to change me. I want to do 'us.' I want to be with you. I'm not saying that everything will be perfect, because it's complicated. But just so you know...you're not fighting alone."

"Syd—"

She brushed her lips against his. He pulled her closer and kissed her with an intensity she'd never felt from him before. And she welcomed it. She'd missed him so much while he was gone. She vowed then that she would make this thing right for him.

When she heard the clearing of someone's throat behind her, Morgan pulled away and glanced above her head toward the bar.

She turned slowly. Kent and Calisa were standing there.

Kent grinned. "Mom called. She wants me to fix her computer. I have to go."

"And I'm going to assume we're not planning anything tonight," Calisa added, a knowing smile on her face. "I'm going to catch a ride with him to my car."

Kent grabbed his briefcase. "So, I'll see you both tomorrow at the meeting—five o'clock."

Once they left, Sydney turned to Morgan. "I guess we're busted, huh?"

Morgan smiled. "I guess so."

"You think they heard us?" Syd asked, sinking her teeth into her bottom lip.

"I think it's safe to say they did. But I don't think they heard anything they didn't already know." He wrapped his arms around her waist, pulling her closer to him.

"So what do you think of the bar?" she asked, changing the subject. In all the excitement, she was interested in hearing his thoughts on the decor. "Nice, huh?"

"Real nice, but..." He leaned down and kissed her forehead. "I'm ready to go—to your place."

"You don't want to finish this conversation?" she asked.

"I think we've already talked too much today."

She patted his chest, grabbed their empty glasses, and walked them to the sink behind the bar. "Yeah, you're probably exhausted from the flight. Besides enlightening, how was the trip?" She wiped the bar down with a wet cloth.

"It was work."

She looked at him and frowned. "That's all? You were gone for a week. Did you do anything besides work?"

He shook his head and pulled the tarp over the pool table. "Not really."

She watched him. Something had changed in his demeanor once she'd mentioned his trip. He shifted about, avoiding contact. She wondered what that meant.

"Let's get out of here." He held out her purse.

Maybe I'm imagining things? She decided to drop it for now. Smiling, she nodded. "Okay."

"I need some uninterrupted time with you," he said, giving her a seductive smile.

"I can't wait…"

* * *

Syd woke up the next morning still thinking about Morgan. They had made love practically all night, cementing their love for each other with every caress, every kiss. She hated to leave him, but he had an early meeting and she wanted to get back to Den's. They'd discussed the appropriate time to tell Den about their relationship and had decided to wait until he was healed from his injuries.

She unlocked Den's back door and stepped into the quiet house. She wondered if Den was still asleep. When she entered the kitchen, she stopped in her tracks. He was sitting at the kitchen table, his leg propped up in one of the other chairs.

"Den? What—what are you doing in the kitchen?" she asked.

He looked up from the papers strewn across the table. "Hi! I was trying to do some work. Where have you been?"

She sighed. "I told you, I stayed at home. Calisa dropped by and we had some wine. Then I took her to the bar. We ran into Kent and Morgan."

He nodded, tapped his pen on the table. "I was worried about you. I tried to call you but it went straight to voicemail."

"I'm fine." She'd turned her phone off so she could concentrate on Morgan. "I went back to my house for a bit after I left the bar."

"Mama called. She is coming back early. My aunt decided not the go through with the surgery at this time.

Mama wanted me to invite you over for dinner tomorrow. She's making her famous chicken and dumplings."

"Yum." She pulled out a chair and joined him at the table. "I love her chicken and dumplings." She grabbed a handful of the popcorn Den was snacking on.

"I know," he smiled affectionately. "I actually suggested it. I knew you'd be happy."

She paused. "Yeah. Um, I probably won't be able to make dinner, though. I wanted to get some work done at the Ice Box. There's so much to do before the opening."

"Well, dinner won't last that long," he said, holding eye contact. "It's just—I thought it would be great to get together and celebrate my recovery with everyone I love."

Oh boy. She nibbled on her lip. "Okay, Den. I'll be there." He smiled and opened his mouth to speak, but she held up her hand to stop him. "But... since Mama is coming back, I think it would be best if I go home tomorrow, for good."

The smile that was plastered on his face when she'd agreed to go to the dinner was quickly replaced with a frown. "Really?"

"Yes. The doctor said that you're well on your way to a full recovery. And looking at you now, sitting at the table working, I think he's right. So you won't need me."

"But I thought..."

She placed her hand on top of his and squeezed. "Den, I don't want to make this situation worse. I just think it will confuse things if I continue to stay here." *What a crock of bullshit.* "I mean—I think it's best if I step aside and let your family take care of you. That way everyone won't think that we're... you know... getting back together."

"Would that be so bad?" he asked softly.

She bowed her head. *Shit.* "Not bad." She looked him in his eyes. "Not realistic either. Nothing has changed. Me and you," she said, bracing herself, "we're better off apart."

He slid his hand from beneath hers and cleared his throat.

"Okay," he said, jotting something on a piece of paper. "Look, I need to get this work done. Do you mind dropping some paperwork by my office today?"

Jarred by the change in subject, Sydney was torn on whether to say something else or roll with it. In the end, she chose to roll with it. She stood up. "I'll take whatever you need on over."

She watched as Den continued to work as though she weren't even standing in front of him. Sighing, she turned and headed toward the guest room she'd been staying in.

* * *

The next morning, Sydney rushed into Den's kitchen. She was running late. After the awkward end to her talk with Den the day before, she was uneasy. She'd tossed and turned the entire night. She ran through the conversation in her mind, trying to figure out what she could've said that would have changed the outcome. Either way, he would've been hurt.

She'd already been in Den's room and left his breakfast for him. Instead of greeting her with a warm smile—like he'd done every day since she'd been there—she received a quick nod of his head and dry "thanks."

The doorbell chimed and she hurried to the door. Mama was standing there with two huge paper bags full of groceries. She grabbed the bags from her.

"Phew," the older woman said. "I'm so glad you were still here. I accidentally left my key at home."

"Oh, wow. Well, it's a good thing I was running late this morning. Den is in his room. I already took him breakfast."

Mama nodded. "Good. Did he tell you about dinner tonight?"

"He sure did," Syd said, emptying out the bags. "I told him I'd stop by, but I have a lot of work to do tonight."

"Aw." Mama's shoulders dropped. "I really wanted the

whole family to get together for dinner. I think it'd do us a lot of good."

Sydney opened the cupboards and quickly started putting things away. "I think it's a great idea. But I think it might be better if I stay away."

The click of heels on the floor signaled to her that Mama was coming closer. She didn't want to get into another conversation about this. She closed the cabinet and waited.

"Syd?" Mama said, her voice soft.

Taking a deep breath, she turned around to face the woman who'd been so important to her. As she looked into her eyes, she wondered what she'd do if the concern in her eyes turned to ire.

"Syd?" Mama repeated. "What's wrong? Did something else happen between you and Den?"

No, but something happened between me and your other son.

"Mama, is that you?" Den called from the bedroom.

"I'm here, son," Mama called. "I'll be right in."

Sydney let out a deep breath, grateful for the interruption. "I better go, Mama. I'm late for work."

Mama eyed her. "We should probably finish this conversation later, then."

"Sure," she lied. There was no way she was finishing this one willingly.

As Mama hurried toward the back of the house, Syd noticed a manila envelope on the table. The Post-it Note stuck to the top had Den's distinctive cursive on it. *Syd, please drop this off to accounting. Thanks.*

Syd stuffed the envelope into her briefcase, grabbed a bagel out of the fridge, and hurried out the door. Once she was in the safety of her car, she dropped her head on the steering wheel. *What have I done?*

CHAPTER TWENTY-FOUR

Morgan knocked on the door and waited. He wondered why he'd even agreed to come. It probably wouldn't make things any better. In fact, he was sure things were going to be worse.

When the door swung open, he smiled. "Hi, Mama." He embraced her.

"Son," she said, beaming, "glad you could come. You're early, though. Dinner won't be ready for another half hour or so."

Morgan glanced at his watch. "Really? Den texted me to be here at six-thirty. I thought I was late."

She frowned. "Six-thirty? I told everyone to be here at seven-thirty." She giggled and patted him on his shoulder. "But it's okay. It works out because I haven't seen you in so long and we can catch up—after I finish the salad. Den's in the family room watching TV. Go on in there."

He rolled his eyes when she turned her back. He'd purposefully arrived late so he didn't have to sit and talk with anyone, especially Den. Morgan wasn't a dishonest person by nature, so it was becoming increasingly harder to be around his brother knowing he was keeping something so big from him.

Den was sitting on the couch with his leg propped up on an ottoman when Morgan walked into the room. "What's up, Den?"

Den glanced at him. "Hey man."

Morgan greeted him with a handshake. "You look like you're feeling better."

"I am. I'll be up and at 'em in a few weeks, according to the doctors. I've been making good progress in physical therapy. The doctors are even telling me I can go back to work next week—with crutches, of course."

Morgan nodded. "I know you're ready to get back in the game. That's good to hear."

"Yep." Den pushed a button on the remote, muting the television. "I'm glad you're here. I've been meaning to talk to you."

Morgan's guard went up at the thought of having a "talk" with Den. He briefly wondered what his brother wanted to say—and if he would like it. "What's up?"

"I've had a lot of time to think since I've been laid up," Den said. "I know that things have been strained between us. Part of that was my fault. Well, most of it was. I've been so tense since the breakup with Syd, and I took it out on everybody in the family."

Den shifted in his seat to face him. "You're my brother." He winced and cursed under his breath.

"You okay?" Morgan asked, assuming Den must've twisted his leg the wrong way.

"I'm good," he groaned. "I don't want my relationship with you to suffer because my relationship with Sydney was struggling."

Was?

"I thought it was over," he continued. "It seemed painfully clear that it was at the time."

At the time?

"And I wanted us to talk about it before any hard feelings develop."

Morgan found it very hard to concentrate on "hard feelings" when he was stumped on "was" and "at the time."

When he finally looked at Den, his brother was watching him intently. Morgan cleared his throat. "What are you talking about, Den?"

"Syd was right. There were some things that happened in our relationship that probably shouldn't have happened. And those were things we couldn't deny. I didn't love her like I thought I did."

Morgan was speechless. What was he supposed to say to that? Den was telling the truth, which was more than he could say for himself. For the umpteenth time, Morgan felt compelled to tell him about his relationship with Sydney. At the same time, though, understanding why the breakup happened was a little different from understanding why your brother chose to go after the woman you were supposed to marry. Somehow, Morgan didn't think Den would understand that.

"You're close to Syd," Den said, interrupting Morgan's thoughts. "You talk to her on a regular basis. With the Ice Box opening, you're going to see her more often than not."

"True. What are you getting at?"

Den shrugged. "Nothing. I was making an observation." He shifted in the chair like he was suddenly uncomfortable. "I have a question to ask you."

Morgan had spent too many years living in the same house with Den to not know when he was about to drop a bomb on him.

"Tell me the truth," Den said. "You and Syd—has anything ever happened between you two?"

That is the understatement of the year. "Why would you ask me that?"

"I don't know. You tell me."

Morgan squinted his eyes. "Is there a purpose to this conversation, Den?"

"We're brothers," Den said simply. "Brothers talk."

"Don't try to play me, Den. I know you. Where is all this *talk* leading?"

"Nowhere. I thought about everything that happened the night of the accident. The more I thought about it, the more questions I have. You're pretty invested in my relationship with Syd. That's evident. You were so angry that night at your house. If I'm not mistaken, you were ready to fight me—literally ready to jump on me like I was some stranger on the street and not your brother, Roc."

Morgan shifted, pulled at his collar. It was too late to bolt, so he figured he'd let Den talk.

"Then there is the fact that you've always been a little in love with Syd," Den mumbled under his breath.

Morgan glared at him. He remembered a conversation he'd had with Den years ago about Syd, way before they'd started dating. He'd basically confessed to Den that he had feelings for her, but wouldn't act on them because of Red.

"What do you expect me to say?" Morgan grumbled. Choosing to steer the conversation away from any feelings he had for Syd, he said, "I'm not sure what you're looking for. The fact is you weren't an innocent bystander that night. Your temper was flaring too hot. You chose to start that conversation with Sydney, even after everybody told you it wasn't the right time. You got angry because she told you something you didn't want to hear. Then you flipped out—destroying my shit," he said, his voice raising as he talked. "Yes, I was pissed off and I could've fought you. But it's not like we haven't had physical altercations before. So, I don't understand this line of questioning."

"We may have had physical altercations before, but never over a woman."

"Den, you walked up on Syd like you were going to do something to her," he argued. "Of course I'm not going to let that happen." Morgan was disgusted that he'd turned this around on Den, who ultimately had a reason to be suspicious. Morgan had never even attempted to hide his anger toward Den that night.

"Touché," Den said. "Forget it, Roc. I guess the problem is mine. I wanted to get this straight with you. Syd's been here, and we've had a chance to talk. I think it's important that I tell you my concerns."

Morgan eyed Den suspiciously, replaying his choice of words. "What do we have to get straight, Den? You were angry—at everyone. There was no conspiracy to gang up on you. The fact is Syd isn't with you because you brought Laney into your bed. And, apparently, it wasn't the first time." He thought about Sydney disclosing the fact that Den had called out Laney's name during sex. Morgan knew that was a low blow.

Den tapped the remote on the table lightly, turning the TV off completely. "Obviously, it didn't matter in the end. But if we're going to work this out, I want to know what I'm up against."

Work it out? Morgan rolled his neck and clenched his fists.

"And we are going to work this out," Den added in a firm voice.

Morgan's eyes flashed to Den's. "Work it out?"

"Yes, we talked last night—extensively. We agreed that things got out of hand and we've both realized the mistakes that were made in the relationship. It's only a matter of time before we put this whole thing behind us and make our way back together."

* * *

Morgan stabbed his fork in his chicken. He still couldn't get the conversation he'd had with Den earlier out of his mind. No matter what Den said, he couldn't see Syd agreeing to work on their relationship. It didn't ring true, and he wondered why Den said it in the first place. Obviously, he wanted him to think that they were working it out. But why? Something was off. Before he'd had a chance to demand answers—not that he felt he was owed any—they were interrupted by Kent barging into the room.

He scanned the faces of his family seated around the table as they merrily swapped old stories and reminisced about better times. Syd was pushed into the seat next to Den by Mama, and that irritated him even more. He felt like a powder keg, waiting to explode. Every time he looked up, Den was all over Syd. In fact, it seemed like Den was going out of his way to touch her. And Syd? She was oblivious to it all. She was too busy laughing at Kent's jokes and smiling at Mama to notice all the ways Den seemed to be up on her. Or was she? Had she noticed and didn't care?

Morgan shook his head, willing himself to stop analyzing every single movement she and Den made. Despite what Den had said, he'd just spent the night making love to Syd—all night. She'd told *him* that she loved him. Him. They had agreed to work this out together. They were going to . . .

"Roc?" Kent shouted from across the table.

Morgan cleared his throat and set his fork down. "What?"

"Can you pass me the dumplings?"

Morgan frowned when he realized the whole table was watching him intently. How long had Kent been trying to get his attention? Without a word, he picked up the casserole dish and passed it to Mama, who was sitting on his right. His eyes met Syd's and held for a minute before she averted her gaze.

"Morgan, you must have something on your mind, son."
Mama said, patting his back.

"I'm fine. Thinking about work," he lied. "I actually
forgot I had to go take care of some business at the bar."
Another lie. When he heard Kent snicker, he guessed Kent
knew it, too. At this point, Morgan didn't care. He was ready
to get out of there before he said or did something he'd regret.

He stood up and dropped his napkin on his plate. He'd
barely touched his food.

Mama grabbed his arm. "You're really leaving? I thought
you'd at least want dessert. It's Texas sheet cake."

He squeezed her hand. "I'm good, Mama. I'll take a piece
with me. But I really should go."

She pouted. "Okay," she said, with a hint of sadness in
her voice.

Way to hurt her feelings, jerk. "I'm sorry, Mama. I'll
make it up to you later." He leaned down and hugged her.
After he said his good-byes, he left the family to continue
their dinner and headed toward the bathroom.

Den's bedroom was on the second floor, but he'd been
moved to the ground level until his leg healed. His stuff was
all over the bathroom—so was Syd's. Her night shirt hung
on a hook on the back of the door; her soap and perfume
were set neatly on the vanity. He scowled at the reminders
that they'd been sleeping under the same roof again.

He turned on the faucet and proceeded to wash his hands.
When he was done, he turned the water off and pulled a
piece of paper towel from the roll on the counter. He dried
his hands and tossed it in the trash.

He gripped the edge of the granite counter. He had to
know. When did they have this supposed "talk"? Was it after
she'd left him? This morning? During her lunch?

"This is ridiculous, Morgan," he grumbled under his
breath. She couldn't have been with him. She wasn't a 'ho.

She wouldn't sleep with him and Den in the same day. She'd never do that to him.

Shaking his head, he told his reflection, "Get it together, Roc."

Taking a deep breath, he wondered if he should re-join dinner with some excuse as to why he didn't have to go after all—so he could keep an eye on the situation. *What the hell is wrong with me?* Morgan had never been an insecure man. And he wouldn't start being one today. He jerked the bathroom door open. It was time for him to leave. Maybe in more ways than one.

* * *

Syd stood on the patio, grateful dinner was over. Morgan had bolted out of the house earlier, but she'd noticed the way the brothers interacted during dinner. Den went out of his way to dote on her throughout dinner, hanging on her every word, asking if she'd had enough to eat. At one point, he'd put his arm around her, which made her extremely uncomfortable. She didn't want to say anything in front of everyone, so she ignored it.

She turned when she heard the patio door open. Kent stepped out.

"Syd?" he called softly. He placed a hand on her shoulder. "Everything all right?"

She bowed her head. "You tell me. I've made a mess of everything, Kent. Something's wrong with Morgan. That much was clear throughout the evening."

"What makes you think that what's wrong with Morgan has anything to do with you?" he asked.

She glared at him.

He shrugged. "Okay, maybe a little to do with you." He nudged her playfully. "But not that much."

A tear drizzled down her face. "You were right. I never should've agreed to help out with Den. It would have been better for everyone."

Kent frowned, tilting his head. "I thought you and Morgan had a talk last night. Did something happen?"

She chewed her lip. "I guess I was shocked that he left so abruptly," she said. "I thought we were good after last night, but something is off with him. He barely said two words to me." Or maybe she was reading too much into everything. Morgan could have had a perfectly good reason for his mood.

"You know Roc." Kent assured her. "He has a lot on his mind—the bar opening, his job." He looked away.

She frowned. "What about his job?" she asked.

"Nothing," he said, waving her off. "Maybe the traveling back and forth is getting to him. Then there's that forbidden love affair between you two to contend with."

When she cursed under her breath, he apologized for the failed attempt at humor.

"Look, Syd," he said. "I hate seeing you upset. You're important to me, like the sister I never had."

She turned to him, hugging her body. "I can't figure out how to make this better. I talked to Den yesterday, told him I wasn't going to stay here anymore. He seemed to be under the impression that we were working things out."

"He told you that?" Kent asked, his eyes wide.

She nodded, replaying the conversation in her head.

"Syd, what else did you think was going to happen?" Kent asked.

"I don't know!" she screeched. "I didn't think at all, apparently. Your mom was so sad and worried about Den. I couldn't tell her no."

Syd knew that Mama wouldn't have held it against her, though, if she had. Mainly, it was her own feelings for Den and her guilt.

"I was worried about him, too," she admitted. "Then there was the guilt, simmering, threatening to choke me."

He pulled her into his side, hugging her tight. "The good news is it's not too late to make this right, Syd. You have to suck it up and do what you can to fix it now."

"I feel sick," she murmured, burying her head in his shirt.

"Take some meds."

Chuckling, she stepped away from him and smacked him on his shoulder playfully. "I guess we're done with our little brother/sister moment then."

He barked out a laugh. "I guess—"

"Syd?"

She turned around toward the patio door. Den was standing in the doorway, leaning on a crutch.

"We could use some help in here," Den said.

"What's going on, Den?" Syd hurried to the door.

"Mama was wondering if you could help with the cleanup," Den said, eyeing Kent suspiciously. "She asked me to come and get you."

Syd slid open the heavy glass door and disappeared into the house.

CHAPTER TWENTY-FIVE

Morgan had driven around for about twenty minutes. There was no real business at the bar and he was starting to think he was overreacting to the whole situation. He was halfway home when he decided to turn around and head back to Den's house.

When he entered the kitchen, Mama and Kent were at the table eating cake. Syd was washing the dishes.

"Hey, man," Kent said, greeting him. "What brings you back?"

Morgan shrugged, joining them at the table.

Mama set a saucer in front of him and plopped a big piece of cake on it. It was his favorite. "He decided to come back and see me," Mama said proudly.

"Something tells me he only came back for cake," Kent joked, winking at Mama.

Syd hadn't turned around to look at him yet.

"I'm so happy that all of my sons are here," Mama said, beaming.

"When did you get back, Roc?" Den said, shuffling into the room. Kent pulled out a chair for him, and he slowly took a seat.

"I just got here," Morgan replied, stuffing a huge piece of cake into his mouth.

"I'm just so happy," Mama squeezed Morgan's hand. "Look at us; we've had a rough couple of months. But we have so much to celebrate." She walked around and hugged each of her sons and placed a tender kiss on their foreheads like they were little boys. "My oldest son is safe, alive, and on the road to recovery. All of my sons are successful businessmen. And my daughter," she added, rubbing Syd on her back affectionately. "I couldn't love her more if she was my own. And from the looks of it, we may be planning a wedding soon."

The piece of cake he'd swallowed seemed to lodge in his throat, and Morgan coughed violently.

Mama rushed over to him and peered into his face. "Are you okay, son?" she asked, concern in her voice.

Morgan gulped someone's glass of water down to clear his throat. "I'm good." He glanced at Kent.

"Are you sure?" Mama asked again. "You need to stop eating so fast." She giggled and patted his back softly, then joined a quiet Syd at the sink.

"Mama, who's getting married?" Kent asked, cutting a sidelong glance Den's way. Morgan's gaze swung to Den, who was watching him. *Something is not right.* "You can't mean me?" Kent quipped. "I'm not ready to get murd—I mean, married."

Mama burst out into a fit of laughter. "Kent, of course, I didn't mean you. I know you're not ready. From what Den told me today, I'm talking about him... and Syd."

A crash from the sink drew everyone's attention to Syd. She scrambled to pick up whatever it was that had fallen.

"Oh my God," Mama said, bending down to help Syd. "What is wrong with my children? Morgan's choking, Syd is dropping glasses. What's next?"

"It's okay, Mama," Syd said with a trembling voice while she tossed pieces of glass into the trash can. "It slipped from my hands."

"I'll finish this. Go and sit down for a bit." Mama grabbed the dishrag and nudged Syd toward the table.

Syd shuffled over to the table as if she were walking off a plank. She plopped down on a chair and met Morgan's gaze across the table, horror in her eyes. He glared at Den, who had a smug smirk on his face.

Morgan muttered a curse under his breath. As Mama continued to gush over a possible reunion and wedding, he thought about telling everyone the truth. Right then and there. Then Den placed his arm on the back of Syd's chair like she was his possession. He didn't know which was worse: the fact that he was jealous or the fact that he was pissed. *Oh wait.* Wanting to choke the life out of his brother for daring to hug Syd was definitely the worst.

Mama closed the dishwasher and joined them at the table, pulling a bar stool over. "Why is everyone so quiet?" Her gaze darted back and forth between everyone sitting at the table. She reached out and squeezed Morgan's hand. "I'd think you all would be happy that things are getting back to normal."

"What's normal, Mama?" Morgan grumbled.

"I think it was nice to have dinner with everyone," Kent added quickly. Morgan knew his brother was trying to keep the situation light. Kent stood up and yawned. "Unfortunately, I think it's time to call it a night. We all have to get up in the morning." He glanced at Den out of the corner of his eye. "Den should probably get ready for bed, too. He looks exhausted."

Den placed a hand on top of Syd's. "I am tired. I may need to take few pain pills." He picked up Syd's palm and kissed it.

Syd yanked her hand away and stood abruptly. "I'll get those for you."

Den grabbed her wrist. "You don't have to get them yet. I'm good right now. Sit down, baby."

Syd peered at Morgan, her eyes widening. "Den, don't—"

Den picked up his crutch and pushed himself up. "Syd, please. You're not here to serve me. I think we're better than that—especially after the time we've spent together since the accident."

Den pulled Syd close to him and she jerked back. "Stop, Den," she demanded.

Clenching his fork in his hand, Morgan opened his mouth to speak, to tell Den to keep his hands to himself. Unfortunately, he was rendered speechless when Den pulled Syd into a kiss. He went to stand up, but Kent's hand on his shoulder stopped him. But Syd didn't need him to jump in, because she shoved Den away from her hard enough that Den stumbled from the force and the shock of it.

Chest heaving, she glanced at everyone in the room. "Mama, I'm sorry. I have to go." Grabbing her purse, she ran out of the house.

* * *

Syd rushed into her condo and slammed the door behind her. *Shit.* Leaning against the door, she slid to the floor and buried her head on her knees.

"What the hell am I going to do?" she murmured to herself.

"I don't know, but you need to figure this shit out."

She froze. "Go away, Red." She'd cried all the way home. Her eyes felt like she'd stuffed cotton balls in them as she peered up at her twin and tried to focus on his face.

He reached out his hand. "Get up."

When she took his hand, he pulled her to her feet. "Go away, Red," she repeated, snatching her hand out of his once she was standing upright.

"Syd, there is no sense in having a pity party. You need to fix this."

She scowled at him. "What the hell do you know about it? Why are you here? Don't you have your own problems to fix? Like telling Cali that you love her and want to be with her?"

He crossed his arms over his chest. "I'm here to help you. Kent called."

She rolled her eyes, collapsed on her couch, and covered her eyes with an arm. "So then you know you can't help me," she grumbled.

He gently kicked her shin. "Can you please stop being so dramatic, Syd?"

Her eyes popped open. "Get out, Red!" she shrieked at the top of her lungs. "I know I fucked up, but the last thing I need is *you* telling me that I fucked up. Leave me the hell alone."

He sat down on the cherrywood coffee table in front of the couch. "You're going to sit here and take it, Syd. I'm not going to leave you the hell alone until we fix it."

She opened one eye and hoped to God she could convey her annoyance at his presence. When he burst out laughing, she knew she'd failed epically. "I hate you," she mumbled. *What am I, a first grader?* Reluctantly, she sat up and finally faced her brother.

He placed a hand on her knee. "Wow, you're a mess, sis. What happened?"

"I'm sure Kent filled you in on everything."

He sighed. "I'm asking you. The only thing Kent said was all hell broke loose after Den kissed you in front of everyone and you almost shoved him to the ground."

As if the night wasn't bad enough. "Yeah, that's about it."

"Son of a bitch."

"He was carrying on all night," she explained. "Acting so sweet and nice, trying to be close to me."

"Son of a bitch."

"I didn't want to cause a scene in front of Mama so I tried to ignore it, until I couldn't anymore." He opened his mouth to speak, but she placed a hand over his mouth. "And don't say 'son of a bitch' again. You're not helping."

"Asshole. Is that better?"

"Not really. Actually, you're probably the last person that I need to talk to about this. You're too biased."

"Well, he did cheat on you," he said.

"And I slept with his brother," she countered.

He waved her off. "After he broke your heart again. He cheated on you more than once. You were engaged to that fool. I still don't get why you're being so hard on yourself. For the last time, you don't owe Den anything. You two weren't together when you and Morgan hooked up." Lowering his voice, his added, "Sure, you could've found someone who wasn't his brother to rebound with, but oh well."

She pursed her lips together. "Shut up!" Needing to hit something, she punched him in his shoulder, getting a small hint of satisfaction when he flinched. "Morgan is not a rebound. It's so much more than that." She groaned loudly and dropped her head on her knees. "Red, I've made a huge mess of things. How am I supposed to make this right?"

"Tell the truth?" Red said, with a shrug. Like it was so simple. He rubbed his shoulder where she'd hit him. "Syd, I can't—for the life of me—figure out why you're still hanging on to Den."

Ouch. "I'm not," she whispered, not even believing her own words.

He watched her through narrowed eyes.

"What?" she asked defensively.

"Don't *what* me, Syd. Maybe hanging on to Den wasn't the right phrase to describe what you're doing. I don't understand this compulsion you have to push yourself to the side for him. It's time for you to end this once and for all. If you don't, you're going to lose Roc."

"I don't want to lose him, Red," she breathed, placing a hand on her churning stomach. "I love him."

"I know." He sat next to her and pulled her into a hug. "But you're going to have to do something about it. You can't go on this way."

"I still feel guilty," she croaked against his shirt. She was sure her tears and makeup were going to ruin Red's silk dress shirt, but if he didn't care...

"Okay, so you feel guilty," he said. "Get over it. And stop crying. I love you, but you just ruined one of my best shirts."

She couldn't help it. She laughed. "You shouldn't have hugged me."

He squeezed her. "Syd, you're the best person I know. Better than me, by far. And I've watched you put everyone else before yourself. Frankly, I'm tired of it. I want you to be happy."

She peered up at her brother and noticed tears standing in his eyes. "You better not cry, Red," she said, pointing at him.

He cleared his throat. "I'm not going to cry. Please. I'm a man." He pounded a fist against his chest.

She smiled and shot him a *yeah right* look.

"You haven't been happy in a long time," he added. "It's time to make *you* happy. I hate to say it, but I told you that agreeing to marry Den was the biggest mistake of your life."

"I believe your exact words were 'I never thought he was the great love of your life. Why would you marry him? You don't even love him like that.'"

"That was pretty harsh, huh?" he said, chuckling.

She nodded. They had gotten into a huge argument the night Den proposed.

"Well, I could've been a little nicer," Red conceded. "But I was right. You would've regretted marrying Den."

Red used to tell her all the time that her getting with Den had immediately put him at odds with him. Before her, Red and Den had been cool with each other. Being the overprotective brother that Red was, though, he couldn't ignore the things that had happened.

"I believe that," she told him, laying her head on his shoulder. "It would have been a mistake to marry him. But I can't discount the good in him."

"I'm not asking you to," Red said. "For all his faults, Den has potential. I hope he can get himself together one day. In the meantime, you deserve to be happy."

"What if I don't?"

Maybe what was happening to her was karma for being with Morgan in the first place? It was the first time she'd done anything so selfish, throwing caution to the wind and not thinking about the consequences. Any choice she made would result in losing one or both of them. If she chose to end things with Morgan, their friendship would probably be over, too.

"Why wouldn't you deserve to be happy?" Red asked. "I do stupid shit every day. I got a woman pregnant and didn't know it. And when I found out I denied it. Now that I'm willing to accept it, I have no idea where she is. Not to mention, I've been sleeping with your best friend for a long-ass time and I'm not ready to stop or to tell her that I want a relationship. That's stupid."

"Well, at least you're not sleeping with your ex's sister," she muttered. "I believe there's a consequence to every action. I could've stopped this a long time ago, but I didn't. Now I love Morgan desperately. If I stay with him, try to make it work, we both lose Den. Everyone in the family would suffer. If I break things off, I lose him and we still could lose Den. All because of my choices."

He cupped her face in his hands and tilted her head to face him. "I don't believe you'll lose Morgan, but if you do, you'll be okay. Could you have handled things differently from the beginning? Yes. But everyone makes mistakes. Nobody is perfect, but like I said earlier—you're pretty damn close. You love with your whole heart. You'll do anything for your family and friends. You forgive when others can't. Maybe I'm biased, but when that man... When you were raped, I didn't know if you'd ever be able to pick yourself up again. But you did. You made a life for yourself. You didn't wallow in it. You're my hero."

"I'm your hero?" she asked, sniffling.

He nodded. "All day."

Syd and Red settled into a comfortable silence. He was right; she had to fix this. Unfortunately, she had no clue where to start.

A soft knock interrupted her thoughts. Red walked to the door and opened it. Morgan was standing there.

* * *

Morgan entered the condo when Red stepped aside. After she'd run out of the house, he'd blasted Den for being deceitful by implying that he and Syd were working things out. Den went on a rampage, destroying the glassware with his crutch before falling and hurting himself. But that didn't stop him from yelling and accusing everyone of being against him, even as they were helping him get up off the floor. Eventually Den calmed down, but not before he blamed everyone else for what happened.

He'd driven straight to Syd's after he'd left Den's house. There were so many things cluttering his mind, so much confusion. For a brief moment, he hoped it had all been a dream. But he was a realist and this was no dream. It was becoming a nightmare with each day that passed.

But she was beautiful.

She was sitting on the couch with her legs tucked under her body. Her swollen, red eyes told him she'd been crying. He hated when she cried.

"What's up, Roc?" Red said, breaking the silence.

He nodded simply at his friend. "I need to talk to Syd alone," he murmured, meeting her gaze across the room again.

"Cool. I'll have my phone on if you need me, Syd," Red said, before making his exit.

Deciding it was best to stay as far away from her as possible, Morgan leaned against the door.

They exchanged no words for what seemed an eternity. Someone had to break the ice, but damn it, he was tired of making the first move.

She cleared her throat. "I—I'm sorry, about what happened tonight."

"Syd, tell me the truth. Did something happen between you and Den while you were staying with him?"

Her eyes widened. "What do you mean? Other than that kiss?"

He closed his eyes, trying to shake the image of that kiss. Thinking about it made his blood turn cold. "Yes, other than the…"

When she didn't answer immediately, his eyes popped open. She was watching him, chewing on her bottom lip nervously.

"Syd, answer the damn question," he demanded, annoyed that he sounded like an insecure fool.

"No," she whispered. "That kiss…It was the only thing that's happened between us since we broke up."

Just what I thought. He didn't really know why he'd asked, especially considering Mama had admitted that Den lied to her.

She frowned. "Why did you ask me that?"

He waved her off, not wanting to get into it. "It doesn't matter anymore."

She stood and closed the distance between them. "Morgan, I've slept in the guest room since I moved in. The only time I went in his room was to bring him food or help him... get dressed."

Damn her.

"Since yesterday, Den and I have barely said two words to each other," she said.

"What happened yesterday?" he asked.

"I told him I wasn't going to stay with him anymore. Last night was it."

As happy as he was to hear her say that, it still didn't change the circumstances. Den's behavior was off. He'd gone to great lengths to portray an image that he and Syd were together. Morgan thought about the talk he'd had with him earlier, how his brother had asked if anything had ever happened with Syd. And after the display at dinner and the subsequent tantrum, Morgan had no doubt Den had wanted him to see that kiss. He just wasn't sure why. *Did he know?*

"Morgan?" Her voice was soft, unsure. "Please believe me. I haven't slept with Den."

He gazed down at her, letting his eyes wander over her face. He reached out, swept his thumb under her chin before caressing her cheek. She closed her eyes and leaned in to his touch. Her tongue darted out to moisten her lips and the urge to kiss her threatened to choke him.

One thing Morgan had become accustomed to—the constant need he had to touch her, to kiss her, to be with her. Even as angry as he was, he still wanted to hold her close to him. But his pride...

"Do you believe me?" she asked.

He surveyed her before nodding slightly. "I believe you. I

don't even know why I asked. I'm glad you decided to leave the house."

"Are you going to tell me what happened after I left?"

He shook his head. "No. It's over. But I do think we should say something sooner rather than later to him about us." He pulled her close to him, resting his chin on her head.

"I'm scared," she admitted softly. "I really think tonight gave us a preview of what will come once we tell the truth."

"I think you're right," he grumbled. "I want to believe that we're going to make it out of this together. But after tonight..." He cupped his face in her hands, still needing the physical contact. It was always like this. He went back and forth between knowing he probably should let her go and wanting to toss her over his shoulder and take her to bed. He was an emotional wreck and he hated the feeling.

"I love you, Morgan. Nothing has changed for me. I meant what I said the other day."

He leaned his forehead against hers. "I love you, too."

The idea that someone could breeze into his life, make him love her, and become his everything, would have never crossed his mind before Syd. He'd tell her every day if he had to. But he suspected he didn't have to. They were so connected, so entwined, he felt like there would be no him without her. He knew he'd do anything for her—even if she asked him to let her go.

CHAPTER TWENTY-SIX

Sydney glanced at her watch. Allina had called and they'd agreed to meet for dinner. Since Syd was working at the bar, Allina said she'd meet her there. But her friend was late, which was not like her. It had been so long since she'd seen her, and she couldn't wait.

Taking long, slow breaths, she prayed the nauseous feeling that seemed to attach itself to her over the last week would go away. She closed her eyes as a wave of lightheadedness swept over her. For a fleeting moment, she entertained the idea that she was coming down with the flu, but she shrugged that off quickly since it was summer. It had to be her nerves. There was so much going on.

She hadn't seen Morgan since the night of the infamous dinner at Den's house. He'd left like a thief in the night after receiving a cryptic phone call the next morning. She couldn't be sure, but it felt like he was avoiding her. Den, on the other hand, wouldn't take the hint. In fact, he'd actually turned up the heat, making it known on countless occasions—and despite her objections—that he still wanted to be with her.

When she saw Allina walk in she stood on shaky legs so

that her friend would see her. Before she knew it, Allina was standing before her with her arms out. They hugged.

"It's good to see you," Allina said, sliding into the booth.

"I know. It's been so long. I love your hair like that." Allina had cut her hair into a cute bob, which was very different from the normal braids and bun she wore. Syd assessed her friend and noted that she was also wearing makeup and earrings. "Girl, what have you been doing with yourself? You're glowing."

"I know," Allina said, beaming. "I met someone. Syd, he's wonderful."

She blinked and flattened her hand against her stomach, suddenly feeling faint. "What? Get out. Who is this guy and is he good enough for you? And what about Kent?"

"He's a minister, an associate pastor at my parents' church in Ohio. We met when I was down for a visit. We got to talking after service and he asked me out...and the rest is history. Oh, Syd, I think he's my *one*."

"Wow. I have to meet this guy." In college, they'd often talked about meeting their *one*—the one person that would complete them, like in all the hot romance novels. Syd had thought she'd already met her *one* in Den. "But you still haven't answered my question. What about Kent?"

"What *about* Kent?" Allina asked, hunching her shoulders. "He was never my man. It's probably for the best, anyway. We're better off friends."

Syd wanted to tell Allina that she was making a big mistake not telling Kent how she felt, but she had no room to cast judgment on anyone.

"And I have some news." Allina grinned.

"More news?"

Beaming, Allina told Syd that the owner of her bridal salon was divorcing her husband and moving to Atlanta for a fresh start. "She offered to sell me the shop."

"Oh my God, Allina!" Syd gasped. "That is awesome. Do you need anything? I'm more than happy to invest in you."

"That's what I wanted to talk to you about. Remember that idea we had back in college about opening up a one-stop shop where we plan events and I do the dresses?" she asked.

"Yeah, of course I do." It was all they'd talked about back in the day.

"I'd like to do something like that," Allina said. "I know you're busy with the Ice Box, but I was wondering if you think Calisa would be down."

Calisa's event planning business was booming, but she was always looking for new opportunities. "I know she will," Syd said. "She still talks about it, too. You should definitely call her. And I'll help any way I can. I'm so proud of you."

They chatted a few minutes, catching up. Syd took Allina on a tour, telling her about all the changes and giving her an update on the grand opening. Syd walked behind one of the bars to grab a bottle of water. As a wave of dizziness passed over her, she stopped and braced a hand on the counter.

Allina frowned. "Are you feeling okay?"

"Yes," Syd lied. Twisting the cap off her water bottle, she gulped the entire sixteen ounces down in a matter of seconds. "Water?" she asked after she tossed her empty bottle into the trash can.

"Are you sure you're okay?" Allina asked. "You look a little pale."

She rubbed her eyes, suddenly feeling exhausted. "Do I? I feel pale." *If there were such a thing.* She wet a paper towel and patted her face and neck. "I might be coming down with something. I'm fine. So tell me what you think of the bar?"

"I love it." Allina glanced around the building. "It's exactly what I pictured when you described it to me all those years ago."

"You have no idea how good it feels to hear you say that."

Actually, it meant the world to Syd. "I can't believe you're finally going into business for yourself," Syd added.

"Yeah, it was time. And I'm happy." Allina hadn't stopped smiling since she walked in. Her friend wasn't the smiling type, so her new beau had to be special. "How are you?" Allina asked her.

"Good." Syd avoided eye contact with her and turned aside to begin unloading a box of glasses.

Allina observed her quietly, making Syd feel like she was under a microscope. There wasn't much she could hide from her friend, but there was no way she was going to spend another minute obsessing about her drama if she could help it.

"How are things with you and Den?" Allina asked. "Is he getting better?"

"He is," she said. Part of her wanted to tell Allina everything, but the other part didn't want talk about it anymore. "Mama asked me to stay with him temporarily to help him out after the accident."

Allina's eyes widened. "Wow. Red must have flipped out."

"He did. So did Morgan and Kent..."

"Well, they love you. They're just trying to protect you." Leaning forward, her hands braced on the counter, Allina asked, "What's going on with you? This is me here. I can tell when something is wrong."

"I'm not going to rain on your happy parade with my problems," Syd said, waving her off. "I need details about this minister."

"We can talk about him later. I'm concerned about you."

"I'm good." *Oh, fuck it.* She blurted out, "I slept with Morgan and have been carrying on a sexual relationship with him behind Den's back, but I'm good."

Allina stared at her, mouth open.

Suddenly, the contents in Sydney's stomach inched their

way up, and she clamped a hand over her mouth. "Oh God," she exclaimed, and rushed to the bathroom.

She pushed the door open and dropped to her knees. Embracing the toilet, she emptied her stomach violently.

Groaning, she fell back on her butt and slid against the wall. She wiped her mouth, lifted her knees up to her chest, and rested her head on them. She yanked the roll of toilet paper off its decorative stand and wiped her eyes. *What the hell is wrong with me?* She frowned, angry at her body for betraying her. She hated to throw up with a white-hot passion. It was disgusting and completely inconvenient.

A soft knock sounded, jarring her from her thoughts. Choosing to ignore it, she thought back to her admission to Allina. She'd have to face her eventually, but she wasn't quite ready.

Another knock sounded—louder. She buried her face in her knees when she heard the door open. *Come in.* She braced herself for Allina's worried face and glanced up.

"Morgan?" she said, surprised to see him there. "What are you doing here?"

Allina poked her head in the bathroom, too. "Are you okay, Syd?"

Morgan walked over and knelt down before her. He placed a hand on her forehead and then raked his fingers through her hair. "Why are you on the floor?"

"I'm going to get you another bottle of water. Maybe some ginger ale to settle your stomach," Allina offered, handing Morgan a towel.

"I'm okay, Allina," Syd assured her. "Do you mind if I talk to Morgan alone?"

Allina hesitated. "I'll be right outside if you need me, okay? And I'll get that ginger ale ready, in case you want it."

Once Allina left, she pulled Morgan into a hug. His body tensed initially, but she held on for dear life. Eventually, he loosened up and he rubbed her back slowly. She buried her face in his neck and brushed her lips against his skin. "How did you know I needed you?"

He pulled back, a confused look on his face. "I didn't. I came to the bar to take care of some business. When I walked in, I saw Allina behind the bar, looking for a towel. She told me you rushed to the bathroom covering your mouth like you had to throw up."

She wrapped her hands around his shoulders again. "I can't believe you're here," she mumbled. "Can you take me home?"

"Are you drunk?" he asked.

She giggled. "No. Why would you ask me that?"

"You drove, baby. Besides, don't you have plans with Allina?" He stood up, pulling her to her feet. "You don't have a fever or anything. Are you sure you're okay? Maybe you should drink some water or something."

Over the past few months, she'd gone back and forth with herself. Knowing that she loved Morgan was one thing. Being willing to step out on faith and be with him was another. She'd tried to avoid conflict all of her life, often choosing to accept what others gave her just so she didn't have to fight or argue. This was one of the reasons she'd gone to live with her father instead of staying with her mother. They never got along and the stress of being around her mother overwhelmed her. So she left. The compulsion to run from this situation was constant as well. Yet as she gazed up at him, she knew she'd endure anything to be with him—as long as he wanted to be with her. "Morgan, you're the one," she said.

His eyes flashed to hers. "I am? Um, that's good."

She smiled at his cluelessness. "No, you're the *one*."

"Are you sure you haven't been drinking, baby?" He asked, arching his brow.

"I'm sure. You're the *one*."

He turned on the water and wet the towel. "Okay, I'll take your word for it. I'm the one."

She cupped his face in her hands. "You're *my* one."

"Oh." He dabbed her face with the damp cloth. "I'm glad I'm your *one*. Not that I know what that is." He ran the cloth under the water again, wrung it out, and placed it on the back of her neck.

"You came in here all protective and took care of me," she said. "That proves even more that you're the one for me."

He scratched his cheek. "I guess that makes sense."

She leaned into him and wrapped her arms around his waist. "I'm sorry, Morgan."

He rested his chin on her forehead. "What are you apologizing for? It's going to be all right."

She sniffed his shirt and burrowed into his strong body. A wave of dizziness passed through her and she squeezed him tightly. "I feel dizzy, like I'm coming down with the flu or something."

"It's not flu season," he said, smoothing his hands up and down her back.

"That's the crazy part. I think it's probably stress. You know, the Den situation..." She peered up at him. "You."

He swept a strand of hair from her face. "Well, you've had a rough couple of months."

"I feel okay now, except for the dizziness—and the nausea." She turned to the sink and cleaned herself up. "Do you have gum or mouth wash?"

He glanced at her in the mirror. "Sure. I happen to have a toothbrush, too."

"Sarcasm evident," she murmured. "I had to ask. I think I have some gum in my purse. I ordered a shipment of mouthwash for the bathrooms. Remind me to call and check on that." She used the running water to rinse her mouth out. "Thanks for picking me up off the floor."

He wrapped his arms around her from behind and she twined their fingers. "I'll always pick you up."

"I missed you," she whispered.

He rested his chin on her shoulder. "I missed you, too."

Their gazes locked in the mirror. "Can you stay for a minute?"

He shook his head. "No. I think you should go home and rest." He gave her a quick kiss on the cheek and opened the door, holding it open for her.

"Are you okay?" Allina asked when they walked into the main room.

"I'm good." Syd grabbed the soda Allina held out to her and twisted the cap off. "Probably a stomach thing." She gulped down the liquid. When she finished, Morgan and Allina were watching her. "What?" She wiped her mouth with her hand.

Syd's gaze darted back and forth between the two of them, noting how they seemed to be looking at her like she was crazy. "Allina, do you want to head to Cali's? We can talk about that possible business venture."

"Okay," Allina said slowly, still frowning. "Syd, maybe you should go to bed or something."

"I'm fine," she insisted.

Syd grabbed her purse and rummaged through it for the pack of gum she knew she'd tossed in there earlier. When she found it, she quickly unwrapped it and popped a piece in her mouth. She turned to Morgan, who was already behind the bar with his pad of paper, jotting down some notes. She told him they were going to dinner at Calisa's. He said he'd talk to her later, and she turned on her heel and left.

* * *

Morgan stared at the closed door. He tapped his pen against the bar counter as his mind drifted to their little encounter in the bathroom. She'd called him her *one*, whatever that meant. He couldn't deny it made him feel good. Really good. He already knew she was the one for him. He loved her beyond reason and it infuriated him that he couldn't be with her like he wanted. They'd done a lot of things wrong. And he wondered if they'd get their happy ending. Then, there was Den. Despite what he'd told Syd, he found himself warring with his emotions even more where his brother was concerned. His childhood would have been that much worse if it hadn't been for Den. He knew that once he and Syd told Den the truth, the already strained bond between them would be ruined.

He heard the side door open and dropped his pen on the bar. Den shuffled into the room on his crutches. *Great.*

"Den?" Morgan asked, walking from behind the bar. "What are you doing here?"

"I saw your car out front. I'm glad I caught you."

"What do you need?" Morgan hadn't seen Den since that debacle at his house when he'd kissed Syd in front of everyone. In fact, he had gone out of his way to stay clear of his brother.

"I wanted to talk to you about the other night."

Morgan rolled his neck in an attempt to alleviate some of the tension he felt. Unfortunately, that didn't help much. "There's nothing to talk about, Den."

"Well, I need your help," Den said. "I want to do something special for Syd, to apologize for what I did. She's helped me in so many ways and I'd like to do something nice for her at the private opening in a couple of weeks."

"Why are you asking me?"

"Because you're my brother," Den replied.

Morgan clenched his fists together. His blood had started to simmer. "Still, you could've asked anyone else."

"And you own the bar."

"Along with Kent and Red," Morgan said. "You couldn't ask Red? He's her brother."

"You know Red and I don't get along. Why? I don't know," he added under his breath.

Morgan chided himself for catching an attitude over a seemingly innocent request and feeling like he wanted to strangle his brother with his bare hands. "What kind of special thing are you trying to do?"

"I'm thinking a nice vacation, to an island in September. It would be nice to get away." Den leaned against a chair. "While we're there, depending on how our reconnect goes, I hope to propose to her again—this time in the right way."

Morgan frowned. *Like hell.* His brother really was delusional. He made a mental note to talk to Mama about whether Den was actually taking his medication. How he could go from wanting to do something nice for Syd as an apology to whisking her away on a romantic vacation and proposing was beyond him. "Aren't you getting a little ahead of yourself, Den? You're not even—"

The door slammed. Morgan glanced toward the front of the bar. Syd rushed into the room with Allina right behind her. She froze when she saw the two of them standing there.

"Hi, Syd," Den said.

Syd glanced at Den, then Morgan, then back at Den. "What—what are you doing here?"

"Talking to my brother," Den replied.

"I forgot my cell phone," Syd announced. She hurried to the bar and grabbed it. Holding it up, she said, "Got it. We should get going."

Morgan watched Syd. She still looked pale. "Are you sure you're okay?"

She shot him a wary glance. "I'm fine—a little tired, but good."

"I've been wondering the same thing," Allina added. "If you want, we can stay around here. We don't have to go to Calisa's house."

Morgan wished she'd take her ass home and get in bed. She didn't look good and it was starting to worry him. Nausea, vomiting…Damn. *Could she be…?*

She shook her head. "We're going. If I feel worse, I'll take a nap or something over there. But we're going."

Den frowned. "Now that you mention it, she does look pale."

"I'm fine. And for the record, women don't like when men point out that they look sick." She clapped a hand over her mouth and bolted for the bathroom.

CHAPTER TWENTY-SEVEN

*S*ydney was, once again, praying to the porcelain god. Once she'd emptied her stomach—honestly she didn't realize she'd had anything left to empty after that first time—she collapsed onto the floor. She felt weak, nauseous, and tired. And according to everyone else, pale. She slid to the wall and leaned her head back against it.

She closed her eyes and took a few deep breaths. *What the hell is wrong with me?* She checked the calendar on her phone. She wasn't feverish. Maybe she was getting ready to start her period? She hadn't had one since...*Shit!* Slowly, she pulled herself to her feet, grasping a small ledge to steady herself. She peered at her reflection in the mirror. *Am I...?* She shook her head. *No. Hell no.* She rinsed her mouth out for the second time that night. Glancing at herself in the mirror again, she observed the dark circles under her eyes that hadn't been there earlier. She pulled at the skin under her eyes and smacked her cheeks lightly.

Pregnant. She glared at herself in the mirror. A gamut of emotions filled her with the possibilities. After countless doctors, numerous tests...*Is this possible?* She smiled at her reflection. Smoothing a hand over her stomach, she examined her frame. If she was pregnant, what would Morgan say? Then the reality of the situation hit her like a ton of bricks.

Never in her wildest dreams had she ever expected to have a child of her own. But how could she explain this sudden nausea? Her period was always irregular, but she hadn't had one in almost two months according to the calendar. A baby? At this point in her life?

For someone who'd been a stickler when it came to using protection with Den, she'd sure let all those principles fly out the window when Morgan took her to bed. He'd never really used protection, not since their first time. And she'd never made him. She was always so caught up in the moment with him that she didn't stop to think about the consequences. Sure, she'd always thought about the fallout from the affair, but never about . . . *Shit.*

A soft knock at the door snapped her out of her thoughts.

Allina poked her head into the room. "Syd, are you going to be okay?"

She sighed. "I'm fine. But I guess you're right. I should probably take it easy. We can still go to Calisa's, though, just not to the bar afterward like we planned."

Allina looked worried but she stepped back to allow Syd to exit the bathroom, then followed her back to the main room. Morgan and Den were still waiting out front.

Syd smiled. *Fake.* "Okay, so we're going to head out," she said, trying to act nonchalant.

"Maybe you should go home and rest," Morgan suggested. "Can't Cali come to your house?"

Their gazes locked. "No," she rasped. "I'm good. Allina will drive." Calisa lived fifty miles away in the Detroit suburb of Troy.

"But you threw up—again," Morgan said, narrowing his eyes. "Do you really think it's wise to drive that far out?"

"It's not that far," she retorted. "And like I said, I'm not going to drive. Right, Allina?"

Morgan glowered at her.

She pushed a piece of hair out of her face. "Come on, Allina. 'Bye, Morgan." She shifted her attention to Den, who had been watching the exchange between them quietly. "Bye, Den. I'm glad to see you're up and at 'em."

She turned on her heels and left.

* * *

Syd locked her front door and threw her purse on the couch. She was finally home. It'd taken every ounce of restraint she'd had to not bawl her eyes out when she saw Cali's face. She wanted to scream about the unfairness of it all. Wail about how life kept smacking her in the face. Allina had given her the third degree on the way down and she'd told her almost everything even though she knew the future preacher's wife did not approve. Mostly it had just felt good to be able to tell her. It had been far too long since they'd kicked it with each other.

Syd plopped down on a cushion and kicked her shoes off. It had taken a good twenty minutes to convince Allina that she was well enough to even go to dinner. She'd quizzed Syd nonstop about her *stomach* issues. But that was just like her college roommate; she'd never changed. She was always concerned about everyone's health but her own. They had that in common.

Leaning her head back against the sofa, Syd groaned. Her life was a complete and utter mess. She pulled the brown paper bag out of her purse. On the way home, she'd stopped at the local Walgreens and picked up her very own e.p.t. home pregnancy test. She tugged the box out of the bag and scanned the directions. *Oh boy.*

She sighed and forced herself off the couch. As if she were walking to her death, she made her way to the master bathroom.

"It's about time you made it home."

She jumped back into the wall, clutching the box against her chest. "Morgan," she screeched. "What the hell are you doing here? I gave you a key for emergencies, not so you can let yourself in on a whim."

He stood up and closed the distance between them. "We need to talk, Syd."

She was pretty sure he saw the box in her hand, but she dropped her hands behind her back anyway. "Morgan, I don't feel well. It's not a good time to talk."

"That's what I want to talk to you about." He grabbed a plastic bag off the loveseat, pulled something out, and held it up for her.

Her eyes flashed to his when she saw the huge plus sign on the box. "What is that?"

"A pregnancy test," he replied.

Unable to help herself, she burst into a fit of laughter. She'd been so worried about what he would think if she told him her suspicions, but he was already on it.

He frowned. "I don't see what's funny about this. This could be a disaster waiting to happen, Syd. It's not a laughing matter."

She covered her mouth with her hand, attempting to hide her smile.

"I've been thinking about this all night. You're nauseous, tired, and you threw up—twice. I racked my brain trying to think of a plausible explanation, but it keeps coming back to this." He tapped the box.

She flashed her box at him then and his eyes widened.

"So you think there's a chance, too?" he asked.

She sucked in a deep breath. "I would say so. Guess I

better get to it, huh?" She pointed toward the bathroom. "I'll be back in a few minutes."

* * *

A few minutes? It seemed like an eternity, Morgan thought. When Sydney emerged from the bathroom—finally—he stood up.

He paused to gauge her reaction. She seemed normal. Not like she'd received bad news. She stared at him from her position across the room.

"Well?" he asked, shoving his hands in his pockets.

"I can't believe this," she said. "I'm—"

"You're pregnant?" he cut in.

"I—"

"What are we going to do?" he asked. His mind immediately counted off everything that could go wrong if Syd was having his baby.

"Morgan, I'm not pregnant. The test was negative."

He let out a breath he didn't know he'd been holding. "Wow. That was close."

She climbed onto the bed and stared up at the ceiling. "It really was. I truly thought I was pregnant, but I'm glad it was a false alarm."

He lay next to her and placed a hand on her belly. "Not that I would've tripped or anything," he lied. "But I have to admit I was nervous."

She giggled and he followed suit with a deep chuckle. She intertwined her fingers with his. "It would've been the worst possible timing," she added.

"Definitely," he agreed.

She glanced at him and smoothed her hand up his arm. "I guess we should probably talk about how careful we haven't been."

"Yeah, we suck." The sound of her soft, airy laughter wrapped around him. He knew he would be no good for any other woman. He'd love her forever.

"Pretty much. I really don't think this has ever happened to me before. I always use protection of some form."

He shot her a look of disbelief.

"Okay, so I haven't had that much experience."

"Well, I've never *not* used protection with anyone," he confessed. "Then again, I've also never felt this way about anyone else."

She cupped his cheek in her hand. "This scare was enough for me, though. We should really rein in that desire."

He smirked. "Good luck with that."

She brushed her lips against his. "We have to. This should serve as a wake-up call."

Yet even as she was firmly putting down the *law*, he found himself unable to resist her. She spouted off all the different birth control methods while he unbuttoned her shirt. He inhaled her scent and bent down to kiss her belly, enjoying her sharp intake of breath. He dragged his lips up to her breasts and unsnapped her bra so he could gain full access to her. Snaking his tongue around her nipple, he suckled it into his mouth. He hissed as her nails dug into his scalp. When she moaned, he muffled it with his mouth covering hers. He rolled on top of her and she wrapped her legs around his waist. *They could start reining in that desire tomorrow.*

CHAPTER TWENTY-EIGHT

Sydney awoke early in the morning feeling like she was hungover. She turned her head and noticed Morgan was knocked out next to her, the thin sheet draped low on his waist. She smirked and guessed it was normal to feel this way after the hours of loving she'd been treated to.

Morgan was skilled in so many ways, so it was no surprise to her that he was an excellent lover. He took his time with her, making sure she got hers every time. She threw her legs over the edge of the bed and sat up. Although the pregnancy test had been negative, she still felt a little queasy. She scanned the dark room, slid off the bed, and shuffled into the bathroom.

After throwing up a third time, she sauntered into the kitchen and poured herself a glass of water. She gulped the water down in a matter of seconds and braced herself against the counter. Closing her eyes, she let out a deep breath in an attempt to calm her stomach.

"You okay?"

She jumped. "Son of a— You really have to stop doing that."

"I'm sorry." He walked up behind her and massaged her

shoulders. "What's wrong? Still sick to your stomach?" He kissed the pulse point in her neck.

"I guess it could be a stomach flu or something." She shrugged. "Or maybe I ate something that's not agreeing with me."

"I think I heard there was some sort of bug going around. Maybe you should stay in today and rest?"

"I can't. I have so much to do before we open."

"Still, I'd feel better if you saw your doctor just in case. You really can't afford to be sick right now."

She nodded. "Maybe it's nerves? I've been working so hard trying to make sure everything is right at the Ice Box."

"Could be. Standing here and thinking about it isn't going to help though. Come back to bed. In a few hours, make an appointment with your doctor."

She promised him she would and they went back to bed.

* * *

Morgan pulled his ringing phone out of his briefcase. "Hey. What's up?"

"Babe?" Syd called through the static. "I'm in the hospital so I may lose you."

"Did you call your doctor?"

"Yes. They had an opening, so pushed back my one o'clock lunch meeting with Kent."

"Good," he said, checking his watch. "Let me know how it goes."

"I'll call you later."

Morgan ended the call and stared at his computer. He'd been sitting there for over half an hour waiting to hear from Sydney. Before he left her house, he'd made her promise again to call her doctor. She'd spent the morning in the bathroom throwing up and he was worried.

The pregnancy test was negative. And he still wasn't sure how he was supposed to feel about that. Of course, he was relieved, but he also felt something else. Something he couldn't quite put a finger on. The first thought that had come to mind when he suspected that she might be pregnant was *Damn*. After that, though, he couldn't deny that seeing her belly swollen with his child was appealing on some level.

He loved her—more than she would probably ever know. And he'd been behaving like a raving lunatic over this Den situation—uncertain, wishy-washy. But he was determined to push those feelings aside to give it a go with her.

Then there was that matter of the promotion he'd been offered. It was the opportunity of a lifetime. His boss had offered him a corner with a view in the new Baltimore office—and partner. He'd worked hard for it, putting in more hours than most and landing huge accounts for the firm. But could he leave? Or more specifically—would he leave her?

A knock on the door jolted him out of his thoughts. Kent poked his head in. "Roc, you have a minute?"

He nodded and gestured toward the empty chair in his office. "Come on in. What brings you down here? Aren't you meeting Syd at one?"

Morgan was surprised to see Kent. His brother hated coming downtown and avoided it at all costs. He figured something must be important.

"Man, we need to talk about this whole Syd and Den situation."

That peaked his curiosity. He gripped his high-priced mechanical pencil. "What about Syd and Den?"

"That whole scene at the house still has me bothered. The way Den told Mama that they were working their way back together. She was pissed. But after you left, Mama asked me what was going on with you."

Morgan raised a brow. "What did you tell her?"

Kent ran a hand over his face. "I told her I didn't know. She probably didn't believe me. I had a talk with Den, too," he said, shooting him a wary look. "I asked him why he insisted on not hiring a nurse to help out."

Morgan had thought about that as well. It wasn't like Den didn't make the money to hire one. But Mama had told him that Den mentioned it was too steep a cost because he'd taken out a loan to refinance the house after Syd moved out.

"I think he's manipulating the situation," Kent admitted.

Definitely. "Well, he does want her back. He made that very clear."

"Which leads me to my next question." Kent twisted in his seat. "I need to know when you and Syd are going to make that move, if you know what I mean? I want to be prepared."

"Shit, I don't know." Morgan shrugged. "We know it has to be done, but she isn't ready to spill the beans yet." Neither was he, if he was being honest with himself. "And what do you need to be prepared for? You're not doing anything wrong."

"I'm keeping your secret. So I want to know when this shit is going to hit the fan. Are you ready?"

He scratched the back of his neck. "I don't know. Honestly, all this talk is giving me a headache. Drama. I've always made it a point to never get involved with it, but all that went out the window when I slept with my brother's ex, huh?"

"What did you expect?" Kent asked.

"I definitely didn't expect Den to wage a 'Win Sydney Back' campaign, especially since she's been so adamant with him about not taking him back. I knew he'd try to get her back, but trying to bring Mama in? That's not even like him."

"I'm just as surprised as you by this whole thing. I'm wondering where this is all coming from."

"Who knows? Every time he starts talking about getting back together with Syd, I'm ready to kick his ass, which is completely ridiculous—on my part. And therein lies the problem. Frankly if Mama hadn't been there when he kissed Syd the other night, I would've beat the shit out of him. Or at least we would've been scrappin' in the middle of his house, crutch and all."

Kent shook his head. "That should never happen, by the way. You need to rein in that anger, Roc."

"I just can't shake the feeling that Den is up to something, though," Morgan told Kent. "His moods are all over the place. One minute he's too calm, the next he's too hyped up. Something is—"

"Morgan?" His secretary, Alicia, called over the intercom.

He pushed the button on his phone to listen as she told him that his eleven o'clock meeting was delayed. He instructed her to reschedule because he had an important lunch meeting that he couldn't be late for.

Kent stood up and grabbed his keys off the desk. "I better get going. You're right, though, about one thing."

"What's that?" Morgan asked.

"He's up to something. I'm going to figure it out, too."

* * *

Syd slammed the door to her condo. *How the hell did this happen?* She tossed her keys on the table and dropped her purse on the floor. Her doctor had squeezed her in after she'd described her symptoms. She'd happily agreed to take any and every test the doctor suggested because she was anxious to know what was wrong with her. Unfortunately, she'd been a little cocky when Dr. Long ordered a pregnancy test. She'd even told the doctor that she'd already done a home pregnancy test and the results were negative. When the doc had insisted, she gave in, knowing that the results would come back the same.

Only they didn't.

She *was* pregnant.

When she demanded another test, the doctor obliged, ordering a blood test and requesting the results be expedited. Syd left the office with little hope, though. For some reason, she knew she was pregnant. But when the first test came back negative, she'd run with it. The nagging feeling she'd had to take the other test Morgan bought had plagued her in between trips to the bathroom to vomit. Yet she'd shrugged it off, even after he had asked her to take the test—to be sure. Ignorance was bliss. *Right?*

Doctor Long informed Syd that she would get a call as soon as the test results were back. There was a possibility of a false positive with the urine test since the other one had come back negative. That was her only solace. What would Morgan say? Or Den? *Oh God! What a nightmare!*

Nothing like the cold, hard truth to put a damper on her world. Kent had begged her to tell him why she was crying hysterically over the phone when she'd called to cancel their meeting. She tried to ignore him, but when she nearly ran off the road, he ordered her to stop the car and spill.

She'd explained everything to Kent in between loud sobs. He didn't say much. He'd simply offered to come and get her because he didn't want her driving in her condition.

Sydney had begged Kent to keep her news between them. She hated herself for putting him in the middle, but she needed time to think. As happy as she was at the thought of being a mother, she was terrified, too. There were so many things to consider.

Her phone's loud buzzing startled her out of her pity party. She powered it off and pitched it across the room. She was in no mood to talk to anyone, let alone Den. She rolled her eyes. Her ex had been blowing up her phone the entire day, texting her, leaving messages.

She stood up and went into her bedroom with every intention of hiding in there until she could figure this out—or give birth.

She stripped out of her clothes and slid into a nightgown and fuzzy socks. Comfort. Then she pulled the comforter back and climbed into the bed.

*C*HAPTER TWENTY-NINE

*A*n hour later, Syd sat up in her bed, staring blankly at the television. She couldn't sleep after all and had gone out for a drive, hoping the fresh air would make a difference. It hadn't done anything. She'd ended up at the Ice Box. While there, she had tried to busy herself with work, but it was no use. She wished she could appreciate her dream becoming a reality. By all accounts, she should feel proud of the accomplishment, but all she felt was despair. *Dramatic, much?*

Now she was at home. Sleep would have been a welcome reprieve. Instead she was treated, in her head, to an endless loop of every single mistake she'd made over the last few months. Her stomach growled. For the first time in days, she was actually hungry.

Climbing out of the bed, she padded to the kitchen to fix herself something to eat. She spotted a coupon to her favorite pizza joint and went with it.

When the doorbell rang later, she went to the door and tugged it open. The pint-sized pizza delivery guy handed her the pizza and proceeded to ask her out for the umpteenth time. She rolled her eyes and slapped the money in his hand, politely declining the invitation before she slammed the door in his face.

She opened the box, pulled out a slice, and took a bite, groaning in pleasure. Nothing like garlic-buttered crust to make a dreary day seem perfect. She devoured the slice in two point two seconds and was on her second slice when there was a knock at the door.

Grunting, she got up and walked back to the door, still holding the box of heaven. She licked her fingers and turned the knob, assuming it was the pesky pizza delivery guy again. "I told you—"

Uh-oh. This time it was Morgan.

"You told me what?" he asked, amusement flickering in his eyes.

She closed the box, embarrassed that she was still holding it in the first place. "Uh . . . I thought you were the pizza guy."

He smiled. "You mean, your lover?"

The delivery man had hit on her countless times since she'd moved in. It was a running joke between her and Morgan. She glared at him. "Shut up. Come in." She backed away from the door to let him in, then kicked it closed. Hurrying to the dining table, she set the box down and wiped her hands with a napkin. "Give me a second . . . I have to wash my hands. There's beer in the fridge."

She rushed to the master bathroom and turned the water on. Grabbing her toothbrush, she squirted paste on it and proceeded to brush her teeth. Once she finished, she washed her hands. She glanced at her reflection in the mirror. She was a mess—hair all over her head, bags under her eyes. She couldn't understand why she'd been wishing he was there looking like she did. This was not a sexy look—at all.

When she returned to the living room, Morgan was sitting on the couch with a slice of pizza in one hand, the remote in the other. "Where did you go?" He glanced up at her. "Well, maybe the question should be, where are you going?"

Sydney looked down at the attire she'd hastily put on. The off-the-shoulder shirt and neatly pressed jeans were definitely an improvement on the baggy sweatshirt and shorts she was wearing earlier. She ran a hand over her hair, which was now in a neat ponytail instead of the wild curls she'd rocked when he arrived.

She scratched her nose. "I figured I should put on some clothes."

"I don't know...I kind of like the look you were sporting earlier." He winked at her. "And I really enjoyed the pizza mouth and greasy fingers. Not to mention, the look on your face when you realized it was me at the front door." He barked out a laugh.

She couldn't help but giggle, too. "I'm glad you found amusement at my expense." She plopped down next to him on the couch and kissed him. *Garlic-buttered Morgan was even better.*

They sat in silence while he finished his pizza and flicked the channels. She studied him. He was still fine as ever, but there was a shadow in his eyes. She wondered what was going on, even as she eyed the last few pieces of pizza. Deciding to go with her hunger, she picked up a piece and wolfed it down.

"Morgan, where—" She stopped when she noticed he was no longer eating, but staring at her. She felt a blush creep up her neck. "What?"

"Wow. You're hungry, huh?" he asked.

She covered her mouth with her napkin. "I—well, I haven't eaten much all day and I had a craving—I mean a taste—for pepperoni and onion. And no one does it better than Marco's Pizza. So I ordered one, even though I knew the jerk who doesn't take no for an answer would deliver.

And do you know he had the nerve to ask can he come in and join me for dinner? I slammed the door in his..." She swallowed, realizing she was babbling. And he was still staring.

"Why don't you report his ass? Better yet, why not let me handle it?"

She shook her head. "No. I can handle him. Besides, I don't order often and he's harmless. He's practically a runt."

"If he does it again, I want to know about it," he said firmly. "And I'll report him for you, after I kick his ass."

"That's exactly what I'm trying to avoid," she grumbled.

"Where have you been all day?" he asked, dropping his crust in the box. "I've been trying to call you. What did the doctor say?"

She struggled with whether to tell him the truth. How was she supposed to tell him he may be a father? With the possibility of a false positive, she wondered if she should even tell him before she knew for sure.

"Syd? You can tell me, ya know? Anything."

"I know," she mumbled, still trying to figure out the right words to say.

"Are you sick?" he asked.

"No. Well, not really."

"What is it?" He observed her with questioning eyes.

His phone blared, giving her a reprieve. He explained it was the office and went in the bedroom to take the call. She waited.

When he finally returned, he sat down next to her. He was quiet, pensive.

He turned to her and a flicker of something passed over his face. Almost like regret. His gaze slipped to her mouth, then back to meet her eyes. And just like that, she felt warm. Her heart rate pumped fast and hard. She sucked in a breath as he reached out and ran the back of his hand down her cheek.

He stood up and walked clear to the other side of the room. She hugged herself, immediately missing the warmth of his body, the safety of his presence near her. *Something's not right.*

"What's going on, Morgan?" she asked, concerned. "Is everything all right? What is it?"

"That was my boss," he told her. "He wants me to go to Baltimore."

"Again?" she asked. "That's... It's really close to the opening. How long will you be there?"

"If he has his way, forever. He offered me a partnership."

Her heart raced. *So that's what's been going on with him.*

"Are you going to say anything?" he asked finally.

She flashed him a sad smile. "What is there to say? This is partner, Morgan. You can't turn it down." She wanted to beg him to stay, but she knew she couldn't. Morgan had been working hard toward partner. It was his dream. He'd made sure she was living hers, and she couldn't keep him from going after his.

"Right now, I'm invested here," he said. "I have the bar, my family... you."

She blinked and a tear fell down her cheek. "I know that. But you've wanted this for years."

He sighed, dropped his gaze. "That's true."

Bile burned in the back of her throat and she struggled to swallow. "If I wasn't in the picture, would you take this job?"

"You are in the picture," he said. "It matters."

She peered up at the ceiling and pressed a shaky hand against her stomach. The pizza she'd eaten seemed to sit like a rock and she wished she could throw up and relieve the feeling.

"What do you want, Morgan?" she asked.

"I want you," he replied. "But part of me thinks it's better if I take the job. Syd, at this point the odds of us really being together are pretty low."

"Wait a minute," she said, finding the strength to stand. "I thought…we were supposed to work on this thing. We knew it wouldn't be easy. But I told you I was in this."

He hung his head. "It's not that easy. I know you. You have every intention of being with me, but how realistic is this?"

She stepped closer, pressing her body against him, yet he wouldn't meet her eyes. "Morgan, why are you doing this? Really? Do you want to take the job or not?"

"If I move to Baltimore, I'll be removed from the situation and no one has to be hurt."

"Except me!" She smacked a hand against her chest for emphasis. "My heart. I love you, Morgan. I don't want you to go." She regretted the words as soon as they left her mouth. She wanted to demand that he stay and keep his promise to see this through, to be with her. But he wasn't wrong. And she couldn't ask him to stay for her.

He wandered over to the couch and plopped down. "I'll stay…if you want me to." His voice was so soft, she wondered if she'd heard him correctly. "I'll give up the promotion and take a chance that everything will work out here. I'll do that for us."

Her heart seemed to crack open at the sincerity of his words. He looked at her then and her heart tightened at the tears standing in his eyes. "I love you," he breathed. "I love you so much."

The room seemed to swing around her and she drew in a shaky breath. She pursed her lips in an attempt to muffle the sobs that fought to fill the silence. Could she ask him to stay and take a chance with her—even without knowing for certain their happily ever after would happen? The answer was no. Plain and simple.

"I can't do that," she whispered. "It has to be your decision."

"So ask me to stay, Syd," he pleaded.

She shook her head. "If you don't go because of me—and this doesn't work out—you'll resent me. As much as I want you, I'm still nervous about making this official. I'm not ready yet. I don't know when I will be ready. And it's not fair—to you. You deserve better."

He leaned forward, resting his forearms on his thighs. The beer he'd been nursing earlier dangled from his fingertips.

Unable to take the distance any longer, she moved closer, sitting on the coffee table in front of him. "Morgan, I—"

"I've wondered if there was anything I could do to make this better for both of us," he murmured.

"Me too. Maybe this is my punishment for sleeping with brothers," she quipped, hoping to lighten the mood. "I guess this is what I get. A broken heart and a…" She stopped short of disclosing her pregnancy.

He was watching her again when their eyes met. "Don't do that. Don't blame yourself. I don't regret being with you, loving you. I want…" He sighed and squeezed her knee. "I need you to be happy. I can see that this situation isn't making you happy. It's destroying relationships already. I can't even stand to see my brother. I'm avoiding Mama. We're lying. We're making excuses when there are none. A broken heart is the least I can suffer through compared to the damage our relationship would cause if it came out."

Unable to stop it, one of her tears escaped and dropped on his hand—the one on her knee. She watched as it drizzled down into the fabric of her jeans. "I'm sorry," she mumbled, her voice unsteady.

He pulled her into a tight hug, smoothing a hand up and down her spine from her shoulders to her hip. "Me too," he murmured in her hair. "Me too."

C HAPTER THIRTY

Morgan taped up the large brown box labeled DISHES/
FRAGILE, picked it up, and set it on top of another box. He figured he'd start packing, even though he wasn't leaving until
after the opening. He'd spent all day packing up the kitchen,
wondering if he'd made the right decision. It was hard
enough moving to another state when he'd built a life and a
home here, but it was torture leaving behind the woman he
loved.

No screaming and arguing. No throwing dishes. No
slashed tires—or death threats. None of those things and
this was still the worst breakup he'd ever experienced. Even
knowing this was probably the right decision, it didn't stop
him from hoping she'd beg him to stay—assure him that it
would all work out in the end. Only she hadn't done that.
Instead, she'd grabbed his hand, taken him into the bedroom, and let him make love to her for the rest of the night.

The next morning, he'd left before she woke up. He'd
decided sometime in the early morning hours, with her
naked body snuggled into his, that he was a punk. He knew
his heart couldn't take waking up with her up against his

body. In fact, he was pretty sure if she looked at him again with those big doe eyes, he'd pledge to continue their affair in secret to be close to her.

"You're a punk."

Morgan's head whipped around to face a clearly disappointed Red. "What are you doing here, Red? Aren't you supposed to be filing some papers with the court or something?" He tossed an empty roll of packing tape in the trash can.

"It's bad enough you're taking the easy way out and leaving," Red said. "But you didn't have to sleep with her and then leave before she even woke up. What the hell is your problem?"

Feeling disgusted with himself, he shifted his attention to the junk drawer. "Look, I know I ain't shit. Tell me something I don't know." He rummaged around in the drawer, randomly tossing things into a small box.

"She doesn't want you to go."

He shrugged. "I know that, too."

"So why are you leaving?" Red shouted, throwing his hands up. "You know, we have a business opening in a week. Investments made, contracts signed."

"That's why you're my attorney. You can take care of all the business for me while I'm gone."

"She's a wreck."

He sighed. Leaving Syd was the hardest decision he'd ever make. He knew she was hurt, but he hated hearing it. "Don't you think this is hard on me, too? I don't want to leave. It's better if I do, though."

"Roc, I can't tell you what to do."

"Good," he said. "Glad you realize that."

Red walked over to him, tossed a pen in a box. "If both of you are miserable with the decision, why make it in the first place?"

"We're miserable anyway. What's the difference?"

When he'd been in Baltimore the last time—as much as he'd missed her—he'd felt a sense of peace there. He wasn't constantly looking over his shoulder to make sure Den wasn't lurking in the background. He wasn't planning elaborate ways to spend time with her on the sly. Most important, he wasn't envisioning pummeling his own brother to death.

"It's not like this isn't something I've been working toward a long time," Morgan continued. "You tell me: Would you pass up partner for guaranteed drama and isolation from the only family you've ever known?" Before Red could even answer him, he held up his hand. "Don't answer that. I already know what you'd do. You'd be on the first plane out of here. But you're too close to this to be objective. You're the only one more protective of Syd than I am."

"Hey, I wasn't going to deny that I'd do the same thing," Red conceded, stepping back with his palms up. "I was going to say you're better than me, though. Somewhere along the line, you've developed a conscience. I guess love does that for you. As career-driven as you are, you'd give it up in a minute if that meant you could be with her in the open— even if that means losing Den. Mama may not like it, but she's your mother. She'll love you no matter what. You know this. You're choosing to walk away because you're a punk."

Morgan shot a dark look at his best friend. "Get the hell out of here, Red."

The other man shrugged. "You know I tell it like it is. You implored *her* to fight for what you have together. But *you're* the one that's hightailing it out of here."

"You're right," he confessed. "I spent all this time trying to convince Syd to take a chance with me. Yet when it was all said and done, she's not the only one who's gun shy."

Red stood silently, arms crossed.

"Shit," Morgan muttered, pinching the bridge of his nose. "I fucked up. This was an impossible situation from the beginning. Can't do dirt and expect to come out clean. So I'm removing myself from the equation. Period."

* * *

Morgan sat alone in his living room, staring at the mounds of boxes stacked in every corner. Red had finally left, leaving him to his thoughts. He'd never expected to fall in love—especially with Sydney. But he had. Hard. And now he was choosing to walk away from her and everyone else he loved.

"Morgan?"

He closed his eyes. *I don't need this right now.* Taking a deep breath, he got up and opened the screen door. "Hi, Mama."

She embraced him. "What are you doing in here all by yourself? You should have your brothers over here helping you pack."

He pulled away, taking a huge bag that smelled like dinner from her. "I'm good. I kind of needed to be by myself right now."

"I'm sorry to interrupt then." She tilted her head, assessing him. "I wanted to make sure you were eating."

He eyed her. The years had been good to her. She was still a beautiful, youthful woman. But her eyes always betrayed her thoughts. She had something on her mind. He dismissed her apology. "I can never turn down a home-cooked meal from you. Come on in to the kitchen."

She dogged his heels as he walked toward the kitchen. Setting the bag on the countertop, he scrounged around for the plastic utensils he'd placed in one of the boxes. Once he located them, he opened the bag and sniffed the homemade roast beef and potatoes.

"Morgan?"

He glanced at her. "Thanks for this."

"Can you reconsider?" she asked, her chin trembling. "I know this is for your job and everything, but I don't know if it's worth leaving everything you love behind. I know I'm not your biological mother, but I love you like I birthed you. Are you sure you're making the best decision for yourself? We always tried to teach you that material things are not as important as family."

"Mama, I've thought long and hard about this." He picked up a piece of beef with his plastic fork and tasted it. "It's the best thing for me. And it's a short flight. If you need me, or if I need to come back, all you have to do is call."

"Is this because of Sydney?"

His eyes flashed to hers. *Uh-oh.* "What makes you ask me that?"

She shrugged and twisted the strap of her purse. His mother was a lot of things, but nervous was never one of them. "Correct me if I'm wrong, but you have feelings for her, don't you?"

He frowned, unsure how to respond to the question. "I— um...I'm not sure what you mean."

"I watch you. I watch all of my boys. Over the past few months, something's shifted between you all. Den is acting strangely. Kent is usually loud, but he's been uncharacteristically quiet lately. And Syd...she's been nervous, distracted—almost guilty. You've been hiding from us. I noticed your reaction during that family dinner a few weeks ago. You can barely be in the room with us. Son, if you have feelings for her, you can tell me. Or not. But don't leave behind everything you hold dear and run away from it."

He studied her for a minute. Her normally flawless skin was riddled with worry lines. Over the years, Mama had often taken on the burdens of the family, especially after

Papa died. She was the ultimate caregiver—gave them whatever she felt they needed at any time, even if it was something as small as cleaning their house when they got too busy to do it themselves. And now she was asking him for the truth and he was going to...

"Mama, I don't have feelings for Syd," he lied. "I'm making a career move. I feel like I need a change."

"You were always my honest boy, even if it got you in trouble." She gave him a loving smile. "You've never lied to me. Most of the time, you just avoid me." *She really had him down.* "So why are you lying to me now?"

CHAPTER THIRTY-ONE

Sydney wasn't surprised when Kent showed up at her house. She knew he'd be by eventually. What shocked her was that he'd been there for five minutes and hadn't uttered a single word.

Kent had never been the quiet one. But you wouldn't know it by watching him today. She waited for him to say something, anything to break the silence.

She shifted, wondering if she should finally make the first move to communicate.

"I guess..." he started, drawing her attention to him. His voice was low, calm. "When Roc told me he was moving, I told myself that he could have every intention of leaving but he'd end up staying because he would never leave you and his child. But I didn't say anything because I assumed he hadn't talked to you yet. Because if he did, he wouldn't be making this move right now. Well, you know what they say about making assumptions because I asked him if he'd told you yet. And he said he had shared the news with you the other day. He told me he came over here and talked to you, even spent the night. But he was still packing. Still preparing to uproot his life and move to another state."

"Kent, I—"

"Why didn't you tell him you're pregnant?" he bellowed.

She bristled at the outburst, suddenly wishing for the quiet Kent that had entered her home earlier.

"Please tell me you're going to say something before he leaves for good," he said.

She wrapped a hand around her neck and swallowed past the lump that had formed in her throat.

He watched her with a quiet intensity. "Well…?" he prompted.

"It's not that easy, Kent. I'm going to tell him."

"When? When he's on the Ohio Turnpike?" he shouted. "You have to say something."

She flinched. She could tell that his temper was dangling on a thin thread and she'd seen Kent pissed before. It was never something she'd thought she'd have to worry about being directed at her though. "I wanted to tell him, Kent. I wanted to, but I just couldn't. I haven't had this confirmed yet. He was…I mean, he's made the decision."

"But you can stop him. You're holding back important information."

"I can't do this to him," she said. "I can't tell him I'm pregnant if I don't know for sure. I don't want to ruin his life even more than I already have. He's doing this for himself."

"He's doing this for you," he said, the words clipped.

"If I tell him, he'll stay. And he'll be miserable."

"You can't make that decision for him, Syd."

"I'm going to tell him," she said. "I will."

"Soon," he warned. "Like before he sells his house."

She wrapped her arms around herself. Closing her eyes, she sucked in a deep breath. Leaning her bottom against the table, she said, "Kent, I wasn't going to keep it from him forever. You should know that. He made valid points for why it was best that he move. While I don't want him to go—and I told him this—if I tell him I'm having a baby, he'll change his mind. I'm just waiting until I know for sure. The doctors told me I'd never be able to carry a baby to term. What if I tell him—and he stays—only to find out that this was a false positive and I'm not really pregnant? What if I just have a fibroid or something and he turns down that job?"

"When will you find out?" he questioned.

"The doctor said she'd call me by tomorrow."

"What?" He groaned and muttered a curse. "Why so long?"

"I don't know," she said "It is a doctor's office. They close at a certain time. Maybe she knew the results wouldn't come back until they were already closed. Kent, please...don't tell him." She wanted to be the one to tell him. "Let me find out for sure, then I'll do it. I promise."

His eyes softened. "I hate lying to him, especially about something this big."

She lowered her eyes. "I know."

"He'll flip the script if he finds out I knew and didn't say anything."

"He won't," she assured him.

Kent stood up and approached her. "Okay. I'll hold off—for now. I need to go." He picked up his briefcase and headed for the front door. "I'll call and check on you later. Get some rest."

Before she could respond, he was gone. She glanced up at the ceiling. *Shit. Can things get any worse?*

* * *

The fifth of tequila gleamed like a beacon of light on the countertop. Sydney stared at it, willed herself to take the shot. One wouldn't hurt, right? She eyed the shot glass, filled to the rim with the amber liquid.

She'd spent the entire day holed up in the house, moping around in her pajamas, ignoring phone calls. Red had left at least ten messages demanding she call him back. Den had texted her numerous times. The only person she didn't hear from was the one person she needed to speak to. Morgan hadn't called or texted her. She'd considered calling him more than once, but decided against it.

Every part of her was screaming to stop this and take a stand, tell everyone the truth and damn the rest. *Can I really do that?*

The jingle of keys outside drew her attention to the door. Rolling her eyes, she guessed it was Red coming to ream her out for daring to ignore his calls. She heard the door open and scolded herself for giving a set of keys to her bossy twin brother.

"Phone off again?"

She turned quickly, caught off guard by Morgan's voice. "What? You're here? Why?"

"Red called." He tossed the keys on the table. "He's at a business meeting and he wanted me to come over and check on you since he can't get here. He told me to cuss your ass out for making him worry about you."

She swallowed and gave the tequila a sideways glance, wishing she could just take it. "I'm fine." She rolled her eyes. "I didn't feel like talking. I wish he would leave me alone."

He looked at the bottle on the counter and then back at her. He pointed to it. "Drinking alone?"

"Not really."

"Well, let me..." He picked up the shot glass, downed the contents, and slammed the glass back down on the counter. He gripped the edge of the counter and muttered a curse.

She raked her eyes over his frame. *God, I love him.*

She wanted to go to him. Needed to touch him, to have him touch her. She longed to hear him whisper that everything would be okay. More important, she wanted to beg him to stay with her, lock him in her room if she had to—forever.

At the same time, she knew he deserved better than her. She was still too scared to be with him the way he wanted. Not at that point. Eventually, though. She couldn't see herself being with anyone else. She knew she'd never love anyone the way she loved him.

"You okay?" he asked.

The question jarred her from her thoughts. "I'm...no."

He poured another shot and slid it over to her.

She shook her head, pushing the glass away. "I've had enough," she lied. Truth was if she wasn't possibly pregnant she'd have been two sheets to the wind a long time ago.

He narrowed his eyes, studied her face. "Sure?" he asked again. When she nodded, he picked up the glass and gulped it down. He drummed his fingers on the countertop and took a deep breath. "You know, this is the nicest breakup ever."

She snorted. "Tell me about it."

He glanced at her out of the corner of his eye. "Maybe it's because we're friends."

"Right. Best friends." She curled her nails into her palms.

"I better go. I'll tell Red I lit into you." He slipped out of the room.

She followed him, torn between outright begging him to stay and throwing herself on his back and tackling him to the ground. "Wait."

He stopped.

"Do you want to have dinner?" she asked, hating that she sounded so desperate. "I haven't eaten yet, and I was going to order Chinese."

He nodded. "Sure. I'll stay."

* * *

Morgan watched Syd clear the plates and load the dishwasher. They'd spent a rather comfortable evening eating Chinese food and pretending nothing had ever happened between them. That was the problem—things were too comfortable, considering his heart felt like a brick in his chest. Something *had* happened between them.

She glanced up at him as she dried her hands with a towel. "Thanks for staying. It was nice."

He nodded, watched as she made her way over to him. "I should go. It's getting late." Lord knew he didn't want to leave. She looked ripe for the picking. He let his gaze travel over her. She was a vision in hot pink. She wore a lightweight pair of cropped pants and a simple T-shirt. Her hair was a mass of loose waves on top of her head, her face red with a blush that seemed to be working its way up her neck and over her cheeks. She was fidgeting. *Is she nervous?*

When his gaze met hers, she was staring at him, mouth parted. His eyes dropped to her lips, lingered there. The air around them changed, sizzled. "Sydney…" His voice was low, husky. It sounded strange even to him.

"Yes," she breathed.

"You look warm. Are you warm, Sydney?"

She took a step back, retreated a bit.

Too late. Something else was controlling him now. And it wasn't nice, sweet, or tender. It was hot, dark, and rough. The voice that told him it was time to go was silent. He wanted her. But worse than that, he wanted her to want it as much as he did. He wanted her to beg for it—feel her tremble with need for him.

She turned her back to him and leaned against the table. He stepped into her, wrapped his arms around her waist, and splayed his hands against her stomach. He pressed down, loving the way her muscles constricted under his fingers.

"You didn't answer my question, Sydney." He heard her breath catch. "Are you warm?"

She nodded. "Hot…"

He leaned into her, lowered his head to her ear, and nipped at the lobe. "You smell so good. So beautiful. God, I love you. I don't know how I'm going to let you go."

"Please," she whimpered.

There it was: the magic word. He lifted her shirt over her head and pushed her pants down to the floor.

He trailed his hand up to the front of her bra and released the hook, letting it fall open. He traced the outline of her breasts, brushing his thumbs against her nipples. She was leaning into him now, arching her back against him. Next his fingers spanned her throat, felt her swallow. Turning her head toward him, he took her bottom lip in his.

He jerked her around to face him and plundered her mouth, hooking his hands behind her knees, lifting her up, and perching her up on the thick wood table.

She looked at him then, eyes wide and puzzled, and bit her lip. She opened her mouth to speak, but he placed a thumb over her lips.

"Don't," he commanded.

Heat radiated from her, blazed in her eyes and across her face. He grazed her cheek with the back of his hand, then around to the back of her neck. Wrapping a hand around the base, he tugged her to him and into an intense kiss.

When air became a problem, he broke the kiss and leaned his forehead against hers. Then he went back in for more, teasing her mouth open with his tongue. She opened up for him willingly. Her small fingers frantically unhooked his belt, unbuttoned his jeans, and pushed them down.

He dragged his lips down to the hollow of her throat, then

lower. Spurred on by the way her nails were digging into his biceps, he moved down further, snaked his tongue around her navel. Kissing his way back up, he took her mouth again.

His thumbs made lazy patterns up her inner thighs until he reached her core. Wanting to make sure she was ready, he slipped his fingers under the thin band of material and found her soft, swollen, and damp. She groaned and dropped her head to his shoulder as he stroked her. Gripping the small piece of fabric with his hand, he pulled roughly and ripped the cotton panties off, flinging them behind his back.

He laced his fingers with hers and entered her in one swift motion. She screamed his name as her first orgasm exploded around him. He gritted his teeth together, determined to hold on to his control.

As she fell over the edge, he watched her. She was glorious. He bit her earlobe. "That's right. Let go. I want you to remember who's making you feel this way."

She leaned back and let it take her over.

Once she stopped trembling, she peered at him through hooded eyes.

He swore under his breath and pushed himself deeper into her. Lifting her legs higher, he thrust in and out of her. He was sure his fingers would leave bruises on her hips, but he didn't care. He closed his eyes, savoring the moment.

They'd been together numerous times, but he could never get enough of her. He wanted this to last forever. Being inside her. Making love to her. He never wanted to let her go. Soon, he felt the trembling that signaled she was close, heard her soft moans as she begged him to keep going.

She twisted under him, letting her head fall back.

"Open your eyes," he ordered gruffly. "I want to look at you."

Her eyes opened and she came with a shrill scream, with him following soon after.

* * *

Sydney opened her eyes, still clinging to Morgan. She held on to him, not wanting to let go. Eventually, though, he pushed himself up on his forearms and smiled at her—a crooked, sexy smile.

When he pulled away from her, she immediately missed the connection. It was as if he were shutting down on her, not simply putting physical distance between them. She gripped his arm. "Stay," she whispered.

Her breath caught as his gaze dropped to her mouth. "I—"

"No." She feathered her fingers across his check. He gripped her hand gently, held it against his face. She shivered when she felt his lips press into her palm. "Morgan, stay. Please."

She felt uncertain—shaky. She suspected it was partly because she was naked and baring her body and soul to the one man who could destroy her.

She placed a hand over the hard muscles of his chest, over his heart. The steady beat soothed her, probably because it seemed to beat in time with her own.

She pulled him into an embrace, wrapping her arms tight around his neck. "I'll fix this. I will," she murmured against his ear. His arms circled around her, squeezing her.

"I wish you could," he said, his voice thick.

"I will," she assured him again.

He pulled away from her. "You can't." He pulled on his pants. "I better go. I'm sorry."

She blinked, his words still ringing in her ears. "Wait." She jumped off the table. "You're really going to leave? After everything we..."

"Syd, sex won't fix this. When it's done all our problems are still here."

She winced, feeling like he'd slapped her. Her hands immediately went up to cover her bare chest.

His eyes softened, flashed a sad smile. "I wish you could fix this. Maybe it wouldn't feel like someone ripped my heart right out of my chest. But I'm still leaving. You're still going to be here and Den is still going to be my brother. You know how I feel about you. That doesn't change. But... I can't stay here and pretend that everything is going to be okay in the morning when we both know it won't."

She told herself to breathe. Sniffling, she struggled to get control of her emotions. She wanted to say something, anything. But what could she say that would make this better? Nothing. Her shoulders slumped in defeat.

"If we continue like this, we won't be able to salvage our friendship. I don't want that."

"Me neither." She swallowed rapidly.

"So I'm going to go." He smoothed a hand over her hand. "I'll... We'll talk soon."

The door shut softly a few seconds later and she was left alone.

CHAPTER THIRTY-TWO

Sydney stared at her reflection in the mirror. It had been days since Morgan had seduced her with wet, deep kisses and deliberate touches. It'd been only seven days since he'd coaxed her into his arms, made her beg him for more. He'd cast a spell on her—left her open—and she'd loved every minute of it. Then he'd left.

Logically, she knew she shouldn't be angry. They had a lot of problems, and it wasn't all his fault. But damn it. She was an angry, scorned, and bitter woman.

She'd gone out of her way to avoid him, even going so far as to turn around and go the other way when she saw him at the mall the other day. She'd purposely scheduled a few last-minute meetings at times she knew would conflict with his work. He'd called her a few times, left messages asking if she was okay. She deleted them without a second thought, never even attempting to call him back. All in all, she was being petty—and emotional. But she was good with it.

With the opening of the Ice Box happening in the next hour, though, she had no choice. She'd have to face him.

"Look at you," Red said from behind her.

She hooked her earring in place and turned to him. It was the private opening of the bar. The grand opening for the public would take place tomorrow. She wore a floor-length, black gown with a plunging neckline. She smiled. "Think I look all right? I feel horrible."

"You're beautiful, sis. Morgan won't be able to keep his eyes off you tonight."

She shrugged. "I don't care. It doesn't matter anyway." Of course, she was lying. It definitely mattered to her what Morgan thought of her. In fact, she'd purchased the dress with him in mind a few weeks earlier—before...everything.

"Look, I'm not going to get in your business or anything."

"Really?" she said, sarcastically. "That's a switch."

"Okay, I hope you're going to leave your bitchy side at home. You don't need to bring her to the opening."

She scowled at him. "Shut up. Let's go."

"Maybe you two should talk about this some more," he continued. "I know it seems like you're at an impasse, but you never know..."

"Oh I know. Morgan made himself perfectly clear."

"He loves you, Syd." He peered at her in the mirror, a slight frown on his brow. "You know that."

"I do. But as I'm always reminded, love is often not enough. It wasn't enough with Den and it's not enough with Morgan."

"You're going to give up?"

"I wasn't the one who gave up. He pursued me. Then *he* walked away."

"Maybe you didn't fight hard enough. *You* didn't show him that you were going to make this work. Did you even ask him to stay?"

"Actually, I did. I begged him to stay." She swallowed, flashing back to her standing in front of him—with no clothes on—pleading with him to stay with her. She shook her head in an effort to clear her mind of the picture. "He still left. So what is there to say, Red?"

"Did you beg him to stay with you that night? Or did you make it clear that you were asking him to stay period?"

I hate him sometimes. It was just like him to point out that she wasn't exactly clear with what she was asking Morgan. But when she'd told him she'd fix things, she'd assumed he understood what she meant when she'd asked him to stay with her.

"Syd?"

She glared at her brother. "Red, you don't understand. What else can I do? I can't force him to stay with me."

He sighed. "Why haven't you answered his calls?"

"I'm ignoring him right now."

"Real mature."

"Luckily, I don't care what you think." She nodded tightly and slipped her bracelet on. "I realize that you've left plenty of women bare and begging for you, but I've never had that happen to me before. So excuse me if I'm a little irritated even though I probably don't have a reason to be."

"You know he didn't do it to hurt you. He's doing what he thinks is best."

"What do you want me to say, Red?" She picked up a piece of tissue and dabbed the makeup under her eyes. "You know I'm dramatic. You're so quick to point it out all the time."

"How about you're pregnant?"

Her body stiffened. "What?" Her hand went up to her throat. "What are you—?"

"You didn't even tell me," he said. "I've been waiting, wondering how long you'd keep this up."

She wondered how the hell he'd found out. She hadn't even told Cali yet. "Why didn't you—?"

"I figured you were waiting on the right time," he continued as if she hadn't spoken. "But then the days ticked by and you kept your mouth shut. Morgan hasn't changed his plans, so I assume he doesn't know."

"But—I . . ."

"Are you insane, Sydney?" he asked.

"What?" She jerked her head back. "Don't call me insane, Red."

"Do you really think it's a good idea to hide this from him?"

"I'm not hiding anything," she said, her hand splayed across her chest "And how did you—"

"Kent called."

Traitor. "When did he call you?" Not that it mattered. Kent had said he wouldn't tell Morgan. He'd never promised he wouldn't tell Red. She still wanted to know, though.

"Don't be mad at him." He shoved a hand in his pocket. "He didn't mean to tell me. It slipped out."

She folded her arms across her chest and wished Kent was there so she could kick the shit out of him.

"Syd, please tell me I'm right about you," Red said. "Please tell me that you're not intentionally holding back this information to get back at him for leaving you."

She gaped at him. "I would never do that to Morgan."

"Then why is he still leaving when you're pregnant with his baby?"

She hurried to the door, cursing along the way. "I don't have time for this shit. As usual, you have the worst timing. We have to go."

He caught her arm, tightened a hand around it. "Syd, you can't let him leave without knowing about his baby."

She yanked her arm out of his hold. "I don't know that I'm really pregnant. The blood tests came back inconclusive, so the doctor wants to schedule an ultrasound to verify. With the bar opening, I couldn't get by there this week. Why should I tell him something that I don't even know—" She held her hand up, shaking her head quickly. "Wait a minute, why do I even have to explain myself to anyone? You should know me better than that." She shoved him—hard. "Get out of my way."

"You know how I feel about this," he grumbled.

"Yeah, I know. That's why I'm hurt that you would even think I'd do that to Morgan after what she did to you. I'd never keep him away from his child. But right now, I need a little time to get things confirmed with the doctor."

"He wouldn't be making these plans if you would fight."

"I—" She lifted her chin. "Red, you don't know what you're talking about."

"I know that you're hell-bent on trying to protect Den."

"I'm leaving."

Before he could argue, she tucked her purse under her arm and walked out.

* * *

The Ice Box was beautiful, Sydney thought as she walked around the open room. She ran a hand over the bar. Her dream had become a reality. She glanced around, smiling at the people mingling and toasting their opening with champagne-filled flutes. Although her personal life was in shambles, her professional life had definitely taken a turn for the better.

She strolled to the other side of the room, taking in the huge fur-covered couches in the corners and the LED lighting that lit up the floor. She marveled at the special bar made of ice that Red had commissioned for the opening. People were lined up to get their cocktails. The world seemed right.

Blue up-lighting set the mood and crystals hung from the ceiling like icicles. They had continued the tradition of selling private booths to VIP customers. Each booth was set against the wall with sheer white draping canopied above. There were lit, high-top tables closest to the bar. In addition, there were sections of lit lounge furniture close to the dance floor. Calisa had done a fabulous job of making it feel like they were hidden inside an igloo for the opening.

· The press was there, snapping photos of everything and everyone in attendance. She guessed it paid to know someone at the local television station. Kent had done work for them and they'd happily agreed to come out to cover the opening. Also in attendance was one of the talented hosts of a radio morning show, along with a top deejay in the city.

Sydney had managed to avoid Morgan for most of the night, except for the times they'd had to pose for pictures. They all worked the room, networking and plugging the business in their own ways.

"Sydney?" Kent called, approaching her.

Her eyes remained trained on one of the pieces of art Calisa had brought in.

"Sydney?" he repeated. "Are you going to ignore me all night?"

"I'm not ignoring you. I'm minding my own business."

"Okay, I should've kept my mouth shut." Kent folded his arms in front of his chest. "Red told me that you two had it out."

She glared at him. "You get on my nerves," she hissed. "How could you? I trusted you. And you told Red of all people."

He shrugged. "I assumed he knew. There's not much about you he doesn't know."

"Get out of my way. I have people to greet."

"How did Morgan take the news?" he asked.

She folded her arms across her chest. "He doesn't know. And if you could keep your mouth shut for more than two seconds, I'd appreciate it. Like I told Red, the doctor still has not confirmed it. Leave it alone."

He frowned. "Why not just tell him about the possibility?"

"Look, I'll tell him when I'm ready!" She glanced around the room, embarrassed that she'd raised her voice. She rubbed the back of her neck, frustrated that she couldn't seem to keep her emotions in check. The last thing she needed was for the reporters to catch her having a nervous breakdown—or to see her kicking someone's ass in the middle of the opening. "I don't want to talk about this tonight. It's not the right time."

He stepped closer to her and leaned in. "Sorry. I won't bring it up again. I want you to—"

"Be happy?" she asked. She was so tired of everyone saying they just wanted her to be happy. "Yeah, I know. That's what every man tells me. You know what? I'm not happy. In fact, I'm angry. I'm bitter. I'm irritated. And I was trying to enjoy the opening of *my* bar with *my* family before I have to possibly drop the bombshell of the century and lose everything. Okay?"

He frowned and gripped her hand. "Why are you so angry? What's going on with you—besides the obvious?"

She closed her eyes and took a deep breath. "Morgan is leaving. He's moving to Baltimore. And it's because of me. I begged him to stay, but he's still leaving. Red said I should've made myself clear to him, but I thought he got it. In fact, I'm pretty sure he did. Now, if you'll excuse me, I have to go mingle."

CHAPTER THIRTY-THREE

Morgan watched as Kent walked away from Syd, slurring some mess about becoming an alcoholic when he walked past him. He wondered what they'd been talking about. They'd been huddled up in a corner having a heated conversation. He'd managed to avoid Den and Mama all night, except for the awkward family picture Mama made them take.

The party was in full swing, people milling around. Laughter in the air, alcohol being poured. An overwhelming success.

He glanced at Syd, who was now chatting with Calisa and Allina. Everything else seemed to fade away, all the people around him seemed to disappear. He only saw her. The way she glided across the floor, greeted the guests. She wasn't even near him and he could smell her. His fingers ached to touch her.

Forcing himself to focus on something else, he scraped a nail on the rim of his glass. This night was turning into a disaster. Instead of being proud of the accomplishment, he'd been sitting at the bar—and not even the special one made of ice that everyone else was congregating next to. He motioned to the bartender, asking for two shots of Hennessy Black.

"Anything else?" the bartender asked.

"No." He eyed the glass in front of him, wondering if it was enough. "Leave the bottle," Morgan grumbled.

When she'd breezed into the bar earlier that evening, he couldn't help but wish she was walking in on his arm. She was beautiful. The floor-length dress hugged her curves like a second skin. The low cut of the front made him want to drop to his knees and beg her to put him out of his misery. It was bad enough that she was showing that much skin in the front, but when she turned around...the dress was backless. Her long, toned legs peeked out of two slits on each side. He couldn't help it. He'd let his gaze travel the length of her frame in slow motion, from the fuck-me stilettos all the way up to her flawless face.

Although she wasn't the type to wear a lot of makeup, when he noticed the dark smoky look around her eyes that made her eye color pop, he found it hard to keep his gaze off of her. She was radiant. Everything about her called to him. And when she walked past him, he was hit with her sweet perfume—that scent that drove him crazy—Vera Wang or something like that.

He'd already told himself that he was going to stay clear of her, but when she looked at him and said "Hey" in that low, husky tone she only used when she wanted him to do her...

He shook his head to clear his mind. *Damn*. She was going to ruin him.

"Are you okay?" Syd was standing in front of him, a concerned look in her hazel eyes.

He stilled, glad that she'd stopped ignoring him.

"Morgan, are you okay?" Syd asked, leaning in close to him. "You look like you're...is everything all right?"

Don't look at her. "I'm good," he lied.

Her arm wrapped around the back of his seat and he inhaled slowly. "If you say so. There are a few people who'd like to meet you. Do you want to . . . ? Or—"

"Who?" he asked softly. "Someone from the press?"

She shook her head and giggled nervously. "No, a couple of my friends from work. I talk about everyone all the time and they want to put a face to a name."

He peered at her then. "You're beautiful."

She averted her gaze and nibbled on her bottom lip. He wanted to kiss her. "Morgan—"

"You've been avoiding me all night," he said.

Her eyes widened. "I—"

"I don't like it."

"I'm sorry." She smoothed a hand over her stomach. "I was—"

"You don't have to explain. I was just telling you how I felt."

She bowed her head and before he could stop himself, he gently grabbed a loose curl that had fallen out of the twist she wore. He rubbed his thumb over the soft strand of hair, loving the way it felt against his skin.

She peered up at him. "We need to talk, Morgan," she whispered.

He nodded. "You want to go in the back?"

She straightened and backed away from him slowly. Shaking her head, she tapped a finger on the bar. "I don't think that's a good idea. But later? Maybe I'll come by your house."

Before he could respond, the bartender was there asking if they needed anything. *He's fired.* He glared at the clueless idiot as he gushed over Syd and offered to get her something to drink. She politely declined, but giggled softly when the guy promised to make sure she was taken care of.

Sydney placed a hand on top of his and squeezed, obviously sensing his aggravation. She then told Peter—the stupid-ass bartender—that she would like a bottle of water.

When Peter scurried to a small cooler to grab the water, she turned to him. "He's nice. Don't scare him away."

As far as he was concerned, Peter wasn't scared, though. He was standing right there—again, with a stupid grin. Morgan noticed the way the man looked her up and down like she was on display for his eyes. And when he asked her if she needed anything else...

"She's good," Morgan grumbled between clenched teeth. "Don't you have someone else you can serve?"

Peter finally looked at him, swallowing roughly. "Uh-I," he stammered. "I'll get to it."

Morgan cursed under his breath and finished off his drink. He rolled his neck to relieve the tension that had set in. If he didn't get a chance to punch something, he was liable to blow. He cracked his knuckles.

She placed a hand on his shoulder and squeezed. "Are you sure you're okay, Morgan?"

He groaned, taking in her scent. "You look good."

The glow of a blush crept up her neck. "Morgan," she whispered. "Stop." She frowned. "Are you drunk?"

"No," he said. *Not yet.*

She picked up the bottle. "Are you going to drink all of this?"

He shook his head and slid a hand over her hip, unable to keep himself from touching her.

She shifted. "Don't do that."

"That dress..." His gaze dropped to the low vee and he reached out to finger the curve, but thought better of it and dropped his hand into his lap. "I can't take my eyes off of you."

The blush rose up to her cheeks. "I bought it for you," she admitted softly.

"You chose the right one." He squeezed her thigh and she gasped. He leaned in and whispered, "Makes me want to do things to you, a lot of things. All night."

"You're making me want to let you," she replied, a seductive smile on her face. Clearing her throat, she eased back a step. "But I don't think that's wise, considering we're not..."

"Together," he finished. "I want you, though. That hasn't changed."

She smiled. "Well, Morgan, sometimes we can't have everything we want, right?"

He leaned back in the chair and picked up his glass, staring at her over the rim. "I guess not. You better be careful."

"How so?"

"It goes both ways. But keep tempting me, and I'll get what I want. Then all hell will break loose."

* * *

Sydney placed a hand over her stomach. Morgan was staring at her like she was a steak dinner. And he was definitely too close. He'd made it clear that he wanted her. But she'd thrown his famous line back at him. Sometimes we can't have everything we want.

Then he'd issued a challenge, of sorts. But he was right. It did go both ways. And Lord help her, she wanted him. His voice, his hands, his...

She hated him.

"I think I should walk away right now," she said, her voice shaky.

"It still won't stop you from thinking about what I said," he teased.

"You won't even remember what you said if you keep tossing back drinks like there's no tomorrow."

"Oh I'm good." He winked at her. "And you know it."

"Shut up," she mumbled. "I hate you."

"No, you love me. That's the problem. No matter how many times we break up, we're always going to end up back in this place. That's why you know I'm doing the right thing by leaving."

She rolled her eyes. "I don't know shit, Morgan. And I don't care."

He snorted.

Asshole. "I'm going to walk away and leave you appreciating this dress..." She ran a hand over her hip, enjoying the way his eyes followed her movements. "And then you're going to go home—by yourself—and wish I was with you so you could do those *things* you're imagining."

When his gaze dropped to her mouth, she sucked in a deep breath. "Shut up." He leaned closer. She closed her eyes. They were only inches away from each other. So close she felt his breath on her lips.

"What's going on over here?" Kent said, stumbling into Syd.

She braced herself on the bar. "Oh God, Kent."

Morgan reached out and gripped her elbow, helping her get her balance.

Kent tapped the bar, motioning for Peter. "Bring me a bottle of champagne. We're supposed to be celebrating here."

Sydney glanced at Morgan out of the side of her eye. Only he wasn't looking at her anymore. He was too busy pouring himself a healthy glass of Hennessey. *Drunk asshole.*

Kent wrapped an arm around her and pulled her into a semi-choke hold, taking her by surprise. She pushed at his arms, scowling at the smell of liquor on his breath. Morgan wasn't the only one hitting the bottle. "Kent, you're drunk as hell. What is up with you and Morgan? This is our opening night."

Kent hunched his shoulders. "I'm not drunk, Syd. I'm having a good time. We should probably have a toast, though," he announced when Peter came back with a bottle of Moët. "Before everything gets blown to hell," he added under his breath.

"What are you talking about?" she asked.

"You have an audience," he muttered, pointing to the other side of the bar. "Mom and Den have been watching this little dance you're doing over here with Morgan. I'm doing Red a favor and breaking this up so he doesn't have to."

"Red sent you over here?" Syd asked, scanning the room for her brother, who was conveniently missing.

"Well, technically, he didn't. But I took pity on him because he just got clocked in the eye by your BFF," he slurred.

Morgan gaped at him. "Cali gave him a black eye?" He burst out in laughter and Kent joined him.

She smacked both of them. "Stop it," she hissed. "This isn't funny."

"Neither is watching the two of you practically..." Kent shrugged. "I don't know what the hell you're doing over here."

"We weren't doing anything," Morgan said. "We're just talking."

Kent shot him a look of disbelief. "Yeah, right. I saw you grip her ass."

She gasped. "He didn't..." Frustrated with the whole scene, she thumped him on the cheek.

Kent flinched and rubbed it. "What the hell was that for?"

"For being a jackass," she said. "He didn't grip my butt."

"I wanted to," Morgan admitted.

Her eyes flashed to his. "This is unbelievable. You two are done. I'm going to tell Peter to hold your liquor for the rest of the night. If I can't drink, neither of you can."

"Why can't you drink?" Morgan asked.

"Oh boy," Kent grumbled.

She pinched her friend—hard. "There's too much riding on tonight so I don't want to get sloshed in the middle of it."

"Ouch." Kent rubbed his arm. "Okay. I'll slow down."

She eyed Morgan. "Don't look at me like that," she hissed.

Morgan shrugged. "What?" he asked innocently. "Damn, I can't look at you now."

"Not like that. And not here." She closed her eyes and took a deep breath. "Please, chill out. The last thing we need is a scene."

When she turned to leave, she stopped in her tracks. Den was stomping toward them.

"What the hell is going on over here?" Den demanded.

She struggled to find words, taken aback by the fury in Den's eyes. He glared at all three of them. She glanced at Morgan and Kent, who were both staring back at him with wide eyes.

"No response, huh?" Den asked, a deep frown on his face. "Am I talking to myself?"

"What is your problem, Den?" Morgan asked. "Why are you over here starting shit?"

"Right," Syd said, stepping between them. "I told these fools to cool it on the drinking. I don't need you coming over here causing a scene. Don't do this here."

"Do what?" he shouted. "You're the one letting him fawn all over you like I'm not even in the room."

"We're talking," Morgan said in an even tone. "In whose world is talking a crime?"

"That's not talking," Den grumbled. "That's foreplay. Damn it! You get on my fuckin' nerves!" he roared, jabbing his finger at them. "You and Syd, in your own little world. You've disrespected me for the last time."

Morgan grunted and waved him off. "Whatever, Den. As usual your timing fuckin' sucks. This is a party—our opening night. And here you are, storming over here like we broke the law. Yet I'm the one disrespecting you?"

Syd glanced around the party, searching for Red. This

couldn't happen. Someone needed to get Den the hell out of there.

"You think I don't know?" Den sneered, nostrils flaring. He snickered. "I've seen the looks. You and Kent both look at her like she's yours."

"Me?" Kent asked, throwing his hands up in the air. "What the hell do I have to do with this? Syd's like my sister..." He hiccupped. "And my sister looks damn good in that dress."

Syd lowered her head. "Oh God," she whispered, rubbing her temples. "Kent, go sit down somewhere."

"Yes, Kent, sit down," Den warned, pointing at him. "See what I mean?"

"Damn, I was just kidding. Trying to lighten the mood." Kent plopped down in the closest chair.

"Caden, what's going on over here?" Mama asked softly, putting her hand on his arm.

"Stay out of this, Ma," Den ordered. "This is between me and Morgan."

Morgan grunted. "I don't have a problem. Obviously you do."

"Hell yeah," Den roared. "And don't act like you don't know what my problem is."

"Boys, what's going on?" Mama repeated.

Den rolled his eyes, groaning. "Ma, why don't you let me talk to my brother? Why can't I talk to Morgan or Syd without their team of supporters jumping in like I'm going to kill them or something?"

Mama coughed, clearing her throat. "Well, you're causing a scene and I..." She mumbled under her breath.

"I don't give a fuck about a scene!" Den blared. Mama gasped and stepped back. "I'm sorry, Ma. I'm...frustrated."

Kent jumped up. "Have you lost your mind?" he asked, his words clipped. "Don't yell at Mama like that. Drunk or not, I'll beat the shit out of you."

Syd's eyes flashed to Den. He *was* drunk. She hadn't noticed before, but now she took a good look at him, noting his wild eyes and jerky movements.

"I'm not the one who's lost their mind," Den snarled. "Morgan has, especially if he thinks I'm stupid." His attention shifted to Syd. "If both of you think I'm stupid."

Syd retreated a step.

Morgan stood up finally, straightening to his full height. "If you have a problem with me, say that shit. Don't take it out on anyone else. If not, get the fuck out of my face."

"Morgan, stop," Syd begged. "Let it go. We can talk about this later."

Morgan and Syd exchanged glances and he sat back down. "Fine. I'll let it go."

"You're so full of shit, Roc," Den growled.

"Fuck you," Morgan sneered. "I'm not getting into this here."

Syd was relieved when Red stepped into the circle. "Can you please keep it down?" he asked. "Luckily, I showed the last of the reporters out. But we still have guests. This is a place of business. This isn't the time for this bullshit."

"Whatever, Red," Den snarled. "I don't care what you have to say."

"You'll care when I beat the shit out of you," Red retorted. "I don't know what the hell is going on over here, but it's time to chill out."

"Maybe the reason you don't know what's going on is because this is none of your business. This is between me and my *brother*."

CHAPTER THIRTY-FOUR

Syd gripped the back of Morgan's chair and scanned the room. She was grateful most of the guests had already left and the ones who were still around were gathering their things. Calisa and Allina were standing close by watching the scene unfold.

She was mortified things had taken such a turn for the worse. She sighed. *What a disaster.*

Her stomach twisted into a knot. "Let's take a step back, okay? The guests are leaving. We can deal with this later," she said, praying the fellas would go back to their respective corners and play nice.

She turned on her heels and headed toward her girls, but Den grabbed her, tightening an arm around her wrist. "Syd, wait. We need to talk. Now."

She struggled to get out of the hold, but felt weak. "Not now, Den."

Out of the corner of her eye, she saw Morgan stand up again. He glowered at Den. And she suddenly felt sick. The tension was palpable. A different energy swirled around them.

"When will there ever be a right time? Don't you think you owe me the truth? Mama said there was a misunderstanding between you and Morgan. What the hell happened?"

She jerked her arm away, stumbling back a step. Then Allina was there, her hand on the small of her back. She flashed her friend a sad smile before turning to Den. "I don't know what you're talking about. What misunderstanding?"

Mama cleared her throat, gaining everyone's attention. "I told you it was nothing, Den. There's nothing to worry about."

One of her co-workers waved to her from across the bar as she left. Syd forced herself to smile back, offering her a half-hearted good-bye. "What's the problem, Mama?" she asked Mama Smith.

The older woman swallowed visibly and sighed. "Morgan admitted to me that he has feelings for you."

Syd's head whipped around to face Morgan, who lowered his head and muttered a curse. *Oh God. Oh shit.* She flattened one hand on the table next to her as a wave of dizziness swept over her.

"But," Mama continued, "he told me that you found out and things have been uncomfortable since then between you. That it's part of the reason he figured moving out of state would be best."

Syd recoiled as if Mama had slapped her. Leaning against a chair, she steadied herself and peered over at Morgan, who hung his head. He'd thrown himself under the bus—for her. Again. "No," she whispered, her voice raspy.

"I'm sorry," Mama said, lowering her gaze. "I probably shouldn't have said anything here."

"It's not your fault," Sydney managed to say. "You didn't do anything wrong. I—"

As she stepped toward the older woman—her second

mother—she felt a strange sensation rush at her. She closed her eyes, cringing at the headache that seemed to come out of nowhere. She seemed to heat up from the inside—like someone had perched her up on a burning stove. She opened her mouth to speak, but nothing would come out and suddenly she couldn't catch her breath. As she gazed over at Mama, everything seemed to lose color. She reached out to grab something—anything. Vaguely, she heard someone calling her name. Then everything went black.

* * *

The shit has finally hit the fan. When Mama had called him on lying about his feelings for Sydney, he'd told her part of the truth. He'd admitted that he had feelings for Syd, but he'd made it seem like it was his cross to bear. That he'd told Syd he had feelings for her, but she'd shot him down. And now they were all uncomfortable around each other because of it. He'd also explained to her that, even though that wasn't the sole reason for moving, he figured it was better if he removed himself from the situation.

And now Mama had told Syd. Morgan watched as Syd's eyes glazed over. She swayed back—and before he could get to her, she fell to the floor like a pile of wet clothes.

He heard Red yell her name, but he was already on the move, rushing toward her. He dropped to his knees next to her limp body.

"Call an ambulance!" Red shouted.

Morgan touched her forehead, then her neck. He placed two fingers under her ear lobe to feel for a pulse. *Thank God.* He reached out and smoothed her hair away from her face, trailing his fingers over her cheek.

"Is she breathing?" Red asked.

He nodded, still focused on her face. Sliding an arm

under her head, he propped her up on his lap. He used his other hand to feel the back of her head.

"She hit her head," he murmured, running a finger over a knot on the back of her skull. He shook her gently, barely registering the frantic voices around him. The only voice he needed to hear was hers. "She must have bumped it against the chair on the way down."

Red swore under his breath.

Morgan shot Red a wary glance before turning his attention back to her. He nudged her again, hoping to get a response. "Syd? Wake up, baby. Come on. Open your eyes."

Her arm fell to the ground limply. Her lips parted slightly. She moaned.

"Syd?" he called again, willing her to open her eyes.

Her eyes fluttered and she clutched her stomach, letting out another low moan.

"Shit," Red said.

The paramedics charged into the bar only a few minutes later, making a beeline for them.

Then Kent was standing next to him, tugging his arm. "Roc, come on. Let them do their thing."

He gently set her head down and stood up, allowing the paramedics to tend to her. He heard Red answering a whole slew of their questions. He wanted to demand they hurry up and get her to the hospital.

"Is there a chance she could be pregnant?" he heard the man ask.

"No," Den answered.

Morgan's eyes snapped up in time to catch the look that passed over Red's face. Red hooked a hand around the back of his neck and glanced over at Kent, who shook his head and muttered a curse.

Red nodded slightly. "Yes," he murmured in a low voice.

Morgan stilled; his gaze dropped to Syd. They'd hoisted

her up and she was stretched out on the gurney. Her neck was secure in a brace. His eyes were fixated on her face. She whimpered, this time like she was in pain. But she hadn't opened her eyes yet. He needed her to open them. He begged her silently to sit up and cuss them out for calling the ambulance.

She frowned and her eyes fluttered. He stepped closer, but they wheeled her out of the room before he could reach her.

Kent nudged him. "Let's go, Roc."

Morgan snapped into action, pulling his keys out of his pocket and following them out the door.

* * *

Syd frowned, lifting a hand up to her forehead. Her head was pounding. She opened her eyes slowly, and tried to regain her focus. Bare walls. Bright light. White everything. Beeping sound. *Hospital?*

She sat up straight, wincing as her head throbbed. Unable to stand the pain, she fell back and groaned.

"Syd?"

Her eyes snapped open. Red was standing over her. "Red," she rasped. "What happened? Why am I here?"

"You fainted," he replied, his face etched with concern. "And hit your head."

She stiffened on a sharp intake of breath. "What's wrong with me?"

"You're fine," he assured her, "and so is the baby."

"What?"

"I heard the heartbeat. It's strong. Your doctor should be in to explain things to you."

She burrowed into the mattress and let out a deep breath. "At least I know for sure now." Her chin quivered and she felt tears well up in her eyes. "Does Morgan?"

He shook his head. "No. But everyone's in the lobby, waiting to see you. I had to tell the paramedics that you could be pregnant and Den's been making a big deal out of it since we got here."

She moistened her lips. "Can I have some water?"

"I'll ask the nurse."

"Can you tell Morgan I want to talk to him?"

* * *

The hospital seemed deserted. They'd all gathered in the emergency department waiting area. Morgan paced the floor with long steps, trying to shake the image of Sydney collapsing to the hard floor. Something else was bothering him, too. It was normal procedure for EMTs to ask about a possible pregnancy. Of course, they'd want to know if they were caring for two instead of one. For all Red knew, Syd could be pregnant. It wasn't the question; it was the way Red had looked. Nervous. Off.

Then there was Kent. They'd driven to the hospital together. The ride was quiet, which was to be expected, but Kent never even looked at him. Didn't say a word.

When they'd stormed into the ER, Red was standing at the registration desk checking her in. His best friend was nothing if not direct, so it was surprising that he avoided Morgan. Even then, as they'd waited for an update, Red had not said anything to him. In fact, he'd gone out of his way not to.

He'd watched a nurse approach Red earlier, and soon after Red followed her through the doors into the restricted area.

Morgan pressed two fingers to his temple and released a heavy sigh. He stretched his neck to the right and rolled it back to the left. Calisa and Allina were seated nearby, worried looks on their faces. Den and Mama sat on the other side of the room. Mama's arms were wrapped around Den, hugging him.

Morgan's jaw was clenched, his nostrils flared. Annoyance shot through him like a bolt of lightning as he replayed the moments leading to her passing out in his head. His eyes narrowed, he studied Den as he let Mama console him like he was the injured party. Den had told the paramedics that there was no chance of Syd being pregnant. Syd had told him nothing had happened between them, and now he knew it to be true. Flashes of Syd lying on the ground rushed back to him—strands of her hair clinging to her cheek, her face pale. He checked his watch. *Somebody better tell me something soon.*

Red appeared in front of them after a while. He shoved his hands into his pockets. "She's okay."

The group let out a collective sigh. Hugs were given, prayers of thanks sent up. Red still wouldn't look at him.

"The doctors said she was dehydrated and that's why she fainted. She did hit her head," Red continued, "but it's not a concussion. She's awake."

Relieved, Morgan let out a slow breath.

"Can I go see her?" Den asked, starting toward the nurse's station.

Red held out a hand, stopping him. "Not yet." He looked at Morgan. "She wants to talk to you."

CHAPTER THIRTY-FIVE

Syd waited. Red had left the room a few minutes earlier after she'd asked him to get Morgan. She shifted and pushed the button on the side of the bed, lifting herself up into a sitting position.

She smoothed a hand over her stomach. "Hang in there," she mumbled to the baby. "It's going to be okay."

Closing her eyes, she wondered how she was going to say this. Come right out and tell him? Or ease him into the idea?

A soft knock on the door snapped her out of her thoughts. Morgan poked his head into the room. "Syd?"

She smiled. "Morgan, come in."

He entered the room, shutting the door behind him.

She motioned him over to the chair next to the bed. "Want to sit down?"

He paused, looking uncertain.

"Please?" She extended a hand. "Come sit."

He watched her with questioning eyes. "Are you good?" he finally asked.

She nodded, struggling to find the right words.

She'd felt a lot of things around Morgan, but awkward

wasn't one of them. Before she could ask him what he was thinking, he closed the distance between them and his mouth was on hers.

The kiss was so tender, she wanted to weep. Her hands fisted on the lapels of his suit jacket. He nipped at her bottom lip, traced the corners of her mouth with his tongue and she opened for him. The feel of his mouth pressed against hers, his tongue sliding around hers, one hand splayed over her heart, and the other cupping her cheek, seemed to flip on a switch inside her chilled body. His presence seemed to engulf her, warming her to the tips of her fingers and toes.

He pulled away slowly, and her eyes fluttered open. "You scared the shit out of me," he mumbled against her mouth. He placed another soft kiss on her lips and quickly retreated to the other side of the room. She immediately missed him.

"I'm sorry," she whispered.

He looked at her, his gaze steady. "You good?" he repeated.

"The doctors said I was dehydrated and that's why I fainted. They want to keep me overnight."

"Um." His was a voice unsure, shaky.

"I don't have a concussion," she added, wringing her hands. "And..." *This is it.*

"You're pregnant," he said.

Her eyes snapped to his, shocked that he knew. Panic coursed through her at that point. Who could have told him? Did everyone know? "How—?"

"I saw the ultrasound machine outside the door," he explained.

She closed her eyes, sighing with relief.

"And it's shift change," he said. "A nurse out there was telling her replacement that the baby's heartbeat was strong and the OB-GYN ordered additional blood tests."

"Oh." She twisted the sheet between her fingers, unsure how to respond. "I—"

"It wasn't a shock, though. I had pretty much figured it out." He continued on as if she hadn't spoken. "Once I heard them talking, everything fell into place. You seemed to be preoccupied. Then there was the pizza."

"I always eat pizza."

"The throwing up..."

"But the test was negative," she pointed out.

"The tequila at your house... You hadn't even touched it. You wouldn't drink at the bar tonight either."

"It was the opening."

He studied her quietly and her stomach churned. He didn't look angry, but she couldn't be sure.

"Say something," he said finally.

"Like what?" she asked, stalling.

His gaze was fixed on hers. "Why?"

"Why am I pregnant?"

He sighed. "You've known for a while. The looks between Red and Kent tell me they know, too. So why don't you start with why they know and I didn't?"

"Well—" she said slowly.

"And end with why the hell you didn't tell me when you first found out?" he demanded.

"I didn't know for sure until tonight," she mumbled, unable to meet his gaze. She ran a hand through her hair.

"Were you ever going to tell me?"

Reflex had her looking down at her chest, searching for the dagger he'd just sunk into her heart. "I'm not even going to answer that." She sucked in a deep breath, determined not to shed another tear. She'd cried entirely too much over the past several weeks.

"I'm sorry," he grumbled. "I didn't mean that. I'm wondering why I had to find out about my baby from a damn nurse."

"I told you; I didn't know for sure. I had that negative test, and then I had a positive test. They ran a blood test and the results were inconclusive. Dr. Long mentioned false positives and she wanted to be sure. I was supposed to go for an ultrasound this week, but it was too hectic. But I wanted to tell you. I did. Not just because you're the father, but because you're my friend. I wanted to tell you that there was a possibility, but that was the night you told me about the job offer."

"Sydney, I took a job in another state!" he yelled. "I packed my shit up. I was going to sell my house. When were..." He pinched the bridge of his nose. "You couldn't have told me about the positive test? Even if you weren't sure, you should've told me."

She grimaced. "I wasn't sure if it was... You know the doctors told me I'd never be able to get pregnant in the first place. Once you told me you were moving, I figured it might be best to be certain before I told you. You'd finally made a decision—your job is very important to you—and I didn't want to ruin any of the plans you made."

"That doesn't even sound right," he barked. "Ruin my plans? My plans were already shot to hell when I chose to be with you in the first place."

"I was going to tell you tonight," she whispered. His eyes flashed to hers, hurt laced in them. She swallowed.

"Is this..." He closed his eyes, exhaled. "Did you really do this to protect Den?"

She shook her head. "No. I wasn't thinking about Den at all. I was more concerned about you. I didn't want to keep hurting you. You're moving to get away from me."

"I'm moving away *for* you," he said.

The only sound in the room was the ticking from the old wall clock hanging above the door.

"Despite what Red or Kent or even you may think of me, I would *never* keep you from your child," she told him. "I wanted to make sure this was real before I destroyed your life even more than this relationship already has.

"And don't be mad at Kent or Red," she continued. "I asked them not to tell you. I wanted to be the one to tell you."

"I know you would never keep me away from my child, Sydney," he said. "I want to be mad at you. Most times I want to throttle you. But before we were *this*...we were friends. I trust that." He sat down on the edge of the bed. "So, what now?"

She shrugged. "I don't know."

"This changes everything," he said. "I'm not going to act like you're not pregnant with my baby."

She didn't expect him to. Her plan was to tell the rest of them herself as soon as she got out of the hospital.

"We have to tell them," he said softly.

"What about your job?" she asked, bracing herself for the response.

He swore under his breath. "I'll talk to Phil on Monday morning. I'm sure we can work something out."

"Can I ask *you* a question?" she asked.

He nodded.

"Why did you tell your mother that you were the culprit in this whole situation?"

"I did it to protect you." He clenched her hand in his, rubbing the inside of her wrist with his thumb. "I couldn't lie to her when she asked if I had feelings for you. So I figured I'd take the heat."

"Why the hell would you throw yourself under the bus?" The thought that he would take all the blame for something that was just as much her doing as his made her angry.

"It doesn't matter, Syd. It's done."

"That's the thing. It's not. What happens when we tell her I'm pregnant with your baby?" she asked. "She'll know you lied to her."

"We'll deal with that when the time comes."

"You don't get it. I meant what I said to you before. I wouldn't be able to take knowing that I caused a rift between you and your family. That's what scares me the most. It's not really about me. Once you lose that…Morgan, you and Den have seen each other through some rough times. And the Smiths are the only family you have. You keep saying it's a risk you're willing to take, but I don't think you really understand the ramifications. I've been around family who hate each other. My parents can't stand each other. They made our lives a living hell growing up. And we suffered for it because both of us grew up without one of them. It's not something I want for you or Den. You've lost so much already."

"I get it, Syd," he said, standing up. He paced the floor. "Believe me. I understand where you're coming from. It hurts thinking about Mama and her reaction to this whole thing. But I can't change it. Now you're carrying my baby. I'm not walking away from this. I hated my own father."

Sydney observed the emotions playing across Morgan's face. His father had always been a sensitive subject for him and he rarely talked about him.

"Hated everything about him." Morgan stared at the monitors. "He was an evil, selfish bastard. He didn't care about anyone but himself. And when he was arrested, I told everyone to stop calling me Nathan. I didn't want anything from him, not even his name. I couldn't wait to change it legally.

"And my mother…she wasn't any better," he continued, shoving his hands into his pockets. "I couldn't help but love her, though. He treated her like shit—and she let him. She even let him treat me like crap. I watched her love him and almost kill herself trying to get him to love her back. He was caught up in money and 'hos. She was caught up in him.

They sucked as parents. They're the reason Den is the way he is. The best thing that ever happened to me was Kent asking his parents to take me in. So I'm aware of exactly what I'm risking by being with you."

"Why?" She cleared her throat. "Why are you willing to risk that?"

He shrugged. "It's not rational. I don't even have an answer. I'm pretty sure Den will never forgive me, but I hope Mama understands why I lied to her."

"Morgan, I'm not letting you take the heat for this," she promised. "I don't care what you say. Can you go get Den—and Mama? I'm going to tell them the truth."

"No, you're not going to tell them anything," he said, his voice stern. "Not tonight."

She gaped at him. "What are you talking about? Didn't we... You said you weren't going to pretend like I'm not pregnant with your baby."

"But telling them tonight is not an option. You're in the hospital. It can wait until after the grand opening tomorrow night. Then we will say something—together."

CHAPTER THIRTY-SIX

$\mathcal{I}$ would like to raise a toast...to us," Red announced, wrapping an arm around Sydney. "May we continue to work well together and make this money."

Syd raised her champagne flute—filled to the rim with sparkling apple cider—and clinked his glass. "Cheers."

They were all gathered around in a circle, glasses held high. The grand opening had been a success. The bar was packed all night. They had sold a lot of alcohol, which made Red grin from ear to ear.

Syd, on the other hand, was nervous. After she and Morgan decided to keep the pregnancy quiet for a bit longer, they'd told everyone that she was fine and simply had not taken care of herself like she should have with the opening and all that it entailed. Den had been curious why she'd asked to speak with Morgan and she'd lied about a business matter. Her doctor had agreed to release her with strict instructions to take it easy and drink plenty of fluids.

Morgan watched her like a hawk all night, making sure she always had a bottle of water in hand. Red and Kent were no better. They'd all taken turns sticking by her side throughout the evening. It was sweet but annoying as hell. She was ready for the night to be over, which was a shame because she'd been waiting for this night for a long time.

The only people left in the bar were close family and a few friends. And all she wanted was a tiny sip of Moët. Unfortunately, Red had filled everyone's glasses and made sure she got fruit juice. She rolled her eyes as she finished her drink.

Everybody was sober—for once. But she knew that was about to change when Kent set a fifth of Patrón on the table. Soon ties were loose, jackets were off, and shot glasses were filled.

"You all right?" Mama Smith asked her.

She jumped, knocking her glass to the floor. Hopping out of her seat, she quickly bent to pick up the pieces. "I'm good," she said, tossing shards of glass into an empty dish she'd grabbed. "Glad this night is over."

"Syd, you really should let someone else do this."

"It's okay. I've got it." Once she picked up the last piece, she stood slowly. "I'm going to go get a broom."

The older woman touched her hand. "Wait. Let someone else clean this up. You've already scared us once this week. Have a seat."

Sydney slid into her seat and watched Mama walk to the bar.

"What's up?" Den asked, sliding into the seat next to hers. "You look worried. You gave us all a scare."

His mood was totally different than it had been the night before, for which she was grateful. She eyed the glass in his hand, the amber liquid sloshing around. She shrugged. "I'm okay—tired, like I told your mother."

"Tonight was good. I'm glad things worked out for you."

"Yeah, well…I'm glad it's over," she repeated for what seemed like the millionth time. "Why are you drinking?"

she asked him as he gulped down the contents of his glass. "It's not good to drink on your medication."

"I've been drinking cognac all night," he said with a shrug. "Why stop now?"

She tilted her head to get a better look at him. "It's not like you, Den. Not while you're taking your meds. Unless you're not. What's wrong?"

"Why don't you tell me?"

She guessed it was too much to ask to have a drama-free night. "Tell you what?" she asked.

"Why you're sleeping with my brother?"

Syd froze as Den studied her face.

He traced the rim of his glass with his finger. "Answer me, Syd," he demanded. "Are you sleeping with my brother?"

"Yes," she whispered, hanging her head. "I am."

He stiffened, pulled at his collar. Letting out a breath, he said, "I didn't know what to expect, but I didn't think you'd actually admit it."

"Den—" She placed a hand on his and he snatched it away.

"Don't touch me," he ground out between clenched teeth. "I wanted to believe that you two hadn't gone that far."

"How did you . . . ?"

"I saw you," he admitted, his skin flushed. His fists were opening and closing. "You two were in the kitchen at his house, kissing."

She gasped. "The night of the accident. You knew—you've known since then?" Her mind raced back to Kent's birthday party. In hindsight, the signs were all there. The mood he'd been in when they got back from the store, the way he'd talked to her and Morgan that night. His rage. It all made sense. He'd asked her to come help him after the accident, seemed to do things deliberately to piss Morgan off. He'd known the entire time and had been playing them.

He released a heavy sigh, tapped his finger on the table. "I wanted to believe that's all it was—a kiss. But I guess I couldn't be that lucky, huh?"

"I'm sorry I hurt you."

"How long has this been going on?" He stopped tapping.

She swallowed and glanced around the room, shifted in her seat. "Den, maybe we should talk about this later. Privately?"

He leaned forward and flattened his hands on the table. "Tell me the truth."

She paused. It was clear he wasn't going to let it go. Sighing, she stood up and walked over to a table on the other side of the room and waited for Den to follow her. When he sat down across from her, she said. "The truth..." She cleared her throat. "Nothing happened between me and Morgan until after we broke up, Den."

"So was this payback?" he asked.

Her head whipped up. "No. Not payback. It wasn't like that."

She couldn't stop trembling. His eyes dropped to her shaky hands. "Then what was it? Was this a fling?"

She averted her eyes again and shook her head slightly. "I'm sorry," she repeated.

"Look at me, Syd." She lifted her tear-filled eyes to his. "You want to know what I think?" he continued. "I think you and Morgan have been fucking around behind my back for a long time."

"I told you..." she said, swiping a tear from her cheek. "Please, Den, let's go in the back. We shouldn't talk about this here."

"Shut up!" he bellowed, the command echoing in the room. He looked around then. Everybody had stopped what they were doing. All eyes were on them.

She grabbed his hand. "Please...Don't do this," she begged.

He yanked his hand free and hurled the bottle of Hennessey across the room. "How could you do this to me?"

She scrambled to her feet and retreated a bit.

Kent appeared next to him, placed a hand on his back. "Den, calm down."

Morgan moved to stand next to Syd, asking her if she was okay. She nodded and told him she was fine. Next thing she knew, Den had grabbed the front of Morgan's shirt and slammed him into the bar. She screamed for Red, who lunged for Den, trying to pull him away. But Den's hands were fisted in Morgan's collar.

"Den, stop." Mama's soft voice broke through the cloud. Red let Den go, so Mama could get to him. "Please don't do this," the older woman pleaded. "You're brothers."

Den planted a forearm across Morgan's throat. "What the hell is wrong with you?" he snapped. "Say something!" He lifted Morgan up and slammed him back into the bar.

Morgan didn't fight back, though. He didn't even move.

"Den, let him go," Kent ordered. "This isn't helping anything."

Den shoved him back and whirled around on Kent. "Don't you think I deserve an explanation? Let him answer me."

Morgan straightened to his full height, brushing a hand over his collar. "I'll answer your questions," he said. "Leave everybody else out of it—including Syd."

Den punched him and he stumbled back. "How long have you been fucking my girl, brother?" he asked, his voice vibrating with anger.

Morgan shifted his jaw and shot him a dark look. "I'm not fucking *your* girl, Den."

"What?" Den said, a scowl on his face. "Should I have rephrased it? What do you call it? Making love?"

Morgan's jaw clenched.

"Come on, Roc," Den said. "Tell me? Answer me."

"It wasn't like that," Morgan said in a low, controlled voice.

"So she tells me. Tell me what it was like, then." Morgan

and Syd exchanged glances. Den pointed at her. "Don't look at him—giving him those big, sad eyes. You two were…I don't even want to think about what you were doing."

"I know you're upset," Morgan said.

"You don't know shit!" Den hollered. "You only think you do. But I have to hand it to you, Syd. For someone who was so hurt that I cheated on her, you sure didn't waste any time bouncing back—hopping back in the saddle, so to speak."

She sucked in a sharp intake of air. "Den."

"Den, I swear, I will fuck you up," Morgan snapped. "Don't talk to her like that. What the hell is wrong with you?"

"What's wrong with me?" Den stepped back. "I'm not the one fucking my brother's fiancée."

"Well, that's the problem," Morgan growled. "She's not *your* fiancée, Den. You two were already done when—"

He waved him off. "I don't buy that shit. It's a little too convenient."

"It's the truth," Syd said. "It happened after I found out you were with Laney. We didn't plan it."

"Maybe not, but you continued to do it. I saw you. Do you have any idea how that made me feel?" Den asked, a mixture of hurt and rage in his eyes.

"What the hell are you talking about?" Morgan asked.

Den's attention shifted to his brother. "Oh, I guess your lover didn't have time to warn you. I saw you two at your house—in the kitchen—all huddled up with each other. You were so into each other, you didn't even know I was there."

"You've known this whole time?" Morgan glanced at Kent. "You knew and you played that shit off. That's why you suggested Syd move in with you after the accident—to get to me. The kiss at dinner." He let out a strained laugh. "Well played."

"You fuckin' piece of shit—"

"You're drunk, Den," Syd said, stepping between them.

Her voice was unsteady. "Let's talk about this in the morning. Please?"

"Go to hell," Den sneered. "All of you."

* * *

Den had been gone for a few minutes but no one had moved. Sydney leaned against a table. Suddenly her knees felt weak, as if they would buckle at any moment.

Then she felt it—a hand—soft against the small of her back. She peered up at Morgan.

"You need to go home," he rasped. "Get some rest."

She drew in a shaky breath. "This is my fault." She glanced at Mama Smith. "I'm sorry. I'm so sorry, Mama."

"I'm sorry, too," Mama said. "I knew there was more to the story. I just wish you two would have handled it differently."

The shame of her actions threatened to choke her. She covered her mouth with her hand. "It wasn't like Den said," Syd told Mama. "I don't sleep around. I wouldn't have sex with just anyone."

"I know that, baby," Mama said.

"Den cheated on me in my own bed," Syd said, feeling the need to explain more. "I was beside myself. And it just happened. Morgan was there for me. He didn't let me drown in my misery. I wish I could say I regret it—"

"Syd," Morgan said, touching her arm. "We can talk about this another time."

"No," she told him. "I'm not running from this anymore." She turned to Mama. "Morgan told you that he was the wrong one in this equation. And that's not fair to him. Truth is, Morgan only did what I allowed him to do. He didn't seduce me or make a pass at me. I slept with him because I wanted to."

"Were you ever going to tell Den?" Mama asked.

"Yes. Eventually. We were going to tell him so many times. But there didn't seem to be a right time. Den has been a huge part of my life. I didn't want him to hate me. I don't want you to hate me, either. More than that, I didn't want your relationship with Morgan to suffer. You're his family, the only one he has."

Syd scanned the faces around her. It was the wrong time, but she wanted to get everything out in the open. "I love him," she admitted. "You're probably so disappointed in me. I'm so sorry for all the pain I caused."

"Syd, first of all, I meant what I told you all those years ago. You *are* my daughter, and I love you," Mama said. "I may not like that you two have carried on behind Den's back, but I do understand the need for comfort. I do understand that things happen. And if I'm not mistaken, I'm looking at a woman who finally knows what she wants."

Mama looked at Morgan. "Son, tell me the truth—the real truth this time. Why did you take that job in Baltimore?"

"That part was the truth," he said. "I took the job because I felt like it was better for everyone if I wasn't here. But I did lie about the nature of our relationship. There *is* a relationship here—and it's not one-sided."

"Wow." Mama dashed a tear from her face. "This is a lot to take in. As a mother, it's hard to know you and Den may never recover from this."

"I'm sorry, Mama," he murmured. "For hurting Den. For hurting you."

"But you're not sorry for being with Sydney." It wasn't a question.

Morgan shook his head.

Mama folded her arms across her chest. "Can I have a moment with my son?"

Syd nodded, casting a lingering glance at Morgan before she walked out.

* * *

Morgan filled two glasses with whiskey and handed one to Mama, who'd joined him at the bar. When Mama asked everyone to give her time alone with him, he'd braced himself for her wrath. He was surprised, though, when she requested a glass of Jameson's on the rocks.

"Is there anything else I should know?" Mama asked.

He hated the fact that he had to lie to her again, but he shook his head. He'd struggled with their decision to not tell anyone else—including Mama—about the baby, but it was for the best.

"Morgan, you've certainly made a mess of this." She twirled the tumbler around before she took a sip. "I can't understand why you felt the need to hide this from me. I asked you and you lied to me."

"It was hard—to lie to you." Morgan studied his reflection in the mirror behind the bar. They'd always had an easy relationship. Mama had given so much of herself for so long in an effort to make up for his parents' misdeeds. She'd had a long, uphill battle, too. He didn't trust easily. It had taken a while for them to reach an understanding. Once they'd turned a corner, though, there'd been nothing he wouldn't do for her—and nothing he couldn't tell her—until now.

"I'm glad you feel guilty. You should."

He chuckled. "You should know I appreciate everything you've done for me. What you and Papa did for me...I can never repay you. My own parents weren't shit. As far as I'm concerned, you're the only mother I've ever had."

She sniffed. "I love you, too, son." Her voice was thick with emotion. She placed her hand on his and squeezed. "I don't like this. I hate seeing my sons at each other's throats. I don't know what to say. I have no idea how to fix this." She finished her drink.

"I don't expect you to figure this out for me. But if you're expecting me to let her go..." He paused to gauge her reaction. "If we can make this work, I want it."

"You really love her?"

He met her gaze. "I do. I think in some ways I've always loved her." And the fact that she was having his baby, that he would get to see her carry his child, made him love her even more.

She flashed him a sad smile. "Tell me something I don't know. I knew something was up with you and I had an idea where it was coming from. I guess I just didn't want to admit it." She placed a hand on top of his. "She's a good girl. Why do you think I wanted her to marry Den so badly?" She sighed. "Your brother may never forgive you."

"I know. I wish things were different. I've given up a lot for Den. There are so many things that will probably never be resolved. He resents me for being the good son. And I hate that he uses that as a crutch. Maybe one day we'll be able to talk about it. If we don't..." He shrugged. "I don't know what to say. If I leave her to appease him, it won't help. The damage is already done."

"But it would show him that he means something to you," she suggested.

"It wouldn't change how I feel about her. I was willing to walk away from her, but now that's not an option."

"Would you have really walked away from her?" she asked, her eyes squinted like she didn't believe him.

"Yes. I had my house packed up, Mama. You know that. I was willing to leave everything behind."

"For him?" She twisted her glass around on the table.

"For her, mostly. He's a part of it though. He's my brother. And I love him. I've never turned my back on him—even after he messed my leg up—until now. There's no excuse so I won't try to offer one. I want to know how to move forward from this—if that's even possible."

"I don't know, Morgan. I would hope that, eventually, you and Den work this out. But I've seen families torn apart over smaller issues—bonds broken forever. I pray that doesn't happen." She pulled her keys out of her purse and slid off the stool. "I'm going to head home. Please...Never mind. Be safe."

He briefly wondered what she was going to say before she changed her mind. He decided not to ask. Instead, he hugged her. "I will, Mama. I'll walk you out. I have some business to take care of."

* * *

Sydney hurried to the door, tying her robe on the way. She peeked through the peephole and jerked the door open. "Where have you been? Is everything okay?"

Morgan entered without a word and headed straight for the refrigerator.

She followed him. "Morgan?"

He pulled out a bottle of water and gulped it down.

"What's going on, Morgan?" She folded her arms across her breasts and waited. Her patience was wearing thin.

"Nothing, Syd," he said. "Mama's not even that mad."

"So why are you so...quiet?" She'd been beside herself, pacing the floor for hours wondering how things were going with him and Mama.

He shot her a wary glance. "I'm tired, shit. It's been one crazy-ass night. I just want to get in the bed and sleep."

She stiffened, suddenly unsure how to act around him. Was she supposed to ask him to stay? Would he stay if she asked? "I hate this."

He tossed the empty bottle in the recycle bin. "What do you want me to do? I told you not to say anything about this tonight."

"I didn't," she hissed. "Den asked me flat out why I was sleeping with you. What was I supposed to say?"

"How the hell should I know?" he asked.

"And Mama...maybe I shouldn't have told her about us, but I was ready to get everything out in the open. No more surprises and no more secrets."

He snorted. "Now you don't want any more secrets." He pulled his tie off as he stomped to the bedroom. He unbuckled his belt and slipped it off, tossing it on the floor next to the bed. The rest of his clothes landed in a heap on the floor as well and he climbed into the bed.

She gaped at him. "You're going to bed?"

He glanced at her over his bare shoulder. "You have a problem with that?"

"I didn't think you...Forget it." She yanked off her robe and threw it on the chair in the corner, climbing in beside him.

She stared at the ceiling fan and wondered how things had come to be so awkward between them. This was a man who could finish her sentences—the one person who understood her without even trying. She thought she knew him the same way. Now she was at a loss—didn't know what to say to him. Or if he even wanted her to say anything. She guessed it was a good sign that he was staying. But why stay if he wasn't going to speak to her?

"Syd," he grumbled.

"Hmm?"

"Go to sleep and stop thinking so much," he said. "It's over. We'll deal with the fallout in the morning, okay?"

"Okay," she answered, feeling stupid that she'd been freaking out.

"I love you."

Closing her eyes, she murmured, "I love you, too."

CHAPTER THIRTY-SEVEN

Sydney let herself into the house and scanned the kitchen. Fiddling with the keychain, she removed her key and dropped it on the counter. She searched the surface for the pad of paper that was usually there.

"What are you doing here?" Den asked, his voice calm.

She froze, and then spun around. "Den? I didn't see your car. I was going to leave a note...and my key."

"A note, huh? What were you going to say?"

She rubbed her hand over the back of her neck. "I was going to ask if we could talk."

"I don't think there's anything to say." He picked up the key. "I think you should go. Thanks for the key."

"Den, I..." She couldn't let it end without talking to him, trying to salvage some sort of relationship if it was possible. "You have every right to be angry with me."

"Angry? That doesn't even cover it," he said.

Rumors were running rampant in their small town. It seemed like everyone was talking about the drama at the opening.

"I don't know what to say," she said. "I *am* sorry. I never meant to hurt you. I wanted to tell you. But I was scared. Breaking up a family wasn't on my list and I didn't handle it well. No matter what has happened between us, I want you to be happy. You're a good man."

"Just not *your* man."

She twisted the strap of her purse around her thumb. "Okay. I hope one day you can look at me and not hate me for what I've done."

"I want to hate you," he admitted, "but I can't. For so long, I tried to push that image out of my mind. I even told myself that if I focused on winning you back, I could get past it. But I couldn't—like you would never be able to forget that I cheated on you with Laney."

"Den, Laney wasn't our only problem. I should've never accepted your proposal."

"Why did you?" he asked.

"I do love you. You mean so much to me. I wanted to believe that we could make a life together—that we could be happy."

"If you believed that we could happy, why did you turn to Morgan?"

"We weren't together."

He stumbled back a step. "You're lying. You owe me, Syd. Why did you go to him?"

"I don't owe you anything, Den."

For so long, she'd had this notion that she owed it to Den to stay with him no matter what. She'd finally realized that being grateful to someone doesn't mean you have to take anything they give.

"I went to Morgan because he's my best friend," she said. "I knew he'd be there for me. But we didn't plan this."

"Don't give me that. I heard the story. You were hurt after you found out about me and Laney, distraught, one thing led to another...I got that part. You know what I'm asking you, Syd. You're not stupid!" he bellowed.

"I don't know what you're expecting me to say," she said. "You want me to tell you the truth. This is my truth. I want Morgan. I need him."

He snickered. "You need him? To what?"

She choked back a sob. "He's my friend. You don't have to believe me. I don't really expect you to, but what happened was not planned and it didn't happen while you and I were together."

"You're right. I don't believe you."

"I don't want to hurt you, but you're not blameless and don't try to make our breakup all about me. You did this." She pointed at him. "You systematically destroyed everything we had together. I know I was wrong to be with Morgan, but—"

"Wrong?" His high-pitched tone made her flinch. "Wrong is forgetting my birthday or taking a couple of bucks from my wallet without asking. I don't know what this is, but 'wrong' isn't the word."

Syd couldn't stand there and listen to it anymore. She was tired of Den playing the victim. "Damn it!" she shouted, slapping her hand against the counter. "I know I was wrong for being with your brother, but I'm not wrong for wanting a man who won't cheat on me!" She ran a hand through her hair. "I'm not in love with you anymore, Den. I'll always be grateful that you took care of me during one the worst events of my life. I'll always love you for that. You always protected me from everyone—but yourself." She walked away from him, needing to put distance between them. Turning to him, she told him, "You fought all my battles, kept all my nightmares away. You were my first love. That never changes. But I don't want you anymore. And deep down, you don't want me either. If you did, we'd already be married."

"And Morgan?" he asked, tears standing in his eyes.

"I love him," she said, meeting his gaze. "I want him. And we're going to be together."

* * *

Morgan rocked back in his chair and clasped his hands together. The meeting he'd had with the partners didn't go like he'd expected, but it could've been worse. He had proposed an alternative to him moving to Baltimore, outlining a plan that would allow him to work in both offices but spend the majority of his time in Michigan. Initially, they'd balked at the plan. They quickly changed their tune when he told them that he had a line on a potential, *local* business owner that could produce millions in revenue for the company. He owed Red big-time for saving his ass at the last minute by introducing him to one of his law firm's wealthiest clients, someone interested in expanding his interests in the area.

The sound of the intercom beeping interrupted his thoughts. Pushing the button, he said, "Yes."

"Morgan, your brother is here to see you," his secretary announced.

He told her to send him in and waited, wondering why Kent would be visiting him this early.

"I guess it's time we talk."

Morgan's eyes snapped toward the door, surprised to see Den standing there. "I wasn't expecting to see you here—ever."

Den shoved the door closed and made himself comfortable in one of the chairs. "Your office is good and neutral."

"This is my job, Den, so if you're here to—"

"Come on now," Den said, interrupting him. "You know I wouldn't do that here."

"I didn't think you'd do that at the bar, but you did."

Den sat back in the chair, crossed one leg over the other. "Look, I didn't come to argue."

"What did you come to do?" Morgan didn't trust that Den wasn't going to start something here. He'd shown them all that he was capable of anything when he was angry. "We haven't been able to talk to each other without arguing in a minute."

"I came to set the record straight. And I expect the truth from you. You owe me that much."

Morgan tapped his pen against the desk. "Okay. What do you want to know?"

"Syd came to see me today."

Morgan's body stiffened. He'd talked to Syd earlier and she hadn't mentioned going to see Den. "And?" he asked.

"We talked. She said some things that resonated. She wants me to forgive you." Den leaned forward, elbows on his knees. "I don't know if I can do that."

"This isn't her fault. I'm the one who pushed this."

"Look at you, defending her," Den said.

"What do you want, Den?"

"I knew I couldn't live up to her expectations when I fell in love with her. I hurt her time and time again. But she made me better. She made me the good brother. I tried to be the man that she deserved, but I always fell short. But you're my brother. I haven't always treated you the best or appreciated everything you've done for me, but you were all I had for so long." He scrubbed his face with his hands. "The Smiths are our family, but me and you . . . we grew up together. We went through hell with each other. It hurts that you would be with Syd knowing how I feel about her. I've heard the pleas from Mama and Kent to try to forgive you, but I can't even look at you without wanting to kick the shit out of you. Of all the women . . . why her?"

"I don't know," Morgan murmured. "We were friends. We talked."

"Talked?" Den shook his head. "Is that all you did while we were together?"

"We didn't sleep together while she was with you." Morgan told him. "I wouldn't do that."

"But you'd do it now? That's…" Den stood up and jammed his hands into his pockets, shot Morgan a dark look. "I guess I shouldn't be surprised. After all, I did know you had a crush on her when I got with her in the first place."

Morgan could have run with it, accused Den of doing the same thing to him all those years ago, but he knew it would only be a copout. He couldn't compare the two. Even if he'd had feelings for Syd all those years ago, he hadn't acted on them. And for a long time, he'd rooted for them. Den did make her happy for a long time.

"You have every right to be angry," Morgan said. "I broke the code. But I didn't disrespect your relationship with Syd like you think I did. I've always defended you. I took care of you when you should've been taking care of me as my older brother. But I didn't set out to hurt you, Den. Things just happened."

"So I've heard." Den picked up the picture that sat on Morgan's desk. It was one of all of them during a family picnic at his house. He set it down on the table. "I didn't come here to rehash all of that. I just felt like you should know how I feel. I don't know if I can ever forgive you. Even if I could, I doubt I'd be able to trust you again."

That was more than Morgan expected, but it still hurt nonetheless. Clearing his throat, he said, "I hope we can get past this one day. Things probably will never be the same—too much said and done to turn back. Stranger things have happened, though. Maybe one day we'll be able to shoot a game of pool or something without hurling insults."

"Maybe," Den said with a curt nod. "I doubt it. In the meantime, I think it's best if we just stay clear of each other. I know we have to see each other at certain events; we deal with the same people, but we're not good. We can't kick it. Not now. Probably never."

CHAPTER THIRTY-EIGHT

Syd?" Morgan called, dropping his keys on her table. He'd come straight over from work. He wanted to tell her about the job.

"Back here!" she yelled from the bedroom.

He set his work portfolio on the table and grabbed a Heineken out of the fridge. Using his keychain, he opened the bottle and guzzled the beer.

He padded through the condo to the bedroom, unbuttoning the top buttons of his shirt on the way. "What have you been—?"

Sydney was sitting in the middle of the floor, surrounded by boxes. "Hi," she chirped.

"What are you doing?" he asked, eyeing the mounds of clothes on the bed and the floor. "You going somewhere?"

"I don't know. You tell me."

He picked up a piece of lingerie off a pile and dropped it back on the bed. "Why are you packing?"

She reached up and pulled herself to her feet. "Ugh," she grunted as she stretched. "My body is on fire. And my breasts are sore. I've had to pee so many times today, it's not even funny."

"Syd, what's going on?" he asked.

"I had so much to do today," she babbled on as if he hadn't spoken. "I had to stop by my doctor's office to get a note. Then I drove to my job and put in a request for a leave, and—"

"Wait. You're going on a leave? Why? Is the baby okay?"

She crinkled her nose. "This baby is giving me the flux, let me tell you. I threw up twice today. Twice." She held up two fingers for emphasis.

He placed his hands on her shoulders. "Syd, focus. You're talking—a lot—but you haven't answered any of my questions."

She threw her arms around his neck and kissed him. "I guess you're right. We have a lot to discuss," she said. She brushed her lips against his again before she threw a pile of sweaters into a plastic bin.

"How about we start with you answering some of my questions?"

She held an emerald green nightgown against her body. "You like this?"

Visions of her treating him to a lap dance and doing a little striptease flashed across his mind. He cleared his throat. "It's...nice."

"I wonder how much weight I'll gain."

"Sydney."

"Okay. Ask away."

"What did the doctor say?"

"Apparently, I'm almost out of my first trimester, which means I probably got pregnant when you pinned me up against your front door."

He scratched his head and reminded himself to try to re-create that—as soon as she answered all of his questions. "Did she give you a due date?"

"February first."

"Are they planning on monitoring you closely?" he asked.

"She suggested I see her more frequently as I grow bigger. I convinced her to do another ultrasound and let me hear the heartbeat again. It's so strong." Unable to help himself, he smoothed a hand down her belly. She caught it and held it against her. "You won't be able to feel it kick yet, but that shouldn't be too long from now." She handed him a small black square with white spots on it. "This is a sonogram of the baby. See." She pointed at a white dot. "That's the head. And this little thing is the heart," she added, circling another dot with her finger.

He swallowed past a lump that had formed in his throat. With all the commotion, he hadn't really had time to think about the baby. Now the proof was staring him in the face. This was real. He was going to be a father.

"Morgan?" Syd asked, squeezing his arm. "Are you okay?"

He ran a finger over the picture again. "I'm good. Next time, I want to go with you."

"Well, it may take a while to find a new doctor."

He frowned. "Why are you finding a new doctor? I thought you liked the one you have now."

She pressed the back of her hand against his forehead. "Are you feeling okay? You're pretty slow today."

He smacked her butt playfully.

She giggled. "I'm just saying…you seem to be behind the curve today."

"Answer the damn question." He groaned.

"I just think it would be wise to have a doctor where I'm going to be living, don't you think?"

"Where are you going to live?"

"Red told me about your proposal," she said. "He also told me your bosses were receptive to it, but they still needed you in Baltimore for a year."

"That fuckin' Red," he grumbled. "I told him I would tell you."

"He didn't want to tell me. I sort of bribed him—with cheesecake and pork chops." She winked.

He barked out a laugh. "Figures."

"So, I figured…" She bent down and picked up a pile of jeans off the floor and dropped it in a different bin. "I better get to packing if I'm going to go to Baltimore with you."

* * *

"You're…what?" Morgan asked, gaping at Syd. She smirked at his cluelessness.

"I told you I would fix this," she said. "I talked to Den. The doctor gave me a few referrals to Baltimore doctors and signed my FMLA paperwork, which I submitted to my job along with the request for a leave. Red and Kent are going to handle bar business while I'm gone," she said, counting everything she did on her fingers. "I'm going with you."

"I'm not moving."

"I know you've decided not to sell or rent your house, so technically you're *not* moving." She spotted the brown skirt she'd been looking for since she moved in and picked it up. "But you do have to travel back and forth for at least a year. So I'll travel with you."

"You're serious?" he asked.

"As a heart attack."

He pulled her against him and kissed her. Hard. When she pulled away, she tried to catch her breath.

"Wow," she said, fanning herself. "That was…intense."

He feathered his fingertips against her cheek and her heart seemed to jump out of her chest and take off at a sprint. The way he was looking at her made her palms sweat and her legs tremble. "You would leave everything and come with me?"

She smiled broadly and linked their hands together. "I would go anywhere with you."

"What about your life here?"

"I'll still have it. But none of that means anything without you. You love me. You might think I talk too much—and I'm pretty flaky. I pretty much suck at making decisions and I'm overly dramatic on occasion. But you don't care. You love me through it. That's what I want to do for you—love you."

"Syd, this is a big step," he said. "Are you sure you're ready?"

"I know. Believe me, I know. Can I just tell you what I've realized in the last few days?"

He nodded.

"It wasn't about the decision between you and Den. It was about choosing to move forward and not be stuck in the past—doing what I want for a change." She stepped into him, placing a hand on his chest. "I hate that I hurt so many people. Can you forgive me for putting everybody through this?"

He frowned. "Me forgive *you*?"

"Yes. You don't have your brother because of me."

"That was my decision, not yours. I chose to be with you."

"Stop arguing with me when I'm trying to be sincere." She smacked his arm. Then she felt the rumble of laughter in his chest. "I'm sorry, Morgan."

"I love you, Syd."

She wrapped her arms tight and hard around his neck. Turning her face into his throat, she clung to him. His arms tightened around her waist. Her body stiffened and she wrenched herself out of his arms, putting an arm's length distance between them. "Wait."

"What?" he asked in a husky voice.

"You have to tell me you forgive me."

"I thought that I was clear that there's nothing to forgive

you for." He hooked a hand in the waistband of her jeans and pulled her back to him.

"You have to tell me you know I never wanted your relationship with Den to be ruined."

"I know," he said, placing a kiss on her forehead.

"Do you want to know why I stayed with Den so long?"

"I think we already went over that, too." He brushed his lips against both of her eyelids.

Her breath caught when his gaze lowered to her mouth. "He was comfortable, safe. I felt like I owed him for saving me. I didn't know who I was without him."

"Okay." He kissed her nose.

"Then there was the fear. I knew a long time ago that Den and I were done. I should've broken it off with him a long time ago."

"Sounds about right." He brushed his lips against the hollow at the base of her throat, then lower.

"And—"

He placed his thumb over her lips. "Syd?"

"Hmm?"

"You talk too much," he said. "I know all of this. And the stuff I don't know, we can talk about later. We have a lot of time to go over the details—forever, to be exact. Let's not ruin the mood."

"One more thing."

He groaned. "What is it, baby?"

"You know I'm kind of OCD. I had this killer line in the speech I wrote out earlier."

"You wrote a speech?" he asked.

"Don't make fun of me. Okay, here it is. The final line. I want to be happy. I don't want to stand still." Tears filled her eyes and she rolled them. *Damn emotions.* She took a deep breath and breathed, "I don't want to be apart. I want to be close to you."

He smiled, and the creases around his mouth came out in full force. "Okay. Shut up. Throw on that green piece of nothing you flashed in front of me earlier and show me how close you want to be."

She giggled. "A lap dance and a striptease?"

"Damn, baby, you read my mind. I love you."

She pressed her lips against his. "I love you, too."

Calisa isn't the chocolate hearts and red roses type of woman. She's perfectly content with a friends-with-benefits relationship...until Jared. She's not ready for what he's asking, but her heart can't seem to keep him out. Now Jared must find a way to convince Calisa to let go and take a chance on him.

Please see the next page for a preview of

His All Night.

CHAPTER ONE

This has got to be the worst date ever. Calisa Harper stabbed at her overdone pasta, twirling it around her spoon. For a minute, she felt guilty even thinking that. Joshua Clayborn was one of the most eligible bachelors in the Detroit area. There were hordes of women waiting in the wings to get to him, but he'd picked her. Still, having dinner with him was akin to watching golf or, better yet, sticking a thousand needles in her eye. One word—no, make that three: boring as hell.

She glanced at her phone, torn between opening up her current game of Candy Crush and browsing through her e-mails. This couldn't be the life.

"Why are you so quiet?" Joshua asked, his dark eyes on her, assessing her.

Eyeing the door, she shrugged. "You seemed like you weren't done talking." She smiled at him. "About your house, your car, your job," she muttered under her breath, not even caring if he heard her.

He reached across the table, picked up her hand in his. Rolling her eyes, she forced herself to at least pay attention to the man. It wasn't every day she was treated to dinner by a hot millionaire. *Hot* was the only thing good about Mr. Clayborn, though. What was the use of having a good face but all the charm of dry paint? At least with paint, she could choose her own color.

"Calisa, you're so beautiful," he said.

She could agree with that, she thought with smile. Her black, low-cut, form-fitting dress left just enough for the imagination, stopping at the knee. Long layers fell down her back like ocean waves. Topping off her look with a pair of five-inch, red-bottomed pumps, she knew she looked good.

"Thank you, Josh. You look good, too."

"What do you want to do tonight?"

"Red." Her eyes widened, mortified that she'd actually said that out loud. Scrambling to cover up her mistake, she tried to think of anything *red*. Red rover, red robin, red… "Redeem my points at the casino," she lied, shifting in her seat.

He seemed to accept her answer because he ticked off the casinos in town and mentioned his preference. Nodding, she agreed to go to the MGM Grand. *Maybe I could lose him on the floor?*

The sound of boisterous laughter sounded in the restaurant, and her attention shifted to the bar. Her body stiffened at the group of men in business suits and the harem of women surrounding them. One in particular stood out, with his smooth golden skin, short wavy hair, and dimpled smile. He chose that moment to look up, locking eyes with her across the room and tipping his glass in her direction.

Knowing he would be in the city and actually seeing him were two different things, since the Detroit-Windsor area boasted a population of 5.7 million. Jared Williams was hard to miss, though. He had a way that drew her to him. Cool, calm, and collected with an irresistible swagger. No wonder she wanted to do him. It seemed as if that was all she wanted to do. Only they had strict rules; rules she tried to never break.

Joshua went on and on about his contacts and his contracts in the city and she...watched as "Red" charmed all the women around him. When she saw one woman slip her card to him slyly, she stood up abruptly, bumping into the table. "I'm sorry," she said, interrupting Joshua mid-sentence. She rubbed her sore knee. "I have to use the restroom." She dropped her napkin on the table, grabbed her clutch, and limped off toward the ladies' washroom.

Closing it behind her, she leaned back against the bathroom door. She did a quick glance under the stall doors to see if she was alone. Once she was satisfied that no one could hear her, she groaned out loud and let out a string of curses. Exhaling, she turned to the mirror and pulled out her compact.

She heard the click of the door latch behind her, but continued to touch up her makeup.

"How's your date?"

Whirling around, she nearly toppled over when she lost her footing. Shocked, she rushed to the door and swung it open, peeking outside. She closed the door and turned to face him. "What the hell are you doing?" she hissed. "This is the ladies' room."

He shrugged, his hazel eyes raking over her body. "I was just checking on you. You bolted from your table so fast, I thought something was wrong."

"How is it that, of all the places in the city, we end up at the same restaurant?"

"Coincidence," he told her. "Holiday party. The firm likes to go all out."

"Really? Red, it's not even close to December yet."

"They did it early this year. They're calling it a harvest party."

"Why didn't you tell me you were coming here?"

"Didn't think I had to. But since you're here, you could always join me." He traced the vee on her dress, sending shivers up her spine. "Why don't you get rid of the stiff and come up to my room?"

Tempted as she was, she wasn't going out like that. "No," she breathed, suddenly feeling very . . . hot. "I have a date."

Slowly, he edged closer to her. She retreated until the hard doorknob dug into her back. Reaching behind her, he flipped the lock on the door, the click echoing in the empty bathroom. She waited, anticipating his next move.

His fingers flitted across the hem of her dress and he inched it up a bit. Kneeling down, he slipped his hands under her dress and slowly pulled her underwear down. She held her breath, wondering what he would do next.

"Step out of them," he ordered in a low, deep voice.

Bracing her hands on his shoulders, she stepped out of her lace panties. With a smirk, he stood up, tucked the thin material into the inside pocket of his suit jacket, and pulled out a tiny key card. He placed it in her hand and closed her fingers around it. "Room 1179," he murmured, his lips a mere breath away from hers. Closing her eyes, she took in the smell of cognac on his breath and leaned closer.

The creak of the door brought her mind back to their location and she opened her eyes. She opened her mouth to speak, but he placed a finger over her lips.

"Shh. Try not to think about what I'm going to do to you while you're on your date." Swinging open the door, he walked out, whistling.

She hated him—in the best way.

* * *

Jared Williams flung his hotel room door open, surprised when Cali burst through it, straight into his arms. He kicked the door closed as she kissed him deeply and passionately. As they backed up toward the bed, touching and kissing along the way, she undid his tie and slid it off. She flung it over her head and went to work unbuttoning his shirt. Grunting when the backs of his knees hit the bed, he struggled to find the hook to her dress. It had a line of tiny buttons going up the back, and he struggled to undo them with his big fingers. *To hell with it.* Frustrated, he gripped the end of it and pulled, sending buttons flying into the air.

"Fuck, Red," she grumbled, shoving him back. "You ruined my dress."

"Sorry," he said, wrapping an arm around her waist and yanking her back to him.

Her head fell back as he nipped at her neck, pushing her dress down to the floor. Pausing, he stepped back to appreciate her. She was standing before him in a black push-up bra and a sexy-ass pair of *do-me* pumps—and nothing else. Her brown skin seemed to glow in the dim light and he hardened at the sight of her.

She tugged on the waistband of his pants and unzipped them, freeing his straining erection. "Step out of them," she said, with a wink and a smile.

Doing as he was told, he kicked the pants behind her and pulled her into another wet kiss. They fell back on the bed, her on top. She straddled his lap and eased herself down onto him. He closed his eyes, gritting his teeth. He wanted to make this last. They stayed like that a moment, staring at each other. Soon, she was moving those hips, grinding into him in a way that often made him forget his name. She was truly the best he'd ever had and he couldn't get enough of her. Gripping her hips, he flipped her onto her back and pushed himself into her harder, enjoying her yelp of surprise.

He looked down at her, taking in her long, dark hair

fanned out on the pillow, her lips between her teeth and her eyes on his, and slammed into her again. They moved, each of them matching the other, settling into a rhythm that seemed innate—like it was meant to be. Hooking his arms under her knees, he thrust into her—deeper, harder each time, until he felt her constricting around him. Knowing she was close, he slipped a finger between their bodies and pressed down on her clit. Her body stiffened, and she screamed out his name as her orgasm shook through her. Soon, he was right with her.

Arms and legs tangled together, they lay there panting, trying to catch their breaths. Lifting his head, he ran a finger across her cheek, smiling at the light sheen of sweat across her brow. Her hair, once flowing down her back like a waterfall, was wet with perspiration. He brushed his lips over her shoulder and rolled off her, onto his back.

She turned to him, propping herself up on her elbow. "You are so naughty," she whispered with a giggle. "You know I couldn't concentrate the rest of the night, right? Imagine Joshua's surprise when I ended our date before he had the chance to bore me with more details of his life."

He chuckled, turning to face her. He slid a hand over her hip and squeezed her thigh. "Mission accomplished, then."

Leaning in, she kissed him and then scooted to the edge of the bed. She picked up her dress and held it up to him. "You are so going to reimburse me for this dress." He watched as she pulled it up and stuck her arms into the sleeves.

"I wish I could say I was sorry and mean it."

"Ha ha." She put on his shirt and buttoned it up. "I'm taking this home."

"Guess you can add it to your collection, huh?"

Over the course of their…relationship, Cali had managed to stockpile many of his clothes, always making up an excuse why he couldn't have something back. He supposed it was par for the course.

"You don't have to leave, you know," he told her.

"You know the rules. No sleepovers." She walked over to him and kissed him again, holding his chin with her hand. "I'll call you later!" she shouted as she flung open the door and walked out of the room.

ABOUT THE AUTHOR

Elle Wright was born and raised in Southwest Michigan near Ann Arbor. She learned the importance of reading from her mother and it was also her mother who, later on in her life, gave Elle her first romance novel: *Indigo* by Beverly Jenkins. From that moment on, Elle became a fan of Ms. Jenkins for life and a lover of all things romance. An old journal she wrote back in college became her first book (which she still wants to publish one day).

You can learn more at:
ElleWright.com
Twitter @LWrightAuthor
Facebook.com/LWrightAuthor

Fall in Love with Forever Romance

DRAGON FALL
by Katie MacAlister

New York Times bestseller Katie MacAlister returns to her fan-favorite paranormal series. To ensure the survival of his fellow dragons, Kostya needs a mate of true heart and soul before it's too late.

FRISK ME
by Lauren Layne

USA Today bestselling author Lauren Layne brings us the first book in her New York's Finest series. Journalist Ava Sims may be the only woman in NYC who isn't in love with the city's newly minted hero Officer Luc Moretti. That's why she's going after the real story—to find out about the man behind the badge. But the more time she spends around Luc, the more she has to admit there's something about a man in uniform…and she can't wait to get him out of his.

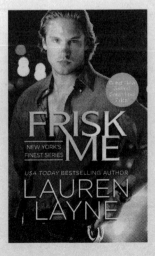

Fall in Love with Forever Romance

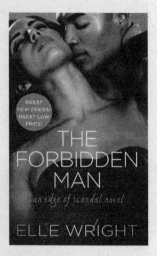

THE FORBIDDEN MAN
by Elle Wright

Sydney Williams has forgiven her fiancé, Den, more times than she can count. But his latest betrayal just days before their wedding is too big to ignore. Shocking her friends and family, she walks out on her fiancé... and into the arms of his brother, Morgan. But is their love only a fling or built to last?

THE BLIND
by Shelley Coriell

When art imitates death... As part of the FBI's elite Apostles team, bomb and weapons specialist Evie Jimenez knows playing it safe is *not* an option. Especially when tracking a serial killer. Billionaire philanthropist and art expert Jack Elliott never imagined the instant heat for the fiery Evie would explode his cool and cautious world. But as Evie and Jack get closer to the killer's endgame, they will learn that safety and control are all illusions. For their quarry has set his sight on *Evie* for his final masterpiece...

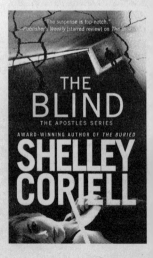

Fall in Love with Forever Romance

THE LEGACY OF COPPER CREEK
by R. C. Ryan

In the *New York Times* best-selling tradition of Linda Lael Miller and Diana Palmer comes the final book in R. C. Ryan's Copper Creek series. When a snowstorm forces together the sexy Whit Mackenzie and the heartbroken Cara Walton, sparks fly. But can Whit show Cara how to love again?

AND THEN HE KISSED ME
by Kim Amos

Bad-boy biker Kieran Callaghan already broke Audrey Tanner's heart once. So what's she supposed to do when she finds out he's her boss—and that he's sexier than ever? Fans of Kristan Higgans, Jill Shalvis, and Lori Wilde will love this second book in the White Pine, Minnesota series.

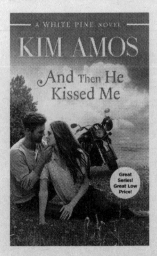